FLOWERS
FOR THE
SLAUGHTERMAN

Copyright © N J Edmunds 2025

N J Edmunds has asserted his moral right to be identified as the author of this work.

FLOWERS FOR THE SLAUGHTERMAN is a work of fiction. Similarities to real people, places, or events are entirely coincidental. The opinions of characters are their own.

All rights reserved. No part of this book may be reproduced in any form or by an electronic or mechanical means, including information storage and retrieval systems, without permission in writing from the publisher, except by a reviewer who may quote brief passages in a review.

No part of this book may be used or reproduced in any manner for the purpose of training artificial intelligence technologies or systems

Hardback ISBN – 9781068593666
Paperback ISBN – 9781068593642
eBook ISBN – 9781068593659

Editor: Bridget Scrannage
Cover artist: Rachel Edmunds (@r.eds.art)

The background image is of Wallfield Place in Aberdeen, near a key location in the story, 20 Esslemont Avenue.

Published by SouthToll. 2025

Also by N J Edmunds

MILES AWAY – Memories Can Kill
Book One in the Flint&Masson crime series

Flint's student life in Aberdeen is disrupted by a growing suspicion that his father is a serial killer. As the bodies pile up, he and PC Masson race across Scotland to stop the killer and save Flint's family.

"Wonderful first novel - gripping and compelling throughout, with many fantastically accurate glimpses of Scottish University life in the late 1970s."

"Many layered story with a strong central mystery – could not be solved without the stirrings of social and technological change that were gathering pace in the seventies."

RAGGED ISLAND
A gripping international crime thriller

2030. World order has been scrambled. Billionaire arms-dealing criminals direct wars from Ragged Island, where they live in luxury and depravity. Quinn Tarrant flees the USA, escaping to Cuba. Blackmailed, bereaved and betrayed, he is forced to take part in a deadly revenge mission to Ragged Island.

"A powerful and very timely novel that will stay with you" – **iScot Magazine, July 2025**

"Brilliantly conceived geopolitical thriller, with elements of espionage, people trafficking and corporate greed" – **John Harkin, Author**

"Pacy, scary and (sadly) all too believable" – **Belle Dean, Author**

To purchase your copies visit: **linktr.ee/njedmunds**

For Rachel and Laura

FLOWERS FOR THE SLAUGHTERMAN

by
N J EDMUNDS

Some notes on Doric Scots are included in a Glossary at the end of Flowers for the Slaughterman

THE FIRST

I didn't realise there would be so much blood.
I'll need a change of clothes.
If I'm going to do more.
If? Of course I'm going to do more. I've got to.
At least it worked, though.
No struggling. Easy to pull him out.
But I should have cleaned him after.
I need to get better.
It's got to be perfect for the big one.
I'll need more practice.
Another one at least.
It's got to be just right.
And he's got to suffer, like that one did.
He felt it. Squirming like that.
He deserved it.
She deserves it.
But the next one's going to suffer more.

Chapter 1

February 1982

Flint's head was banging and his lips were glued to his gums. A wiry hair was stuck between his front teeth. Rolling his head to see his watch set a kaleidoscope spinning inside his skull. Ten to eight, and it was still dark. Isla stirred beside him. Her back was towards him, one arm stretching out behind her and lying across his belly. It was pressing on his full bladder, and felt podgy when he tried to lift it away. She's putting on weight, he thought. It suits her, but when did she start biting her nails?

Isla, Isla, Isla. They must have caught the last bus back to Hillhead, or maybe walked? He became aware of how quiet it was, the only sound something scraping at his window. Normally there would be the morning sounds of students rousing. Muffled radios through walls, footsteps in the corridor, and conversations from outside as straggles formed on the way to the refectory or the bus stance.

Turning his head left he was blinded by a dull streetlight. Open curtains hung in limp ripples at either side. They should be mustard yellow, but were offensive pink and too far away. The room was huge, not like the narrow box of space he'd been allocated in the university halls of residence. This wasn't Esslemont House, he decided.

The blushing curtains were nothing compared to the electric pink of the rumpled candlewick. He'd always preferred the blue one his mother kept for summer. She thought pinks were warmer for winter. The air smelled of his mother, the perfume she'd worn since his infancy. I'm at home. Oh God.

Reality began to surface.

But how did Isla get here, his childhood home in Auchmoor, where he'd been since leaving Aberdeen? He hadn't seen her since she'd thrown him out.

He could remember being in the Arms last night, as usual. Tich had been there, and flashes of disco lights meant he had gone on somewhere. The Royal Hotel for the Friday night late licence? The rest remained elusive.

Flint shuffled onto his right side, and the old mattress creaked. A moan emanated from the shape beside him as it shifted. He looked at the back and shoulders presented to him, pale in the rosy hue. Wider, longer.

It wasn't Isla. Or the familiar disappointment of waking after dreaming about her. Someone else was in his bed.

A wicked smile of guilty pleasure cracked his lips away from his teeth, and he managed to extract the curling hair. He'd pulled, he thought, as Nudge would've said. Nudge, his best pal at university, had loads of tales of similar conquests. Some of them were probably true. He wished he could meet Nudge again, in the Dungeon Bar. As memories washed over him, he felt himself drifting back into sleep.

When another movement in the bed beside him brought him back from Aberdeen to Fife, Flint surfaced from a dozy slumber to a restive awareness. Something wasn't right. Who was it lying beside him? And why did Mum let me sleep in her bed with a strange girl?

Bang!

A crashing tidal wave of horror washed away the doubt he had been floundering in. Paralysed, he didn't dare breathe. He didn't care if he drowned.

He could smell his mother and he was between her sheets. Bile filled his mouth and he gagged, his heart punching against his ribcage. How could he be so depraved? How could she? Had he added to the list of men who'd abused her?

Flint let out a deep moan, and the body beside him stirred. Holding himself rigid as his mind writhed with self-loathing, a new burst of adrenaline blew the fog from his head. Ecstatic relief flowed in.

He had waved his mother off in Janet's car yesterday.

Aunt Janet, his mum's snobby sister, had invited Eleanor away for a couple of days, to 'take her out of herself.' It was now more than four years since Alun had died, Janet had said. Time Eleanor moved on.

Flint smiled as he remembered the cheeky smirks he and his mother had exchanged as she climbed into Janet's latest car. They both knew his aunt didn't need to worry about his mother 'moving on.'

Exhaling, Flint sank into the mattress. He didn't know who the slumbering girl beside him was, and stifled a guilty laugh. What might she think if she knew he'd mistaken her for his mother? Watching her wide back move rhythmically with her breathing, he felt a transient swell of feeble passion, but his hangover made him sleep before he could summon the energy to reach his arm around her.

The girl was gone when Flint woke and he still didn't know who she was. The scraping noise went on. Now in daylight he saw spidery branches of a silver birch brushing glass. The sapling he'd watched his neighbour plant all those years ago, now reaching the upstairs window.

Stepping round the creaking floorboard on the landing, he made his way downstairs to the kitchen to gulp icy cold water from the tap. He sat at the red Formica table with empty nausea. There were biscuits in the cupboard above the sink but it was some minutes before he could make himself move again. A few rich teas helped. Idly flicking crumbs into the crack where the drop leaf folded down against the woodchip wall, he remembered eating biscuits at the same table just hours before his father had died. He shivered the thought away before it brought the guilt back.

A welcome noise distracted him, a car door banging shut outside. It can't be anyone coming here, he thought. Seconds later there was loud rapping at the front door. Flint pulled himself up from his stool and leaned out of the kitchen to see along the hall. A shape shuffled outside the wavy glazed door. Flint stayed out of sight, but instead of going away the figure knocked again and again.

"Flint. Are you in? Flint?" A male voice, muffled but familiar.

Who the hell would visit me? Spake's in Edinburgh. While Flint wondered, the shape outside crouched down and the low letterbox flapped inward.

"Flint! It's me, Craig. How's it going?"

Craig Masson. He hadn't seen the young policeman since not long after The Mount. The events and emotions of that day now played like a cinema film trailer, key scenes flashing over his mind.

The exciting, terrifying chase around the Fife landscape of his boyhood as he and Masson tracked the killer down. The murderer's body writhing in its death throes, suspended like a butchered carcass 100 feet up in the winter sky, with a metal spike protruding through its eye socket. Flint's fears and relief for his mother, after that day's revelations about her tragic past.

As he swung the door inward Craig Masson stood up, grinning broadly.

"Christ! Flint, what is it about you and being naked? You've no excuse this time!"

Now shivering as the February air rushed in to the Auchmoor semi, Flint remembered he was only wearing his Y-

Fronts. When they'd escaped the Mount, Flint had only had Craig's jacket to cover his bottom half.

"Wait there, I'll find my jeans." He ran along towards his own ground floor bedroom, before remembering where he'd spent the previous night. About-turning, he pushed past bemused Craig to run up the carpeted stairway.

"I take it your mum's not in?" said Craig when Flint returned, pulling his Aberdeen University sweatshirt on.

"Err — no. She's away for a couple of days."

"I see you're making sure you look after the place," said Craig, grinning as they sat down at each end of the kitchen table. Flint realised he must have brought beers back to the house as well as the unnamed girl.

"Fuck! She was smoking," he said aloud. Three damp fag ends balanced on one of several open Tartan Special cans. The ring pulls were on the floor.

"Entertaining last night?" Craig's grin was even wider, his eyes glinting cheekily. Weak sunshine through the kitchen window highlighted his prominent ears.

"Aye, just — erm — had a friend round. Heavy night." He didn't know why he felt he had to try to hide what had happened.

"You'd better clear that up if you want to invite your girlfriend back again when your mum's away." Craig wasn't pointing at the mess of cans and ash, but out into the hall. And it wasn't the open condom wrapper on his mum's velour telephone seat the police constable was presenting as evidence. It was the pair of twisted lace knickers against the skirting board.

"Oh, Jeezuss!"

###

"I can't get over how short your hair is," said Craig with a grin.

Flint ran his hand over his head. "Aye, and this is it growing back. It was a lot shorter when I was working for the Council."

Flint had made them coffee. He now put his mug on a coaster and looked out of the living room window at the red Escort parked outside.

"Still enjoying your car, then?"

"Yeah, but I'm saving for a Cortina. A sergeant at work bought the latest model as soon as it was launched. You should see it. I'll not be able to afford a new one, though."

Flint had almost given up the idea of ever being able to buy a car. He couldn't even drive. Looking across at the PC, he wished he'd made more effort. It was good to see Craig. They'd kept in touch by letter and phone for a few months while the furore around the Limb Collector continued, but as soon as it died down Flint wanted to forget it all.

But why had Craig turned up now, all of a sudden?

As if he had read Flint's thoughts, Craig said, "I have today and tomorrow off and I thought I'd take a wee drive."

"Back to Fife, though?" Flint grinned. "Still breaking the rules? I'm surprised they let you out of Edinburgh after what happened."

"I got a transfer to Aberdeen nearly a year ago. I think the Lothian chiefs were glad to see the back of me."

"Aberdeen! You've been up there?"

"Yeah. And it's not too bad. They're not all sheep shaggers."

"But how come I never saw you?"

A lash of rain blew hard against the window. Craig was silent for a moment. "Aye, sorry. I was busy, and by the time I got round to looking you up you'd gone. Isla told me."

Flint winced on hearing Isla's name spoken out loud. His mum had learned not to mention her soon after Flint returned to Auchmoor.

Looking at the rain outside, Craig said, "She didn't tell me what happened. Why you left..."

"It doesn't matter. I'm over it."

Neither spoke for a moment, then Craig stood up. "Can I use your toilet? Long drive."

"Aye." Flint pointed over his shoulder with his thumb. "Upstairs."

Alone in the living room, Flint's thoughts jumped back a few months to his life with Isla in Aberdeen.

"For the love of God, Flint! I can't stand this!"

"What? What'd I do? Sorry. You not sleeping?" Flint went straight back to tortured nothingness. His next awareness was of Isla moving in the kitchenette. He'd never heard of a kitchenette when they found the flat, but agreed that a sink, cooker and fridge in an alcove off the living room didn't merit more. It was still dark outside their second-floor window. He slipped out of bed and pulled on the heavy Norwegian jumper his mum had embarrassed him with when he got his job in Aberdeen. It was October and the flat was cold already.

"Come back to bed," he said, entering the living room where Isla was now hunched over the two-bar electric fire.

"I'm going in to work early," Isla replied without looking round at him. "I've been awake half the fucking night again, anyway. I might as well get out of here."

If she ever swore, he knew it was serious. He must have done it again.

"Was I–?"

She twisted to face him. Without standing up she shrank him with a glare. "Thrashing. Moaning. Kicking your legs up and down. All night. I can't take much more of it."

"I'm sorry. I don't know I'm doing it. I—"

"Shut up. Just do something about it."

But he hadn't known what to do. He'd continued in his ways, coming home from work, opening cans of beer or persuading Isla to come out to the Silver Slipper. Without drink, he knew the early part of his night would be awful. The dream would be more vivid and he would remember some of it the next morning. What he dreamt no longer frightened him. What did was the increasing certainty it left that he had killed his father. He'd given up telling Isla: she would only remind him that the Police had cleared him.

In late 1977, when at last Flint had learned the truth, confronting his father led to a fight. Flint had been knocked unconscious, and came round to discover his dad was dead. Isla was right, the Police had proved Alun Flint's death was a tragic accident, but Flint's twisted nightmares hinted otherwise. Even hypnosis was now useless in dismissing the dreams, and only blotting himself out with alcohol meant any peace from them. For him, at least.

So the routine continued. Disturbing dreams were followed by unconscious writhing and calling out for help, before eventually he reached an empty blankness that lasted until morning. Then Isla's ire. And still a nagging doubt about his part in dad's death.

By November she had had enough. "I love you, Flint, but I can't do this anymore. You're 23 now and it's all starting again, as if we've gone back years."

Craig's clumping down the stairs brought Flint back to Auchmoor.

"So, what are you doing with yourself now? When you're not picking up women, I mean."

Flint shook his head, exhaling. "Christ, I've never done anything like that before. D'you think she's alright? I mean, I don't know what happened."

Craig laughed. "It looks like she knew what she was doing. You obviously shared a few drinks when you got back here then retired upstairs for what comes naturally."

"She must've brought the rubber johnnie," said Flint. "It wasn't mine."

"There you are, then. She got what she wanted."

"Jesus, I really can't remember."

Craig picked up the mugs. "Can I make us another coffee?"

Flint followed Craig back into the kitchen and started clearing away the cans and fag ends.

After he'd filled the kettle, Craig said, "Anyway, what are you up to? Working?"

"Aye. Hamlyn's Mill in Cupar. Filling up sacks of animal feed. I know all about calf pellets. It's fascinating."

He heard Craig laugh. "Sounds it."

"It's fucking freezing as well. The wind cuts through you. The auld bugger I have to work with doesn't like the dust; keeps every bloody windae open to keep the stoor down."

"And you're fair getting back your Fife accent. No other jobs going? What was it you said you were doing in Aberdeen?"

"I got a job with the Council. 'Parks Department Assistant Manager,'" he said with a sarcastic sneer.

"Sounds OK. Got to start somewhere."

"They said my botany degree would make me just right for the job. Shite! All I did was check up on guys cutting grass and pruning shrubberies. Fucking shrubberies!"

Craig appeared to smile sympathetically but soon let a laugh escape. "Sorry. You haven't lost your sense of humour at least. Anyway, I wanted to ask you something. Are you still doing the hypnosis?"

"You must be joking. Look at the trouble it caused me. Why?"

"It was just an idea I had." Flint thought Craig looked unsure of himself, as if he wanted to ask something but didn't know how.

"Idea?"

"It's just — I wondered if — well — you know the dreams you had, and how you thought they meant you were a murderer. Do you think—"

"What the fuck? I don't want to drag all that up again. And here's me thinking you'd come to visit your pal. Long way for a '*wee drive*'! I thought you'd just come from Edinburgh. And all along you want to fuck with my head!" Flint was shocked at how quickly his hackles had risen.

"No, I don't, but — well — you know how you used hypnosis, and you found out why you were dreaming that stuff — and…"

Flint heard the young policeman's words dry up and could tell Craig was uncomfortable. Shrugging and shaking his head, he said, "If you think I'm going to hypnotise you or anyone else, you can forget it. Hypnotising myself nearly made me go mad. And why the hell d'you want to do that, anyway?"

"And you say this nutter dreams about cutting guys' nuts off? Fuxake!"

"Well, it might just be the cock — like, err, penis — y'know, rather than the balls. But yeah, 'genitalia' it said in the psychiatrist's report."

"Aw, just the cock, that's OK then! Not a nutter after all!" Flint laughed and saw Craig's face relax. The toast popped up from the toaster and he stood up with their plates and a buttery knife. "But how d'you know he didn't do it? Kill the guy and stuff his balls in his mouth?"

As Flint buttered more toast and poured a third coffee for each of them, Craig repeated the doubts he had about Ian Soutar's guilt. "He claims it was the penis he cut off when it was actually just the balls. And he's too small, not strong enough, y'know."

"But you said he knew all about the place it happened, I mean the golf course where the body was, and the car and all that. And he confessed. Why the fuck would he confess if he didn't do it? I'm no detective, Craig, but even I can work it out."

"The psychiatrist wrote that he's been having these dreams about cutting off men's *'genitalia'* for years. Or at least she thinks they are dreams but he says they might be real."

Flint was shaking his head and smiling sarcastically. "You're not making much sense here, y'know."

"Oh, God, I know it sounds mad. But I can hardly think about anything else. Christ! I've got a date with a cracking lassie tomorrow night and I'm bound to be going on about it even to her! It's driving me nuts."

Flint was glad of the chance to change the subject. "Tell me more. What's she like?"

"She's the sister of my mate at work, the guy I'm teamed up with."

"Lucky bugger! I never meet anyone stuck here. I'm not much of a catch anyway, stinking of cattle feed."

It was Craig's turn to grin ironically. He stood up, opened the litter bin and pointed in. "Err — you did OK last night!" Reflected in the chrome of the underside of the bin lid Flint could see the black lacy knickers the unknown girl had left behind. Stuck to them was the condom wrapper.

"Aye well — that was a one-off. I've never done anything like that before. I've not thought about anyone since — you know — " He looked at the floor. "Isla."

They were quiet for a minute. Then Flint stood up and looked out of the kitchen window.

"But I know how real and scary dreams can be. Even if he did cut the guy's cock off, I feel a bit sorry for your man in the jail."

"Balls, not cock. But anyway, that doesn't matter. If his dreams make him *believe* he did it, maybe that's why he confessed." Flint didn't say anything, and Craig continued. "The psychiatrist said he needs therapy to get to the bottom of the dreams."

Flint turned round from the window. "I'm not fucking hypnotising him! Anyway, they wouldn't let some amateur do it!"

"Aye, I know, but I just wanted your opinion." Craig's head was down.

"Forget it. I can't believe you drove all the way from Aberdeen to ask that!"

Staring at his clasped hands, Craig spoke quietly. "There's another one. The exact same thing — balls cut off and head smashed — that guy from Cupar. They found his body a year ago. At Tentsmuir. Just the same."

Flint stood shaking his head, his eyes fixed on Craig. "Naw! Fuck, you're taking that too far. Don't tell me you think there's another serial killer?"

###

When Craig Masson had left to drive back to Aberdeen, Flint had a bath, went for some chips, and spent an hour tidying up the house. His mum would be back the next day, and though she might have been glad to hear he'd had a visit from Craig, he didn't think she'd want to know about the unknown girl. He emptied the kitchen bin and left the windows open as long as he could bear the cold, trying to get rid of the smell of cigarettes.

He smiled to himself, thinking how Eleanor Flint's life had improved in the four years since his dad had died. Far from being a lonely widow as her sister Janet thought, Flint knew she had transformed herself. No longer the timid, cowed victim in Flint's childhood.

How the ongoing deception of Janet had started Flint couldn't quite remember, but it had become a shared joke between him and his mum. It would have surprised Janet that Eleanor and Granville Sutton had kept in touch after Alun Flint's death. If she knew that within a few months they had rekindled a secret love they'd shared years before, Janet would have shit a brick, Flint thought.

And if Janet ever did find out, he knew his mum would handle his aunt's disapproval with a new confidence. He wondered what Janet's 'taking Eleanor out of herself' would have entailed. He strongly suspected it would have meant an opportunity for Janet to visit her favourite Edinburgh shops.

Chapter 2

Four months earlier

1st October 1981

Detective Constable Barry Cummings tried not to look as a hulk of a man in a green gown carried a shining steel tray past him. The man started to wash out the contents of an opened colon in a deep, white sink.

From the dissecting table to his left, Barry heard the pathologist's voice. "George, I have to say you've excelled yourself this morning. The reek in here is about turning my stomach."

"Sorry, Bill," said the hulk from the sink, "D'you want me to open a windae?"

Thank God, Barry thought, his hopes rising. I don't know how they can stand the heat and the stench in here.

"Don't let the cold in. Just breathe the other way, for God's sake," said the pathologist. In pin stripes and neat white coat, Dr Bill McHardy leaned closer over the corpse in front of him.

When George, the mortuary assistant, walked back past him Barry discovered what McHardy was objecting to. It wasn't strong chemicals and putrid gut contents. A fug of stale beer fumes dominated the atmosphere.

Barry remembered where he had seen the mortuary assistant before. The Black Sabbath t-shirt, the fat backside hanging over the sides a Prince of Wales bar stool. Come to think of it, George's occupation might explain the acrid smell that sometimes affected the far end of the long bar.

"Detective, you might want to see this."

Bill McHardy's words drew Barry's attention back to the gruesome task the forensic pathologist was poring over. With his nose almost touching the forehead of the corpse, he appeared to be probing into its mouth. Keeping his eyes aimed over the body at the pale green wall above, Barry edged forward a little, but McHardy waved impatiently.

"Come on, man! Get in close, you'll love this. If these are what I think they are you'll remember them forever."

Trying to hold his breath, Barry took two small steps forward.

"Here we go. As I thought. It's like delivering twins."

What on earth is he on about?

"That explains where they went!"

Barry had to look. With a pair of forceps, McHardy was carefully withdrawing something purple from the corpse's mouth. With a pop and a slurp, a walnut-size lump appeared. McHardy suspended it in mid air, smiling as the looked over his glasses at DC Cummings.

"What the f..? Oh, sorry, sir. I mean…"

"Give me a sec. I'll have the second twin out in no time, then you can give them names."

The pathologist put the orb carefully onto a green sheet — it looked like a ripe plum — and seconds later his gloved hand placed another beside it. Briefly distracted from his disgust, Barry couldn't help being reminded of the smudged attempts at still-life paintings on the wall of the art classroom at St Machar Academy.

As it dawned on him what he might be looking at, Barry Cummings felt sick. Holding on to the cold edge of the steel table, he felt a shrinking between his legs. Reflexly, one hand moved to cover his crotch. George moved round from the sink to lean in for a closer look.

"Christ! I've never seen that before."

"Well, Detective, you'll be able to report back that while they weren't quite in the usual order, all his body parts were present and correct. If you'd like to look down here, you'll see how neatly the work was done." With the glinting forceps, McHardy led Barry's reluctant gaze down over the torso and abdomen. Deftly, the pathologist pulled bloodless flaps of floppy skin aside to display the inside of an empty scrotum.

The dam burst. Barry's breakfast bacon softie travelled back up his gullet, mixed with stomach acid. When he turned back round from the huge porcelain sink, wiping from his chin a swinging slaver of mucoid sick, George was guffawing.

A sympathetic look on McHardy's face was spoiled by upturned corners of his mouth. "It's alright, laddie, it often happens. But I'm afraid there's more. You'll need to see this. It'll be important in your report."

Still facing the wall above the sink, Barry fixed his eyes on cracks in the green paint, trying to focus and prepare himself for whatever else Dr McHardy could want him to look at.

"George, could you lift his head for me for a moment, please?" McHardy said to his assistant. Barry relaxed a little. He wasn't going to have to look down there again. When he turned, George had a thick arm under the corpse's shoulders and with his other hand was supporting the neck to elevate the head. Barry was relieved to see that sheets covered the empty chest cavity and abdomen, and what lay below.

"Round here, Constable." McHardy beckoned Barry round the head of the dissecting table. The face on the cadaver looked different now that its mouth was empty. Relaxed, unblemished, eyes closed, he could have been asleep. But as the right side of his head came into view Barry tried not to recoil, hoping he wouldn't embarrass himself again. The first thing he saw was a stain on the green sheet. Above it, towards the back of the head there was a crater the size of a golf ball, its jagged margins smoothed by congealed, bloody hair. It was shocking after the serenity of the face.

When he made himself speak, he thought his voice sounded like he was talking through a cardboard tube, muffled but loud. He hoped to be professional.

"Can I report back that the man was killed by the damage to his head, and then the killer cut off his — er — you know — and put them in his mouth, sir?"

"Very good assumption, Constable, but that's just it, you see. Wrong way round. Look." McHardy waved him along the table to where he was standing. He drew back the sheets to reveal the man's groin and legs. "See? Blood. Lots of it."

The insides of the thighs were blackened by dried blood, and scattered spots fanned out in disordered lines that reached as far as the dead man's knees.

"When this man's scrotum was sliced open, when his 'you knows' as you call them were removed, his blood was circulating well. He was alive." Dr McHardy had a satisfied grin on his face.

Chapter 3

Barry Cummings was still feeling sick half an hour later when he walked into Grampian Police HQ in Queen Street. He was now beginning to understand why witnessing the post mortem had been delegated to him.

Detective Sergeant Alan McCann looked up from his desk and blew out smoke. "Aye, yer lookin' a bittie green about the gills, man. I can't stand the smell in that place."

"Thanks, Sarge. Yeah — um — interesting."

It was less than a month since he'd been told he was to be made detective, and Barry was still unsure about McCann. He was sure Detective Chief Inspector Blackie had meant them both to attend, but McCann had made Barry go to Foresterhill alone.

Blackie still wasn't referring to the death as a murder, even though the mutilated body seemed to make it more obvious than the shiny cyst on Blackie's forehead. Now that Barry could report back that there was no way the injuries could have been self-inflicted or accidental, he guessed they would officially be investigating a murder. His first. Feeling excited and important, he was even able to ignore the lingering smell in his nostrils and the sting at the back of his throat.

"The doctor said it's definitely murder, Sarge." Barry looked at his notebook and continued, "'Massive blunt force trauma to the head,' that was what he told me was the cause of death. But there's more. Should I go and tell DCI Blackie, Sarge?"

"No, just write everything up. I'll let him know it's been confirmed. We'll get the formal PM report on paper tomorrow, most likely."

Barry was disappointed. He'd have liked the chance to report the news directly to the boss.

McCann stubbed out his cigarette and lit another before he lifted the phone. Barry sat down and started writing, listening in as McCann spoke to DCI Blackie.

"DS McCann here, sir. The pathologist has told me it's a definite murder, sir. 'Massive blunt force trauma to the head,' he said, and no way it could have been any sort of accident."

Told me, thought Barry. He shook his head and decided he was going to use that trick one day.

Half an hour later he gave his report to McCann to read over.

"Jesus H Christ! Balls in the mouth? Bloody hell. And that was done while he was alive? Why didn't you tell me? I'll need to let the boss know."

"You didn't give me a chance, Sarge." Barry smirked to himself as McCann lifted the phone again. Seconds later DCI Blackie flung his office door open and shouted.

"For Christ's sake, McCann, why didn't you tell me that? I've already spoken to the Super and told him it was just the head injury. You didn't think castration was worth mentioning? See one of them every day, do you?"

"Sorry, sir, I—"

Blackie slammed his door.

###

Barry needed a lager. He hurried straight along from Queen Street after his shift. The Blue Lamp was unusually quiet when he walked in, but the pub would get really busy after the Dons match. He was still buzzing about being involved in a murder case. DCI Blackie had been instructed to put a team together. They would all gather the next day at nine o'clock to review progress.

His first few mouthfuls of lager did little to wash away the lingering taste of sick and formaldehyde, and he asked for a packet of tomato sauce crisps. As he was opening them, Davy

Jepson walked in. He waved at Barry and came to sit on the next bar stool, his hand reaching out to the crisp packet.

"Don't mind if I do, thanks. And a fine pint of McEwan's Lager, please."

"Cheeky bugger. It's your round."

"C'mon, man!" said Davy, "you can afford it now, seein' as your mixin' wi' the grown-ups."

Barry was still on the same salary as his uniform PC colleagues but he liked the idea that they would see his move into CID as a promotion.

"Ach, OK, since it's just you, Davy. As long as you get me a date wi' your sister." He waved to the bar owner and ordered two more pints. "Anyway, how come you're not at Pittodrie?"

"I couldna get a ticket. European games sell out quick." Davy was a big Dons fan. After lighting a cigarette, he went on. "Anyway, fit's it like, min? Bein' oot o' uniform?"

Barry and Davy had lived a few blocks apart on Hilton Terrace, and been in the same class at Woodside Primary School.

"Still finding my feet a bit, I must admit. But I'll get there. Blackie likes me, that helps."

"DCI Blackie?"

"Aye. He wanted me on his team."

"Wait 'til he finds out you're a lazy bas..." Davy stopped mid-sentence and grinned.

The pub was beginning to fill up. A man in a brown suede jacket edged past to sit at the next table. "Can I take one of those?" he said, reaching in front of Davy for a beer mat and placing it under his pint.

"Aye, help yersel', min."

"Wait 'til you hear this, Davy." Barry leant forward and spoke more quietly. "You know how they found that body out at Girdle Ness?"

"On the golf course? Aye, just this morning."

"Well, you should have seen what they did tae him."

"Was it definitely a murder, then? That's going to make us all busy. Who's the SIO? Christ! If Blackie gets it, you'll be working a murder already."

"Shut up, listen tae this. I am on the case, and in fact, I got to go to the PM."

"Jeez. Did you puke? Did you have tae watch it all?"

Barry sat back proudly. "Aye, it's no bother. Quite interesting, really. All pretty routine. But listen to this. He'd had his bits cut off." He pointed towards his groin.

Davy put his pint down. "You mean — his — wedding tackle? Surely no'!"

"Aye, I'm tellin' you. But that's not the best bit, they found —"

"You mean that's how the mannie died? Jeez!" Davy was still shaking his head at the thought.

"Nope," said Barry, smugly. "The cause of death was 'massive blunt force trauma to the head', actually, and it was obvious that the guy was still alive when his bits were chopped off. He'd have seen it happening."

"Aw! Jeezuss Christ!" Davy's hands shot down under the table to cover his groin.

Barry was still itching to see his pal's reaction to the next detail, but he waited until Davy had dared to lift one hand to take a mouthful of lager.

"And what he'd had chopped off was stuffed in his mouth."

"Fuck!"

The man in brown suede left a third of his pint and stood up before hurrying to the door.

"Haha! I think we might have put that loon off his Guinness."

Barry was looking the other way. A girl with a Princess Di hairstyle had bent down to pick up something she'd dropped.

###

Tom Jordan couldn't find a cab. His car was parked about half a mile away outside his flat, and he thought it would waste time walking there. But it turned out to be just as far to the taxi rank in Back Wynd. Not for the first time he cursed Aberdeen and his decision to move north.

"How come there's hardly any cabs?" he complained to the driver as they made their way up Union Street.

"Plenty taxis, min. Fit's yer hurry?"

This really is a dump, thought Jordan. He sat back in the seat and pulled his notebook out of his inside pocket. As the car turned into Rose Street, the driver said over his shoulder, "Writing a letter to yer girlfriend, loon?"

Distracted from his scribbling, Jordan said, "No, this is work. How long will it take to get to the Lang Stracht?"

"Ye dinna ken Aberdeen well, son? I didna think it. It's the accent, ken. I can aye tell. Ye fae Glasgow? Edinburgh?"

Jordan hadn't caught much of what the man had said, and decided explaining he had lived and worked in both cities seemed pointless. Sitting quietly was easier, and he went back to his paper and pencil.

"Suit yersel, min." Jordan then heard the driver mutter what he thought was 'bloody ootsiders'.

Why the hell did I move here?

He'd been in Aberdeen three months and was regretting the move. The city and its people had been something of a culture shock to him when he'd left the central belt, but the contrasts between the *Daily Record* and the P&J were even more stark. He'd thoroughly enjoyed his two years at the *Record* as a junior crime reporter. Here in Aberdeen, although nominally a more senior position and certainly a much better salary, he had been disappointed by the relative lack of big news. The odd fatal fight between Peterhead fishermen and housebreakings in Torry were small beer compared with the steady flow of stories he'd written about organised drugs gangs in Edinburgh and Glasgow.

But tonight, luck might have been on his side. He had a potential story he could claim as his own. He just had to write it up and get it to the editor by the nine o'clock deadline. But if he missed the first edition of tomorrow's P&J someone else might break the story.

I don't need to make my own luck this time, he thought as he walked through the main doors of the *The Press and Journal* offices. The clock on the office wall said eight twenty-three.

Chapter 4

Friday 2nd October 1981

Craig Masson counted eleven policemen gathered in the incident room for the nine o'clock briefing. Detective Superintendent Charles 'Chic' Morrice called their attention by knocking on the desk. At six foot seven, he had to bend down to reach it.

Behind him, a noticeboard bore four photographs. From where Craig sat the faces of two men were unclear, but there was an image of a body lying beside a red car, and one of the car itself, a Ford Escort Mark 2. The T-registration plate showed Craig it was a 1978 model, and his practised eye told him it was a Popular Plus. His own red Escort was three years older, but it was an XL.

When he arrived on duty, PC Masson had been told to be ready to assist the murder investigation team being set up by the superintendent. In the room he could see a number of other PCs he knew, and guessed that like him they had been seconded from their own teams. All he had heard was that yesterday a body had been found on a golf course near Torry. When he arrived that morning the Queen Street HQ was alive with anticipation. Murder had been confirmed.

When Morrice spoke, there was absolute silence.

"You all know by now we are dealing with a murder. On Wednesday, the body of a man, as yet unidentified, was found on Balnagask Golf Course out at Girdle Ness. The man is in his fifties, and had suffered massive trauma to his head. Bill McHardy says in his report that the weapon was possibly a hammer. Multiple blows, all concentrated on one area of the skull. But before he died his genitalia were mutilated, and body parts were placed in his mouth." Muttering and intakes of breath filled a short pause in Morrice's account. "It's a strange one, and we're looking for a real nutter. The pathologist estimated the time of death to be between twenty-one hundred hours and midnight the night before, 29th September." He looked around his rapt audience. "Any questions so far?"

After a few seconds a hand went up.

"Yes, DS Ovenstone?"

The officer who rose to speak was stocky, with a small bald patch. Craig didn't know him and wondered if he was based at Bucksburn.

"We have the car reg, sir. Is it the victim's car?"

"The car is registered to an Ivan Skilling, at an address in Newmachar, but so far there has been no reply at the house, and near neighbours have as yet shed no light on the occupant or the car. We can't be sure it's him." Morrice looked to his right. "DCI Stuart Blackie will be the SIO."

Blackie stood up and faced the room as Morrice continued, "and his core team will be DS Ovenstone, DS McCann and DC Cummings."

Barry bloody Cummings! thought Craig Masson. Cummings had been one of the first PCs Craig had met when he'd arrived in Aberdeen. Despite being two or three years younger than Craig, it had been clear from the start that he'd viewed Craig as a rival, if not a threat. Craig's attempts to fit in had been, it seemed, deliberately thwarted by Cummings, who taunted him for not being fluent in Doric. Several times he referred to Craig as "Fae Ootbye"*, to emphasise his incomer status.

Morrice moved aside, letting DCI Blackie take over. Craig thought Blackie looked about forty. His thick curls were greying and receding from his forehead and his shirt strained against his belly.

"Two priorities: confirm the identity of the victim and find the murder weapon, presumably a hammer. There's already been a search of the immediate surrounding area, and the car has been removed for forensics to take a good look at it. I want to press them on that." He pointed towards McCann and said, "Alan, you and DC Cummings work on the car and arrange a proper search of the locus. And check at the golf club to see if anyone reported anything. They must have greenkeepers — start with them."

Blackie now looked over the room. "DS Ovenstone, stand up again, will you?"

Ovenstone stood up smartly. Heads turned and there were one or two nodded greetings.

"This is DS Murray Ovenstone, Bucksburn Station. DS Ovenstone is here in the absence of DI Maggie Sangster who's on sick leave."

Craig heard a murmur behind him from near where Barry Cummings sat. He thought he heard the words 'women's trouble,' and a snigger.

"Murray, I'd like you to concentrate on confirming the ID."

"I'll get on to DVLA, sir. Ask them for any other addresses for Mr Skilling. We might find some of his relatives. Have we got good pictures of his face, sir?"

Blackie pointed at the notice board. "One's from SOCOs, and the one without swollen cheeks is from the pathologist." There were groans of disgust and a few muted laughs before Blackie continued. "Now, before we all get to work, has anyone got any questions?"

Craig Masson put his hand up. "Has the operation been given a title, sir?"

He heard muttering behind him, and 'bloody Edinburgh', and, 'thinks he's in the Met'.

"For now let's just say it's unnamed."

Blackie was turning away when Barry Cummings called out, "Operation Nae Baws!" Immediate laughter broke out and Chic Morrice had a smile on his face while Stuart Blackie tried to look furious. Morrice stood up.

"Enough. Get to work."

(Some notes on Doric Scots are included in a Glossary at the end of Flowers for the Slaughterman)

Chapter 5

It was cold, wet and very windy out on Balnagask golf course. DC Barry Cummings was delighted. After a quick look around the taped-off area where the car and body had been found, he and DS McCann had retreated to the relative warmth of the car, but six uniformed PCs had to brave the elements. Barry smiled as he watched them slowly searching the rough between the second fairway and Greyhope Road, which skirts around a wide promontory to the south of Aberdeen harbour. Through the misting windscreen, he could just see the white tower of Girdle Ness lighthouse. Beyond the tower and out of sight near the rocky shoreline he knew there was a huge red foghorn. Directed seawards, its deep, penetrating lament could vibrate eardrums miles inland as well as out to sea. An effective warning to approaching vessels, the lowing of the "Torry Coo" also meant Aberdonians didn't need to open the curtains to know it was a foggy morning.

"If this was six weeks ago you'd be out there, Barry. Glad you're not in uniform nowadays?"

"Aye, Sarge. Those poor bastards'll be soaked through," he said, laughing.

"Drop the 'sarge' when it's just the two of us, Barry. Right, I've seen enough here, take me round to the golf club and let's see if anyone there knows anything."

They found the small clubhouse closed, but nearby a man in overalls was crouched down, working on a mower outside a wooden hut.

"I'm DS McCann. Can I ask you some questions?"

The man didn't look up from the blades he was cleaning. "I've nae been here the last couple o' days. I dinna ken nuthin' about the body."

"Has anything been found on the course? Handed in?"

"No."

"How do you know? If you weren't here yesterday."

"I'd have heard."

"Is that your store shed? Where you keep tools? Anything missing?"

"I telt ye. I wisna here."

McCann said nothing, and stared at the man, who eventually stood up and walked round the big tractor-drawn mower to open the wooden doors of the shed.

"Help yersels, why don't ye." The man spat into a rusting oil drum.

McCann waved Barry into the shed. By the light of his torch, he could see three smaller mowers lined up along one side of the shed, leaving space enough to store the tractor mower. On a bench at the back stood assorted cans of oil, petrol and paint, and above it a rack for hanging tools. Screwdrivers, spanners, and pliers, but no hammer.

Back outside he told McCann what he'd found.

"Where's your hammer? You must have a hammer," said McCann to the greenkeeper.

The man reached down beside him and lifted a claw hammer with a thick wooden handle.

"We'll take that," said McCann reaching out with an evidence bag in his gloved hands. "Put it in here."

"No chance," said the greenkeeper, "I need that."

"Want me to arrest you for obstructing an investigation?"

Barry Cummings stepped forward, ready to assist, and the man meekly dropped the hammer into the bag, shaking his head and muttering.

"That's got to be the murder weapon, Sarge," said Barry in the car on the way back to Queen Street. "Don't you think we should have taken him in?"

"Dinna be feel, loon. If he'd used that tae batter the mannie's heid in he would of got rid of it, nae keep it beside him for us tae find."

When Barry had parked back at HQ, he asked, "So why did you take the hammer off him?"

"Didna like his attitude," said McCann, opening the door. He smiled. "And I was needin' a hammer myself. Saves me going all the way out to B&Q."

The forensic report on the car was on the notice board in the incident room when Barry and his sergeant got back. It contained little of interest. The only things noted were a letter in the glovebox from a daughter and a toolbox in the boot. There was no blood inside, and although the driver's side doors had been spattered, most of it had been washed off by the rain. They were able to match the blood type to the victim, though, and their initial impression after examining the scene was confirmed. The victim had been mutilated outside the car, lying half on the rough gravel of the parking area the car had been found in, and half in the long grass of the golf course rough. The man's fawn-coloured cardigan appeared to have been snagged on the inside car door handle, where loops of thick wool had been found matching a tear in his right sleeve.

"I don't get it," said DS McCann. "It looks like he was dragged out of the car, but why didn't he put up a fight?"

"Drugged?" Barry Cummings was enjoying being involved in solving the case, and sure they would soon be able to tie it up. He still thought it was obvious that the greenkeeper was guilty.

"Aye, most likely drugged. The PM report said 'toxicology to follow'. We'll have to wait for the lab tests to know for sure. Might be a day or——"

The door to the Incident Room flew open and crashed into the desk behind it, knocking a mug of cold tea onto the floor.

Ceramic shards skidded across the lino under their feet and Barry Cummings saw brown splashes on his pressed grey slacks. Before he could protest a deep voice roared from the doorway.

"Who the fuck did this?"

Chic Morrice stood in the doorway, red-faced and his neck bulging against his white uniform collar. He was waving a newspaper.

"Who the fuck did this? Who spoke to the press? What fucker is responsible for this?"

Morrice was towering over McCann and Cummings, the only two in the room, who stood up dumbly, shaking their heads.

"When I find out who's behind this, I'll…" Morrice threw the newspaper on the desk and stormed out.

When Tom Jordan saw his headline in that day's *Evening Express* it made up for the disappointment of his piece not making the front page of the morning's *Press and Journal*. He'd finished writing his copy in time but the editor hadn't been sure enough about it to displace a planned story about job losses. Front page space was also being reserved for the Aberdeen match report. The Dons were expected to progress in Europe.

There was a bonus to having his exclusive held back. It may have been relegated to the *Evening Express*, but it meant he would have a follow-up piece on the front page of tomorrow's P&J.

Jordan spread his copy of the *Express* on the bar of the Prince of Wales with a satisfied smile of pride.

'GOLF COURSE GORE', he read. The subheading went on 'Murder Victim's Penis Found in his Mouth.' By Tom Jordan, Crime Reporter.

The editor had refused to have the word 'penis' in capitals. He read on through his report which he'd filled out with speculation and sensation. He particularly liked his references to the victim's 'blood-red car', and the possibility that there might be an 'Aberdeen Ripper'. He had outlined Peter Sutcliffe's 'horrific crimes of mutilation' and the editor had allowed a small picture of heavy-browed Sutcliffe in his wedding day bow tie. The picture had been reproduced a thousand times in the press over the course of the multiple killer's trial earlier that year. All this padding out of the story was to distract from Jordan's lack of hard information about the Aberdeen killing, which he grandly referred to as being from 'reliable police sources'. He'd broken the story, and would have that forever, even though he knew he'd have to fight hard to keep follow-up stories for himself. He was already planning tomorrow's P&J front page, but knew he'd need to find out more about the case, and that the police would be very unlikely to be cooperative.

For now, though, he was treating himself to a well-deserved afternoon pint.

Chapter 6

Word about the leak to the press spread faster than secret gossip. Craig and DS Ovenstone got wind of it over the police radio when they were on their way back from Ivan Skilling's house in Newmachar. They stopped in Dyce to buy a copy of the *Express*, and Murray read most of it out as Craig drove. He had felt his stomach lurch when he knew the reporter was Tom Jordan, and felt no better when he read the details for himself back at Queen Street.

There was an air of sombre expectation when the team gathered in the incident room for the planned five o'clock debrief. DCI Blackie stood up holding the *Evening Express*, and the room became silent.

"Before we hear what progress we've all made with the investigation I want to know who spoke to the press." As he glared round the room, faces looked at the floor or studied the noticeboard. "Well? Which one of you was it? I hope you're pleased with yourself." He slammed the newspaper down on a desk. "You know what this means? This means our job will be much harder. I want to nail the vicious, perverted bastard who killed Skilling, and I want to do it quickly. Having the fucking press watching our every move's gonna make that a lot more fucking difficult. When I find out, I'll fucking…" He stopped, red-faced, and picked the paper back up. "It says 'information from reliable police sources.' Well — who *was* the '*reliable police source*'?"

Silence.

"And who is this 'Tom Jordan, Crime Reporter' anyway? I've never heard of him."

DS McCann offered, "He's a new bloke, boss. Came from Glasgow. *Daily Record*."

"Well, he'd better fuck off back to Glasgow. He's getting nothing more from us."

Blackie was still glaring, teeth gritted. "The switchboard has been ordered to block any calls from reporters. We're promising them a statement from me at ten o'clock tomorrow. That means the bastards'll have nothing new for Saturday's P&J."

No one owned up to leaking the information, and eventually DCI Blackie calmed down. DS Ovenstone was able to report that the victim was indeed Ivan Skilling, aged fifty-three, of 54 Greens Way, Newmachar. The photograph provided by forensics had been shown to neighbours nearby, and two of them had confirmed that Skilling had lived at that address for two years. Both had described him as a quiet man who they thought lived alone.

"I'd like authorisation to enter his property, sir, to take things further. I was able to get DVLA to provide two previous addresses for him, both in Fife, and I plan to make enquiries there about next of kin, but a search of his house would help."

"Good, Murray, thanks. Get on with that first thing tomorrow, will you?"

'Yes, sir.'

Blackie looked towards Alan McCann. "Now, where are we with a murder weapon?"

McCann reported that a thorough search of the golf course had yielded nothing, but that the forensics team had finished with the car. He went on to describe the snagging of Ivan Skilling's clothing and how bloodstaining outside confirmed he had been dragged from the car, the injuries inflicted after.

"Did you get anywhere with the golf club, DS McCann?"

"The clubhouse was closed, sir, but I spoke to a greenkeeper. He wasn't much help, I'm afraid, and although he did have a hammer it was just one of his tools, and—"

"He had a hammer? On the golf course? Why didn't you bring him?"

"Sorry, sir. It's just—"

"It's just a fucking mess, that's what it is!" A spray of spittle followed Blackie's words. "Get out and bring the bastard in. If we can nail someone for this, we might be able to avoid a media circus. I said now!"

McCann left with Barry Cummings. Craig watched as they made their way towards the door. Cummings looked angry, whispering at his sergeant.

DCI Blackie spoke to the rest of the team. "Right. We know the victim, and we know he was pulled from the car before this freak did what he did to him. Does anyone have any ideas? Observations?"

"Sir, the victim was quite a big man, I think, five foot eleven the PM report said." It was DS Ovenstone. "I guess that means we're looking for a big bloke as the killer. To overpower the victim. The Doc said, I mean Dr McHardy said he was alive when he had his genitalia — err — incised."

"I would have been fighting back, that's for sure!" Another of the uniformed cops Craig didn't know had spoken, and there was a release of tension and some muffled laughter.

"Sir, can I speak?" Craig had his hand up.

"Aye, son, who are you? Stand up."

He stood, feeling watched. "PC Craig Masson, sir. I wondered — well—"

"C'mon, son," snapped Blackie. "We're nae goin' tae bite."

"Sir, forensics said there was no blood or damage inside the car. If the victim didn't put up a fight, I mean even when he was pulled out of the car, he must have been asleep, or unconscious. Drugged?"

"Good, son. That's one thing DS McCann got right — he's chasing up the lab for toxicology to see if he was drugged, or just pissed." Blackie scanned the room again. "Anyone else?"

Any satisfaction Craig might have had from the DI's praise was smothered by his sick fear that someone would find out about his connection to crime reporter Tom Jordan.

###

The greenkeeper had gone home by the time Alan McCann and Barry Cummings made it back to Balnagask Golf Club through the rush hour traffic. In the clubhouse they found a helpful lady in an apron. She put down a tray of hot sausage rolls to find the address for them. Barry was starving.

"Here we are, son. Paul MacNaughton. Do you want his phone number?"

"Just his address, please." McCann was brusque.

"Is it to do with that awful thing? You know, the body. The man who had his—"

"The address."

"Paul wouldn't have anything to do with that. He's a fine mannie. A richt family mannie."

McCann's silent stare and outheld hand did the trick. The woman scribbled an address on a notepad and tore off a sheet.

"Here you are, officers."

Back in the car, McCann had lit another cigarette by the time Barry had his seatbelt on.

"Let's get this bugger arrested and back to the station. I'll need to buy my own hammer now!" McCann was grinning through his fug of smoke. From under his seat, he lifted the hammer in its evidence bag. "Good thing I hadn't been home yet."

"Sarge, I told you we should have arrested him this morning." Barry was annoyed he had to stay on into the evening. He had a date at the Star and Garter with the Princess Diana lookalike he'd met in the Blue Lamp.

The traffic was thinning a little as they made their way to the address in Kincorth, but by the time they'd taken the handcuffed and protesting greenkeeper from his crying wife and children it was after seven o'clock. They still had to process him back at Queen Street.

"Blackie's bound to want to interview him tonight, and I want this done right, Barry. No more fuck-ups, right?"

Barry was getting used to taking the blame for McCann. He waited while the desk sergeant logged Paul MacNaughton's details and belongings, before having him fingerprinted and escorted to an interview room.

"This is nae right!" MacNaughton said when he was seated and cuffed at a plain table. "I never did onythin'. I telt you I wisna even working that day. Ask ma wife, I took her tae Foresterhill on Monday and I'd tae mind the weans the next two days. Cost me my wages. Get me out of here!"

Barry stood by the interview room door and said nothing. Plenty of people would surely be able to confirm MacNaughton's story. McCann had been right after all, and Paul MacNaughton was going to turn out to have nothing to do with the body out at Girdle Ness. But Blackie wanted an arrest and McCann wasn't going to cross him by not doing as ordered.

At least a uniformed cop would be found to guard MacNaughton, Barry thought — he'd done it often enough himself. He'd probably be allowed to leave soon. Blackie and McCann would do the interview, and if they got themselves organised quickly Barry still might be in time to get to the Star and Garter for his date.

###

It was ten minutes to eight when Barry hurried past the desk sergeant calling, "G'night, Kenny," over his shoulder as he strode to the glass doors. No chewing the cud with Big Kenny tonight. If he hurried, he could still make it along to Crown Street. He'd have to go in his work suit instead of changing into his chinos, but didn't want to stand the girl up. He was fairly sure she'd said Natalie, but had a nagging feeling she might have been Natasha. She looked like a Natasha.

Before he had even reached the end of Queen Street he heard a voice behind him, and footsteps catching him up.

"Excuse me, Officer."

Barry hurried on. It would just be a punter who had seen him exit the HQ. Probably a wiseguy trying to avoid having to tackle Kenny on the desk.

"Excuse me, can I have a word?" The steps behind him quickened, and the voice became louder. Reluctantly, Barry slowed and turned round. A man of about five foot six was hurrying up towards him. He thought he might have seen the man before.

"Sorry, sir, I haven't time. On duty." He held his warrant card out and the man's eyes flicked down at it quickly.

"Sorry to bother you, Detective Constable Cummings, can I just ask you something?"

"Who are you?"

The man's right hand stretched out in greeting. "Tom Jordan. I've been waiting to catch you. I just have a couple of questions."

"The reporter from — you!" It was the man in the brown jacket, the man he'd seen in The Blue Lamp.

"Can I buy you a pint, Officer?"

"No you bloody can't! I don't know where you got your story from, but it's rubbish." Barry could feel his face heating up and hear how unconvincing his words were.

"Well, I suppose 'DC Cummings had no updates for me last night' will have to do. Along with what I have found out for myself." Jordan's smile was both inviting and threatening.

"Are you trying to—?"

"No, no nothing like that, DC Cummings. This could work for both of us. Let's go and get that pint." Smiling and without relaxing his focus on Barry, Jordan half turned, arm outstretched and beckoning towards Broad Street.

"I have to meet someone in ten minutes," he said, looking at his watch but taking hesitant steps to follow Jordan.

"Ah, well. Shame. It would have been an opportunity. And not just for you to avoid — you know — the headlines."

To improve his chances with her, Barry wanted to be at the Star and Garter before Natalie/Natasha. He knew she would soon be arriving, but as the reporter walked away the angry rants of Chic Morrice echoed. If Jordan published more, the super's fury would be worse, and all directed at Barry.

"What do you mean, 'opportunity?'"

"I'm sure we could come to some arrangement. C'mon, man, your pint awaits." Jordan strode off across Queen Street and round the corner. Barry followed, uncertainly at first, before picking up his pace and drawing level as they passed the towering granite frontage of Marischal College.

"Listen, I can't tell you any more," he said.

Jordan raised his eyebrows and nodded towards the bar across the road.

It was Friday evening and the Kirkgate Bar was busy. A few old men sat on bench seats smoking. Standing between them and the bar was a loud babble of students, thronged together and swilling. Tom Jordan carried two pints close to his chest and edged his way through the crush with nods and smiles. Barry wedged in beside him in the back corner near a cigarette machine, just outside the toilet. Jordan knew Barry was a lager man.

Barry felt conspicuous, but none of the drinkers had appeared to notice two more bodies squeezing in.

"So, what do you think?" Jordan supped at his Guinness, smiling eyes boring into Barry. "How about you keep me abreast of things and I keep your name out of the paper? OK?"

Tom Jordan had the front page of Saturday morning's P&J almost all to himself.

Chapter 7

Too junior for a parking space at Queen Street, Craig Masson was used to the top deck of the bus down Union Street. The traffic was quieter on Saturday mornings, and familiar shop fronts were whizzing by below him. He was in two minds. He could keep quiet about knowing Tom Jordan, or he could come clean and admit that it was Jordan's piece about him in *The Scotsman* that saved his police career.

Two women in overalls helped him decide. Trying to hear more of their chatter meant he almost missed his stop.

"Did you see they named that mannie? That een they found oot by the Torry Battery?"

"Nah. Oor paper's aye late at the weekend. Fa wis it?"

"He wis ca'd Skilling. Ivan Skilling. Fae Newmachar. And they've charged a mannie for it already."*

Someone had given the P&J more information. It was still hours until DCI Blackie was scheduled to give his press statement. Craig would have to make it clear the leak hadn't come from him. He had to speak to DCI Blackie as soon as possible. Admitting his link to Jordan before someone else found out about it might help him convince the bosses he wasn't the source of the leak.

He whirled his way down the bus stairs to leap out as the doors were closing. When he entered the incident room it went quiet, a few faces flicking in his direction. It was obvious everyone had read the newspaper. Barry Cummings muttered something about "ootsiders." Craig was already their top suspect.

Blackie strode in and rapped hard on a desk with his knuckles.

"Right. I want to know everything about this 'Tom Jordan, Crime Reporter' bastard. And he's going to tell me which one of you his contact is. And then I'll have your guts for garters." Blackie swept a vicious stare round the room, and Craig looked at the wall behind the DCI, desperate to avoid eye contact.

Barely pausing for breath, Blackie said, "Murray, you get up the Lang Stracht and have a wee wordie with the editor, and if you can bring back Jordan's balls with you I can wear them round my fucking neck when I speak to the press later. We've postponed the statement until this afternoon."

"Right, sir." DS Ovenstone beckoned to Craig to follow him as he stood up and made for the door. With moist palms and prickles up his nape Craig followed. He could feel the eyes of his colleagues boring into him as he fumbled his notebook into his breast pocket.

Murray Ovenstone was as furious as Blackie. As they hurried towards the P&J offices he said, "It doesn't matter that they got it wrong with their '*Man Charged*' crap, it's the fact that the shits think they're a step ahead of us,"

"So, they released the man MacNaughton?" Craig said. He had thought the greenkeeper was still in a cell.

"Aye, last night. Clear alibi. It was obvious if you ask me. Blackie should learn to be a bit more like a bloody detective."

###

The P&J editor wore a nylon shirt and cufflinks. He refused to tell them anything, and spoke in a superior manner about journalists' integrity and the impossibility of revealing their sources. Craig thought the man was barely disguising his glee at Grampian Police's discomfort, and that he definitely knew Tom Jordan had a police insider. For Craig, the editor's only redeeming feature was that he said Tom Jordan was out of town working on a story and wouldn't be back that day. Craig had been dreading he might meet Jordan.

From Murray Ovenstone's first words when they closed the car doors before returning to HQ it was clear he shared Craig's view of the editor.

"Obsequious, crawling, slimy creep! He was enjoying every minute of that. Did you hear him bumming up his new crime reporter, how he'd worked on *The Scotsman*? And the *Daily* bloody *Record*, as if that's meant to impress!"

Craig's resolve to come clean about his previous association with Jordan crumbled when Murray went on.

"I can't believe this Jordan character's got one of us tipping him off. Letting us all down. What kind of bastard speaks to the press?"

(Some notes on Doric Scots are included in a Glossary at the end of Flowers for the Slaughterman)

Chapter 8

"Call for you, DS Ovenstone. It's Sgt Tawse, Bucksburn station. Craig handed the receiver across to the DS. The voice was loud enough for Craig to hear the conversation.

"Aye, he's not long out of Kingseat. Been back and forward there a few times I think."

"Kingseat?" Murray said.

"It's the nuthoose — I mean the hospital — it's out by Newmachar."

"And he's claiming to have killed Ivan Skilling?" Murray covered the mouthpiece, sighed and rolled his eyes up as he listened. "Aye, OK, John," he said. "Tell him to go home and we'll see him there. You've got his address?"

"Aye, Sergeant, the loon bides just along the road in Miltonfold."

###

On the way to Bucksburn from Queen Street the Monday morning traffic was heavy. As he nudged the car along in a queue on Great Northern Road, Craig Masson said, "You reckon this'll be a waste of time, Sarge?"

"Aye, Craig. Total waste of time. But I know John Tawse has been around a long time, and he seemed to think it was worth passing this Ian Soutar laddie on to us."

Craig had only been out to the Bucksburn station a couple of times, but remembered Sergeant Tawse. He was a big man, near retiring age, and Craig had thought there must be nothing he didn't know about the people from Bucksburn.

Murray went on, shaking his head again, "But he claims to have cut Skilling's cock off. That's not right, he's obviously just read it in the paper."

"Aye, Sarge, but he seems to know the area where the body was found. Or thinks he does. And about the car."

They said no more until they were approaching Ian Soutar's address. Craig had looked at the map, but Murray knew the way.

"He didn't have far to go to turn himself in," said Murray Ovenstone.

Number 64, Miltonfold was on the first floor of a squat block, just a stone's throw from Bucksburn Police Station. *Real to Real Cacophony* was booming out from below as Craig knocked hard on the pale green door. Someone on the ground floor was a Simple Minds fan. He could feel the music through his feet as they were shown into the maisonette by a frightened, fat woman in a nylon overall.

"Fit's he been deein'?" she said, after Murray asked to speak to Ian Soutar. She turned to shout up the stairway. "Ian! Get doon here. The Polis want you." After a drag on her cigarette and a cough, she went on, "Oh, I'm sorry, Officers, fit's he done?" Waving them to a low, floral sofa where a cat lay, she rasped, "Cissie, get doon. Shoo!"

They remained standing, and Thomasina Soutar called again to her son.

Ian Soutar was short like his mother. But he was thin, so slight his footsteps made no sound on the uncarpeted stairs. He stood in the hall, squinting in at the bright light from the living room window. Framed in the doorway, Craig thought he looked puny and pale. Not his idea of a crazed killer.

"Fit've ye been deein'?" Mrs Soutar blew smoke towards her son.

Murray introduced himself and Craig to Ian Soutar, then turned to his mother who had sat down beside the gas fire.

"Is it OK if we take Ian upstairs, Mrs Soutar," he continued, "we've a couple of questions for him. It shouldn't take long."

Mrs Soutar sighed and rose to follow them upstairs until Craig turned round. "It's OK, Mrs Soutar, we'll manage."

The bedroom was a mess. Piles of comics and scattered brown tablet bottles. Craig picked one up and read the label: 'clomipramine tablets 50mg'. Ian Soutar sat on his bed. Behind him there was a Status Quo poster and hundreds of what appeared to be random magazine clippings. Around the head of the bed, the off-white woodchip had been picked smooth.

"OK if I move these, Ian?" Murray lifted a jumble of clothes from a chair near the window and sat down. Craig stood by the door.

"Ian, I think you told Sergeant Tawse something this morning? Something about the golf course? That's a long way from here."

Without looking up, Soutar said, "I go there sometimes. I get the first No. 12 in the morning. Can't sleep. That's where I cut his thing off."

Murray caught Craig's eye.

"Want to tell me exactly what happened?"

Soutar looked up and stared as if he could see out of the curtained window. He spoke quietly, monotone.

"I battered him. I left him lyin' on the grund, aside his car." He looked round at Ovenstone, then straight at Craig. "Then I got my knife and cut it off." He was grinning and Craig noticed his small teeth. "Stuffed it in his moo." The smile he wore melted away and his eyes widened, a look of terror and disgust. "I'm fuckin' sick! I need locked up." He looked at the grimy, threadbare carpet between his feet and Craig thought he was hiccoughing, until he heard sobs.

"Can I come up? Is he awright? What's he greetin' at? Is it his arthuritis?" Mrs Soutar was humphing herself up the stairs, and Murray gestured Craig to shut the door.

"He's fine, Mrs Soutar, could you just leave us a bit longer?" Craig called through the gap as he forced the door over a ridge of carpet until it would shut.

"Ian, tell me exactly what you were doing on the golf course. Maybe we can sort all this out." Murray spoke gently.

Soutar looked up with wet cheeks. "Stiff. Dinna call me Ian. A'body calls me Stiff."

Murray threw a quizzical look towards Craig. "Err — OK. But where exactly was this? And what time?"

"If I canna sleep I just get up. It's the dreams. They ken all aboot the dreams. At Kingseat, I mean. So I get the bus. I walk up the Howes Road and the driver kens me. It's often the same driver. The No. 12."

Murray let him continue without interrupting. Craig was struggling to follow Soutar's account.

"Then I get off. Torry, that's far it goes, y'ken? The No. 12."

"And then you walk round the golf course?"

"Nah. I dinna like the golf. I like the Torry Battery."

The Torry Battery was a ruined fortification overlooking the entrance to Aberdeen harbour. Craig had been there on one of his days off.

"So, you were near the Torry Battery? Where exactly?"

"There's a flat bit for the cars to park. That's where I did it. Lyin' on the grund aside his car. Like I telt ye."

"What make of car was it, Ian — sorry, Stiff?"

"A red een. That's all I ken. Ah wisnae mysel, I telt ye. I battered his heid and then I cut his cock off." The grin was back. "Then I got the bus hame. I had to get my mither's paper, P&J, like. The mannie in the shoppie in Auchmill Road pits it aside for me, I pick it up every day, even if I hinna been on the bus, I walk down fae here. Every day, ken."

###

"So what? Cock? Balls? What's the difference?" DCI Stuart Blackie raised his fists in celebration, screwing his face up in delight. "We've fucking got him!"

After giving his formal statement Ian Soutar was now in a detention room. Blackie was beaming, waving the statement in the air.

Murray Ovenstone had asked Soutar to come to Queen Street for some more questions, and he'd agreed willingly. Ovenstone radioed brief details ahead while Craig drove, and when they'd walked into Queen Street, Blackie and Barry Cummings were waiting for them. They immediately arrested Soutar and marched him into an interview room, closing the door. Murray had calmly accepted Blackie's move to shut them out, but Craig felt dejected. He'd thought he would be involved in the interview.

It had taken less than half an hour for Blackie to emerge, grinning and pointing at Soutar's scrawled signature.

"He's admitted he prowls the area regularly. Described the car, the location, the injuries, the fucking lot! We've got him!"

"Did you press him on the penis, though, sir? When I did, he stuck with his story. He's got it wrong."

"I'll have you locked up next, Murray, pressing on his penis!" Blackie was guffawing.

"Want me to check the bus drivers, sir? And the newsagent? Make sure we've got sound witnesses?"

"Yes, better do that, but we're charging him anyway! Less than a week since the killing. Fucking magic! What a team!"

Chapter 9

The main door made a scraping noise each time it opened or closed. It wasn't loud, but it grated on Craig Masson's ears. Worse at night. When he'd first moved into the flat, it was like someone had placed a microphone behind the door, wired to a speaker under his pillow, the volume set to painful screech. After a few sleepless weeks though, his imagined tormentor had given up and unless the students upstairs had company he could sleep.

This evening the noise was just one more irritation to remind Craig what a shite day he'd had. At least Soutar being charged had lessened some of the speculation about the press leak. For now, he thought, as he stepped out into the cold, pulling the door shut against its useless draught excluder. Instead of anticipating a night out with friends it was like going back to work.

Walking along Springbank Terrace, hands in his bomber jacket pockets and shoulders hunched against the wind, he reflected on whether the move to Aberdeen had been a good idea. He had been glad to escape the fallout from his disgrace in Edinburgh — lucky to keep his job at all. But most of the luck went to Lothian Police. They'd taken the credit for smashing a major drug smuggling operation, when it had been his idea. Just like they did after he'd caught the Limb Collector with Jack and the PNC. And Gordon Flint.

By the time he walked up the slope towards Union Street, he was still turning it all over in his head. He was thinking back about Flint and their adventures in Fife as he approached the Bridge Bar. Standing aside to let a stream of bus passengers empty onto the pavement, he was about to push the bar door open when a voice behind him called, "So, yer joinin' us the night, then, loon?" A large hand slapped between his shoulder blades.

Craig was relieved to see Davy. When he'd first arrived in Aberdeen in April, he'd felt isolated by the different accent and Grampian Police's ways of working. But PC David Jepson, who was 26 and three years younger than Craig, had seemed patient with him. "Ah can translate for ye," he'd said with a broad grin when Craig's blank look showed he was lost.

It was even better now Craig had been partnered with Davy. Jepson's sister also made him good to know. He'd seen her dropping Davy off one morning, driving a blue Renault 4. She'd given Craig a nice smile, and he'd remembered her since.

"Hi, Davy. Aye, it's about time I met up outside work with you guys again." Craig felt a sickening cringe as he listened to his own cheesy lowland words and waited for some sarcastic Doric reply.

"Ach, c'mon in an' hae a pint wi' us. Wir nae 'at bad, min!"*

Craig was soon on a low stool with a pint of export. He'd been to The Bridge once before and knew it was a regular haunt of the off-duty junior cops. Almost all were PCs in their civvies, and all were male. There was no ladies' toilet, but so far Craig had come across no female PCs in Aberdeen.

By the time he was two-thirds into his pint, he was wondering if he should offer to buy the next round. Or would that make him look too eager? Maybe they already expected him to have bought a round by this time?

He waited for a lull in the noisy bantering. After six months in the Granite City, he could follow most of it. On shift, everyone used more or less the same police language as he did, with only the odd Doric word dropped in. Outside work, his fellow PCs relaxed. In his early weeks Craig had struggled with what seemed like their own impenetrable code.

Before he could make his offer to buy drinks, the group's attention shifted away to behind him as the heavy door from the street swung open. The sudden noise of traffic was soon drowned out by cheers from his colleagues.

"Here's the man o' the moment!"

"Well done, min!"

"Someone get the loon a pint!"

Craig took his cue and stood up to go to the bar. Then he saw who it was. Oh fuck. That's all I need.

Still in his work suit, Barry Cummings strode in as space was made for him on the bench seating. Craig could see him in the mirror behind the bar as he waited for the pints to be poured. Cummings was already holding court. Sitting back against the worn varnish of the wood panelling, he was accepting plaudits and revelling in his small part in the arrest of Ian Soutar. Wearing the work suit was deliberate, too, thought Craig. Rubbing it in that he'd made detective before any of the others.

"It was up tae me and Blackie tae tak his statement. DS Ovenstone widnae even have unnerstood fit the loon wis sayin'! I'd 'ave had tae translate for him!" These words from Cummings were accompanied by a swift glance directly at Craig who was returning with three of the pint glasses. Cummings was having another dig at the ootsiders.

On his way home later, Craig's hunger steered him into a chip shop in Crown Street.

"Can you add two pickled onions and a pickled egg?" he said as his smoked sausage supper was being wrapped. Within seconds, the large jars had been opened and Craig's favourite meal was ready. He walked towards his flat, ignoring the wind and savouring the strong sausage and runny red sauce. He always saved the vinegary egg for last.

Four pints of lager had helped. Barry wasn't so bad. Quite a good laugh. Craig would need to get over his disappointment that he and Murray hadn't been able to finish the job with Ian Soutar. He was only a PC, after all, and still in uniform, unlike Barry. There'd be other killings.

He thought now about Soutar. 'Stiff', he reminded himself. It was good they'd tied the case up, and DCI Blackie had been ecstatic. But Craig knew Murray Ovenstone wasn't so sure, and that there were inconsistencies. The 'cock or balls' discrepancy between the true injuries and Stiff's account was one thing, but Craig was also struggling to believe that a puny waif like Soutar could have overpowered and manhandled a big man like Ivan Skilling.

Licking a rivulet of red sauce from his wrist before it disappeared up his sleeve, he started to scrunch the P&J page his feast had been wrapped in, pausing when something caught his eye. 'Cupar Man's Killer Still at Large.' Under the orange glow of a streetlight he could just about read smudged words. 'Tentsmuir', 'Tay Estuary', 'mutilat...', 'no clue after nine mont...'

Cupar, that's near where Flint lives, he thought. Picturing Flint, freckled and always dishevelled, Craig threw the paper into a rusty bin on the lamppost.

(Some notes on Doric Scots are included in a Glossary at the end of Flowers for the Slaughterman)

Chapter 10

DCI Stuart Blackie's early delight at Ian Soutar's arrest didn't last. When Soutar appeared in court the duty solicitor advised him to enter no plea and he was remanded to Craiginches Prison.

"We'll just have to wait. If the Procurator Fiscal decides the case isn't strong enough, we'll need to dig up more on the freak. For now, Chic Morrice wants to make sure we get the bastard who spoke to the P&J." Blackie looked into Murray Ovenstone's face.

Ovenstone took the cue. "Yes, sir. Can I help with that?" He had wondered why the DCI had turned up at Bucksburn asking to talk with him. Blackie now explained that Morrice wanted someone from outside HQ to investigate the leak. It was clear that Blackie wasn't pleased.

###

Arriving for an early shift a week after Soutar's arrest, Craig walked past the desk sergeant with a wave.

"Message for you, PC Masson," the sergeant called out to him. "Can you ring DS Ovenstone over at Bucksburn?"

Murray had returned to his Bucksburn duties after Ian Soutar was charged.

"Hello, DS Ovenstone, it's PC Masson. You wanted me to call?"

"Murray is fine, Craig. Listen, I need to speak to you, in private. Can we meet after your shift?"

"Err — yes, sir. What's it about?"

"Call me on this number when you're finished." Craig put the number in his notebook, wondering what DS Ovenstone wanted.

Craig had been paired with Davy Jepson not long before the Skilling murder case had blown up. Until then, Jepson had been partnered with Barry Cummings. Although the pair had been friends since primary school, Craig had the impression that Davy was a bit relieved when Barry moved over to CID. They'd only done a couple of shifts together before Davy commented, "You dinna bullshit me like Barry did."

Murray Ovenstone's call distracted Craig, but the day was soon taken up with chasing a GP for a statement about a sudden death. It was obvious to Craig and Davy that the old woman had just died in her bed — after breaking the door down they'd found her lying cocooned in blankets with a cup of cold tea at her bedside.

"They should ban they electric blankets, min," Davy had said, "Christ, the reek off a deid body that's been well and truly cooked!" But no one had seen the poor woman for a few days, meaning the Fiscal had to be alerted, and medical statements sought.

It was hard to get the harassed GP to find time to give a statement, and they also had to contact the woman's brother in Dudley. By the time the two PCs returned to Queen Street to do their paperwork, they were late finishing their shift.

Craig was nervous when DS Ovenstone rapped on his door, and not only because Murray was his first visitor to the flat. The sergeant had been cagey on the phone, insisting they speak in person. Though desperate to know why, Craig was scared to find out.

When he'd shown Murray to the armchair and sat down on the unmatched orange sofa, Craig tried to smile.

"What did you want to talk about, Sarge?"

"How do you know Tom Jordan?"

A lump grew in Craig's throat, and he looked at the mirror behind Murray. He noticed the bald patch again. His ears were pounding, but no words came.

"He tells me you knew each other in Edinburgh. You gave him a big story?"

"I didn't — I mean I did — but not here — I didn't speak to him here — I—"

"It's OK, son, I know you weren't the leak. He told me that. But you're under suspicion, and Blackie thinks it was you."

"But—"

"Calm down. Jordan has assured me it wasn't you, and I believe him. But he won't tell me who it was."

Murray Ovenstone explained that via Blackie, he had been asked by Chic Morrice to investigate the leak. Until he had interviewed Tom Jordan, Murray had also wondered if Craig was the culprit.

"I was glad Morrice gave me the task. He's less wary of outsiders than some of the Aberdeen force. It showed he had some confidence in me." Murray sat back in the chair. "Listen. Blackie's a bit of a bastard. Not his fault, he is Aberdonian after all." Murray was grinning and Craig thought he might even soon be able to relax a little. "Some of them take longer than others to trust 'ootsiders'," Murray went on. "You can't blame them, really, with all the coming and going, yanks, bankers, businessmen, all buying property and office space and then moving on when they've made a few deals. But Blackie can't seem to believe one of his own could be the leak, so he's gunning for you."

"It really wasn't me, Sarge, I—"

"I know it wasn't, Craig. Jordan told me, remember. But if word gets out that you're connected to him, unless you've backed up his statement, I might find it harder to convince Blackie and Chic Morrice. I'm on your side, Craig."

Craig knew he was going to have to tell the story of how he met Tom Jordan.

###

"Christ! That's some story. I'd heard about the Limb Collector, of course, but I didn't know you were involved." Murray Ovenstone leant back in the chair with his hands behind his head. "And you used the PNC unofficially? I'm not surprised you were in trouble. No wonder you moved away from Lothian."

Craig had recounted his chance contact with Gordon Flint, whose unbelievable theories had eventually turned out to be true. Flint had claimed that somehow — he didn't even know how — he had knowledge about the slayings of four young girls. The crimes were in different areas of Scotland, and no one else had connected them. He had presented himself at Oxgangs Police Station with a fantastic story of serial dismemberments, only to be dismissed as a lunatic and shown the door. Craig had pitied Flint and taken his details, more by way of humouring him than anything else.

Craig was keen to prove to his Lothian bosses that the newly-introduced Police National Computer could change police work forever. Even though the murders Flint raved about were figments of his crazed imagination, a selection of cases spread over different forces presented an ideal dummy run to test the PNC. He and a computer enthusiast friend had accessed the system unofficially, expecting to prove nothing but that Flint was indeed a nutcase. But it turned out Flint hadn't been imagining connections between the murders, and Craig went to see him to find out more.

Flint had been using hypnosis to confront repressed memories of childhood trauma, but had started to suspect he was connected to the sadistic killings. Now Craig had given his outlandish ideas some credibility.

Flint and Craig teamed up with Flint's psychologist, and after more surreptitious use of the PNC, there was a frantic hunt across rural Fife. They caught up with a serial killer the police didn't know was at work. Craig and Flint were trapped by the murderer and only just avoided being mutilated and killed themselves.

The press soon dubbed the killer "The Limb Collector" for his obsession with collecting human and animal body parts.

"But where does Tom Jordan come into it," asked Murray, after Craig had explained the background.

Craig looked at the floor. "I met him when I was under suspension—"

"For using the PNC? This 'limb collector?'"

"Well, no." Craig looked up briefly, then away from Murray's gaze. "I met Jordan during my second suspension. It was for using the PNC again, though." Murray was shaking his head. "But it solved more cases," said Craig, his voice weakening.

Sighing, Murray said, "Go on."

"I just met Jordan in a pub. I was moaning about being in trouble, even though I'd helped break up drug gang."

He looked up at Murray now, "Being in the police is all I ever wanted to do, to become a detective."

"So, you gave Tom Jordan a big story?"

"Aye, and the bosses still managed to take all the credit. Claimed they had solved everything by using the PNC, even though they didn't have a clue how to! And made me apply for a transfer out of Lothian. Bastards!"

Murray smiled kindly. "Let's make sure you don't get into trouble in Grampian as well. You definitely didn't tell Jordan about Operation Nae Baws?"

Craig couldn't help smiling and began to relax a little more. "No, I didn't even know he was with the P&J until I saw his first report about Skilling. Last I knew he'd got his new job in Glasgow with the *Daily Record*."

When Murray left, Craig was exhausted. He had only outlined some of what had happened over the last four years, enough to confirm for the sergeant that while Craig had met Jordan before, he wasn't the source of the leaked information.

By the time he went to sleep Craig had resolved to keep his head down and enjoy being a policeman. He certainly wasn't going to tell anyone in Grampian what had led to his second suspension.

Chapter 11

November 1981

After six months in Aberdeen Craig was keen to make the most of one of his twice-yearly long weekends. Even more when he found out his break coincided with Jack's annual leave. He'd finished an early shift at 2 o'clock on a Thursday, and made it to Edinburgh in time to meet up with his two old pals. When the three of them got together the Canny Man's was their automatic choice of venue.

They had been at Napier College together before Craig and Jack joined the police, where they'd shared an interest in all things computing. Predictably, Phil was already raving about the eagerly-awaited Sinclair ZX81.

"I'm going off computers," said Craig.

"What? Even with that massive mainframe PNC to play with." Phil's cheeky smile only grew wider when Craig flicked the Vs at him.

Craig took a swill from his pint. "Fuck, I'm never touching that thing again!" He looked at the wooden floor between his feet. It was a year since his second suspension.

Phil laughed, but patted Craig's shoulder, shaking his head. "I couldnae believe you did it a second time, and then went to the press! You knew they only didn't sack you the first time cos you promised not to do it again."

"There's more to it than that," said Craig.

Jack sat forward. "Tell us, then, Luggy. We read about the case in the paper, but you've hardly told us anything."

Craig stared at his pint for a moment. Jack had got away with a slap on the wrist after the Limb Collector, his Tayside bosses being more forward-looking. Craig had been ashamed of his second suspension and hardly spoken about it. He could trust his friends, though, and looking up, he drew a deep breath.

"I got frustrated. They could get so much out of the PNC. But all they do is set up committees to talk about fucking protocols and safeguards. Nothing bloody changes."

When Craig had returned to work after his first suspension, he'd been cautioned: no access to the PNC in any circumstances, and no mention of the Limb Collector case to anyone. He was so relieved to still be a cop he'd have licked the Chief Constable's boots.

Transferred from Oxgangs station to Haddington, he was back doing the job he'd wanted to since he was wee. At first it was easy to put aside his ambition to make detective. Frustration grew though, when it was obvious that the potential of the PNC was being wasted.

Despite the plaudits Lothian Police had accepted after the Limb Collector case, and their pledges to "capitalise on the possibilities the PNC offered to advance policing into the 1980s," there was a notice in the office warning against access to the system without senior management approval. Authorisation meant agreement between the various enthusiastic committees that had been set up to exploit "the undoubted and wide-ranging, transformative benefits of the PNC."

Craig looked at Phil and Jack now and said, "The bloody committees enjoy their fancy jobs too much. It'll be out of date before they get round to cranking it up."

Jack said, "It's not like that in Tayside. We use it all the time."

"Aye," said Craig, exhaling and shaking his head. "But with us they only allow a few big bosses at Fettes HQ, and they don't even know what it is." He took some beer.

"So how did you manage to get into it?" said Phil.

"One time I was on a training session over at Fettes. The new personal radios." Craig looked at the ceiling as he went on, "Christ, they thought we had to be shown how to switch on a walkie-talkie."

"Fuck's sake," said Jack. "Go on."

"I was the only one who could help the Assistant Chief Constable boot up one of the computers," said Craig. "He had a piece of paper on his desk. 'PNC, Johnspassword'."

Jack and Phil rolled their eyes and shook their heads. Craig smiled with them and drank more lager before going on. "Aye, I know. Something made me remember it."

"Bloody useless," said Phil. "And they're in charge of our security."

Months later on a routine day in Haddington, Craig and his partner had picked up two neds for possession.

"It was about October '80. They were complete tossers, trying to sell heroin in the Long Bar. The barman called us straight away. They didn't have a clue what they were doing, but were mixed up with some dealers in Muirhouse."

"I'm going to get another round." All evening, Phil had been glancing towards the fruit machine just beside their table. He now stood up quickly. The old man playing the bandit had gone to the toilet and Phil took his place, pulling a handful of change from a pocket in his bondage trousers.

"Look at him," said Jack, smiling, "still playing at being a punk." He turned back, "Go on — the smack boys..?"

"I can still hear you," said Phil, smiling down from the whirring machine. "Go on, Luggy."

"They kept calling the smack 'scouse'. Said it again and again, smirking and giggling."

A week or so later Craig saw a report in *The Scotsman*. The headline had read "Samaritan Cops Seize Smuggled Heroin." Traffic cops had stopped to a broken-down car on the A74 near Lockerbie. They found a package under the spare wheel and the driver and passenger had tried to run off.

It was well known that much of the heroin in Edinburgh was brought in from Amsterdam and Liverpool. The A74 was the main road route into Scotland, and the neds' use of the term 'scouse' had set Craig thinking. Other cars carrying drugs might have been stopped between Liverpool and Scotland. Lancashire? Cumbria? Strathclyde?

"It kept bugging me. I mean, maybe Lothian wasn't the only force ignoring the PNC. Liverpool gangs branching out? Nationwide?"

A month or two later Craig had to write up a report on a domestic. A husband had beaten his wife for the umpteenth time and Social Services had taken the four children into care, just weeks before Christmas. The sergeant had told Craig to write up a report, and in the back office he found the secretary had left the computer switched on. Bored and saddened by what he was reading, he had been tempted by the winking cursor in the corner of the blue screen. Before long he had opened up the PNC and entered the ACC's password he'd remembered from Fettes.

Like a child reunited with a favourite toy, he scrolled up and down, familiarising himself with the system. He soon worked out how to search for stolen cars and was about to look into what other databases had been installed when the door behind him opened and the sergeant walked in.

"That's why I got suspended again. Interviewed by CID. Thought I was going to be charged, and definitely sacked."

Jack nodded him to go on.

"I told them what I was thinking about, the 'scouse' thing, and looking for other seizures on the motorway in other force areas."

Two weeks later, an announcement was made to the press that pioneering detectives in Fettes HQ had used the PNC to link several drugs seizures, and by liaising with forces in Cumbria and Merseyside they had arrested a major heroin smuggling gang. Lothian and Borders Police were credited with changing the future of policing.

"Bastards!" said Jack.

"Fuck! I can see why you were angry," said Phil, sitting back down. "You showed them tons of heroin were being driven up the A74, they caught the bastards, and still you got suspended again!"

"Aye," said Craig, exhaling. "And just think, Jack. If I'd been in Tayside like you I'd have been given a medal."

All three were quiet for a moment.

Craig drained his pint. "And the disciplinary process seemed to drag on for fucking ever. I was scared to go out."

He had been in a frustrating and idle limbo, still employed but unable to work. Not daring to tell his parents, he made things up when his mum asked him how work was going. He rarely left his flat except to buy necessities, and on one clandestine trip to buy food he felt sure he saw his mother looking at him from a passing bus. He worried for days, wishing they'd just sack him and get it over with.

"I wondered why you stopped coming to the Canny Man's," said Phil.

Craig did risk an occasional afternoon drink in Burlington Bertie's. Tarvit Street is a quiet side street in Tollcross, and Bertie's faces onto the high, windowless wall of the King's Theatre. The sun never seemed to reach down to street level, and the pub suited Craig's need for discretion. And his mood. It had been a few pints in Bertie's the previous February that saved his police career.

Nine months earlier, February 1981

"Cheer up, son, it might never happen." Craig looked at the barman who he was now beginning to recognise. "Yer face is aye trippin' you. Have you nae got a job to go tae?"

He tried to grin, but knew his eyes wouldn't smile.

"Sorry. Aye, I've got a job, but they'll not let me back."

"Eh?"

He could feel his anger rising, but at the same time, he felt glad to be asked. He still hadn't spoken to anyone about his suspension.

"I got suspended."

"What's your job?"

Unsure whether to reply, he lowered his voice, but said, "Police constable."

"Fuck!" The barman looked sympathetic but turned away as another customer ordered a pint. A man put down a sheaf of papers on the bar and searched in the pocket of his suede jacket, pulling out a scuffed wallet. He smelled of tobacco and had melting sleet in his red hair.

"Sorry, carry on. I didn't mean to interrupt." The man smiled expectantly, and Craig felt himself relaxing a little.

"Erm — I got suspended from the police. Sorry, I'll—"

Before he could turn and walk to his corner seat, the man put his hand out. He did the same, and the man gave him a warm, firm handshake.

"I'm Tom. I'm happy to listen if it helps you."

An hour or so and three pints of 80/- later Craig had told Tom Jordan the stories of both of his suspensions. Jordan listened intently to his catharsis, encouraging him and prompting him to continue. Jordan had shared information about himself, and Craig soon felt he had known the man for years.

By evening Craig was back in his flat, feeling better than he had in ages. It felt like it had been his idea for Jordan to write a piece in *The Scotsman* about the injustice he'd suffered, and that Jordan was doing his duty. It was a real stroke of luck that he'd bumped into Tom, and that he was a journalist.

Tom had said the top brass at Fettes would be embarrassed, and reinstate Craig. As the beer wore off, though, his confidence in the plan wavered. It was too much of a gamble. They were more likely to just sack him straight away.

The scales tipped the right way. Tom Jordan's article made page two of *The Scotsman*, with the headline 'Hero Cop Suspended Twice', and the subheading 'Computer whizzkid punished despite solving two major crimes.' Jordan laid out details of Craig's involvement in the infamous Limb Collector case, and highlighted the 'witch-hunt' which had led to a second suspension for exposing a gang of drug smugglers. Letters were printed the next day from concerned citizens, who avowed that the breathtaking lackadaisy of the police hierarchy was abhorrent to them, a symptom of continual decline in societal standards, and the failure to capitalise on the obvious and manifold benefits of the PNC was a scandal they had felt obligated to bring to the notice of their MP.

Days later Craig was called into Fettes HQ and given his job back, subject to his "requesting" a transfer to Grampian. He was also, though, instructed to follow all procedures to the letter, including protocols for accessing any and all computer systems. He was only too pleased to agree.

Chapter 12

November 1981, The Canny Man's

"So, you've been back in the job more than six months, now. Not been tempted to sneak onto the PNC?" Jack smiled wickedly. He and Craig had stayed on in the Canny Man's. Phil had left about ten o'clock, saying he had another job interview the next morning.

"I'd be scared if I saw it. I'm enjoying sticking to normal policing. I missed out on making detective, but I'll get another chance."

"You had a murder case in Aberdeen a month or so back, right? Got the guy pretty quick, I think?"

Craig felt vague unease. "I'm not sure they got the right guy. He confessed, but it was full of holes. I don't know what to make of it."

"Holes in it?"

"Well, things that didn't sound right. He was just out of the loony bin, and he was at the scene, but he got some stuff wrong about the injuries."

Jack was shaking his head and grinning. "For God's sake, Craig. You say the guy confessed, and he was at the scene? If he was a nutter like you say, he probably just got mixed up. Or was out of his head on drugs. Let it go."

Craig went to the bar. As he watched the pints being poured, he thought Jack was probably right. He decided to drop it, and when he sat down, he was glad Jack asked him what books he'd been reading. Jack was an avid reader.

Later, though, inevitably their chat meandered back to work topics. Jack was moaning about how busy he was, and Craig asked him, "By the way, was there a murder near you a few months ago? Tay Estuary somewhere? Cupar man?"

"Tentsmuir. It's a big forest area near Tayport, across the river in Fife. Aye, he was a Cupar guy. Head mashed in with a boulder. How'd you know about that? Sure you haven't been at the PNC on the sly?"

"Fuck no. I read it on my chip wrapper."

"You'll make a detective yet!"

Chapter 13

January 1982

Now that he'd been in Craiginches for weeks — months really — Stiff could just about cope with the smell. At first it had been the thing he hated most. A mix of stale sweat, feet, tobacco smoke, and disinfectant. He'd always been sensitive to smells.

He could remember it was the first thing he noticed that afternoon. As he was being taken to his cell, shuffling along the second-floor landing, the stench had made him retch. He had stopped and grabbed onto the metal rail with his cuffed hands, taking deep breaths. The warder behind him, the kind one, nudged him on his way.

"Nerves, son? First time, son? You'll get used to it. Next time you'll stride along waving to old pals."

Next time?

He'd looked round at the old man in the black uniform, the strip lights above reflecting in his shiny cap peak and silver buttons.

"I'm not nervous. It's the reek in here."

"You'll get used to that'n all! C'mon, son, in you go."

Clang.

But the smell was worth it for the relief of being in jail. He was safe there, and all the horrors were coming to an end.

His cellmate Paco had the upper bunk. Stiff could see and hear the strain his bulk put on the wire grid supporting the bed above him, the diamond shapes distorted and the 64 springs around the edges stretching. The underside of the stripy, stained mattress was convex, and every night appeared to Stiff to be sagging ever closer to where he lay. He was by far the slighter occupant of the little brick box they shared, and it would have made sense for Stiff to have the top tier, but he was outranked and intimidated by the older man. Stiff had always been at the bottom of the pile.

The bangs, slams and shouts were diminishing as he had learned they always did about an hour after lights out. One by one, he imagined, the occupants of the rows of cells would drift off to sleep. The persistent ones would keep banging on the doors, shouting to each other or to no one in particular, and doing their pointless press-ups until even they settled themselves for a night of snoring and coughing. Eventually, the background noise was of creaking beds, interrupted sporadically by noisy nightmare screams or loud pissing into toilet bowls. Stiff rarely slept, though. He tried to make sure he didn't. He'd taught himself not to, years ago.

He lay watching Paco's rhythmic breathing expand and contract the wire grid, and when he'd counted the 64 springs a few more times he looked out into the cell. The dim light from the floodlights outside threw a faint pattern on the wall opposite. He stretched his neck round slowly in case the creaking of his bed roused Paco, and looked up at the grimy window.

Stiff spent much of every night staring at that window. By day he barely noticed it, but while Paco slept, he would count the squares between the crossed bars. Over and over. Anything to stop him from sleeping. It meant he counted squares and rhomboids for 49 hours every week, and knew that after nine or nearly ten weeks that made 20 whole days and a bit more. Mrs Milne had told him he would always be good at sums.

He liked thinking about Mrs Milne. Shiny hair, red lips, floppy skin under her chin. He didn't know why the other boys all seemed to make fun of her. He wanted to poke them with his pencil when they sniggered about her big bosom. His mum had told him he had a dirty mind when he'd tried to tell her he loved Mrs Milne. Old bag like her, she'd said. His mum didn't understand. It wasn't like that.

He'd thought when he was locked up it would all stop. The barred window and the loud steel door meant he couldn't do it again. He was safe. They were safe from him.

But sometimes he did sleep. He just couldn't help it. And then the dreams came back.

Chapter 14

It was Craig's first winter in Aberdeen, and he had begun to believe the stories he'd been told about the cold. The P&J had reported that Aboyne had been colder than Antarctica.

One morning he and Davy Jepson were on their way back to base from a downstairs flat in Hutcheon Street, where the owner had just returned to find his door forced open and his hi-fi gone. When they'd taken a statement about the burglary and had a look around, there was little more they could do than give the man the number of a locksmith.

"Did you see the ice hanging off the flats back there?" said Craig as he drove. He'd forgotten his gloves and thought the steering wheel of the panda car was going to take the skin off his hands. "It's like being at the north pole."

"C'mon, Craigie-boy, ye like it really. It's nae aye like this." Davy was laughing.

Craig had to admit to himself he was settling into Aberdeen life. Work had helped. They'd been very busy, especially over Christmas and New Year, and he'd barely had time to think. The phone call to his parents on Christmas Day had been cut short when word had come in of a fight on the street outside the Grampian Bar. Worse than that, he'd had to leave the pie and chips he'd been stuffing down while his mother talked.

"Aye, you're not a bad bunch of *loons*, I suppose," said Craig with a smile.

It was later that day when Craig was in the Queen Street HQ writing up reports that he had a call from Murray Ovenstone.

"Hello, sir?" Craig hadn't spoken to DS Ovenstone since he'd come to his flat in October. No more had been said to him about the leak, and he'd guessed Murray had cleared him of all suspicion. Whether anyone else had been found responsible he didn't know. Murray's unexpected call made him wonder if the investigation was still going on. "Erm — thanks for..."

"No need. Don't worry, it's not about that. I've spoken to your sergeant and you're coming across here tomorrow for an hour or so. I want to talk to you about Ian Soutar."

Craig had barely thought about Soutar or the Skilling murder. When his shift finished and the paperwork was done, he spent what was left of the afternoon at the laundrette. He watched his clothes rotate in the dryer drum behind his distorted reflection in the convex glass, and wondered how Soutar was coping in Craiginches.

By that evening Craig had a vague sense of foreboding he couldn't explain. He slept badly, and woke the next morning unrested. He was still unsettled, but at least now he knew why. His subconscious had worked it out. It was because he still thought Ian Soutar was innocent. There was nothing he could do, though. None of his colleagues seemed to care.

When Craig arrived at Bucksburn Police Station at half past nine as arranged, Sergeant Tawse waved him in and told him to wait in one of two interview rooms. Murray Ovenstone joined him a short time afterwards carrying a heavy pile of files and papers.

"Morning, Sarge."

"Murray's fine." Ovenstone stood at the table and pulled out a sheet of paper from one of the files. "Read that first. I'm going to get coffees." He thrust the sheet towards Craig and walked back out.

It was a memo from the Procurator Fiscal. The defence counsel in the case of Ian Soutar had indicated that they would be calling Murray and Craig as witnesses. Having been the first to question Soutar they would be asked under oath about their initial impressions of the accused.

"They'll probably only call one of us, most likely me as the senior, but I thought you'd better have a look at the files so we both say the same," said Murray as he returned with two mugs of coffee. Before he could sit down, there was a knock on the door he'd just closed, and John Tawse poked his head in.

"Sorry, Sergeant Ovenstone, Queen Street on the phone for you. Detective Superintendent Morrice."

Murray had to leave. Chic Morrice had called a meeting.

"God knows what this'll be about, but I'll have to go. Have a read through that lot, Craig, and we'll talk later."

The buff folder Murray had left him had been organised in date order. At the back he found the statements given by the golfer who had discovered Skilling's body and from Paul MacNaughton, the greenkeeper who had been arrested for nothing more than possessing a hammer. There were crime scene photographs, reports from DCI Blackie and DS McCann, and the letter found in Skilling's car. Craig paused to read it. Typed on pale blue paper, it was from Ivan Skilling's daughter. He skipped to the end, feeling he was intruding. The letter finished '*I'm not ready to meet you yet, Dad*', and finished abruptly with '*Yours, Sandra.*'

He came next to Ian Soutar's confession, and then a stapled document with a bold title. IAN SOUTAR, PSYCHIATRIC ASSESSMENT. Written by Dr Muriel Trickett, it was long and detailed.

Ian Soutar has been a patient of mine for some three years. Prior to that, he was under the care of the Department of Child and Adolescent Psychiatry.

Typed under the Kingseat Hospital letterhead, it ran to three pages. Craig expected the report to be beyond his comprehension and full of medical jargon, but Dr Trickett had written it for a lay readership. There was a detailed account of Ian Soutar's life from his birth to the present. He was born in Bankhead Avenue in February, 1960 and attended Bucksburn

Primary School. Dr Trickett presented a list of dates under the heading "Life Events."

- *1968–death of father*
- *1969–moved to Miltonfold address*
- *1971–hospitalised, Royal Aberdeen Children's Hospital, Juvenile Rheumatoid Arthritis*
- *1971–Bankhead Academy*
- *1975–School truanting; behaviour change noted by teachers; isolation from peers*

Soutar's health problems seemed to begin in the early 1970s, but from 1975 onwards it appeared to Craig that he descended into serious mental illness. He skipped through Dr Trickett's summaries of multiple assessments by her Child and Adolescent colleagues. When she had quoted terms he didn't understand he found she had translated them for her intended audience, with references to "bizarre ideas" and "fantastic beliefs." His "possible hallucinations" she decoded as "disordered conscious dreams." Her report finished with a summary of her own more recent assessments of Ian Soutar's mental state.

"*Since his last inpatient admission (17th December 1980 - 26th February 1981) I have continued to see Ian Soutar as an outpatient. During that admission as usual his preoccupation was with what he described sometimes as dreams, at other times as real experiences. Many of the experiences he described involved bizarre rituals, possibly sexual in nature but in any case involving mutilation of the genitalia of men or boys. While at no time has he expressed or displayed any homosexual orientation, and in fact, he has displayed vigorous heterosexual attraction to female staff and patients he has encountered, this apparent obsession with the mutilation of the sexual organs of men raises questions. In my more recent contacts with him, I have become less certain about his diagnosis of psychosis. The question of the exact nature of his ideation with respect to genital mutilation may not, as has long been thought, be true psychotic thought disorder or hallucinosis, and in fact may, as he has repeatedly stated for several years now, be partially-remembered disturbing dreams he* has had. Mr Soutar has repeatedly stated that he is frustrated by his dreams, and that there is some importance to them that he cannot understand. Whether there may be some forgotten trauma behind his dreams is something I continue to keep under active consideration. Before his confession to murder, I had been considering a referral to a psychiatrist with special expertise in clinical hypnotherapy, Dr D Slinn. I hoped that Dr Slinn might be able to regress Mr Soutar under hypnosis to determine whether there is indeed a traumatic event or events in his past which may be behind the dreams. It is my recommendation to the Court that Dr Slinn is consulted about Ian Soutar's case."

Craig read this summary with increasing confusion. Was she saying Soutar was mad or not? He can't be right in the head if he's obsessed with cutting off men's bits, surely?

As he drove back to Queen Street, Craig's discomfort about Ian Soutar's situation grew. Not only was there the obvious discrepancy between his account of the injuries he had inflicted on Ivan Skilling and those found by the forensic pathologist, but Soutar might simply have been recounting something he had dreamt.

The psychiatrist's comments reminded Craig of Gordon Flint. "Forgotten trauma behind his dreams" — Flint said that was what caused his phobias.

It would have been good to talk to DS Ovenstone about Soutar. He thought Murray Ovenstone might also have misgivings about the confession, and he wondered what he had made of the medical reports, if he had read them. But even if they both thought Soutar was innocent, what difference would that make? Blackie had led the case and he didn't seem to care as long as he got someone nailed. It was up to the Fiscal, and later the court and jury to decide if Soutar was guilty or not.

Chapter 15

Craig's unease about Ian Soutar continued. At times he wished he hadn't read the psychiatry report. When he woke in the small hours, his mind often turned to Soutar and the disgusting 'dreams' he claimed to have.

It seemed plain the little man was a complete nutcase, and hard to believe that Dr Trickett could have any doubts about that. She'd described Soutar's awful *'obsession with the mutilation of the sexual organs of men.'* But in the same report she'd written, *'I have become less certain about his diagnosis of psychosis.'* How could a specialist psychiatrist like Muriel Trickett be taken in by a manipulative freak?

Trickett seemed to think hypnosis might uncover some meaning to Soutar's dreams. If she was right, the truth behind his obsession might help prove his innocence.

Several times, though, Craig would wake to memories of Gordon Flint. It was a welcome relief from Soutar, but it was some time before he worked out why the Fifer with the wavy fair hair had come to mind.

Flint had spoken about dreams with deep, hidden meanings. And by using hypnosis, Flint had revealed that his dreams concealed awful events from his past. Events so terrifying to him that his mind had blocked them. Dr Trickett was suggesting hypnotherapy for Soutar. That must be why Craig was thinking about them both.

Having worked out what was disturbing him, Craig thought he'd be able to move on. But he still tossed and turned, waking unrested. There was something he couldn't quite put his finger on. Something else that connected Soutar and Flint.

Then one morning on the way to start an early shift it came to him.

"Jesus!" he said out loud to himself. A man across the bus aisle looked at him and went back to his P&J.

The elusive link between Ian Soutar and Flint wasn't only their dreams, or hypnosis. It wasn't The Mount. It was Fife. More specifically, the man from Cupar who died in the woods. On the chip wrapper Craig had read 'mutilat-'. Mutilation was a word linked to Ivan Skilling and to Soutar's obsession. Could the murder in Fife be linked to Skilling's mutilation?

If there did turn out to be a link, that would mean a new line of enquiry. One that might rule Soutar out. Or implicate him in another killing.

###

Craig was soaked after walking to the phonebox on the corner of Great Western Road. When his 12-month rental of the flat in Hollybank Place ended, he decided his next flat must have a phone.

As the pips went, he pushed two ten pences into the slot. Jack's voice in his ear transported him back to their time at Napier College.

"Hi, Jack, How are you doing?"

"Craig? Hiya! You coming down at the weekend? I'm meeting Phil and his new girlfriend on Saturday."

"Another one? You mean he's split from Crazy Carol?"

"Aye, a few weeks ago. You coming down?"

"Nah, sorry. Can't get enough time off. Listen can you do me a favour?"

He heard Jack sigh. "What? As long as it's not the PNC."

Craig cringed. He *had* been going to work up to asking Jack if he might access the PNC for him again, but Jack had closed it down before he'd even raised the topic. Damn it.

Craig said, "No, it's OK, not the PNC this time, Jack, just a question."

"Thank fuck. I thought you were going for a hat-trick. Three suspensions in a row."

Craig moved on to his plan B.

"No, I'm keeping clear from here on in. But listen, remember that mannie from Cupar that was killed in the woods somewhere? The one I read about on the chip paper?"

"Mannie! Christ! It must be infectious. You're Aberdonian now?"

Craig hadn't realised what he'd said. "God, I must have caught it!"

When they stopped laughing, Jack said, "D'you mean the Cupar, guy? Body found out at Tentsmuir?"

"Aye, that's the one. I couldn't remember the place. Tentsmuir."

"What about him?"

"Well, was there anything unusual about it?"

"Unusual apart from having his head battered to a pulp and his cock and balls cut off, you mean? That's what I heard happened." Jack was laughing again. "They're all unusual, Craig, but that one stood out a bit!"

"Jeezuss H Christ!"

"Yeah, and rumour has it they never found his tadger. Pretty weird, eh?"

Rumour? thought Craig. He rushed on, "Did they get someone for it?" He was feeling sick at what Jack was saying, but his pulse was racing, beating up into his neck and head.

"Not as far as I know. It'd have been in *The Courier* if they had. It's almost a year ago now, I think."

Even in his excitement, Craig had to laugh at the irony. "You mean that's how Tayside police talk to each other? Read the local paper?"

"Everything I know about the case is from *The Courier*." Jack must have sensed the puzzled look on Craig's face. "I mean, it's not one of ours. It's Fife's case."

###

Craig dialled another number after finishing the call to Jack.

"Hello?" The pips went and he pushed in another ten pence.

"Maureen? It's me, Craig Masson."

"Oh hi!"

He hated the sound of his own voice, jangling in his ears as he spilled the words he'd prepared.

"Could we meet for a drink sometime? I mean—"

"Yes, that would be great. This weekend?"

The wave of relief that washed over him was followed by a surge of excitement. They chatted until the pips went again.

Maureen, who asked him to call her Mo, was Davy Jepson's sister. The last time he'd seen her, when she'd come to pick Davy up from the Bridge Bar one evening, Craig had found her easy to talk to while she waited for Davy to finish his pint. She'd smiled when he commented on her new hairstyle. Her brunette perm had been replaced with a neat, short cut, and he liked the sparkle in her dark eyes. During the call he'd been picturing Mo's thin-lipped smile and the few fine freckles on her cheeks. Davy had said she was two years younger than him, making her 24. Craig had a spring in his step as he made his way back to Hollybank Place in driving rain.

The excitement of Mo Jepson agreeing to go out with him wasn't the only thing that kept Craig awake that night. Try as he might, he couldn't help himself replaying his conversation with Jack, and the coincidence that the Tentsmuir victim had also had his cock and balls chopped off. Coincidence? If they'd been using the PNC, the Fife and Grampian forces would surely have noticed the similarity between their cases.

If the same person killed both men it couldn't have been Soutar. The Fife killing had been about a year ago, and Craig was sure he remembered from the psychiatry report that Ian Soutar had been in hospital at the time. Soutar was innocent. He had to be. Craig rolled and thrashed as he tried to sleep.

He must have slept, because the next morning his head was full of half-remembered dreams. Nightmares. They had to have been prompted by thinking so much about Fife. He'd been back at the top of a high tower on a windy winter afternoon. The Mount stood on a hill outside Cupar, and four years ago Craig had nearly been murdered at the top of it. He woke with swirling visions of mice escaping from a cage and a wardrobe filled with body parts. Flint had a jacket round his naked lower half, and a man hung impaled on the spiked parapet that encircled the Mount's top.

Craig had stopped having nightmares about The Mount a couple of years before, and thought he'd put it all behind him. But thinking about Flint and his dreams, and then hearing from Jack about the Fife murder had brought it back as vividly as ever.

Flint knew all about dreams, he thought. Poor Flint and his mixed-up family. He wondered how Flint was doing and realised with a vague feeling of self-reproach that he hadn't been in touch with him for years, even though he knew that Flint, too, was living and working in Aberdeen. Craig had his address somewhere.

All that day, Craig had a nagging feeling that he was missing something. Something else that kept making him associate Flint with Ian Soutar. Almost at the end of their shift, as Davy was driving the panda car along Holburn Street, it came to him. He knew how he might be able to help Ian Soutar. The little man called Stiff.

###

Poor Flint, thought Craig as he closed the rusting iron gate outside the Jamaica Street flat. Poor Isla. She'd looked well. Dark, shiny hair and a lovely smile — although she hadn't smiled once while she'd told Craig she and Flint had split up.

Flint had moved out, and was back in Auchmoor. Isla hadn't gone into detail, but it was clear the break-up had been her decision. I'd had enough of his dreams and drinking, she'd said. There had been tears in her eyes.

Craig tried not to think about Flint, Soutar or the body found at Tentsmuir. He was looking forward to two days off at the end of the week. He had the Saturday to himself and would be going out with Mo Jepson on Sunday night.

THE TARGET

Now I've cut them off, I don't…
I don't know what to do with them.
Something special? Just for him?
I hope he likes his lovely bouquet. Ha ha.
He was the one.
He felt the knife!
He twitched.
His eyes opened.
The bastard suffered.
He deserved it.
They all deserve it.
I've waited for this.
I deserve it.
And so do they..
That rock was heavy, though.
And there's blood on my nice leather jacket.
It'll wipe off.
Oh God! The hammer. They'll find the hammer.
They'll come to me then.
Should have worn gloves. But I used his Spirit.
I like the blood, though.
Running between my fingers. Dripping.
I know what to do with these!
I'll leave them in here. Perfect.
Save them looking for them.
But I'm throwing *this* to the foxes.

Chapter 16

It was the day before his first date with Mo Jepson that Craig drove to Auchmoor to visit Gordon Flint. On the drive back north, he chuckled to himself about Flint and his mystery one-night stand. But he'd failed to get Flint's help, and by the time he was back in Aberdeen he had told himself again he had to forget about Soutar, innocent or not.

On Sunday evening he waited for Mo on the corner of Union Street and Union Terrace, at the foot of a huge granite statue. 'Edward VII' was inscribed in gold letters on its base. Craig stood a little awkwardly near a group of punks and skinheads. They were often gathered there when he drove past in a panda car. He hoped none of them would recognise him from the time he'd had to move them on one Saturday afternoon. It was a relief to see Mo walking towards him with a wide smile.

"Sorry, am I late?" she asked. She was right on time, 7pm.

"No, I was a bit early. Nervous," Craig replied. He had been nervous all day and hoped he sounded like he was joking, being cool.

"I won't bite you. Not on a first date," she said with a laugh. "Fancy going to Radars? I thought that would be good. Been there before?"

He had driven past the American-style diner on Belmont Street but never been in. They walked the short distance and took seats in a wooden booth.

"Try a root beer. It's amazing."

An hour later, Craig used the last of his burger bun to mop up some ketchup and mustard from his plate, sat back in the red vinyl booth and exhaled. "That was brilliant," he said, before taking another mouthful of root beer.

"Good. I was hoping you'd like it here."

"It must be like this in the US. I'd love to go to America, but I doubt if I ever will. Not on a police salary."

"I'm hoping Rigman keeps getting bigger and sends me to Texas."

"Rigman?"

"I'm in the accounts department. Rigman Services. My dad works with another American lot, and once he was sent over to Houston for six weeks. He said it was amazing, but he came back with a stupid accent. For a while he wanted us to move there, but it'll never happen. My mum likes it here."

"What does he do?"

"Something to do with valves for drilling oil. Listen, d'you want to go round to Ma Cameron's?"

They split the bill and sauntered along the cobbles. Craig's spirits soared when he felt Mo's woollen-gloved hand take his. Ma Cameron's was busy, even on a Sunday night. A noisy throng of mostly youthful bodies filled the old stone passageways and snug bars. To understand each other in the hubbub Mo had to tiptoe and talk loudly, and he had to stand close in to answer her. Perfume behind her ear tantalised him and the possibility that they might kiss later made Craig conscious of the lingering taste in his mouth. He wished he hadn't chosen beer after pickles and mustard.

"Fit r'ye daein' wi' an ootsider, quine? Run oot o' Aiberdeen loons?" The raised voice behind him made Craig wince. He saw a sparkle in Mo's eyes as she looked past him, smiling.

"If there wis ony fine loons in Aiberdeen, it wid be different!" she said with a cheeky smile.

Barry fucking Cummings! "Oh hi, Barry," Craig said, turning. "Can I get you a drink?"

"Nah, loon, I'm here wi' someone, ken?" Cummings winked conspiratorially and tapped the side of his nose. Over his shoulder, Craig could see a stunning girl. It must be the Natasha he's been bragging about, he thought.

The way Mo and Barry had interacted so naturally, and the way her attention was instantly drawn to him sucked away all Craig's confidence. He should have realised they would know each other. Barry and Mo's brother Davy had been at the same school, and Mo was bound to have been there. They'd have known each other since they were infants. They'd probably been in each other's houses, played together. Her eyes had sparkled at Barry more brightly and quickly than at him. They had probably been a teenage couple, for God's sake. He watched Barry and his date make their way through the clamour, both chatting to everyone they passed.

"Thank God he's gone!" Mo said.

Craig looked back at her, his smile slowly returning.

Smirking, she went on, "He's always been a chancer. Tries it on with every girl. As far as I know from my friends he's never got anywhere, either."

Craig was intrigued. "I thought you—"

"Don't even say it. He's great for a laugh, a bit of banter, but you keep him at arm's length."

Craig was relaxing, until her next words.

"You ready to go?" She had an empty glass, and Craig quickly drained the last of his pint.

"Err — yes. I'll walk you home," he said, uncertainly.

"Home? It's only half past nine. That's no night out. I meant let's go somewhere quiet."

Craig woke with a serene feeling of contentment, his bed warm and his limbs loose and relaxed. He was more used to waking abruptly and jumping up, no matter what shift he was working. Even on days off, he was up in time to get to work for a 7 o'clock start.

This morning he had slept longer, and the sun shining through his thin yellow curtains gave his room a golden glow. He lay going over the evening he had spent with Mo. After Ma Cameron's they had walked hand in hand to a quieter bar where they had sat chatting until closing time. They'd laughed and shared stories from their past, and Craig had been surprised to find himself telling Mo about his trip to Fife the previous day. He didn't tell her what he had asked Flint to do, but he did mention Flint's experiences with hypnotherapy. She had commented that her flatmate was a psychology student and was fascinated by hypnosis. He'd then walked Mo to her tenement door in Rosemount. He could still taste their passionate kiss.

His sunny mood was clouded only by the unfortunate timing of their first date. Craig was about to start a run of seven night shifts, and he wouldn't be able to see Mo again until after that.

As he walked into Queen Street that night the desk sergeant called out to him.

"Evening, Craig. There's a phone message for you."

Mo? he thought, his hopes rising. He grasped the folded note the sergeant had put on the desk before he'd turned away to answer the next call.

TO: PC Masson

Message: call PC Storrie, Tayside Police

01382 233444

Why was Jack calling him at work? He stuffed the note into his jacket pocket and trudged to the locker room to change. Seven nights, 11 at night until 7 in the morning. Oh God.

A heavy slap on the back made him jump. "What the f—?"

"Hiya Craigie-boy! Ready for this?" Davy was always on form, whatever time of day or night. "How'd it go wi' ma wee sis?"

Craig was already rushing along the busy morning pavement towards the bus stop when he found the note in his jacket pocket. He had forgotten about Jack's message.

Damn it! I'd better call from here and find out what shift Jack's on.

He'd been hoping to get straight home to bed. As he hurried back into HQ, the morning desk sergeant said, "Want overtime? Can't get enough of us?"

"No chance, Kenny. Can I use the phone in your back office? I've got to call a PC in Tayside."

"Help yersel, son. Shut the door, will ye, I dinna want ti hear yer private business. 'Calling a PC in Tayside!' That's a new excuse."

Before Craig could explain it was true and he was using the phone officially, Kenny had pushed the door closed behind him.

"Hello, PC Masson from Grampian here. Is PC Jack Storrie on shift?"

"Yes, I'll put you through," said a friendly female voice, "Jack's on earlies this week, at his desk already. Loves his computer, that laddie."

A moment later Craig heard Jack's voice. "Hello, PC Storrie speaking."

"Jack, it's me, Craig. What are you calling me at work for?"

"Oh, sorry, PC Masson," said Jack's voice, "I'll just put you on hold for a second." The phone went silent, and Craig was about to put the phone down thinking his friend had been playing some silly trick on him when there was clicking on the line, and Jack said in a hushed voice. "Craig, listen, I can't talk for long. Listen—"

"I am bloody listening. What the hell—?"

"Sorry," Jack hissed, I can't talk loudly, I'm in a shared office, and if someone comes in I'll have to hang up."

Craig sighed. "C'mon, Jack, I've just finished a night shift. Knackered."

"I was thinking after you told me about your man with his balls cut off. You know, same as the Tentsmuir guy. I was alone in the office this weekend for a few hours. I had a look on the system. I found another one."

"Another what?"

"A man who died the same way. I can't talk now."

Craig said nothing.

"Craig, phone me tonight at home," Jack went on. "There's at least one more. But I can't talk now — oh, hi Sergeant, I was just phoning technical support, I think there's a problem with the—"

The phone went dead, and Craig was left wondering. His mind was foggy after his night shift, as it always was after the first of seven. By the end of the week he would be fresher when he came off duty, until the day shifts restarted and his sleep pattern was disrupted again. He thanked Kenny as he sauntered out past the desk, yawning.

On the bus, Jack's truncated call played back to him. Had Jack risked accessing the PNC without permission again? Like he had when he'd helped Craig and Flint trace The Limb Collector. Craig was still scared to even think about the PNC. But Jack seemed to be suggesting there'd been another identical murder. 'At least one more', he'd said.

Three victims? More? Linked by the killer's MO? But not linked by the police. Another undetected serial killer?

Craig needed sleep.

###

He still needed sleep when he got up out of bed that evening. Familiar excitement and frustration had kept him tossing and turning. There could be another serial murderer at work, but because neighbouring police forces were not sharing information, he was getting away with it.

After a big bowl of rice crispies and a ham sandwich with plenty of butter he put on his jacket and walked along to the telephone box. As well as some tens, he had two fifty pence coins, and hoped he wouldn't need to use one of them. It was after six o'clock and Jack would be off duty by now. He was surprised when the phone was answered after only two rings.

"You'll need to get a bloody house phone, Craig! This is a pain in the arse."

"My next flat. The lease is up on this one in—"

"Doesn't matter. Listen to this. Got a pen and paper?"

"Yeah."

"The two men have got to be connected. Same killer, I mean. I was thinking about it and used the PNC. Listen to this."

"But I thought hardly anyone was using it? I mean only Tayside mainly?"

"Well, since you and Flint connected four murders, one thing that *has* happened is details of *all* murder cases in Scotland now get added to the database. That means at least we can find out if there are any similarities. The information is pretty basic, but one thing they record is any suggestion of a sexual nature to the killing."

"I don't get where that takes us. We're not talking about rapes or anything—"

"Stop interrupting. Since they started putting murders on the PNC, in about May '78, there's been 203 murders added to the system."

"203! How the hell—?"

"But we're only looking at males, so that's 144 men, in about four years." Craig was shaking his head. He could see a man standing outside, stamping his feet to keep warm. Even through the misty glass of the phone box he could see the man's breath in the cold night air. Jack hadn't stopped. "I thought if we include sexual aspects in the search that should catch anyone who's had his nuts cut off, don't you think?"

"I suppose so." Craig was beginning to understand what Jack had been doing.

"Murders with a sexual element, there were only eleven—"

"Only? Bloody hell!"

Jack kept going. "But four of them were little kids, so that leaves seven. And guess what? Your man in Grampian *and* the Tentsmuir guy are two of them! You know what that means?"

Before Craig could think properly Jack rushed on. "It means the search works! Fucking computers, man, I tell you, fucking brilliant!" Jack didn't often swear. "And another bloke was found lying beside a car, with 'genital mutilation'. That's three. Two of the cases are still open, and no one's made a connection."

The man outside was knocking angrily on the phone box door.

Back in his flat before he had to get ready to go to work, Craig pondered what Jack had told him. It seemed possible — or even likely — that there were at least three unsolved killings of men, all involving genital mutilation. The chance that they weren't linked was small. That would mean that he and Jack had identified another serial killer, but only by accessing the

PNC without clearance. Again. There was no way they could do anything about it without risking the end of their police careers. Or his, at least — Jack's part in The Mount had never been disclosed, and he would be seen as a first offender.

There was something positive, though. He was even more certain that Ian Soutar had to be innocent. He couldn't have killed the man found at Tentsmuir because he was in hospital at the time, and now that they knew about other possible victims it was even less likely Soutar's confession was true.

Craig decided he had to find out why the man called Stiff had confessed to a murder he didn't commit. If it was something to do with his dreams, surely someone should hypnotise him to find out why. It worked for Flint.

Chapter 17

"Blue, wi' a cream roof. It's ma pride 'n' joy. Ah polished it again last nicht."

If I hear once more about his fuckin' Cortina with a cream roof I'll fuckin'...

There were still 40 minutes before the morning break, and listening to Tommy go on about his car was making Flint's ears nearly as sore as his wrists. He was filling bags of cattle feed. As usual, Tommy had the easy job, pulling a trapdoor handle to let the flow of 'nuts' out of the huge steel hopper.

Flint had to hold a sack underneath the hopper, and signal to Tommy when it was full. It was hard work humphing every half-hundredweight bag onto a pallet, and Hamlyn's mill produced animal feed by the ton.

"Ah'll take a shot after the piece-break, son, gie you a bit o' a rest."

Flint knew Tommy would do no such thing. The dust would set off his cough and he'd say between rasps, "Sorry, son, could you—? It's the stoor. Ma chest, y'ken."

It's the fags, more like, Flint would think before stationing himself under the hopper again. And he still had to cycle home to Auchmoor at the end of the day. There must be a better job than this.

On that crazy Saturday, nearly a week ago, after Craig left Flint had moped around feeling unsettled. He had told Craig more about Isla than he had to his mum, but as he tried to watch TV it wasn't his familiar ruminations about the break up that was bothering him. He couldn't put his finger on it. Flint had no difficulty brushing aside Craig's mad notions about hypnosis and the man called Stiff being innocent, but his mind kept returning to their conversation until he gave up and went to bed.

After Craig's visit Flint tried to cut down on the drink again. The incident with the mystery girl in his mum's bed had scared him, although he'd had a laugh once Craig pointed out that she clearly knew what she was doing. His sleep was patchy, but unlike previous attempts at abstinence, when he'd got up sad and exhausted, this time it was different. There were no half-remembered dreams to frustrate him. Instead, wherever his mind had taken him overnight was somewhere that left him stimulated.

Now, watching calf nuts tumble into sacks and blanking out Tommy's moans, some of what his excited subconscious had been trying to lay out for him began to emerge. Fleeting notions mingled with resonant echoes, melding together and drifting apart in Flint's mind as he hefted yet more heavy sacks. When a solid concept finally floated to the surface, Flint was compelled to express it. Out loud. Two words. 'Serial killer.'

Tracking down the killer of Inga Sabiston, Sarah Kibble and the rest of the Limb Collector's victims had been exhilarating. A successful team had come together over the course of one frenetic and terrifying day. Flint, Craig, Isla and Dr Sutton had worked together with focus. Even his mum had played her part.

He wanted that again.

By day, the idea that there could be another madman committing gruesome crimes would occur to Flint again, flicking a switch that started his pulse racing. Tracking the beast down would be so much better than his awful job.

By the time he tried to go to sleep, though, reality would depress Flint. Craig had no proof that the two similar killings were connected. It was fanciful to think there could be another undetected series of slayings. Even if there was, Craig was living and working in Aberdeen while Flint was stuck in this dead-end job a hundred miles south.

With no prospect of escape, Flint's sleep deteriorated again. If he continued to steer clear of alcohol, he might have to risk resorting to his old remedy.

###

Another bloody Saturday. Flint slumped down the stairs towards the sound of the kettle boiling and dishes being washed. Through the little window above the front door he could see it was a bright day but windy, spindly branches of the birch tree waving in and out of view. He'd promised to cut it back for the neighbours. If he could be bothered, he could do that today.

"Is that you, Gordon?" *Who else would it be?* "I'm glad you're up. Granville's coming for me soon."

"Morning, mum."

"Aren't you going to get dressed? What are you going to do today? You could go for a haircut. It's getting long again." It wasn't long since Craig had commented on how short it was. Flint said nothing and Eleanor went on, "We're going for a drive. I want to go to the Woollen Mill sale."

Taking a mug from the cupboard, Flint grunted, "I'll probably watch the sport. Not much else to do."

He took his coffee into the living room and switched the TV on. He'd missed most of Tiswas, but World of Sport would be on soon enough. His mum was singing as she went back and forth, opening and closing cupboards and tripping up and down the stairs.

"At least put this on, Gordon." Eleanor threw his dressing gown to him. "I wish you would do something, Gordon, instead of moping around all the time. Can't you go and visit Spake, or someone?"

"I'd need to get a bus and a train, and by the time I got there he'd probably be out or something." He dragged himself off the couch to go over to the TV to turn the volume up. Spit the Dog was on.

A short time later, Eleanor came back into the living room. "You should learn to drive. You could save up for a car. I might be able to help you out."

Flint knew his mum's meagre widow's pension and her wage from the library job didn't stretch very far. There wouldn't be money she could give him. He managed to smile thanks to her, but shook his head.

"Mum, I couldn't even afford the driving lessons.

Hours of horse racing and wrestling later, the football scores were coming in when Flint heard the car draw up outside. Minutes later he was talking football with Granville Sutton while his mum made a pot of tea. She brought a tray in with cups and saucers and Granville stood.

"I'll take that, Ellie. Sorry, I should have helped you."

"It's OK. Did you ask Gordon what he thought?" She was looking at Flint, expectantly, and he wondered what she was going on about.

"Err — not yet, I was distracted by the football."

"Granville's offered to teach you to drive." There was a broad smile on his mum's face as she looked back and forth between them. "He can take you out tomorrow."

He'd been in his car a number of times, but before this afternoon he hadn't been back to Granville's home since before The Mount. As he sat in the passenger seat of the old Volvo his mind went back to his first visit, when he cycled all the way from Auchmoor and spent a hazy summer day with Dr Sutton and his elderly mother, discussing hypnosis and the subconscious mind. He drank homemade beer and Granville had whisky. He had only vague memories of Morna Sutton driving him home, with his bike tied to the roof rack and

Granville snoozing. Flint had spent the journey trying to keep together the psychological jigsaw puzzle Dr Sutton had helped him complete. He could just about understand how self-hypnosis had uncovered memories he had repressed, and how those memories had, until that afternoon, convinced him he was linked in some way to multiple murders.

Today the sun was shining as it had been that first afternoon, but beneath the hedges there was still frost. Granville had talked all the way from Auchmoor, telling Flint about the clutch and brake pedals, and the importance of using the mirrors. He gave a running commentary on which gear he was in and by the time they pulled into the narrow road to his smallholding Flint was thoroughly confused and sure he would never master driving.

They'd come to Motray Den for Flint's first driving lesson because Granville knew there were quiet, straight stretches of road nearby. As they drove on past the row of cottages Granville and his mother occupied, Flint had a brief view of the field behind. It was where the goats and chickens were kept.

When he took over driving, after a few lurches and crunches Flint found he could propel the car forwards. It took more practice to stop it smoothly and keep the engine running. All the time Granville was looking forward and back to check for an approaching car or tractor.

"What's that smell?"

"That'll be the clutch," said Granville.

"The pedal?" Flint's mind hadn't connected the lever under his foot with the workings of the gearbox.

Half an hour later, Flint felt confident enough to steer the big car into the bumpy driveway that led into Motray Den.

"That was ace. I never thought I would drive a car. Can we do it again?"

Granville smiled as he unclipped his seatbelt. "Yes, Flint, I'd be glad to. You might need a couple of proper lessons, though. I don't know the highway code as well as I should. Before I take you home, I'll need to pop out and feed the goats. Mother's joints are getting a bit too stiff. Come on in, she'll be pleased to see you again."

Morna Sutton looked exactly the same as she had when Flint first met her, the corners of her smiling eyes etched with diverging lines, pale against her weathered face. "Lovely to see you, Gordon. I hope I still look as young as I did when we met before." Flint felt himself blushing. When he'd first met her, he'd assumed Morna was Sutton's wife. She'd been delighted.

"Hello, I…"

She had turned away and was already filling the kettle. Flint could smell baking and the familiar goaty smell the car had.

When Granville came back in he had changed into wellingtons. He kicked them off at the kitchen door. "Ooh, tea, lovely. I'd offer you a beer, Gordon, but we're driving." Flint saw water forming around the little clods of earth on the tiles as the frost melted. He could now see the obvious age difference between Granville and Morna. Four years ago he'd have put anyone over about thirty in the same ancient category.

They set off an hour later. "I want to get back before it's too dark. Mother worries. She doesn't drive much now; her eyes are not so good." As he drove, Granville glanced towards Flint from time to time and seemed unusually distracted. As they passed through Cupar he said, "Flint, there's something I want to say."

Granville usually forgot to call him Flint. He wondered what was coming.

"It's about your mother and me."

Flint squirmed. Granville's relationship with Eleanor had developed, he knew, and he had wondered if he was getting in the way now that he had moved back in with his mum.

"Granville, I'm OK with it."

"When I met your mum again after — you know — that day, I didn't know if she'd keep speaking to me. I had tried to forget her for years before, and seeing her again — it stirred me…" He went silent.

Flint had never known Dr Sutton to be lost for words. He realised the older man was asking for his approval. Granville had never discussed his relationship with his mother, even though Flint had known about them for nearly four years. He looked straight ahead, keeping from his face the ironic smile he could feel inside. He had no idea how to respond, other than to repeat, "It's OK."

After another silence, Granville went on. "And I'm very sorry about you and Isla. I was upset. I know your mum was too." Flint couldn't speak. "Are you still in touch with her?"

"No. I don't know what to say." Now it was Flint who had no words. He stared out of the passenger window, tears gathering.

"Are you still having the dreams? I'm sorry, but Eleanor said she thought that was something to do with the break-up."

"Not as much. I don't remember them."

"And your acrophobia?"

"That's all in the past. I can climb ladders at work. Anything."

Out of the window, behind Granville's head, Flint could see The Mount in the near distance. His experience there was terrible, but it proved he had conquered his fear of heights.

"Do you have other friends in Aberdeen you keep up with?"

"No. No one. Mind you," he said, looking at Granville, "d'you remember Craig? PC Masson?"

"Of course. How could I forget that day?"

"Craig visited me the other day. He wanted me to hypnotise someone, I think."

"I'm not sure I would approve, Flint, even though you were successful in treating yourself."

"Don't worry, I told him to bugger off." They both smiled, and Flint went on to outline some of Craig's theories about another serial killer.

Granville shook his head. "I don't want to know."

In Auchtermuchty he took a left turn.

"Where are you going?" said Flint. "It's quicker to go straight through 'Muchty."

Sutton said nothing, smiling as he drove on. In half a mile he pulled in.

"It's quiet from here on. You're driving."

Oh shit.

###

Flint's spirits lifted over the next few weeks as he developed an interest in cars. Cycling to and from Cupar each day, he began to notice Fords and Vauxhalls, and matched up road signs to the diagrams in the dog-eared, coverless booklet Granville had lent him.

One Friday, Flint's mum let him off with his dig money, enough to pay for three lessons. The driving instructor had laughed at Sutton's out of date copy of the Highway Code, and told Flint to buy a new one.

He needed more driving practice, but waiting for Granville to take him out in the Volvo was frustrating. He even considered asking Tommy for a go in his Cortina, but knew the old bugger was too proud of it.

Flint would never be able to buy a car of his own, he decided, but as soon as he had passed his test he was going to find a job driving. He imagined himself as a travelling salesman, roaming the countryside in his company saloon car with a boot full of samples, after being waved off each morning by proud, smiling Isla.

Chapter 18

March 1982

On the Monday after Craig's night shifts finished he picked Mo up from her flat in South Mount Street. They went to a hotel along Queen's Road, and after he'd had a couple of soft drinks and Mo some white wine and soda, he took her to see his flat. By the time he drove her back to her own flat their embraces had become steamier than he dared hope.

By Thursday evening they were on their third date. As they left the Silver Slipper after a couple of drinks, Mo stopped, poking Craig in the ribs.

"You going off me already? You forgot to hold my hand." Her nervous smile was lit by an orange glow. "What's wrong? You hardly spoke in there."

Craig had been distracted all evening, and now pulled her in close and hugged. The collar of her jacket was poking his neck, but he relaxed a little.

"Sorry, just tired."

"It's more than that." Mo didn't move.

Hesitating, he told her he thought a man charged with murder might be innocent. Instead of glazing over, she leant against a wall and asked more. He told her a little about Ian Soutar, and his bizarre dreams.

"So that's why you were interested in hypnosis? I wondered what that was really about. But you'll be able to think about something else tonight, won't you?"

"Aye, said Craig, taking her hand. "Sorry, I've been prattling. I've got some beer in the fridge. Let's go back to my flat for a while, then I'll walk you home."

"I've got a better idea." She winked at him. "Unless you really are tired." Squeezing in even closer, she blew warm air as she whispered in his ear. "My flatmate's away overnight."

They hurried up Rosemount Viaduct, and soon she was welcoming him into her flat with a deep kiss, reaching for his belt as he pulled off his jacket.

At twenty-past six the unusual ring of Mo's alarm clock startled Craig. He jumped out of the warm bed and threw his clothes on. Mo stirred and managed to smile at him before pulling the duvet tight around her. "See you tonight?" she mumbled, snaking a slim wrist and hand out into the air to wave at him. He smiled yes and leant in towards her but she drew back with a giggle. "You'll let the cold in."

He paused on his way through the living room, picking up a small flyer from the coffee table. He'd noticed it the previous night, and Mo had said it was her flatmate's. It advertised a psychology lecture by a visiting professor. 'Exploring the Subconscious Through Hypnotic Regression — aberrant behaviour patterns explained?' The lecturer was named as Professor Dante Slinn, from the Department of Clinical Psychiatry at the University of Dundee. There was a picture of a man in a leather jacket looking at the camera like a film star.

Slinn. I've heard that name somewhere before, thought Craig.

Most of Craig's spare time was taken up over the next few weeks with finding and then moving into a new flat. With his 12-month rental in Hollybank Place due to expire at the end of March, he didn't have long.

After just a few weeks in Hollybank he knew he'd been a fool to sign a year-long agreement. The landlord's promises had been empty, and agreed repairs remained undone even as Craig prepared to move out. It explained the low rent.

As well as a phone, on Craig's wishlist was a working hot water supply. He looked at several flats, and it was soon clear that unless he took another slum, he wasn't going to be able to afford a flat of his own. He was going to have to find someone to share with, but knew no one he could ask. He was moaning about his predicament on shift one evening, when Davy surprised him.

"I'd move in wi' you."

Craig was driving and turned briefly to look at his colleague. "I thought you were happy living with your parents? 'Hot dinner any time of day,' you're always saying."

"It's not that good. And I'm twenty-six. I'd like to get away."

Craig felt a mixture of surprise, relief and unease. He liked Davy and enjoyed working with him, but he didn't really know him that well. They were teamed up to work the same shifts, and sharing a flat would mean they would spend even more time together. He'd shared loads of flats, but never with someone he was working with. All of this went through his head in a flash, but it was something else that made him hesitant. Something he hadn't told Davy.

His partner must have sensed his discomfort. "It's alright, loon, I'll no' cramp yer style wi' Mo." Davy had a big grin on his face. "Ah ken yer no' just haudin' her hand, min."

Craig hadn't told Davy he'd kept seeing his sister after their first date. Mo had said not to. He would be 'funny' about it, she'd said, wearing the same grin as her brother wore now. Craig had been excited to share something secret with her, but didn't know if she was serious. He played it safe, though, unsure how protective of his wee sister Davy might be. Now it seemed she had been teasing him.

He squirmed as he drove, his face heating, but Davy moved on. "And if you're feart we'd be spendin' too much time thegither, we'll no. I'm getting sent oot tae Bucksburn in April. You'll hae plenty o' peace tae *entertain* ma sister!'

A week later, they had moved into a top-floor flat in Esslemont Avenue, opposite the grammar school. Sharing the rent meant a bedroom each, a living room with a Baxi gas fire, and a little kitchen with two hotplates and an electric frying pan. And a phone.

Craig and Davy had one more week of night shifts to work together before Davy transferred out to Bucksburn. It was in the early hours of that Wednesday when Craig almost lost a leg.

Chapter 19

April 1982

Something wasn't right. He was trapped in blackness. Paralysed. Cold rubber was smothering his face, and he seemed to be inhaling Barr's cream soda from a tin cup. There was a pain, but not as intense as before, no longer overwhelming. It was now concentrating in his right leg.

Deep, rumbling voices. Something happening to his left arm. A tiny sharpness pierced his wrist, and cold liquid flowed up his arm. He wanted to laugh.

His head shaking, his mouth shouting, "Fuck off," into the rubber. A hand on his face, a latex finger pulling at his eyelid. A flash of lightning, blinding until a black silhouette moved in. A head, upside down.

"He's coming round. Get another drip in, Ronnie. Now! And where's that fucking Orthopaedic Registrar?"

"And you still don't remember anything? The blue Corsa?" Davy was shaking his head, smiling. "Ah tell you, you should have let me drive, min!"

"Last I remember was the call coming in."

It was now two days after the accident and Craig was on a bed in Ward 14, Aberdeen Royal Infirmary. As far as he knew, he'd been taken from Casualty straight to an operating theatre. Reality had returned when a deadpan, unshaven youth in a bloody white coat had stuck needles in him. He'd retreated with a cheery, "Your ankle's gubbed. Mr McWhan said he thought he was going to have to amputate."

Davy explained they'd had a call to marshall boy racers on Beach Esplanade. It happened at least once in every week of night shifts. Davy said they had the blue light flashing and were following a white Escort XR3i as it sped towards the

Beach Ballroom. From the links golf course, a single-track road climbs up to join the wide Esplanade. It had been from here that a blue Corsa had roared out, just as Craig drove the panda car past. It broadsided them and Craig had been lucky to survive with only a broken leg.

"I thought you were deid. Ah wis thrown out, right doon the embankment, I wis lucky I didna hae the seat belt on. Ah tell you, I thought you were deid, man!" Every time Davy told the story he seemed more excited and the story was more embellished. Craig knew, though, that he had been lucky. What worried him was how his leg would be when the plaster cast came off. Whether he would get back to work. The young doctor's words stayed with him. 'Your ankle's gubbed.'

###

The plaster cast stretching from below his knee to his toes was heavy, and meant Craig was more or less confined to the flat. He'd lied to the consultant, saying he was going to his parents' house to be looked after, and when Davy and Mo picked him up he had to sit with his leg across the back seat of their dad's Cavalier. Getting out of the car was difficult, but nothing compared to climbing to the top floor flat, supported on each side by Mo and Davy while he carried his wooden crutches.

On his first day alone in the flat, he had to wait with an expanding bladder until Davy finished his shift and could help him to the toilet. Davy then repositioned furniture, and with enough piled up cushions he could get out of the low chair and hobble around on the crutches. He still kept a milk bottle beside his chair.

The embarrassment of relying on others to cope with everyday living was bad enough, but the boredom was worse. There was only so much Pebble Mill or Crown Court he could stand, and the plaster cast was to be on for at least eight weeks.

"You should maybe go back and stay with your mum and dad," said Mo one evening when she came in after work.

"That's a bit awkward, really."

"Oh, right. You mean you don't get on with them?"

Craig looked away. It was something that had been bothering him.

"Well, yes, we get on fine. It's just — I haven't actually told them."

"Haven't told them? You mean — jeez! Why not?" Mo shrank back in obvious surprise. "I wondered why they didn't visit you in ARI."

"It just sort of happened. I kind of knew my mum would be upset, worried, y'know. I decided to wait a day or two, and then I thought they'd be angry I hadn't told them, and then I thought it was too late, and..." He knew he wasn't making much sense, and didn't really know why he hadn't told them.

"That's weird. You should tell them."

"I know. I'll phone them tonight."

When Mo had gone back to her own flat, Craig spent some time looking at the phone. He imagined it ringing at the other end, and his mum walking along the carpeted hallway to answer it. He'd have to tell her, and she'd be upset that he was "hundreds" of miles away and she couldn't visit. She'd ask again why on earth he chose to move "up there" when he had been doing so well in Edinburgh. He still wouldn't tell her about the suspensions. Instead, he'd let her go on telling her friends how he was rising through the ranks, and that the move to Aberdeen was good for his career.

Eventually, he lifted the receiver and dialled.

"Hi, Jack."

Chapter 20

Late April 1982

When Jack suggested he come to stay in Dundee for a few weeks Craig agreed immediately. His spirits rose at the thought of a change. Ten days had passed since he'd left hospital, and while it was fun with Davy when he was off duty, and Mo made regular visits when Davy was on late or night shifts, being imprisoned in the flat was driving him mad.

"But, Jack, how can I get there? I can't drive, and I couldn't get the train. Not like this, with these fucking crutches."

"Easy. Someone's sick, and they're making me change from early shifts to lates on Wednesday. That means I can come up there on Tuesday and drive you back on Wednesday morning before I go to work."

"You've got a car, now? Brilliant. What did you get?"

"No, I mean I'll drive you back in your car. I'll get the bus to Aberdeen. What's your address?"

Craig was excited for the rest of that evening. The next day he hobbled about the flat gathering some clothes together and packing a grip. He was zipping it up when Mo rang the bell.

"I got off work early. A power cut. They sent us all home. What are you doing with the bag?"

When he told her the plan Mo went quiet.

"It'll only be a few weeks. I'm going mental shut up here all day."

"You'll be shut up in his flat instead," she said.

"He's on the ground floor. At least I'll be able to get out a bit." She looked sceptical. "I'll miss you," he added.

He saw her face soften with a smile. "Aye, that'll be right. You'll have a great time, talking about computers and police stuff all day."

He had to admit it would be good to spend time with Jack. It was years since they'd been at Tulliallan Police College together. He promised he would phone Mo regularly and come back at weekends, if Jack was off duty to drive him.

"And when I get this bloody stookie off I'll make it up to you."

"You'd better phone me," she said with her arms round his neck. "Look how long it took you to phone your poor mum."

He didn't tell her his mum still didn't know he'd been in a car crash.

Jack slowed as they approached a junction, just after they'd been through Stonehaven. A road sign pointed left to Montrose and Dundee, right to Brechin and Forfar.

"Which way? The bus came up through Forfar."

"Six and half a dozen," said Craig. "Takes the same time anyway. Go left, there's a good chip shop in Inverbervie."

"You getting used to life up north, then?"

The chip shop wasn't open, and it was nearly half-past twelve before they bought sausage rolls in Montrose.

"I'll need to eat and drive," said Jack. His shift started at two o'clock.

They made it to Dundee and parked on Pitfour Street with only time for Jack to help Craig in with his bag before getting into his uniform. When he had gone, Craig sat in the front room of the flat, very tired.

Jack's tenement flat was on a sloping street, and when he had told Craig he lived on the ground floor he hadn't mentioned that the main door was elevated above street level, seven steps up. When he'd moved into Esslemont Avenue just a few weeks ago Craig had always run up the four flights of stairs. It annoyed him how quickly he had become so unfit. Even when the plaster cast came off, it would be ages before he was strong enough to return to work.

In his rush, Jack hadn't said which bedroom was which. His flatmate, a medical student, was away at some hospital in England for two months, and Craig was to have his room. Pushing himself up to stand, he walked with one crutch to the nearest door off the narrow hall. This was clearly Jack's room. A shelf crammed with books, a pile of records, and an unmade bed were all clues, but the clincher was the revolving record on the turntable. The stylus was crackling its way around the LP's run-off groove, as it must have been doing since Jack left Dundee the day before. He'd always done that, Craig remembered, smiling. The last record of the night was always still revolving the next morning and only stopped then if Jack happened to notice. It was *Combat Rock* this time. With his free hand, Craig lifted the needle and switched the turntable off.

The other room was no tidier, but the books were medical texts and there was a small rubber hammer on the bedside table. A huge poster of Siouxsie Sioux looked over the bed, where Jack had dumped Craig's grip.

An hour later, after a cup of cheap coffee while he tried to adjust the aerial on the portable black and white TV, Craig was as bored as he would have been if he'd stayed in Aberdeen. The change of scene he'd looked forward to had lost its charm already, and it was still his first day in Dundee.

The view outside was of the roofs of cars parked a few feet below, and over the street a dim tenement like the one he was in. Soft, reddish-brown sandstone instead of stern, grey granite. At least his Aberdeen flat looked out over the turrets of Aberdeen Grammar school, gothic silhouettes against a dull, unwelcoming sky.

Surely I can't be homesick, he told himself. He'd phone Mo later to hear her voice.

Having explored the flat and found it easy to get around, he decided to borrow one of Jack's books. He had just chosen a John Le Carré he hadn't read when he noticed the corner of a buff file showing under Jack's bed. He recognised his friend's writing. '*Not the*' was all he could see. He couldn't help putting his crutch aside and sitting on the bed to reach down. Pulling it out he read on the front of the file '*Not the PNC (haha!)*'. He smiled at Jack's weird sense of humour and pushed the file back.

He couldn't get into Smiley's People the way he had expected to. Something was distracting him and he knew what it was. He wanted to know what was in Jack's file. Would he really have kept printouts from the PNC? Surely not.

Chapter 21

Craig was relieved the pages in Jack's file were handwritten. He hadn't printed PNC files. It wasn't Jack's writing on the first page, but he knew instantly what it was. Flint had shown it to him after The Mount, when they had discussed the deaths of four girls and how they were linked. When he'd written them, months before, Flint had still been trying to prove his dad wasn't the killer.

Craig scanned through the familiar words. Seeing the girls' names again chilled him.

1. Inga Sabiston.
~~*Fraserburgh*~~ *village near Fraserburgh. 1974.*
In a ditch. (Power station?) Arms cut off.
FAKE. (David Thom!)
2. Mhairi (?)
Summer 72? Crianlarich, Glen Dochart.
River. Leg cut off.
DEFINITELY HAPPENED. (Big Alick)
3. Name unknown.
Date unknown. Location unknown (Perth?)
Hand removed. Floating.
I MADE THIS CRAP UP ? ? ? CARTOON!!!

Despite the grim subject matter, Craig smiled to himself, remembering the times he had argued with Flint about which was more important in linking the cases: the buried memories Flint had uncovered using hypnosis, or Craig's unofficial use of the PNC. Craig remembered Flint meeting Jack once, in the aftermath of The Mount. Flint had brought his notes to Edinburgh, and he must have given them to Jack.

The next page was in Jack's hand, and Craig's mouth dried when he read the first words. *Ivan Skilling (CM)*. Jack had made notes about Skilling. It must have been after they'd talked on the phone. In Jack's untidy scrawl, there were details he remembered telling his friend.

"*Confession — (CM doubts)*", "*injuries — check, what injuries?*".

Craig was shocked by what he read next.

"*From Grampian file: Ivan Skilling, 53. golf course, outside car, head injury, genital mutilation. Letter in glovebox -- from daughter? (previous addresses in Fife. connections???)*"

Jack had accessed the PNC for this. He had to have. Warily, Craig looked at the next sheet in the file. There were details of another killing, again a male victim.

The notes read: "*Harkan Gaska, 49, divorced, known as Harry. 1980, Hammer, lay-by, A811, near Cambusbarron, Stirling. (Central case). Body left outside passenger side door. Genitalia removed. (letter)*

NOTE: ground marked where body dragged. Into cover of wall??"

Hairs bristled on the back of Craig's neck. He knew before he turned to the next page what was coming next. Jack had also recorded details of the Tentsmuir killing. Alex Narloch, a widower from Cupar, was 58 when his head was mashed with a rock. He had also been found beside a car. In bold capitals, Jack had written,

"*PENIS REMOVED? CHECK DETAILS!!!*"

When he'd carefully replaced the file under Jack's bed Craig sat quietly in the living room. The TV had drifted off the station and he stared distractedly at distorted outlines of what he thought were cowboys herding cattle. Still unable to concentrate on his book, he searched the flat until he found batteries for the transistor radio. Peter Powell's voice irritated him and he switched it off.

Jack had made notes about three very similar murder cases, details he had read after an illicit search of the PNC. For the rest of the afternoon and evening, no matter how he tried to distract himself, Craig could think of little else. On the last page in the file Jack had drawn a neat table, with a column for each of the murdered men. There were rows for name, age, responsible police force, location, and mode of death. And one for details of the genital injuries the victims had all suffered.

What disturbed Craig most was the fourth column in the table. It was completely blank apart from the heading '*4*'.

Craig woke early the next morning, relieved that Jack hadn't seemed to notice the file had been disturbed. He'd been vaguely aware of his friend coming in well after midnight; Jack must have been delayed after his shift finished, and Craig had soon heard snoring.

Jack didn't surface until after nine-thirty, and by then Craig had managed to have an awkward bath. He was becoming adept at tying a plastic bag round his plaster cast and leaving his right leg dangling over the side to keep it dry. It wasn't conducive to a relaxing soak, but he was getting used to it.

When Jack wandered through, yawning, Craig was looking for something to eat. "Good shift?" he asked, fishing in the bottom of a waxed plain loaf wrapper. Only the heel left.

"Don't ask. I had to go out with a probationer. I spent the whole shift doing everything for both of us."

Craig smiled to himself. It wasn't that long since they were probationers.

"Got any food?"

"Aye, I mean — sorry about that. No, not much. There's some tins in that cupboard. I'll pick up bread on the way to work."

Craig had become used to having Mo and Davy bring supplies in. "It's OK. I'll get it. I've got to get out on my own sometime. The hospital said to keep using the crutches, and I'm managing OK now."

"There's a corner shop just down the road."

Jack had a few hours before his shift started, and the two friends toasted the heel of bread and shared a tin of spaghetti hoops. Eventually, Craig couldn't resist asking a question.

"Remember we discussed those murders? The Tentsmuir man and our Grampian one? Did you say there were more?"

He was cringing internally. Jack might already know he'd looked in the file. He scraped the last of the spaghetti sauce off his plate with his knife.

Jack looked away. "I gave up thinking about it," he said. "Pointless. I'm not talking about it again." He stood up. "I'm going to the shop. I'll get a paper, and we need milk if we're going to have coffee."

"But — I was going to go later..." Jack had thrown on a jacket and left. Craig sat for a few minutes. It was unlike his pal to rush off like that.

When Jack returned ten minutes later, he sat down opposite Craig, still in his jacket and holding a plastic bottle of milk in one hand and *The Courier* in the other. "Sorry. It's just, I can't..." He looked at the window, and Craig thought the foil lid on the milk was going to give way as his friend's hand tightened on the flimsy bottle. "There's three cases, all pretty much identical, but I can't risk it. I mean I can't go any further with the PNC. I nearly got caught last month." He stood up abruptly and dropped the newspaper on the coffee table.

While Jack was making coffee, Craig hobbled past him to the toilet. As he passed Jack's room, he could see the file open on the bed. A pen lay on top of it. Given up thinking about it! he thought, with a smile.

When he returned, Jack was sitting with *The Courier* open. With a pencil, he was circling some of the small-ads.

"Looking for something?"

"ZX80s."

"I thought you had an 81? And the Spectrum is coming out soon. Why d'you want an old computer?"

"Just thinking ahead. There's still loads of folk buying the 81, and when the Spectrum comes out even more people with the 80 will want to have the latest one."

"You mean folk might change computers the way some people are beginning to trade in cars after only four or five years."

"Yeah, and I'll be able to sell ZX80s. It's still a good entry-level. Soon, they'll even be buying them for kids." Jack was always happy when he was talking about computers, and good at finding ways of making money.

"You going to open a shop or something?" Craig was joking, and taken aback at the reply.

"Not straight away. I think I'll just sell from here. Free ads in the paper, that sort of thing. And when I buy a car, I might look at those car boot sale thingies people are talking about. I heard they might be starting one near Perth."

Jack was losing interest in the police, thought Craig. It had always been the computerisation of police work that interested him most.

"Giving up on the police?"

"What?" said Jack, looking up from *The Courier*.

"Fed up that we're not all using the PNC properly?"

Jack shrugged, looking distracted, but he closed the paper.

"Not officially, I mean," Craig went on. "Never tempted to explore for yourself?"

Jack turned to the window.

Craig took a breath, then blurted, "I read your file about the murders."

To his relief, Jack looked back at him, asking, "What did you make of them? They're too similar not to be connected, d'you not think?" He went to his room, returning with the file. Putting the spaghetti plates on the floor, he spread the five pages on the coffee table.

Craig picked up the Alex Narloch page, reading again the notes he had quickly scanned the day before. This time he noticed Jack had used three different pens. Some of the scrawl was in blue ink, some in black and a few underlined words were in green.

"No, let's do this in order." Jack pulled the sheet from him and lifted Harkan (Harry) Gaska's page. This was the first one. Well, the first connected one."

The two discussed the Gaska killing. The body beside his car in a lay-by near Stirling.

"It was a Central case," said Jack, "a woman found the body on a Sunday morning. July." The Central Scotland force had impressed Jack. "They put quite a lot of detail on the PNC."

It was clear Jack had memorised a lot more detail from the PNC than he'd dared to write down.

"The body was left outside the passenger door, but a bit of his jacket had caught on the inside of the driver's door. The gravel showed he must've been dragged round the car."

"So, it had to be someone big," Craig said.

"Aye. Had to be. Strong enough to overpower him, and move him."

"And he would've been kicking and struggling," said Craig. "What injuries?" asked Craig.

"The sick bastard cut Gaska's cock and balls off, but the bleeding meant he was alive when it was done."

Like at Girdle Ness, thought Craig. His mind was back in Queen Street when he'd heard about Ivan Skilling's ordeal.

"And killed after."

"Yeah," siad Jack. "Pathologist said it was the head injury that killed him. A hammer, he reckoned. Gaska was butchered, then killed."

Craig reached again for the Narloch page. "This one's a bit different. Killed by a rock, not a hammer. And I know you said 'penis removed', but..." He scanned Jack's notes again. "Was there some doubt? You wrote, 'check details'." He looked up at Jack.

"The PNC just said 'genitals'. It was *The Courier* that said something about 'rumours' that his cock had been chopped off. Well, they said 'manhood,' believe it or not." He rolled his eyes. "But think about it. Three men all about the same age, all killed outside their own car, and all had their bits cut off before they had their heads mashed. Cock and balls or just cock. Hammer, rock. What's the difference?"

Craig immediately thought of Ian 'Stiff' Soutar. His story was inconsistent, and that might be because he was innocent.

"It could make all the difference," he said.

Jack suddenly gathered up the sheets of paper and stuffed them into the folder. "What's the point? I can't go any further with it. Fuck!" He strode across to his room and threw the file in, pulling the door shut with a bang.

Unsure what to say in the face of Jack's obvious frustration, Craig pulled himself up, lifting the mugs. "More coffee?"

Jack ignored him, slumping back down into an orange nylon armchair in the corner. "It's a fucking nightmare. Those cases are bound to be linked. It's got to be the same guy going around doing it. But I can't do any more or I'll lose my career."

Craig sat back down, surprising himself that he managed to take a step backwards and lower himself into the seat with two mugs in one hand and a crutch in the other. They sat in silence for a minute.

"Can I keep taking a look at your file? I mean, just for something to do."

"Aye, but what's the point? You're on your own. I can't help you. I'm not risking it."

After another pause, Craig spoke again. "Just one question then I'll shut up about it. In your notes, you drew a table with four columns. Why four? There are only three murders."

"In case I found another one. I hadn't finished going through the search when I was interrupted. I wouldn't be surprised if there are more we don't know about yet. But I mean it. I'm having nothing to do with it."

Chapter 22

Before Jack left for his shift, Craig had moved to the orange chair and watched him toing and froing as he stuttered into his work life, like a car on a cold morning. From their time training together, Craig knew that on the job Jack would be focused and efficient. The contrast with his haphazard off-duty life was stark and comical.

Jack went in and out of his room as he forgot this and remembered that; each time, Craig had a glimpse of open drawers and the bed strewn with discarded pages from the file on the mutilated men. Craig smiled when he heard, "Where's my fucking wallet?" Seconds after he'd finally left, Jack had burst back in saying "Keys!" to himself, before finding them in his trouser pocket.

Shopping on crutches was harder than Craig had anticipated. He'd been pleased with himself for managing to get as far as the corner shop a few hundred yards away. He wished he'd thought to take a bag with him, but the smoking man behind the counter had handed him one with the bacon, rolls and cheese. Getting back to the flat was slow and tiring. Staying balanced was hard with the bag of messages* tied to his left crutch handle. When he reached the steps outside Jack's tenement block, he had to leave one crutch against the railing to haul himself up one step at a time. Opening the flat door, he dropped the bag on the floor. He had forgotten to buy margarine, and by now was in a foul mood.

Summing up his situation, he became even more downhearted. Having jumped at the offer to let him spend some of his recuperation in Dundee, he had realised how alone and helpless he was while Jack was at work. Even when off duty he wasn't quite the perfect host. Jack took most of his meals at the work canteen and had little need to keep supplies in the flat. Craig missed having Mo for her care as well as her affection.

Exhausted by his first exercise for over two weeks, he slouched in an arm chair. Across the hall he could see the door to Jack's room.

Thinking about the file lifted him a little. Jack had made it obvious he wasn't willing to take any more risks by accessing the PNC without permission, but at least he'd said Craig could keep looking at his notes. He passed the time concentrating on the possible links between the crimes.

The similarities were stark. Three men with almost identical injuries, all found lying outside their own car. The man in Stirling, Harkan Gaska, seemed to have been pulled out of his car, like Ivan Skilling. Gaska had also been dragged into the cover of a wall, Jack had written. It meant both of them must have been overpowered, and only someone big and strong could do that, surely. Not a waif like 'Stiff' Soutar.

After making himself another coffee, he sat looking at Jack's door. He could gather up the scattered pages of the file, and start working to prove Stiff's innocence. But as the coffee cooled on the table in front of him, reasons to hesitate lined themselves up like a barricade outside Jack's room.

Not least was that discovering more about the three crimes would mean making enquiries. Unofficially, and in secret. He'd never considered whether a serving police officer was permitted to work as an unpaid "private detective," but he knew in his bones what the answer would be if he asked the question.

But the main thing holding him back was his leg. He could see the roof of his Escort outside, where Jack had parked it the day before. Without Jack and the PNC, he couldn't investigate any further without visiting other police force areas, and he couldn't drive. Looking down at his plaster, he swore out loud, "Fucking leg!"

He spent the rest of the day moping and watching TV. Jack had shown him how to position the aerial cable to keep it tuned. Each time he struggled across to make coffee or a dry bacon roll he took the opportunity to switch channels. BBC2 had tennis on, but the signal was poor and he couldn't see the ball. Both the other channels were showing horse racing which wasn't so bad, but when Little House on the Prairie started, even with his heavy plaster cast it was worth the effort to get up and switch off. The radio was no better.

Trying to concentrate on Smiley's People, he reread the same dozen pages again and again. His mind was nagged by an unknown irritant, a pest that wouldn't show itself or go away. He'd missed something crucial that was in Jack's notes.

In the story he was reading, unconnected words, names and phrases were a frustrating puzzle. If put in the correct order, they would turn a key; open the box holding the identity of Le Carré's concealed traitor. The notes Craig had glimpsed scattered on Jack's bed also held a secret, but not a fictional one. He had those pages neatly ordered in his mind, the key already turned. But he couldn't open the box.

Craig rose the next morning unrested. He felt as if he hadn't slept at all. He lay preparing to drag himself out of bed, confused images, sounds and sensations flitting through him. Faces, voices, and snippets of conversation from his dreams. A crawling unease began to build.

He forced himself to clump his plaster along to the draughty bathroom, trying to piece together his dreams. Mo had been with him, until she had morphed into Jack and then Flint, who she'd never met. They were in a boat, then a plane and a car, travelling with an unstated purpose.

He shook his head trying to dismiss the nonsense as he turned to fill the bath. Words continued to resonate, though. A soundtrack, a commentary. In a distinct and cultured voice he recognised. A newsreader?

He watched the water bubbling into the tub, full enough now, and turned the taps off. As the surface turbulence smoothed itself, he saw his reflection backlit by the strip light above. Instead of his face, though, it was the commentator's he was looking at. Granville Sutton. Dr Sutton, Flint's childhood psychologist. Craig had met him only once, on the fateful day with Flint and Isla that ended in Cupar police station, and led to his first suspension from work.

He didn't tie the plastic bag properly and the top of his cast got wet. After his bath he sat in front of the three-bar electric fire with its convector fan on the high setting. It made him remember he was due to attend a clinic in Foresterhill next week. He'd have to find a way of travelling back to Aberdeen.

Trying to read yesterday's *Courier* while he waited for the kettle to boil, his mind kept returning to his dreams. Sutton! What the hell?

It was like the living nightmares Soutar endured. Dr Trickett's report suggested he might not be mad after all. She'd thought a specialist, from Dundee if Craig remembered correctly, might show that Soutar's crazy ideas and confession were caused by 'disordered conscious dreams'.

However Craig tried, for the rest of that day he couldn't sweep his dream away. At least it had only played once. Gordon Flint had also been disturbed by the elusive meaning of his nightmares. But Flint's had played over and over, and searching for their significance had almost killed him. And Craig.

The days continued to drag. The strange dream didn't recur, but there was little to divert his thoughts from the killings detailed in Jack's notes and his misgivings about Soutar.

Though Craig was tempted by Jack's folder, he knew looking any further into the murders was too dangerous to their careers. But another idea was forming. One that he suspected had somehow developed after his weird dream. It scared him, but was becoming irresistible. It was OK when Jack was around, but when Craig was alone he had to do his utmost to stave off his crazy notion.

It was Friday afternoon, after a week cooped up in Jack's flat, when Craig gave in.

*(Some notes on Doric Scots are included in a
Glossary at the end of Flowers for the Slaughterman)*

Chapter 23

Flint was only a mile from home when he had a puncture. Pushing his old bike along the busy road was hard work. The rush hour traffic meant he had to walk on the high verge to stay safe, and his back was sore from work already. He dumped his bike against the garden shed knowing he'd have to repair the puncture before it was dark.

When he and Isla had parted, they'd agreed to keep writing to each other. Her too-polite replies were taking longer to arrive, and once again there was no letter waiting for him on the telephone table in the hall. He cursed.

He saw the look on his mum's face as he went into the kitchen, knowing she shared his disappointment.

"Good day?" she asked, hopefully. He grunted, looking away. He felt guilty every night that his mum took the brunt of his frustration, and each morning told himself he wouldn't snap at her again.

Sighing, she continued, "At least it's Friday and you're off the weekend."

Flint looked up, forcing a smile. He'd forgotten what day it was, and wouldn't have to fix the bike tonight after all. "Is Granville coming tomorrow?"

"No, not this weekend. Morna's being admitted for her cataract operation. Granville's taking her to the Vic, and he'll have to visit her every day."

No driving lesson. Flint's spirits fell again, but a thought occurred to him.

"If he's going to Kirkcaldy every day he'll be passing here. He could pick me up."

Eleanor Flint strained boiled potatoes at the sink. "I don't think he'll want to this weekend, Flint. Oh! I forgot. Craig Masson called for you. PC Masson. I didn't know you kept up with him. I liked him. Very polite and smart." She turned her attention to the mince.

"What did he want?"

"I don't know. He just asked if you could call him. He left a number."

"Is that you, Craig?"

"Flint? Hiya. Good, I wanted to ask you something." There was a pause before Craig went on. "Erm — how've you been?"

"Fine. Well, just the same. Pretty bored. Same job. Nightmare, really."

"Good, that's great. Listen, I wanted to ask…"

Flint shook his head and smiled. Same old Craig.

"Get to the point, Craig. Why d'you phone?" It had been two months since Craig had visited him that Saturday morning. He'd wanted something that day and he was bound to want something now. The first time Craig had ever visited him had been four years ago at Aunt Janet's house in Edinburgh, and that time he'd wanted to hear what Flint knew about dismembered girls.

"It's just — I wanted to ask you about your dreams. I mean, more like about how the hypnosis works—"

"No. I don't do hypnosis now, and I'm not teaching anyone else."

Prickles of guilt were crawling up Flint's neck. He'd lied to Craig. When sleep had deserted him again, determined to avoid reverting to alcohol Flint had restarted self-hypnosis. He'd convinced himself the risk was worth it; surely there couldn't be any more forgotten trauma in his past for him to uncover.

He was right. Entering a trance had been like riding a bike, and any crazy notions that he'd killed his father were easy to banish. With no alcohol his moods didn't see-saw so violently, and his relationship with his mum became smoother. It irked him, though, that he couldn't explain why hypnosis hadn't worked for him when he'd still been with Isla.

He hadn't told anyone he'd restarted hypnosis, but Granville Sutton noticed the change in him and guessed. He'd raised it on one of their driving lessons, and Flint had been pleased and relieved to talk about it. Sutton had listened, and later suggested that perhaps the fear of losing Isla had been one factor too many for Flint's busy subconscious to deal with. Once she'd made him leave, painful though that was, one obstacle had been removed.

Now Craig had mentioned hypnosis, and Flint became defensive. It's probably because I don't want to give myself another complication, he thought, something that might rock the boat.

Craig's words continued in the earpiece, even more hesitant now. "It's alright, Flint, I —erm — wasn't going to ask you to teach me. Erm — Sorry, I won't mention it again. But…"

It was obvious Craig had more to say, and Flint couldn't help smiling to himself. Aye, same old Craig right enough. "Go on," he sighed.

He heard Craig draw breath. "Do you ever see Dr Sutton? It's just that I was thinking about him and something I've been trying to work out, about a case in Aberdeen, and — sorry, I'll shut up. It was just an idea."

Flint laughed. "Can't the police get their own experts? Shrinks, psychologists? If they need that sort of help."

"It's unofficial. I'm off work at the moment."

###

The bus was packed with Saturday shoppers heading to Dundee. As it crossed the Tay Bridge in late April sunshine, Flint looked down at the water below. He'd been going over the same bridge in the other direction the first time his acrophobia had made him collapse. His dad had been furious when Flint was sick in his work van. Seven years later Flint finally understood what caused such a severe attack. Eleven-year-old Flint had just seen a severed human hand in a freezer.

He thought back to last night's phone conversation. When Craig Masson had explained that he had a broken leg and was off work, Flint had asked what he was doing with himself to pass the time. He'd assumed Craig was still in Aberdeen, and when he'd explained he was stuck in Dundee, with his car but unable to drive it, Flint had mentioned he had a provisional driver's licence and was taking lessons. Minutes later the plan was hatched.

By the time he was walking from the bus station with only a vague idea of how to find Pitfour Street, Flint was buzzing. He was going to drive a different car. He had never driven in traffic before, but traffic lights and roundabouts couldn't be that hard.

Dundee was bigger than he had known. Having only ever been in the compact town centre on shopping trips with his mother, or later alone to browse the LPs in Bruce Miller's, it hadn't occurred to him that all the people must live somewhere.

He'd written down the Pitfour Street address, and when he'd asked at the bus station, a busy, fat woman in a uniform had said, "Off the Lochee Road," before turning her attention to a steel ticket machine hanging round her neck on a leather strap.

Flint wandered into the city centre, automatically turning into Reform Street. In Miller's, a boy he'd remembered flaunting brown flares and a perm now had a mohican and ripped tartan drainpipes. The punk told him politely which way Lochee Road was. In all it took nearly an hour to walk to Jack's flat.

Chapter 24

Saturday afternoon

Since their phone call the previous evening Craig had been excited. He still hoped to interest Flint in Stiff, and the three murder cases. With Flint as driver, making enquiries might be possible.

But now he was having second thoughts.

"I'm not so sure this is a good idea. I thought you'd been driving for a while. I want to be able to trade my car in later this year."

"Ach, it'll be no bother. I'm a quick learner. A good driver already."

"Anyway, I don't have L-plates."

Flint smiled and reached into the big inside pocket of his army surplus jacket. "I brought mine with me. And some string."

Craig insisted on making Flint practice clutch control in Pitfour Street. He made him stay in first gear and crawl along a few yards at a time.

"Not bad."

"I told you, I'm good at this. Let's go somewhere."

Craig relented and soon they were on the busiest road Flint had been on, heading east.

"This is brilliant. Much faster than Granville's Volvo." He tried to put on an air of confidence, but he was terrified by traffic lights. On Arbroath Road he was able to relax a little, until a van behind him blared its horn.

"Get stuffed," Flint shouted, grinning sideways at Craig, who was ashen.

They were soon in Broughty Ferry, which Flint thought was quite like Cupar with a beach. After numerous right and left turns he drove them past a small castle which appeared to rise out of the sea, and onto a wide, quiet road near the beach. He pulled to a stop, put the handbrake on with a flourish and said, "Well? Pretty good, eh?"

"I should never have agreed to this. But we made it, and at least the car doesn't reek of burning clutch now."

"Yeah, sorry, I kept nearly stalling. It's just different from the Volvo."

Craig wound the window down and the smell of the estuary filled the car.

"Walk on the beach?" said Flint, opening his door.

"With this? Craig pointed at his cast. The crutches would get stuck in the sand." He looked over his shoulder. "Did you put the crutches in the boot?"

"Oh, shit. Sorry. I must have left them on the pavement." Flint remembered helping Craig into the car and then laying the crutches down.

"Aw jeezuss, Flint! Some bugger'll nick them."

They drove in silence back toward the city. On a wider, four-lane road that passed a huge gasometer, Flint hugged the nearside lane. "I don't really like these wider bits."

"Stay in this lane, you'll be alright."

Flint did as he was told. The road widened even more and he concentrated on staying between white lines. They curved left.

"Not here, you idiot! You're taking us onto the — fuck!"

Flint was confused, shaken by Craig's cursing. He soon saw his mistake. Looming in front were toll booths guarding the Tay Bridge. He'd accidentally moved onto the slip road, and with no way to turn they were committed to crossing the estuary.

"What do I do?" He could feel panic rising. The narrow space between the booths was getting closer, the striped barrier barring his way. He was going to have to stop exactly at the window.

"Just stop at the booth, pay the man and drive on."

He managed to line up with the booth, but couldn't wind the car window down. The little grey handle wouldn't turn, until Craig pointed out he was pushing it the wrong way. A car behind honked its horn.

"I don't have any money," he said.

"Not even $12\frac{1}{2}$p?" Craig was delving awkwardly into his jeans pocket.

"I left my wallet in the flat."

"You paying or not?" the man in the booth shouted down impatiently.

Handing over Craig's 50p coin Flint was amazed that the man had little piles of change lined up. $37\frac{1}{2}$p was instantly dropped into his hand, before slipping through his fingers into the footwell.

"Just drive!" shouted Craig, as the barrier lifted. Flint revved and lurched forward.

The low car window meant Flint couldn't see the drop to the swirling River Tay he had seen from the bus earlier. He'd been taught in primary school that the bridge was just under $1\frac{1}{2}$ miles long and an 'engineering marvel'. At the other end was Fife, with its quieter roads.

At the end of the bridge, Flint pulled off a roundabout and into a small car park. Built to allow sightseers to view and photograph the bridge, it was empty.

"I came here for a picnic once," he laughed. "A school trip. We'd been to Tentsmuir for nature studies."

"Tentsmuir? That's near here?"

"Yeah, just a few miles along the way." He pointed east along the estuary. "Just the other side of Tayport. You can get there other ways; we just came this way to—"

"Let's go. Come on, I want to see it."

"Why? There's nothing there except paths, trees and a beach. It's good for walks, but — look at you…" He pointed at Craig's right leg. Safety pins held together the outside seam of his jeans, ripped apart to accommodate the grubby cast. Flint couldn't help laughing.

"Just take me to Tentsmuir. I want to see what it's like."

"OK. It's great if you like trees and marram grass," said Flint, starting the engine. He pulled back out onto the road beside the Tay. "What is it about Tentsmuir?"

Craig said nothing until they were driving through Tayport a few minutes later. "D'you remember I told you there were some murders? One of the bodies was found at Tentsmuir."

He's still on the trail of a serial killer, Flint thought, smiling inwardly. "Aye. The man they found on Hogmanay? My mum went on about it when I was home from Aberdeen. Must have been before me and Isla…"

The road into Tentsmuir Forest was narrow, with passing places. It was a dull day, and the tall pines on either side seemed to lean in over the car. As they went further into the forest, it was as if night had fallen. Flint bent forward, his chin almost touching his hands on the steering wheel.

"Third gear?" Craig pointed at the gear stick, and Flint tore his eyes from the narrowing track ahead while he tried to ungrip his left hand from the wheel.

"Watch where you're going!"

Instantly panicked and befuddled, and knowing he had to do something with both feet in an emergency stop, Flint jammed his right foot onto the brake pedal and pulled his left away from the clutch. The car jolted to a halt as the engine stalled and the gearbox groaned. He looked helplessly at Craig, who was shaking his head, but smiling.

"Jeezuss, you nearly lost control. Start the engine, I can't drive the bloody thing. Just don't take us into the ditch."

"How far do you want to go?" Flint was already worrying about how he was going to turn round.

"Apparently there's a parking area somewhere. I thought you knew this place?"

"I only came here twice. Once with my mum and dad in his van, and once on the school trip."

Flint managed to restart the car, and drove on even more slowly.

"You trying to break my steering wheel? Relax a bit, Flint, you're doing fine, but don't panic again."

The tree canopy seemed to thin, the road now mainly straight, its tarmac fairly smooth. In places, the surface was lightly covered with pale orange pine needles. At one point there was a slight bump, and a loud crack. Flint made a perfect emergency stop this time.

"You just went over a stick." Craig was laughing.

"I'm sorry, it's difficult. I've never driven on roads like this."

"You're no rally driver, right enough."

As they rounded the next corner, Flint saw a patch of grey sky, growing larger and whiter as they moved towards it, like a welcoming beacon lighting the way. With the road widening, and light now penetrating the walls of lichened tree trunks, he let himself relax.

A clearing paved in compacted shingle opened up, pocked with puddles like acne. Beyond it was the beach he remembered playing on as a child, and later capering on the school outing. He stopped the engine, winding down the window and throwing a sardonic smile at Craig who mimed applause.

"Well done. See? It's easy if you wind it the right way."

"You think this is the place they found that body?"

"Must be. I haven't seen any other places you could park." Craig was looking around him. "I wonder where the body was left?"

"Do they know his name?"

"Narloch. Alex Narloch," said Craig, still looking left and right.

"How did he die? I mean, stabbed or what?"

"His head was mashed in."

"Christ. What'd he done?"

"I dunno, it's a Fife case. I only know from newspaper reports. Well, Jack does. He looked at the PNC but said there wasn't much on this one."

"He's been on the PNC again? After last time?"

"Aye, I know. You'd think we'd learn, eh?"

Flint was thinking about Craig's visit to Auchmoor February. "I think you said this one had his nuts cut off, like the man in Aberdeen?"

"Well, yeah, but it might have been his cock. And before his head was battered. Before he was dead."

"Fuxake! And that happened here? Jeezuss." Flint looked around the parking area. Beyond the strip of beach the North Sea was grey but calm. Seagulls were circling just offshore and the air was chilly. As he started to wind the window back up Craig spoke.

"Flint, can you see what's on that tree? Over there." He pointed through the passenger window towards nearby trees at the edge of the clearing, a few yards away.

"Something hanging on it?"

"Aye, what is it?"

"Canny really tell," said Flint, opening the car door.

"Ach, it doesn't matter, Flint. I just thought it was a dead animal or something, like the gamekeepers do."

Flint was walking towards the trees. "No gamekeepers here," he called over his shoulder, "it's a nature reserve. Someone's left a bunch of flowers."

"Flowers? Where the body was found? A tribute?"

A bunch of sticks and leaves hung suspended by a loop of bright blue nylon string tied round the tree trunk. The twine stood out against what Flint now saw were the drying heads of thistle flowers, their purple faded. There had been nothing like it at his dad's funeral.

"Aye, flowers, yes, but not the usual type," Flint said as he got back in the car. "Thistles. And anyway, who ties a bouquet of flowers with baler twine?"

"Strange thing to leave. Maybe it's just a coincidence."

"Or some sick bastard that didn't like him."

Chapter 25

On the way back to Dundee Craig was quiet. He had the coins ready for Flint to pay the bridge toll. Flint was confident enough to think more about Craig's interest in the two murders.

"Tell me again what it is makes you think the guy they got for killing the Aberdeen man didn't do it? Just because there's a similar thing in Fife? He could have done them both."

After another silence Craig said, "He was in hospital when Narloch was killed, and he's in the jail now so he couldn't have done the…"

Craig's words tailed off and in the corner of his eye Flint saw him turn to look out of the window. *He was going to say something else…*

After the quieter roads and the straight bridge, the journey across Dundee to Pitfour Street made Flint's hands sweat. Roundabouts and traffic lights were ganging up on him, hiding round corners and jumping out to surprise him. He stalled as he parked the car, some way along the road from Jack's flat to allow him room to pull in without reversing.

"Fuck!"

"You did not bad. My car's in one piece."

There was no sign of the crutches when Flint walked along to check. He was about to go back to the car and huckle Craig along to the flat when he heard rapid knocking from across the road. A grey-haired woman was waving at him from a ground-floor window opposite the main door to Jack's block. He could tell she wanted him to come across to her, and he walked uncertainly over the road. She held an off-white net curtain to one side with a gnarled hand, and he could hear her muffled voice through the window.

"Come. Come." She was waving towards the door along the wall. Flint went to what he guessed was her flat and knocked.

The high-pitched, weak voice continued. "Come. Come." Then coughing. He opened the door wondering what the old lady could want. "There. There." She was sitting near the window, and he could now see one side of her face was drooping. Pointing with her right arm, she said again, "There. There."

Propped against the wall behind the door he found Craig's crutches.

"Thank you."

She pointed now to a picture on the wall beside her, a black-and-white image of a soldier. "My man." Then she pointed to the crutches Flint was holding in one hand. "My man." A lop-sided smile lifted the right side of her face and her eye sparkled.

"Thank you." Flint couldn't think of anything else to say. He waved and left.

"I think her husband must have seen them in the road and taken them in. God knows where he was."

"He'll be in the pub," said Craig as they made their way along to the flat. "I've seen a wee bloke come out of there wearing a blazer every afternoon since I've been here. One night I saw him staggering back. Could hardly walk."

"Poor old woman."

The Polepark Bar was less than a mile from Jack's flat but it was by far the furthest Craig had walked on his crutches. He was pleasantly surprised that he didn't feel too exhausted, even if Flint was obviously struggling to walk slowly enough not to leave him behind. It had been Craig's idea that Flint should stay the Saturday night in Dundee. Jack was starting a run of night shifts that night and his room would be free.

When Jack had come in after playing football, he agreed to Flint using his bed, but pulled a sleeping bag out of his wardrobe. "But use this. And don't make a mess of my room."

Jack wanted to have a sleep before he went out to work, so going to the pub meant they could give him peace.

As they left the flat, Craig said, "Don't worry about making his room untidy." He was laughing. "It couldn't get any worse."

The bar was busy and they could only find a seat for Craig next to the fruit machine. Flint had to stand, and was jostled by the constant flow of drinkers as they went to and from the toilets in the corner. With the hubbub and loud music, it was pointless trying to talk until a man next to Craig stood up and put a blazer on. He was short, old and had a neat moustache.

"Ye can sit here, son. Ehm awa hame."

After he'd gone Flint squeezed in beside Craig who said, "That was the wee guy from over the road. The one who lifted the crutches."

A couple of pints later, it was Flint who raised the subject of the two murders.

"So, you really think the mannie in Aberdeen and the one in Fife were both killed by the same bloke, but not the one in Craiginches?"

"'Mannie'!" said Craig with a grin, "You're slipping back into your Aiberdonian."

"Aye, it gets to you. Anyway, d'you really reckon the same man did the two of them?"

"I think it's got to be. Both had their genitalia removed before the head injuries killed them."

"It could still be a coincidence."

Craig hesitated, then said, "There's another one. The same. Three all the same."

"Fuck! Three?"

By the time they got back from the pub, Jack had left for work. Flint pulled *London Calling* out of the heap of LPs leaning against the end of Jack's bed. "Combat Rock's good, but they'll never match this," he said as he put it on the stereo.

They'd stopped at the chip shop on the way back from the pub, and Craig made mugs of tea. Jack had left the TV on when he went out, and with The Clash still playing loud from across the hall, they watched highlights of Celtic beating Hibs 6-0.

"I didn't expect it to be that bad," was Craig's verdict on his team.

"I didn't even know the Dons were at Dens Park today," said Flint, through a mouthful of white pudding when Dougie Donnelly described Aberdeen's 5-0 defeat of Dundee. "I've sort of lost interest a bit since — well — since I had to leave Aberdeen."

Craig switched the TV off and they sat listening to the music and finishing their suppers.

"What happened between you and Isla? I thought you were set for life there."

Flint looked at Craig, shaking his head. "Fuck, it was my fault. I don't blame her really. I knew it was coming."

"But why? I mean what did you do?"

"I started all the nonsense about my dad again. Every night in my sleep I convinced myself I'd killed him."

Craig was silent for a while, before going on, "She threw you out because you were having bad dreams? That doesn't sound like her."

Flint explained about his night terrors and how much he had disturbed Isla. "I didn't know anything about it, but I was thrashing, kicking my legs and stuff. I just hope I didn't kick her. Fuck, what a mess I was."

Craig took a slurp of his tea.

"And I kept drinking to try to knock myself out. It was mental. Without drink I was scared to go to sleep. But even with it I still had the dreams, about my dad, I mean, and the thrashing started. At least with the drink I didn't remember the dreams the next day. What a mess. I don't blame her for kicking me out. I—"

"Do you still have the nightmares?"

"No." Flint looked up from the grubby tartan rug he had been staring at as he spoke. Threads were fraying from its edges. He'd counted seventeen of them. Now looking Craig in the eye he said, "I sorted myself out with hypnosis. But don't ask me to use it on someone else, OK?"

Lying in the sleeping bag on Jack's bed Flint stared at the ceiling. Yellow light from a streetlamp fanned out from the gap at the top of the curtains, distorted by the folds of the fabric. His mind meandered here and there: driving Craig's car; the poor old woman over the road who he thought must have had a stroke; Isla alone in Aberdeen (was she alone?); the tall pines of Tentsmuir. Again and again, though, he fought the temptation to think about what he knew he wanted to. The three murders Craig had outlined. The file was under Jack's bed. He'd seen it when he was choosing a record. '*Not the PNC (haha!)*'

A lamp lay on the floor beside the bed. He switched it on and reached for the file.

Chapter 26

Sunday morning

Flint was up and dressed by the time Jack came in from his night shift, just before 9 o'clock.

"I need to go to bed. Don't make a noise, I've got another six bloody night shifts." Throwing a screwed-up paper bag towards a wicker bin in the corner, he went into his room and shut the door.

Flint crept about trying to keep the noise down, cringing at the knocking water pipe as he filled the kettle. Its ill-fitting lid made a metallic screech when he tried to close it. They'd used the last of the milk the night before, and he sat cradling a mug of black tea and shivering. He was reading Thursday's *Courier* when Craig clumped through holding onto the wall.

"I'm getting more and more fucking fed up with this stookie," he said lowering himself into an armchair. "Shit. Now I've got to get up again to piss."

It wasn't long before Craig shook off his morning mood. "I'm starving. What's that smell? Bacon?"

"I think Jack brought back a bacon roll or something." Flint pointed to the bag, ketchup-stained and stuck to the carpet by the bin.

Craig stooped down to reach the soggy bag and tipped some crumbs out. "Magic!" he said, holding up a scrap of bacon rind and sucking ketchup from the paper.

They made toast. It wasn't long before Flint reached below the chair he was in and held out Jack's file. "I read this last night. What were the letters about?"

Craig's eyebrows went down in confusion. "Erm — what?"

Flint went on, "At the end of the notes about Harkan Gaska, the body found near Stirling, Jack wrote 'letter'. There was a letter in Skilling's car, too."

"I didn't really think much about it."

"It sounds like the one in the Aberdeen car was from his daughter," said Flint.

Craig furrowed his brow, "Aye, you're right. So what?"

"Must have been important if they entered it in the computer, surely? Your famous PNC."

"Aye, I suppose. Not much we can do, though, we can't get any more from the PNC."

"But you must have noticed the other similarities," said Flint. "Between the victims, I mean?"

"Yeah, they all had their nuts cut off and their heads battered." Craig laughed. "Well done, you should join the polis."

"No, there's more. I mean, like, they all lived on their own. Or, I mean, one of them was divorced, and one's wife had died. And you said the mannie in Aberdeen lived alone. He had a daughter, too. The letter in the car."

"You seem to be getting pretty interested in this. But don't bother, there's nothing we can do."

"But there's a definite link. If there's nothing you can do, why did you want to go to Tentsmuir?"

Craig looked out of the flat window, and then back at Flint. "OK, I mean it's interesting, and I keep thinking about it, but..." He looked out of the window again. "But I got in hellish shit after The Mount for using the PNC, even though Jack used it more than me. And then..." Craig paused, biting his lip and his face flushing. "I got in even more shit for doing it again."

"What?" Flint stared at Craig, wide-eyed. They had both been arrested after The Mount, and he knew what trouble Craig had been in, but he had no idea there had been something else.

There was a slight shaking of Craig's head as he went on, "Yeah, stupid, PNC again. But I'm not going into details." He was screwing up the paper bag from Jack's roll. "And I'm not doing it a fucking third time," he said, throwing the bag at the wall.

They were both quiet for a moment, until Craig mumbled, "Anyway, without investigating cases in three different Force areas we can't do any more."

"But hasn't Jack got access to the PNC?" said Flint.

He could tell from Craig's resigned smile that he had anticipated his question. He shook his head. "He's ruled that out. He almost got caught as well, doing what he has so far. He's having nothing more to do with it."

There was silence again until Craig pushed himself up from the chair, clumping towards the adjoining kitchen. "I need a drink of water."

Flint followed, picked up the kettle and said, "I need tea. Can we get some milk?"

"We? You live here now, then?" Craig smiled "Maybe we could pick some up if we go out driving."

"Brilliant. I didn't know if you'd let me drive again."

"I want to phone Mo first."

"I'll just go down to the corner shop for milk while you're doing that, then. More time for driving."

When Craig called her flat, Mo was getting ready to go out. Her brother Davy was coming to pick her up and take her to the family home for Sunday lunch.

"When are you coming back?" she asked him. He felt a pang of guilt for being away and a glow of pride that she wanted to see him.

"I've got to be back by Friday. Got a clinic appointment about my leg."

"Good. Oh, hang on, that's Davy arriving." A doorbell chimed. She put the phone down and Craig heard Davy's deep voice in the background.

"Can I have a quick word with Davy?" he asked when Mo picked the receiver back up.

"D'you want to go out with me or my brother?" She laughed, and went on, "Here he is, I've got to get my make-up done and get ready. See you Thursday. Kiss kiss."

"Hiya Davy."

"Craigie Boy! Foo's yer doos?"* Craig smiled at the familiar Doric greeting.

"Aye peckin'!"

"Well done, loon! Ye'll mak a fine Aiberdonian if ye keep iss up!"

Flint returned from the shop, and had to squeeze past Craig in the hall. He waited to ask Davy his question until Flint was in the kitchen. He lowered his voice. "Davy? Remember the man Skilling? The body at Girdle Ness. D'you know what the letter in the glovebox was about?"

"Nah, min, I wisna really involved."

"No bother. It doesn't matter."

Flint overheard what Craig said to Davy. As the kettle began to hiss, he smiled to himself. Craig was still trying to find more links between the three murders. Still trying to prove the wee man in Aberdeen jail was innocent.

On this driving lesson, Flint negotiated the roundabouts with aplomb. On the road towards Carnoustie, he said, "I've been thinking. You can't do anything about the serial killer, but there must be something you can you do to stop the laddie in Aberdeen from getting the jail for life? You seem pretty sure they've got the wrong person for it." He glanced across at Craig, who had turned towards him with an ironic smile.

"Have you changed your mind about hypnotising him for me?"

"I didn't say that." Flint made clear why he was unwilling to hypnotise Stiff, and neither of them raised the subject again. After their drive, they watched TV with Jack until it was time for Flint set off back to Fife. He had to work in the mill on Monday morning. Jack told him which bus would take him to the town centre, and he got to the bus station in time to catch one that stopped in Auchmoor. For most of the journey he stared out at the passing dusk, thinking about Stiff Soutar and his dreams.

Craig was right. Hypnosis might help unlock the deep subconscious box which Soutar's torturing dreams escaped from. That might help explain why he had — or hadn't — killed the man on the golf course. But that would depend on a lot of things.

First of all, Stiff would have to be susceptible to hypnosis. Not everyone was. Flint had been lucky, and Dr Sutton had even described him as 'super-susceptible'.

Next, Stiff was locked in jail. There was no way an amateur would get into a prison to hypnotise one of the inmates. Craig would need to find himself a qualified specialist.

Most of all, Flint knew from his own experiences that hypnotic regression could be more harmful than helpful, especially if the subject was mentally unwell. Stiff was definitely that — he'd been in and out of a loony bin. It would need a real expert to tackle something like that, and it might be too dangerous to try.

Flint had explained all this to Craig, and told him not to bother asking again.

When he walked towards his home in Rothes Park the light was fading. His mum would still be up, though, and there was a chance she might make him something to eat.

As soon as The Good Old Days started, Jack walked across to the TV to click the dial round to STV. "I hate Sunday television. Never anything on."

Craig had noticed Jack's mood was volatile. He'd been up and about when they came back from the driving lesson, and quite animated, asking where they'd been and offering to make tea. Now he was restless, and there were empty mugs all over the flat.

"I hate bloody night shifts. It's always the same. A few nights into a run of seven and you're all messed up sleeping. Then you adjust a bit by the end of the week before you have to get used to sleeping at night again. I've been up and down, in and out of bed all day. I should be in bed now, but bugger it, I'm never going to sleep."

Craig knew exactly what he meant. He waited until Jack seemed to have calmed a little, before he spoke.

"I was going to ask you, Jack. Remember in your file, y'know, '*Not the PNC?*'. You wrote 'letter' against Harry Gaska's name. Who was it from, d'you know?"

"What? Oh, yeah." Jack's head shuddered for half a second as if he was trying to shake off cobwebs. "I don't know. I was just about to look further when I got interrupted. That was when I nearly got caught." He looked hard at Craig. "I tell you, I'm *not* going unofficial on the PNC again."

(Some notes on Doric Scots are included in a
Glossary at the end of Flowers for the Slaughterman)

Chapter 27

The sweat running down his face gathered in a dusty brown moustache, and the tons of grainy calf nuts kept on coming, dropping into the massive aluminium hopper. However many half-hundredweight bags he filled, the flow of cattle feed dropping from a clanking conveyor belt above meant the level in the hopper never dropped below halfway.

When Flint started his job at Hamlyn's it was winter, and the constant heavy lifting had served to keep him from getting unbearably cold. Now, in early May sunshine, under its corrugated iron roof the mill heated up to what felt like boiling point. The thought of the approaching summer was too much. And Tommy's endless moaning. Now, it was the heat going for his fucking chest.

When midday came and they stopped for dinner, Flint went outside and sat in shade at the side of the shed that served as an office.

The previous evening as he'd tried to listen to what his mum was saying, thoughts had kept popping into Flint's head about the murders in Fife, Stirling and Aberdeen. They had continued on Monday, at first only random images or words from Jack's file. Over the course of the morning the cases had been like a magnet drawing his mind. Over the dinner break, the seed of an idea germinated.

After work, it wasn't until he'd had a bath and eaten cold meat and chips that he checked whether there was a letter from Isla. His mum must have noticed his distraction.

"Don't you want to watch the Mastermind final?" she asked. The TV schedules were all mixed up for the May Bank Holiday, even if Hamlyn's hadn't noticed and had worked as usual.

"Sorry? What?"

"It's the general knowledge bit in a minute. You usually like Mastermind. Will I make you some tea?"

"Nah, thanks," he answered, "I'm going to bed."

Tuesday 4th May

"Where are you going, laddie? Come back. It's no near piece-time yet. And the fuckin' hopper'll overflow."

With only a brief glance over his shoulder, Flint ignored blabbering Tommy and kept walking. He grabbed his dusty jacket and started down the splintering wooden staircase from the bagging floor to the ground.

Fuck their bloody job. Fuck Tommy and his bloody knackered chest. And fuck calf nuts!

He could have simply not turned up, but had started the day at the mill as usual just to see the look on Tommy's moaning face when he walked out.

He crossed the yard, swung his leg over his bike and cycled out onto Millgate, the movement of the air cooling his brow and drying his sweat-plastered hair. When he smiled to himself, the brown veneer crusting his face cracked.

"But what are you going to do for money? You shouldn't have just walked out. What will they think? What about references? That's *two* jobs you've walked out of!" He'd known his mum would be furious with him, but the feeling of release was worth it.

"Stuff it. I'm going to find something else when I can be bothered. I'll sign on the dole."

"Gordon!"

He should have asked his mum to lend him some money, but that didn't occur to him until he had stuffed his chequebook and a few clothes in his grip and walked along

Rothes Street. He only had three pounds and some change on him, and not much in the bank. He'd have to hitchhike instead of paying for a bus.

On the way through town, he thought about going into the Auchmoor Arms for a pint. He had hardly been out for the last couple of months, and the idea of a celebratory beer or two almost swayed him into walking down Kirk Wynd towards the pub. He'd given up that awful job, and would never have to see or hear Tommy again, or his bloody Cortina, cream wi' a blue roof. He walked on, though, and was soon positioned on the Dundee Road with his thumb out. Standing at the roadside, jobless and almost penniless, he felt released. There was nothing keeping him from putting his idea into action.

Chapter 28

Craig didn't recognise the man who knocked on the flat door, and it was obvious that whoever it was was surprised to see who answered it.

"Luggy?"

The voice hadn't changed. "Phil? Bloody hell, what have you done?"

A bouffant hairstyle meant Phil looked six inches taller, but it was his eyes that drew Craig's attention.

"Make-up?" was all he could manage.

"Aye, I'll explain. It's my new look. Usually only at night but I'm working today."

The voice and accent confirmed it. Geeky Phil, his classmate from Napier. Craig waved him into the flat, his eyes drawn to the light reflecting from the back of tight, shiny trousers.

"Jack not in?"

"Erm, aye, he's in bed. Night shift. What the fuck? Phil?"

"We always get that reaction."

"We?" asked Craig, lowering himself.

"New Romantics. It's the latest big trend. Sort of underground, you know, and all the best music. But you have to be in the know."

"In Dundee?"

Craig had heard the term but dismissed it as another London gimmick. He couldn't imagine an Edinburgh disco filled with men wearing make-up and hairspray, or women with white faces. He chuckled inwardly, but Phil looked serious, going on to explain that his latest job was in a disco with a New Romantic theme. A 'club', he called it.

"And you came to Dundee dressed like that?"

Phil did admit to feeling a little threatened as he'd walked through the Overgate shopping centre on the way to Dazzle. The new night spot was opening up in the next few days and Phil had been sent from Edinburgh by the sister club.

"I'm an ambassador."

Craig laughed out loud, spluttering the tea he'd made for them.

Jack's door creaked open and his sleepy head poked out.

"Fuckin' noise!" He started at the sight of Phil and came out of his room. "What the fu...?"

When Jack had heard all about Phil's metamorphosis he returned to bed. It was just after two o'clock, and Phil had a gap between meetings.

"What's this?" he asked, picking up the buff folder with PNC on the front. "'Not the PNC?' What's that about?"

Craig tried to reach over the coffee table to pull it back but Phil already had it open.

"More fallout from The Mount?" From the number of preserved body parts found in the cottage in Luthrie, it was widely expected that the "Limb Collector" had dismembered more victims than the four Craig and Flint had identified.

"No. Listen, Jack won't like it if he sees you looking at that. But it's about——"

"I know one of these girls. Or knew her." Phil had grabbed a page of Jack's notes.

"What?" Craig was terrified Jack would come back in and find the sensitive file being shared, even if it was with their old pal. He was also excited. More details about the murders.

"Patricia Gaska," said Phil. "Her dad's on this list. Harkan Gaska. He was killed a couple of years ago. Murdered apparently."

"How do you know that?"

"It was all in the papers. Gaska's not a common name."

Phil now had Craig's undivided attention. This Patricia was bound to have information they could use. His mind showed him a fleeting image of Ian Soutar, the way he imagined him in Craiginches jail. Even smaller, cowering, bullied and innocent.

"What happened to her? I mean where did she go after school? Job?"

"No idea. The parents had split up. She left the school when we were in about third year, I think. She was off a lot. Rumour was she was seeing a shrink or something."

"Where did they go? The mum and daughter I mean."

"Somewhere up your way, I think."

"Dalkeith?" Craig still thought of his home area as Midlothian.

"No. Sheep shagger territory. Aberdeen way. Stonetown or something. Stone something anyway."

"That'll be Stonehaven," said Craig.

"Why's Jack got this?"

The questioning look on Phil's face made Craig want to giggle again at the eye-liner and helped him check himself before he said too much. "No reason. Just interested. It's Jack's stuff."

Phil shrugged. "I've got to get away. Another PR meeting. Say 'bye to Jack."

It was Craig's turn to look quizzical. "PR?" But Phil had gone.

Craig had hardly sat back down when there was more knocking on the door. Thinking Phil had forgotten something he groaned and pushed himself back up to stand. Using one crutch and the wall to hold on to he made his way back to the flat door.

"For God's sake, Phil, what–?" He swung the door inwards. "Flint?"

"Hiya, Craig. Can I stay here a bit longer? I've got an idea."

A muffled but angry "Stop the fucking noise!" came from behind Jack's door. Craig put a finger to his lips and mouthed *"Jack's sleeping,"* before ushering Flint in.

"What are you doing back here? Off work?" he asked when they were in the living room.

"I walked out. Couldn't take it anymore. Anyway, I've got a better idea, listen."

As he sat down, Craig said, "I don't know what you want, Flint, but I'm only a guest here, and Jack finishes his night shifts at the weekend, and…"

"I'll sleep on the couch in the living room. If I do the driving we'll be able to check out the links between these dead men." With rising excitement, Flint rushed on to stop Craig interrupting. "I've been thinking. We can go and see the daughter, the one who wrote the letter. In the car. The man Skilling. Jack wrote about previous addresses in Fife. We could find the daughter, see if we can find out more, and—"

"Stop, Flint. I'm police. I'm off work. I can't work unofficially."

Flint grinned, standing up and pacing back and forward. "I know. I can be a private detective. You can tell me what to look for and I can do the legwork. Like in a film. 'Masson Flint Inc. — Private Eyes.' Or 'Flint Masson'? And with Jack's help with the PNC, we can—"

"Flint, shut up. Are you pissed?"

Flint sat down. He looked at Craig who was shaking his head.

"But we must be able to do something."

Craig stared into space. "There's nothing I can do about the three murders. And I've told you before Jack's not going to help us. Not with the PNC."

Flint frowned and said, "So that's it? The killer gets to carry on?"

Craig ignored Flint, as if he wasn't there. "To tell you the truth, I'm more interested in anything that proves Stiff's innocent. Ian Soutar. If I can do that, they'd have to look for someone else for the Skilling murder. And they might consider a connection to the others." He looked back at Flint and said, "Sorry, I was just thinking aloud."

"Can I help you with that, then?"

Craig grinned and shook his head. "You're keen, right enough."

"Tell me again about Soutar. I know what you said about the dreams. A mad dream that he killed the bloke. But you said there was something else that made you think he couldn't have done it."

"He's five feet tall and eight stone. A right wee boy. Skilling was a six-foot hulk. He was overpowered and dragged out of his own car, so the killer has to be a big man."

"Maybe he poisoned him? Drugs, I mean."

"Toxicology was negative," said Craig.

Flint sat back in the chair. "But they charged the wee man anyway?"

"Aye. The DCI just wanted to get someone for it."

"That's hellish. Did no one complain?"

After a pause, Craig looked out of the window again. "It's not like that."

Flint saw a look on Craig's face he couldn't read, and said nothing. Craig rose and limped out. "Want a cup of tea?" he said over his shoulder.

Craig was smiling when he returned. "If you're staying, are you goin' to take your jacket off?"

Flint threw his jacket on the floor beside the chair. "Any food? I left my piece bag at the mill and I'm not going back for it."

Flint made coffee and fried egg sandwiches. "Red sauce on a fried egg! Nothin' better." After wiping his chin and licking yolk and sauce from his fingers, he took the plates and mugs away to the sink. "Right. Can we go out driving now?"

It was after four o'clock on a busy Tuesday afternoon, and Craig told Flint the rush hour traffic would be too much for a learner. "We could go out somewhere tomorrow."

"That mean I can stay?" Flint grinned and turned back to the sink. "I'll even wash the dishes."

They watched kids' TV programmes with the sound turned low. After the news had been on Jack came out, moaning about having to do another night shift.

"He'll be in a better mood in a while," said Craig. After he had dressed and shaved, Jack humphed around a bit but gradually joined their conversation.

After they'd had pie and beans Jack sat back in his seat and farted. "That's better. So, what are you doing here?" He looked at Flint. "You sleeping on the couch?"

"If it's OK."

"No bother if you can be quiet when I'm sleeping. You not working?"

When Flint had explained about walking out of Hamlyn's the chat returned to the three murders.

"It's pretty clear the three men were killed by the same bloke," said Jack. "And if the wee boy in jail in Aberdeen couldn't have done one of them because he was locked in the nuthouse that means he's obviously innocent. It's simple. You should concentrate on him if you want to get anywhere."

When he thought about it later, Flint realised that it had been Jack's neat summing up of the situation that seemed to spur Craig on.

"So if we get anywhere we've got to show that Stiff just dreamt he killed Skilling? We keep coming back to that, but we'd have to get a shrink to hypnotise him or something."

"I don't really understand hypnosis. How can it help?" said Jack. Craig encouraged Flint to explain.

Jack hadn't heard the full story of Flint's experience with hypnosis and dreams. Flint found himself telling Jack and Craig most of what he'd only told Isla and Dr Sutton. Both the cops listened without interrupting as he gave details about how his childhood had been affected by acrophobia.

"And you only cured it when you got hypnotised?"

"Well, I had to hypnotise myself. But yes, in trance I was able to go back to what made me scared of heights in the first place."

Jack and Craig both nodded him to go on.

"I fell out of a window when I was eight. Broke my wrist. I always knew I'd broken my wrist but I had no memory of the fall. When I started hypnotising to help the heights problem I sort of went back to that moment, when I fell, I mean. I could see stuff happening that I didn't like. Granville Sutton explained it. He said what I saw was so shocking my brain couldn't cope with it, stored the memory away where I would never find it."

"What was so shocking? I mean, it must have been bad to —"

Flint spoke over Jack as if he wasn't there. "I saw my mother with another man."

"Oh fuck, I'm sorry."

But Flint was shaking his head. "It was all a misunderstanding. She wasn't *with* him. He was helping her. It's just — when it came back to me under trance years later — I *thought* she was..." Flint stood up. "I need a piss."

While Flint excused himself Craig said quietly to Jack, "I know it sounds like he's covering for his mother, but it really did turn out she was innocent. So was the bloke Flint saw her with."

"Fuck!" Jack still looked bemused. "And didn't you say he thought his dad was a serial killer?"

"Aye," said Craig, now whispering. "He even thought he was a killer himself at one point."

"That's mental."

"He dreamt all that mad stuff. The hypnosis kind of explained it, I think." The toilet flushed, and Craig hissed, "Don't say any more. I think he still has the dreams. That's what made his girlfriend chuck him out."

For the rest of the evening, they didn't speak about hypnosis, Stiff or the three murders. When Jack went out on shift, Craig went to bed and Flint tossed and turned in the living room. If he was going to stay there for a while, even if Jack's bed was empty for another few nights, he might as well get used to the lumpy couch.

Chapter 29

It must have been talking about his childhood fall with Craig and Jack that brought it back. After the third time he'd woken in a sweat convinced he was falling to his death, Flint spent a few careful minutes trying a modification to his hypnosis induction.

It worked. The next thing he knew was someone bumbling around the flat. Jack had come back from his shift. Flint lay on the couch, serene and as comfortable in the knowledge that it was morning already. He really was good at self-hypnosis.

"Morning. What day is it?" he asked through a delicious yawn.

Jack's startled look as he turned was soon replaced by one of tired bewilderment. "Oh, hi. It's Wednesday. I forgot you were here, even though I saw you lying on the couch when I came in. Weird. Night shift messes with my head. Sorry. Fuck, I'm tired. I'll be alright when I get a cup of tea." The ramble of spoken thoughts tailed off and he turned round to fill the kettle.

Flint pulled his jeans on and sat wishing he'd brought a toothbrush. When Jack had made the tea, he put mugs for both of them on the coffee table and sat opposite Flint. He appeared to have shaken off his fug.

"Anyway," he said, "I was thinking about this hypnosis business. Was it the psychologist, the man who was involved that day with you and Craig at The Mount, was he the hypnotist that helped you?'

"Dr Sutton? No. I taught myself. He'd been my psychologist when I was a kid, and he helped me understand why hypnosis did what it did. Why it brought out all that stuff from my memory, I mean. Why?"

"I just thought Craig could maybe get him to hypnotise the wee man in Aberdeen. Stiff."

"He doesn't do hypnotherapy."

"But he suggested it?"

"No, it was all a kind of chance. A flatmate of mine was doing it and he taught me."

"Maybe he could help? The flatmate."

Flint looked away, his mind suddenly drawn back to sickening images. His flatmate's grey face screamed silently at him through plastic. He had suffocated himself, no longer able to tolerate his disabling mental illness.

"No. He couldn't." Flint was glad to hear Craig's door open. He wouldn't have to repeat the details.

"Is that tea in the pot?"

"I need to go to bed." Jack stood up, yawning and stretching. "But, Craig, I was thinking. You really need to do something about that boy in Aberdeen if he's innocent."

"I know. And I think I know how." Craig was grinning, excited. "I was dreaming about Mo last night, and I kept seeing a poster, well, a flyer, y'know. It was mad. But when I woke up it made sense."

"What are you talking about? I'm going to bed." Jack was walking away.

"No, listen. I remember now. Stiff's shrink in Aberdeen, Dr Trickett, she said she wanted him seen by a specialist in hypnosis. To regress him or something, to find out about his dreams."

Flint could see Jack was as puzzled as he was.

"Aye, but listen, listen to this. The bloke she recommended was a guy called Slinn."

"So?" Flint was shaking his head, not really following.

"That's the same name that was on the flyer. Slinn. It was advertising a lecture in Aberdeen."

"I've really got to get some sleep," said Jack, standing up. "I don't have much clue what you're going on about, but this specialist fella might be just the man to hypnotise Stiff." He went into his room and shut the door.

"This stuff was all in your dream?" Flint got up to pour more tea.

"The flyer said Slinn was from Dundee."

Flint shook his head as he put more mugs of tea down, frowning in confusion. "You're not making any sense. You dreamt it."

"No, it's real; it's just it only came back to me last night. Weeks ago at Mo's flat I found an advert for a lecture Slinn's giving in Aberdeen. It said he's a Professor from Dundee University. I didn't make the connection until last night that this was the same bloke Trickett recommended. He's here in Dundee."

"So what?"

"Didn't Dr Sutton work at a hospital in Dundee?"

"Yeah, Liff Hospital. Why?" At the mention of Liff, a familiar melée of emotions stirred in Flint. He could picture the letters on Liff Hospital stationery he had found secreted in his mother's wardrobe. He'd read them in the early hours of a December morning, and had no idea what they meant. Later that day he had fought with his father.

Flint forced the memory away. "I mean what has Granville got to do with anything?"

"I've been thinking about this half the night. Dr Sutton is bound to know him if they worked at the same place. We could ask him to speak to this Slinn man, find out if he's seen Soutar. Like Trickett recommended, I mean. Obviously, it would be up to the Fiscal to involve Slinn, and if he's like DCI

Blackie and just wants the case wrapped up, after Stiff's clear confession, I mean, well, the Fiscal might not ask Slinn, and —"

Flint had to interrupt Craig's flow. "Hold on. Hold on, Craig. Dr Sutton's not going to ask another doctor stuff like that. Anyway, he retired, ages ago. And Slinn isn't going to reveal details about a patient anyway."

"But if Sutton tells him about Soutar and how important it is he gets hypnotised Slinn'll surely—"

"Craig! Dr Sutton won't get involved."

"Even when he knows about the three murders? And that Stiff's innocent? He knows all about hypnosis. You said so. He explained how it affected you, you said."

"Jeezuss!" Flint was used to Craig being calm. Only yesterday Craig had been the one slowing him down when he'd arrived all excited by his private detective ideas. He could see now that had been unrealistic, but today, here was Craig getting all fizzed up by wild ideas.

It was unfair, though, that an innocent man — boy, by the sound of it — was going to be locked up. And a serial killer would be left to get on with killing.

"All right. I'll phone Granville. But just to ask what he thinks. About Stiff Soutar, I mean, and whether hypnosis would help. But he won't get involved, I'm telling you."

Craig smiled. "Bring the phone through from the hall. It's got a long wire. That way you won't wake Jack."

"Oh, hello, Flint. Where are you? Ellie's — erm, your mum's worried."

Flint hadn't thought to let his mum know where he was going.

"Yeah, sorry, tell her I'm OK, I'll give her a call. I'm in Dundee. But anyway, Granville, can I ask you something?"

"Of course, wait for just a moment, Flint, — Morna, could you check the gate's closed? — Sorry, Flint, I was out feeding the goats." Granville always addressed his mother by her first name.

"It's about hypnosis." There was a silence on the other end of the line, and Flint sensed Sutton's apprehension. "It's OK. Granville, it's not about me this time."

"Are you doing alright?"

"Yes, fine. It's all sorted. Really."

"Still treating yourself? And keeping the ideas about your dad under control? I know from your mum that you're not drinking nearly as much. I'm not interfering, you know, Gordon, it's just I can't help asking how—"

"Really, Granville, I'm doing OK. It's not about me. Do you know Dr Slinn from Liff Hospital?"

He could almost hear Sutton thinking. He could picture him sitting in his comfortable study by the small square window cut into the thick sandstone walls of his old farm cottage.

"Yes, I think, so. Dan Slinn. Yes, of course. He was something of a high flyer. Made Professor a year or so ago, I heard. I'm not surprised. Always starting this clinic, that service. To be honest, he really shook Liff by its foundations when he arrived. Rather threw himself into things after his wife died. Such a tragedy. They'd only been married a year or so. Leukaemia, I think it was. Sorry, I'm rambling again." Flint heard Sutton taking a drink and then a cup being placed on a saucer. "What about him?"

"I think he does hypnotherapy? Deep regression, that sort of thing?"

"Yes, that's right. He was very interested in trauma. I mean the after-effects of severe emotional trauma, not physical of course. He ran clinics for people no one else could help. Gosh, I haven't thought about him for some time."

Flint was getting impatient but didn't like to interrupt.

Sutton went on, "His first senior post was at Stratheden Hospital, near your home. That's where he started his trauma clinic. Come to think of it, you might have been referred to him yourself, Flint, when you were a boy, but I was the one who tended to take on the school-related referrals. Oh, and he had a clinic for people who'd been abused in their childhood. That sort of thing. He seemed to have some success, too, if his papers and publications were anything to go by. Oh, I'm sorry, I'm going on and on again. Why did you want to know? You are OK, really, aren't you?"

"Yes. Yes, honestly, I'm fine" Flint looked over his shoulder to where Craig was sitting listening to his half of the conversation. He rolled his eyes and with the fingers and thumb of his free hand he imitated a jabbering mouth. Craig smiled. "But can I ask you if you think Dr Slinn would be able to help someone whose dreams have made him believe he has killed someone, even though he really hasn't?"

"Are you sure you are OK? It sounds very like some of your — you know — experiences. You can tell me, you know."

"No really. It's a man who's in jail, in Aberdeen, and we think he is innocent."

"We?"

"Me and Craig."

Another silence. "What are you up to?"

"D'you remember I mentioned Craig thought there might be another serial killer on the go? That day you took me on the first driving lesson."

"Erm, yes, but I didn't think you were going to get involved."

Flint thought for a moment before going on. Can I tell you a bit about the man in jail, and why we think he's innocent?"

Flint held the phone at an angle to let Craig hear Granville Sutton talk. "It sounds very much as if the psychiatrist in charge of the man's care thinks Professor Slinn should see him. Her impression seems to be that he has suffered some deeply traumatising event. There are some striking similarities to your own experiences, Flint, in that this poor man may have found something that happened to him — or something he saw, perhaps — so distressing that he has buried it as far away in his subconscious as he can. I think you said he has some kind of fixation on men's genitalia?"

"Yes." Flint looked to Craig who nodded. Flint went on to explain that Soutar seemed to believe that he had taken part in ritual mutilations.

"But," Sutton said, "I don't see what you can do if the Procurator Fiscal has decided not to seek Professor Slinn's assessment of the patient."

Flint could see Craig waving at him, asking to take the phone. "Hang on, Granville—"

Craig took the phone from Flint, "Hello, Dr Sutton, it's PC Masson here. Sorry to butt in, but what about if you contacted Professor Slinn and told him he should see Soutar? It's just, I don't think the Fiscal will have asked him. They think the confession's enough. Surely they'd have to let Slinn see him if he says he wants to. Especially because Dr Trickett has already recommended it, I mean. Is there any way you can contact Slinn and find out?" He paused, his face reddening. "Sorry, I shouldn't have asked." Craig shook his head, looking embarrassed as he handed the phone back to Flint.

Flint had never heard Granville Sutton speak so forcefully. In no circumstances would he interfere by speaking to Professor Slinn, even though he and Slinn had at one time shared an office and a secretary. He advised Flint and Craig to leave all decisions about Soutar's care to the involved clinicians, and decisions about his guilt or innocence to the police and legal system.

After Craig's interruption of the call and Dr Sutton's firm admonishment of their interference, they didn't discuss Soutar or the murders any further. Flint went to the corner shop for more bread and tins of spaghetti hoops, and when he returned Craig was in the bath. He could hear Jack snoring.

"Christ, another bath. You had one yesterday," he said when Craig emerged cursing that he'd got his plaster wet again.

"I don't sleep well with this bloody thing on my leg and I get all sweaty with the tossing and turning. I'm fed up with it."

"How long have you got to keep the cast on?"

"Another four bloody weeks. I think so anyway. I've got to go to Aberdeen on Friday. Clinic appointment."

Flint unloaded the bag with the bread and tins. As he chewed on a heel of the loaf, Craig said from behind him, "Flint, are you going back to Auchmoor today? Or are you definitely not going back to your job?"

"Fuck, no. You don't know how bad it was. The work was hard but I didn't mind that. I was thinking last night, the heat was awful, but really it was that bloody Tommy and his coughing and whining and—"

"D'you want to take a trip to Aberdeen?"

Flint paused, puzzled for a moment. Then his eyes lit up. "How are you getting there?"

"You're driving me, if you want to. I was going to have to get the bus."

"Fucking magic!"

"We'd need to go tomorrow though, the appointment's on Friday morning."

While they ate spaghetti on toast Craig interrupted Flint's excited jabbering. "I think you'd need more practice before driving that distance. Let's go out this afternoon."

"Yes! Brilliant. I'll wash these dishes, then let's go."

Chapter 30

Craig told Flint to pull into a petrol station as they approached a busy roundabout where the Coupar Angus Road crossed the Kingsway. When he was sure the handbrake was on, Flint reached into his jacket pocket and brought out his wallet.

"I've got two pounds left."

"Forget it. I'm not spending much since I've been off work, and I'm still on full pay."

"Really? You get paid even when you're not working?" Flint had never been off sick from his job at the Parks Department in Aberdeen, and hadn't thought about it. Before that he'd only had casual jobs.

Craig had to tell Flint how to use the petrol pump. "Fill it right up if we're going to Aberdeen tomorrow."

The pump dial read £6.73, and Flint took Craig's cheque and bank card to the cashier in a hut. He had spilled petrol on his hands.

"You really get full pay if you're off ill?" he asked once they had got going and the busy roundabout was behind them.

"Yeah. You must have had some arrangement, working for the council. What did your contract say?"

"I never read it."

They continued on the road towards Coupar Angus. There was little conversation other than Craig's occasional reminder to change gears or speed up a little. After about an hour they were on the way back towards Dundee when Flint spoke. They were just passing through a row of houses called Birkhill.

"Can we turn right here?"

"Aye. No harm in taking a different road back."

About a mile further, on a long, downward slope and with the River Tay visible in the distance, Flint indicated again and slowed to take another right turn.

"This takes us away from Dundee, it's the wrong direction."

Flint said nothing and Craig shrugged. A couple of minutes later Flint slowed and pulled in at the side of the road. They were parked next to a stretch of pavement, outside a squat, sandstone cottage. Its roof had corbie steps.

"Why are we stopping?"

Flint nodded through the windscreen, and Craig followed his gaze. Next to a wide entrance, a painted board was mounted on a stone wall. He read 'Royal Dundee Liff Hospital.'

Craig sat staring at the words, eyebrows down and lips pursed. He said nothing.

"Didn't you see that road sign for Liff? On the way out of Dundee," said Flint.

"Yes. But I didn't think we'd go near it."

"Well, we're here now."

Silence from Craig.

"What d'you think? I mean, we could at least go and enquire?"

Craig looked at Flint now, eyes wide. "But what? I mean —"

"I've got an idea," said Flint, putting the car into first gear with a crunch.

"Hey! Be careful."

Flint drove between the gateposts. The driveway swept right then left between tall trees. Soon they emerged into an open area in front of a huge gothic building. Flint parked in a space between a grey van and an Austin Princess, switching off the ignition. Over the sudden quiet, crows cawed.

"What are you going to do? You can't just go in there."

Flint grinned mischievously at Craig and opened the car door. "I told you. Got an idea." After pulling his khaki jacket from the seat rest he swung the door shut and walked lazily towards an impressive door with stern, square columns to each side. Above it, a large window was framed by two round turrets, and higher still he could see more corbie-stepped roofs. Still trying to affect nonchalance, he opened the door with palpitations and a dry mouth.

Inside, there was a surprisingly narrow hallway with plain walls and flaking paintwork. A door to his left bore a 'Reception' sign, and through a square window he could see two women sitting at desks. One, a middle-aged lady with a cardigan and thick make-up, looked up when she saw Flint. He tried to smile, and knocked on the door as he opened it. He was greeted by cigarette smoke and the clitter-clatter of a typewriter.

The woman stood up. "Hello? You can't come in here. What—?"

"Sorry, I'm Gordon, a psychology student. I've come to see Professor Slinn. Am I in the right place?"

The woman seemed to relax. "You shouldn't really come in here. Didn't you see the bell by the window? Anyway, I don't think he's in the hospital today." Now Flint was in the office he could see a typist in the corner. She was much younger. Smiling at him, she rolled her eyes and looked towards the older woman. His shoulders loosened.

"Oh, sorry, it's just that he asked me to leave something. Will he be back?"

"His office is just upstairs. You could ask his secretary." It was the girl at the typewriter. Her pale face and black punky hair reminded him of Siouxsie.

"Thanks," he said smiling at her past the older woman as he turned to go. He walked along the hallway and found a stairway, his shoes catching on the metal stair trims as he climbed. A corridor stretched left and right, with doors spaced at irregular intervals along the walls, and a cracked linoleum floor. He could hear chatter, a phone ringing, and more typewriters. The third door on the right had a newer, larger sign than the rest, and there were screw holes where other names had been removed. Professor D Slinn. He knocked as confidently as he could.

"Come-in." A cheerful voice.

He knocked again as he opened the door, saying "Hello, I was hoping Professor Sl—"

"Come in, shut the door, quick. This place is like an ice-box."

Flint had to search the room quickly to locate the speaker. Poking up behind an enormous typewriter he could only see smiling eyes, a forehead and a frizz of blonde curls. He closed the door, and as he turned back he saw that the typist had now stood up.

"I'm sorry, Professor Slinn's away for a while. He does private clinics in Inverness once a month and he's been asked to give some lectures. Aberdeen next week, I think. Sorry, I'm rambling. Can I help?"

Flint realised he had very little idea of what he had been going to say when he met Slinn, and felt a wave of relief. There was a picture of a moustached man in a corduroy jacket on the wall opposite the door.

"Erm, I'm one of the students, and I'm interested in hypnotherapy. Regression mainly. I know he's an expert."

"Oh, yes, he's wonderful, isn't he?" she said, looking at the picture on the wall. "I've been with him for years." She blushed. "Well, not with — I mean, I've been working for him." She cleared her throat. "What did you say you wanted? You're one of his students? I'll check his tutorial lists and leave him a note. What's your name?"

She pulled a notepad from her desk and took the pen from its clasp on a chain around her neck.

"Erm, Gordon." It still felt strange using his first name.

"He hasn't got a Mr Gordon. I know the names of all his students. Are you new?"

He wondered what to say. His thoughts raced, and he fought against panic. It had been a stupid idea. He'd learned nothing about Slinn. He shouldn't have come here. Thinking he could have just turned up and magically persuaded the eminent professor to hypnotise the truth out of Soutar, or Stiff or whatever he was called, it was just mad.

Backing towards the door, he took a deep breath and said, "I shouldn't have just turned up on the off chance."

Then a sudden idea flashed as he remembered something Sutton had said. He paused. "I'm actually a student in Aberdeen. It's just that Granville Sutton suggested I might speak to Professor Slinn."

"Dr Sutton? Oh, I *loved* Dr Sutton. Such a gentle and kind man."

"You know him?" Flint turned back from the door and smiled at her.

"I'm Rosa. I used to work for both of them. Dr Sutton and Prof— erm — Dr Slinn as he was then, before he became Professor." She said the word with reverence. "That used to be Dr Sutton's desk," she said, pointing to her right. With no chair behind it, it was almost covered with piles of buff folders.

Opposite, an embossed nameplate sat on Professor Slinn's much neater desk.

"I talk to Granville quite often. We spoke this morning, in fact."

"Oh, how is he? He hasn't been back to see us since he retired."

"He's fine. He's a friend of my mother's." He was getting used to his mother being 'with' Granville Sutton.

"If you're a friend of Dr Sutton, let me see what I can do to fix you up with Professor Slinn. If you'll give me a moment I'll go and fetch his diary. I left it in the coffee room. Oh, and I might pop to the ladies' while I'm along there." She moved out from behind the desk and he saw that although short and slight, she wasn't the young girl the big desk had made her appear. As she passed he saw dark roots near her scalp, and guessed she was probably somewhere in age between his mother and a young teacher. It was his usual way of assessing stage of life. Kid, teenager, normal, young teacher, mum, old teacher, ancient.

When the secretary had left and clicked down the linoleum corridor, Flint looked around the office. Filing cabinets, certificates on the wall and shelves of books. And more heaps of buff folders. He looked at some of the files, idly reading the labels on their spines. Trauma; Trauma – Male; Trauma – Female; Trauma – Recent; Trauma – Past. It was clear trauma was Slinn's speciality.

Flint's eyes drifted to the secretary's typewriter, and he moved around to look at what she was working on. Earlier that day, seeing the name of the hospital had taken him back to that cold December day more than four years ago. The full letterhead had more impact.

Department of Psychiatry
Royal Dundee Liff Hospital

Dundee

Ref. DS/RF

He couldn't read on, and not only because he knew it was wrong to read confidential information. The letter looked almost identical to the one he had found in a shoebox of his mother's old letters. Later that day he had discovered the real truth about his parents, and his father died.

He wandered over to Slinn's desk. With a glance towards the office door, he pulled open a drawer. A folder with a typed label lay on top of some other papers: Survivors of Childhood Trauma, 1971. Granville Sutton had said Professor Slinn might have been able to help Flint unearth his own buried memories, and he was intrigued to see what was in the file. He looked again at the office door, and then out of the window. He felt like he was being watched, but from the first floor the view was only of grey sky above trees. Leaning forward, he could see the top of Craig's red car.

Turning back round, he eased the drawer fully open and lifted the old, faded file. Before he opened it, a sheaf of papers underneath caught his eye, punched in the top left-hand corner and bound together by a treasury tag. The top sheet showed a table of three columns; number, surname, and date of birth. As he scanned down the list of names, he could feel the hairs straighten on his nape.

The secretary's footsteps echoed in the high-ceilinged corridor outside. They click-clacked louder as she approached. By the time the door opened, the folder was back in the closed drawer, on top of the list it had concealed. Flint was looking out of the window. He was glad the Slinn's secretary wouldn't be able to see the shock and confusion on his face.

"Here we are, I'll have a look in his diary. When would be a good day for you? I'll see if I can find some free time."

"Erm, no, thanks. I've — changed my mind." He walked towards the door without looking at the woman.

"Don't you want—?"

Chapter 31

"Did you see him?"

"No."

Flint closed the car door and immediately started the engine.

"What's your hurry?"

They'd pulled out of the main hospital gates before Flint spoke again. "Am I going the right way?"

"Aye. This is the way we came. What's wrong?"

Flint said nothing. A mile or so later Craig tried again. "How did you know the way to Liff? Been there before?"

"No," was the eventual reply. "When I saw the signpost it started me thinking. Then when you went to the toilet in Coupar Angus I found the map book." He pointed at the glovebox.

"I'd forgotten that was in there. Hey! Watch it!"

Flint had taken his eyes off the road, veering towards the kerb.

"Bloody hell, Flint."

Flint gripped the steering wheel.

After they entered the city and had stopped at traffic lights, Craig said, "I take it the man Slinn wasn't there?"

Flint turned to look at Craig. "No, he's in Inverness, I think. Doing lectures. Or was it clinics? Going to Aberdeen as well, his secretary said."

"Probably for the lecture I saw the flyer for. What got to you in there, anyway? Looked like you'd seen a ghost."

Flint shook his head and said nothing more until they were in the flat. Jack was up and dressed.

"Where've you guys been?" he said.

"Went for a driving lesson. Flint's going to drive me to Aberdeen tomorrow so I can go to the clinic on Friday."

"You trust him?"

"Only just. He nearly drove us off the road on the way back from Liff."

"Liff? Why'd you go there?"

"Flint had an idea he could speak to the shrink. Slinn."

Flint came in from the kitchen. He'd been washing the petrol smell from his hands and came out shaking water on the floor. "No towels?"

"At the loony bin? What did Slinn say? He's the bloke who's supposed to hypnotise this Soutar guy, right?" Flint looked away.

"He wasn't there," said Craig, "but something freaked Flint out. I think he must have run into some scary nutters or something."

Wiping his hands on his jeans, Flint said, "Want to go for a beer, Craig? Then I'll tell you something that'll freak *you* out."

"Lucky bastards," said Jack.

###

Flint put two pints of lager on the table and sat down. "I've got less than a quid left. I'll need to cash a cheque somewhere tomorrow."

Craig had asked again on the way to the Polepark Bar what it was about Flint's visit to Liff Hospital that had so obviously unsettled him. "There was something you saw or heard in there, Flint, I know there was. You couldn't wait to get out." Flint had thrown a blank look at him and walked on, slowing every few yards to allow Craig to catch up.

They were seated in the pub before he tried again. "Are you going to tell me, or what?"

Flint took a long swig from his pint and put it down on a beer mat, wiping away a foam moustache. "It was something I saw in Slinn's desk drawer."

Craig's pint was almost at his mouth when he held it still, staring at his friend with wide eyes.

"You went through his stuff? Are you mad? You need a warrant for that!"

"I'm not a policeman." Flint was grinning.

"But you still can't do that. You didn't take anything, did you? Fucking idiot!"

"Relax. I didn't take anything. Just slipped a drawer open and read some stuff."

"I don't want to know. I could lose my job. I've been in enough trouble."

"You will want to know when I tell you what Slinn's up to."

NUMBER SIX

He's the heaviest one yet.
Somehow he doesn't look so big now.
Peaceful though.
Now he's gone.
When I'd tidied. Wiped him clean.
I'm too good at this!
And to think I was going to stop.
That's three more now, since the target.
He's long gone.
And I've still got a taste for it.
I shouldn't.
They deserve it, though.
And *they* deserve it.
I know I ought to stop.
But the List…

Chapter 32

Thursday 6th May 1982

"I still can't believe it. Are you sure you got the names right?"

"I'm telling you. I know the names from Jack's file."

They had taken the coast road back to Aberdeen. Craig thought it would be quieter for Flint to drive, but the traffic was much heavier than on the way south. After an hour and a half, they were not far past Montrose. Every few minutes Craig returned the conversation to the list Flint had seen in Professor Slinn's desk.

"And you're definitely sure they were all spelled the same way?"

"Yes. I told you, I know the names. Gaska. Skilling. Narloch. All easily remembered, especially Gaska, for God's sake."

They drove on in silence for a few miles.

"And you said there were others? Others crossed out, I mean."

"Aye. That's what's bugging me. There were definitely more crossed out. But I can't remember the names. One of them began with *t–h*. Crossed out."

"Thomson? Thomas?"

Flint shook his head. "Nah. I remember it definitely started with a th- sound. Like thimble, or throttle. But I can't think of the rest of it. I spent half of last night trying to remember. Aw! Magic! Turn it up. Loud."

Craig leant forward to the radio and turned Joan Jett up to maximum. Flint started singing and thrashing the steering wheel in time to the chorus. "—dah-dah-dah-dah-daaah, dah-dah, **dah-dah! ba-by!**"

"Hey!" shouted Craig, turning it down a bit. "Two hands on the wheel." He was stomping his left foot in time.

They were caught in a long queue on the road between Stonehaven and Aberdeen, crawling along past roadworks behind an artic loaded with dozens of long steel pipes.

"They're always doing something on this road," said Craig. "They should leave it alone, there's nothing wrong with it."

Flint was idly tapping along to the next song. "Slinn's got to be the killer," he said.

"A list of names doesn't prove anything."

"But it proves he's connected in some way to three dead men with unusual names. Maybe he saw them all in his job. Patients, I mean."

"I thought you said the file was about children. Childhood survivors, or something, right? They're all men."

"They haven't survived very well!" Flint was laughing.

"For God's sake, Flint, that's sick."

"You're trying not to laugh."

A few minutes later, Craig said, "Why were some of them crossed out?"

"Some detective you're going to make." Flint's voice was heavy with sarcasm.

"I just can't believe it," said Craig. "There must be another reason."

"I'm telling you. The famous Professor's a psycho. He's working his way through the list. You know that means he's killed more, don't you?"

"I don't believe it."

Once the traffic started moving again, they were soon on the long slope down towards the River Dee. A wide banking on their right was a sea of spent daffodils. Flint knew which council team would be sent out to trim and mow it for the summer. On the left, and across the river, was Aberdeen's dry ski slope. He'd gone there for lessons with Isla.

As they crossed the Bridge of Dee, Craig broke their silence. "How many were on the list?"

"Dunno. Eight? Ten? About half of the page."

"Oh jeez."

###

"Christ, I'll be glad to get this stookie off. Four more bloody weeks. I'm knackered."

They'd reached the top landing outside the Esselmont Avenue flat and Craig was struggling to find his keys, leaning awkwardly on the wall. Flint idly tried the door, and it opened.

"Davy must be home." Craig waved Flint in.

Carrying his canvas grip and Craig's rucksack, he squeezed into the hall.

"Fa's 'at? Craigie-boy?" The voice came from a room on the left, and a big grin appeared as the door opened. "Hiya, min. You Craig's pal?"

"I forgot you'd be in, Davy," said Craig as he followed Flint. "Is it OK if Flint stays on the couch for a few days? He's a pal of mine from Fife."

"Aye, the mair the merrier. Wantin' a coffee?"

Flint moved into the living room. "Aye, thanks. Just milk."

"Flint drove me up the road, I've been giving him lessons," said Craig. "I'm just going to call Mo." He went back out to the phone on the wall in the hall.

Flint knew Craig would call Mo the minute he got in. On the way from Dundee, when they'd not been talking about Slinn and his list, he'd spoken about her several times. It was obvious he was hoping the relationship would get serious.

Flint could hear him talking, and before he pushed the door closed to allow Craig privacy, he heard him say, "Yeah, great. Can you pick me up?"

Mo arrived twenty minutes later, and she and Craig soon left to go back to her flat. Flint watched her walk towards the door. He caught Davy's eye and mouthed a lustful, conspiratorial 'phwoar'.

When the door had shut Davy grinned and said, "You like my wee sis, then, eh?

Flint's face flushed. "Sorry — really — I didn't know she was your sister."

He was relieved when Davy smiled back at him and winked. "It's alright, loon, ah ken she's braw. It runs in the family, eh?" He pointed at himself with both index fingers, gurning and laughing. Petite, dark-haired Mo couldn't have looked more different from big-boned, sandy-haired Davy.

Flint couldn't help laughing. "At least your ears don't stick out as much as Craig's."

"Aye, when he taks he's hat off it's like the lid comin' off the Scottish Cup!"

Davy was cooking mince. Flint liked his easy manner and the two shared more laughs. He had missed the Aberdeen accent, and remembered how difficult he'd found it when he first arrived in the city six years before.

As Davy brought two plates to the small square table he said, "How d'you know Craig, anyway? You're fae Fife, right? How'd you get in tow wi' a posh Edinburgh boy?"

"That smells magic," said Flint, lifting a fork and starting with the mashed tatties. Between mouthfuls, he described his first meeting with Craig, in a small police station in Edinburgh four years before.

"Hang on, have I got this right?" Davy's face showed he was struggling to understand, let alone believe what he was hearing. You mean you turned up claiming your dreams made you think you'd killed someone? A young quine? I'm nae surprised they sent you away." Brow furrowed and head shaking, he went on, "And for some reason, bloody Craig decided you *weren't* a headcase? But then the pair of you ended up nabbing a serial killer?"

Flint had been over and over it all a thousand times, and this time it sounded no less crazy.

"So this freak was going to do that to you? And then kill you? And kill Craig? Fuck's sake, min!"

Flint filled in more details as Davy tried to get the story straight.

"I'm no sure I unnerstaun it all, the stuff wi' the dreams and the hypnosis an' that, but it sounds like you did the work o' aboot four polis forces."

"When you put it like that I suppose we did not bad. At the time I just wanted to get out alive. And with all my body parts."

"So *that's* what Craig got suspended for. He's nivver telt me fit happened."

Chapter 33

Davy was going to the Bridge Bar to meet the usual group of cops. Flint could have gone with him but chose instead to go for a walk. He told himself he didn't know where he was going, but he did. He passed the Silver Slipper and didn't stop. He went left up Rosemount Viaduct. Ten minutes later and with no memory of crossing at busy junctions he turned into Lamond Place, as a long Inverness-bound train rumbled by behind him.

Before he reached the next corner he stopped, leaning against cold granite, still out of sight.

She might not be in, anyway. If she is, she might not want me. You're pathetic, go and ring the bell.

As he turned the corner into Jamaica Street his eyes went straight to the one window that mattered. The light was on. She was in. The wrought-iron gate across the path to the main door was latched, as always. He had to lean down to open it, but it was just at the right height for her, he remembered

The light went out and his hand stayed still on the latch. He recognised the noise of the flat door closing. Her footsteps on the stairs, louder like his heartbeat.

It was after six o'clock, meaning he could hide behind the red Transit that always parked there overnight. With his back to its rear door, Flint listened to her footsteps on the path. The gate opening, then closing. If she turned right, he would have to move round to the side of the van or she would see him.

She turned left, and as her footsteps receded up the slight slope, he risked a glimpse. She had a new jacket, but she was wearing the boots he had bought her.

###

It wasn't quite closing time when Flint left the Silver Slipper, but the barman made it clear he wasn't going to serve him another pint.

"You said you're staying in Esslemont Avenue, son. Turn right when you go out the door." Flint couldn't remember telling the barman where he was staying. He wondered what else he might have told him. He had often been in the Silver Slipper with Isla, and it seemed the natural place to bring his sorrow. He'd sat alone cursing himself for his cowardice, then telling himself it was just as well. She was bound to be going out to meet someone anyway. A man.

Now, after walking past granite tenements and concrete tower blocks he turned right when he recognised the silhouette of the Grammar School. He knew Craig's flat was on the top floor and about halfway along the level section of Esslemont Avenue, but he didn't know the number. With one hand on a lamppost, he stood for a moment, swaying. When he spotted Craig's parked car, he gave himself a thumbs up. All the street doors looked the same. His maudlin spirits had lifted a little and he chuckled to himself at his situation, standing back and looking up the tall tenement frontage.

He was lucky. He chose the correct front door, and managed to haul himself up the four flights of stairs. Shushing himself loudly, he burped and then heard himself mumbling "Don't wake the neighbours." His words resonated between his ears and he started laughing again. Luck ran out on the top landing. He was tapping as gently as he could on the flat door when a young woman in a housecoat swung it inwards as he was leaning on it.

"Stop banging on my fucking door! Fuck off!" she shouted, slamming the door against him. Shrugging, Flint turned to the opposite door, which he found had been left unlocked again.

Chapter 34

"Flint, are you getting up? It's after 11 o'clock."

The words echoed between his ears. Beginning to remember where he was, he shuffled himself to a sitting position to make room for Craig on the end of the couch. The zip of the nylon sleeping bag was jagging his hip.

"Sorry. It was a late night," said Flint, struggling out of the bag to get up. He belched.

"God, what were you drinking? You smell like a pub drain."

Flint smiled. "Aye, a few too many beers."

"Who were you out with? Davy?"

"No, just myself. I went for a walk and got a bit pissed off." It would have been good to tell Craig about trying to visit Isla but he was too embarrassed. He'd chickened out and hidden from her.

"Look at this," said Craig, straightening his right leg.

Rubbing his eyes, Flint saw that in place of Craig's tatty, white plaster cast was a much thinner, bright blue one. From the way he was easily lifting his leg up and down it was obvious it was much lighter.

"They call it a walking cast. Made of 'Baycast'. It's brilliant. They said the bones are healing well and it's time to start walking a bit. Look at the heel."

Flint could see a tough, rubber ridge embedded in the blue material to take Craig's weight.

"Is it strong enough? Looks more like a bandage."

He could hear how solid it was when Craig knocked hard on the cast with his knuckles.

"Best of all, I can get a pair of breeks on over it. Loose ones. I've got tracksuit bottoms somewhere." Craig was still wearing the same pair of butchered jeans. "And I can walk. Without bloody crutches."

Flint hadn't noticed they were nowhere to be seen. A wooden walking stick was hanging over the back of a chair.

"I got the taxi to drop me at the corner shop." Craig held up a bag of sausage rolls. "And I won't need to get a bloody taxi again. I can walk to the bus stop now I've got this on."

Ten minutes later, having splashed his face and gulped some water, Flint could feel his hangover receding. He remembered where Craig had been last night, and his mind flashed an image of Mo's figure walking away in her tight jeans.

"Good night, was it?"

Craig met his grin with an easy smile and a sigh. "Aye. I really like her."

"I'm not surprised, from what I saw. A cracker."

Craig didn't say more and seemed content to finish his sausage roll. As he was emptying the flakes of pastry into his palm Flint couldn't resist another probe.

"Get much sleep, then?"

Craig's smile widened. His eyes appeared focused on something beyond the beige anaglypta. "Not really."

"Lucky bastard!"

Craig's smile slipped away and he shook his head. "To tell you the truth, I was awake half the night thinking about the names on Slinn's list. I found this again." He took a folded sheet of paper from his pocket and passed it to Flint. It was the flyer advertising Slinn's lecture on 10th May.

"Christ, he looks like Jason King," he said, laughing and dropping the advert on the table.

Craig didn't laugh and turned to look straight at Flint. "You really think he's killing the men?"

Flint shrugged. "He's got to be. Why else would he be scoring their names off his list?"

"I've been thinking about that list. We don't know why the men's names were on it."

"Go on."

"We need more. We can't go to Blackie or Chic Morrice with only an idea that Slinn *might* be connected to the men. We've got to prove what the connection is. If we're going to get them to look at the case again, I mean."

Flint looked at Craig, shrugging. "Who?"

"My bosses."

"Are you really thinking about going to the police with this?"

"We have to at some point, but with all we've got they'd just dismiss us as mental. Especially because Blackie will lose face if Stiff is innocent."

"This guy Black, is he involved in the case?" asked Flint.

"Blackie. He was the SIO on the Skilling murder."

"SIO?"

"Senior Investigating Officer. He was determined. Even though Stiff couldn't have done it he was going to charge him anyway. Bastard."

"But if he sees the list Slinn's working through, that's got to make him think again, surely?"

"We'd have to show some motive. The men might just be his patients. He might not even know they're dead."

"That's ridiculous. There's got to be a reason why he's crossed out the names of the ones who've been murdered."

"Yeah, but that's what Blackie would say. We need to get more. Proof he's got a motive to kill them. And evidence."

"But that's the police's job."

"Aye, but Blackie's never going to admit he's got the wrong man."

"Maybe the connection is the daughters," said Flint. "There was a letter from Skilling's daughter in his car, right?"

"Yes. I saw it. So what?"

"And Gaska had a daughter. She might have been seeing a psychiatrist."

"Go on." Craig sat forward.

"What if the daughters were Slinn's patients? The list was in a file called something like 'child abuse survivors'. Maybe Slinn's patients had all been abused."

"And Slinn was — like — taking revenge for them?"

"That's what I've been thinking," said Flint. "There's your 'motive'."

"It's too mental. And we don't know if the Skilling girl was seeing a psychiatrist."

They sat drinking their coffee until Craig said, "I'm going to get rid of these." He pointed to his cut-off jeans with the safety pins.

Flint laughed. "Thank fuck. I thought there was a dead dog in the car yesterday."

"At least they washed my leg before they put the blue stookie on. You should have smelt what was inside the old one."

While Craig was away changing, Flint closed his eyes and dozed. He was jolted when Craig returned and swung his leg onto the coffee table, knocking over an empty mug. He sat admiring his tracksuit bottoms and the protruding cast. His toes were exposed, white against the royal blue.

"Wake up, Flint. I've been thinking. Didn't you say Slinn's list had dates of birth?"

"Aye, three columns. A number, a surname and a date of birth. But I can't fucking remember any of them. The names sort of stood out, but it was like the rest of the page was out of focus."

"Shit. The ages would show if it was the daughters or the fathers."

Flint sat forward. "Maybe it doesn't matter. Slinn's the common factor. He's taking revenge for the daughters."

"But why would a man like Slinn take the risk? He's a professor, for God's sake."

"But think what it's like listening to kids telling you about the awful shit done to them. Maybe it got too much for Slinn?"

Craig took his leg off the table and stood up. "I'm going to make coffee."

Flint stared out of the window. The granite spires and gables of the Grammar School were silhouetted against a milky sky.

Craig returned and put a mug in front of Flint. He said, "We've got to find some proof."

Flint nodded, biting his lip. "What do we know about the daughters?"

"Not much," said Craig with a sigh. "Only that Skilling had a letter from his daughter in his car, and Phil told us Gaska has a daughter."

"And there was a letter in Harkan Gaska's car. It might have been from his daughter."

"But all we know about Narloch is he was separated. He might not even have had a daughter."

"I bet he did," said Flint, lifting the picture of Slinn. "If we can prove the daughters were patients of this guy, all victims of abuse…"

Craig put his elbows on the table and his chin in his hands. "There's got to be some way we could trace them. Ask them, I mean."

"I'm going to get dressed," said Flint standing up and rummaging in his grip. He grabbed his jeans from the floor and went to the bathroom.

Craig was standing up near the window flipping the pages of the phone book when Flint returned. He looked up, grinning. "Phil said the Gaska wife and daughter moved to Stonehaven. We might be able to find her. The daughter, I mean. And he also said something about her seeing a shrink."

Chapter 35

"This isn't the way to Stonehaven."

"Just keep driving where I tell you."

Flint shook his head, but kept going down a sloping dual carriageway. Heavy traffic slowed to a stop as they approached a junction with another busy road.

When Craig had found just one 'Gaska' entry in the phone book he'd smiled to himself and shaken his head. "Right, this is got to be where she lives," he'd said.

Craig insisted they go to the address. Flint couldn't believe he might be going to approach the girl, but was happy when he said to drive him there. More practice.

"Turn left here."

"But this is the wrong direction," said Flint, turning left at traffic lights. "Look, the sign says Inverness for fuck's sake. We're supposed to be going south."

"We're not going to Stonehaven." Craig appeared to be enjoying taking Flint on a mystery tour. A right turn past a bakery that made Flint hungry took them through Bucksburn, and a mile or so further on Craig told him to turn left.

"Aye, up here, Market Street. Auchriny Circle's up at the top on the right, if I remember."

Flint was still mystified. A roaring noise filled the car, and ahead of them, he saw an SAS jet rise above the rooftops. The noise intensified as it swung upwards at an impossibly steep angle. Craig motioned him to turn right, and when the jet was far enough away to allow speech said, "Welcome to Stoneywood," said Craig. Flint looked at him. "When Phil said 'Stonetown' I thought he meant Stonehaven." He pointed at terraced houses. "I was in one of them at three in the morning one time. A domestic."

Flint said, "You just going to go and speak to her? Since you're polis, I mean."

But Craig was shaking his head, his eyes closed. "Christ, what was I thinking? This was a mental idea. Look at me, a tracksuit and a plaster cast? Anyway, I'd lose my job for doing something like that. I'm not getting suspended *again*. We can't do anything. Let's go." He made circles with his hand.

But instead of turning round, Flint unclipped his seatbelt, opening the car door.

"Where are you—? Flint! You can't."

"Got an idea," said Flint, winking and turning away as the car door closed.

"Thank God there was no one in. Flint, you're a bloody headache."

Flint was grinning as he drove. "I just thought it was worth a try."

They were on Auchmill Road heading back towards the city, and Craig was only now beginning to calm down. Ten minutes before, with Craig watching open-mouthed, Flint had sauntered to the door of the Auchriny Circle house. After ringing the bell and knocking several times, he'd turned away with a shrug. Getting back into the car, he'd handed Craig his warrant card.

"You dropped this yesterday. I forgot to give it back."

"You had my fucking warrant card! Impersonating a police officer? You would have been jailed, you stupid bastard. Drive!"

Flint was laughing now. "Sorry. I just thought I could pull it off."

"But fucking look at you! And you're still reeking of beer." Flint had never heard his friend swear as much. He had to admit to himself, though, that in his army jacket, dirty jeans and scuffed baseball boots he didn't look much like a detective.

"I could have said I was working undercover."

Craig shook his head, but the corners of his mouth turned up as he tried not to smile. "Thank fuck there was no one in."

###

Friday afternoon

Craig had gone out to buy another pair of tracksuit bottoms, saying he wanted to test drive his walking cast. Left alone in the flat, Flint took the opportunity to have a bath. He realised the immersion heater wasn't on, and the water ran cold when it was only two inches deep. He was still cold and damp an hour later.

He'd forgotten to bring the Le Carré book, and after reading all the small ads in an old copy of the P&J he switched on the TV. He had an idea there might be some cartoons on ITV.

When the main door slammed two floors below, running footsteps on the stairs meant it wasn't Craig. A few seconds later the flat door opened.

"Onyb'dy in?" It was Davy's voice, and the big face grinned round the living room door. "You made a fine racket when you came in last night, min. You were bangin' aboot for ages." Flint thought he'd gone straight to bed.

"Aye, sorry. Had a couple of beers."

"Mair than a couple by the sound o' it." Davy didn't ask where Flint had been.

They were watching Roadrunner together when Craig returned. They hadn't heard the door and both were startled. Flint turned back to the cartoon but Davy stared at Craig.

"Fit in hell's 'at?" he said, pointing at Craig's new cast with an expression of distaste.

"Good, eh?" said Craig. "It's dead lightweight. I can walk no bother."

"You canna go aboot with that on, min. Look at the colour o' it!"

Flint laughed as he realised Davy's problem was with the royal blue. "Aye, you should have asked for a red one, Craig." The rivalry between the Dons and Glasgow Rangers fans had been intensifying in recent years.

"Christ, I never thought of that." Craig sat down and pulled the hem of his tracksuit bottoms as low as he could.

"Ach well, at least yer nae workin'. The Casuals wouldnae like a hun polis goin' about." Davy was laughing. "Remember the last time they played at Pittodrie? We were on night shift and cells were stowed out."

"Aye, and we took a good few to A+E as well."

When Craig returned from making coffee, Davy pulled a folded sheet of paper from his trouser pocket. "I forgot. You asked me about this a while back," he said, handing it to Craig.

The puzzled look on Craig's face quickly turned to one of shock.

"What the hell? Where did you get this? Davy, for fuck's sake."

"I had to work for a while at Blackie's desk today, and the Skilling file was just sitting there. I found that letter you were asking about."

"Davy, you stupid bastard. You can't take something out of the file." Craig held the letter as if it was going to burn his fingers.

"I'm nae that stupid," said Davy with his trademark grin, "that's a photocopy. What's so important about it, anyway?"

Craig dropped the letter on the low table. "I don't even want to see it."

Flint leant forward and took the flimsy sheet of copier paper. "I'll read it, it might..."

When Flint stopped in mid-sentence Craig lowered his eyes from the ceiling to look at him. "What is it?"

Flint continued to look at the paper, his eyes scanning slowly back and forth as he read and reread the letter. "Slinn." He flopped against the couch, letting his head hang back. His turn to look at the ceiling. Craig pulled the letter from his hand.

"What is it that's so bloody important about this letter?" said Davy.

"More guys wi' their goolies cut off? And you two think this psychiatrist is doing it?" Davy was smirking in disbelief.

Craig was glaring at Flint. Until now they hadn't mentioned the other murders to Davy. Flint was clearing the dishes away after spaghetti bolognese. He'd made far too much spaghetti and the sink was choked.

"I'll sort that mess after," he said. "Can I just make a quick phone call?"

Craig looked at his watch. "Aye, it's after 6 o'clock. Phoning your mum at last, now it's cheap rate?"

Flint mumbled a reply as he closed the door behind him.

Davy was holding the letter, reading it again. "I mean, it's a simple note to a bloke from his daughter. Just 'cos it mentions the shrink it doesn't mean much."

"There's something linking Slinn to three men who were all killed the same way." Craig was still annoyed at Flint for involving Davy, but it didn't matter now.

"Look, I keep telling you. Just because the letter says Ivan Skilling's daughter was seeing this Prof Slinn mannie, it disna mean he's got anything to do wi' his murder. Or any others. You can't blame Grampian."

"Davy, I'm not blaming anyone. Anyway, even with the link between Skilling and two other murders we can't use the letter. You'd get suspended for taking it. Christ, you know what happened to me."

"Fuck." Davy dropped the letter, his smile gone. During one of their long night shifts together, Craig had told him about being suspended for using the PNC without permission. Davy had said he would never do anything like that. His worried look then softened a little.

"But the letter's still in the file. No one knows I took the photocopy. I can bin it and say I just happened to read it in the file. Nae bother."

"But you're not working on the case now, Davy. You'd no business looking." Craig talked on, as if to himself. "Anyway, we need more than just one of the daughters seeing Slinn. We need a lot more before we can tell Blackie he's got the wrong man. Slinn's involved in this, but there's SFA we can do about it."

Davy was now tapping his hand rapidly on the wooden chair arm. "Fuck's sake, min," he said through pursed lips. "That's *your* problem! How come you asked me about the letter, eh? Why'd you involve me? When you knew I wasn't on the case?"

"I thought you might have heard something about it, that's all."

"Christ, I dinna want tae be involved." Davy stood. "Anyway, why the fuck did Soutar confess if he didna dae it? I dinna want tae ken ony mair." He stomped to his bedroom, passing Flint who was putting the phone receiver down.

Davy's door slammed shut as Flint came back into the living room. Craig was on his feet. "Shit. I'm supposed to be at Mo's at seven. I'd better get changed into my new breeks."

Before Flint could ask what was wrong with Davy, Craig walked out, also shutting the door.

Flint had no one to tell what he'd just discovered.

Chapter 36

Saturday morning, 8th May 1982

Flint couldn't get back to sleep after the flat door banged when Davy left for work. Now, four hours later, he was angry and deflated. He'd been waiting for Tiswas to start, but it had been taken off air and it felt like Christmas had been cancelled. Every Saturday he and Isla had snuggled under a blanket in whichever flat they'd shared to watch and laugh at Spit the Dog.

He swore at the TV. Baby cartoons and a series about Black Beauty. His coffee tasted sour and his rice crispies went soggy.

Craig came back from Mo's just before 11 o'clock. Flint was itching to share what he'd learned on the phone the previous evening, but before he could speak Craig said, "You shouldn't have told Davy about the other murders. He's bound to tell someone, and I'll get suspended again. So will he, most likely."

"But what are you doing wrong? I thought it was your job to catch baddies."

Craig sat down, still in his jacket. "I'm not supposed to be doing anything when I'm off sick. Especially not poking into cases in different areas. And now Davy's nicked that bloody letter."

Flint got up and went to the sink to fill the kettle. "At least it's proved Slinn was seeing Skilling's daughter."

"So what?" said Craig. "It doesn't get us anywhere. I can't go to Blackie and say he's got the wrong man locked up just because the victim's daughter was seeing a shrink. He'd send *me* to a fucking shrink." He got up and dropped his jacket on the back of the couch, reaching for the switch above the sink to turn the immersion heater on.

Flint was spooning coffee into mugs, and said over his shoulder, "Well, you can tell him Slinn was seeing two of the daughters."

About to sit back down, Craig stopped. "What? What do you mean?" He lowered himself slowly, placing his cast on the coffee table. "How do you know?"

"I phoned Patricia Gaska."

"You did what? When?"

"Last night, before you went out."

"After you phoned your mum?"

"I didn't phone home. I called the Gaskas' number. The one in the phone book." Flint grinned at the look of disbelief on Craig's face. "Smart, eh? I tried the student thing again."

"Student? What? Wha—?"

"I said I was one of Slinn's students again. Doing a research project. Following up his patients. She—"

"Jeezo, Flint! You didn't even know she *was* one of his patients." Craig withdrew his leg from the table and sat forward.

"Aye, I know, but if she wasn't I'd just have said it was a mistake. Sorry to have bothered you. Stuff like that." Craig was shaking his head, but with a hint of a smile in his eyes. "She wanted to help. Said what a great man Slinn is, and I was lucky to be working with him. How much he'd helped her." He paused. "She had a sexy voice; I quite liked her."

"You fancied her down the phone?" Craig was laughing now.

"Well, she's a Fifer. Reminded me of a lassie at school."

Craig looked at the ceiling, exhaling. Flint put two coffees down.

"But, you're really sure she was a Slinn patient? That's definitely two of them?"

"Aye. *At least* two of the victims had daughters that Slinn was seeing. I bet you he was seeing Narloch's daughter as well. And the other two he'd crossed out."

Craig took a sip of his coffee and turned to look out of the window.

"Well? What do you think," Flint continued, "is that enough to get your wee Stiff man out of jail?"

"Pass me that bit of paper, will you?" said Craig, indicating an advert for a handyman service that Flint had found on the doormat that morning.

"Got something needs fixed?"

Craig ignored him and took a pen from the coffee table. He started writing on the back of the paper.

"What have we got?"

Flint watched him write.

> *Three killings, same MO*
> *Injuries: head injury, genitals removed*
> *Names Skilling, Narloch, Gaska, all on list in Slinn's office*
> *5 names on list crossed out (includes S, N and G)*
> ***2 MORE DEATHS?? !! **!*
> *Two daughters of victims being seen by Slinn*

"Remember the bit about Soutar. Or 'Stiff' if you like. He was in hospital when Narloch was done in," said Flint.

Craig looked up, grinning. "Aye!" He added to the notes.

> *Ian Soutar charged for Skilling (confessed!!)*
> *Soutar in hosp at time of Narloch killing.*

"Fuck! Soutar's got to be innocent." Craig threw the pen down. "But that means someone's got to tell DCI Blackie he's got the wrong man in Craiginches."

"I'm telling you, the famous professor is going around killing men that abused their daughters," Flint said. He stood up and looked out of the window. For a moment neither of them spoke, the only sounds the wind through whistling telephone wires and seagulls squawking as they fought over scraps around a litter bin two floors below. "Maybe we should let him carry on. Bastards deserved it," said Flint.

"I know what you mean, but no one should take the law into their own hands."

"The law didn't do much for those girls, did it?" said Flint. "If those men abused their daughters and then were able to carry on as normal, I mean."

"If the victims don't report the abuse, well..." Craig's words tailed off. He was still staring at the notes he had written. "Some coincidence, though," he said. "I mean Slinn kills Ivan Skilling and then gets asked to give an expert report on the man we've charged for the murder?"

Flint shrugged and said, "One thing's for certain: his report's going to say Soutar's as guilty as sin. There's no way he's going to say they've got the wrong man. With someone charged it means they're not looking for him."

Chapter 37

It had been Craig's idea to go out for a lunchtime pint. Now, five hours later, they were being swept along among thousands of men, women and children streaming away from Pittodrie after the St Mirren game. They'd met Barry Cummings on the way to the Silver Slipper, and he'd been all smiles and handshakes.

"I heard you got your leg smashed, Craig. Nightmare. How're you doin', min?"

"Erm, OK, thanks."

"On yer way to the game? Quite a lot of us goin' the day. Fa's yer pal?"

Craig introduced Flint, and soon Barry suggested that they all go to the Bridge Bar. Barry's bonhomie continued and Craig wondered if his injury in the call of duty meant he would not be such an *ootsider* when he returned to work. He and Flint had ended up joining Barry and several other off-duty cops in the crowd at Pittodrie. They agreed to take a bus along King Street to save Craig from walking all the way with his stick, and made plans to paint his blue cast with red paint.

Flint was caught up in the excitement of Aberdeen's continued success, enjoying the collective euphoria of the crowd. The chants and jeers during the match, mostly good-natured, had amused and excited him to a level he hadn't reached in a long while.

Now as the chanting red mob surged along Merkland Road East, Barry was joining in. "5 - 1! Magic! Come … on … you … reds!"

Flint said excitedly, "It's St Mirren again midweek, then Rangers next weekend. If Celtic drop a point that's the title!"

Barry grinned toward Flint and said, "'At's right, and then the cup final, Rangers again. Come … on … you … reds!"

Flint looked round to check that Craig was keeping up. He had stopped, leaning on his stick and staring down and to his left. Flint followed his gaze and saw a newspaper hoarding outside a corner shop.

Evening Express
SKILLING MURDER
Suspect Released
after
Shrink Intervenes

A minute later he watched Craig come out of the shop. Leaning on his stick and with his other hand steadying him down the low doorstep, he was holding a folded newspaper between his teeth. Flint knew he had to wait with Craig but was disappointed to see the gang he had become part of leaving him behind. He watched the tall figure of Barry Cummings lead his troupe across to the Pittodrie Bar on the other side of King Street, the impatient traffic no match for the surge of red and white.

Craig leant against the shop window, unfolding the paper.

"That's your man Stiff let loose, then?" said Flint.

Craig seemed taller, somehow, when he turned to Flint with a satisfied grin. "Aye, and you know what it means? It means they'll have to reopen the case."

"But you still can't tell them about the others. I thought you said you'd lose your job if you did that. And Jack. And Davy, you said."

"Yes, but not if someone else tells them."

"Me?" he said, hairs were pricking his neck. He'd been brave enough to blag his way past the Liff Hospital receptionists and gallus enough to mislead Patricia Gaska, but he didn't think he could face the police.

Craig simply smiled back at him. "Come on, let's go and get food."

Craig's leg meant they sat downstairs on the bus. Nowadays, Flint preferred the upstairs. The front row of the top deck always made him think of Isla. Her delight when he'd first shown her he had overcome his fear of heights still swelled him with pride. He'd just mastered self-hypnosis and felt like a God.

"Look," said Craig, drawing him back to the present. "See who wrote it? That's who'll help us."

Flint followed Craig's pointing finger. Underneath 'MURDER ACCUSED RELEASED' he read, 'Bail for Soutar after Psychiatrist Intervenes'. Then, 'Special Report by Tom Jordan, Crime Reporter'.

"Who's that? You know him?"

"Come on, this is our stop," said Craig, pressing the button.

The Light of Bengal was just a short walk along Rose Street, and though it had only been open for an hour it was already half-full with Saturday evening diners.

"You've lived in Aberdeen for years and you've never been in here? I can hardly believe it," said Craig.

"I didn't really like curry until the last year or two. We used to go to the Raj Dulal. Isla and me, I mean."

"Have you decided to go and see Isla while you're up here?"

Flint sat back in the red booth and looked at the ceiling. He still hadn't told Craig about his abortive visit to Jamaica Street two nights before. "Let me have another look at that paper."

Craig folded the *Express* so that they could fit it on the table between them. They took turns to read it again.

"So they actually let him out this morning," murmured Flint, reading below the picture of Ivan Skilling. "When does it say Slinn saw him?"

"It doesn't, but my guess is it would have been at least a few days ago. He'll have had to send a report to the Fiscal."

"What does it mean? 'Bail'?" asked Flint. "Does that mean he's completely free, or what?"

"He'll still have to go to court unless they drop the charges altogether. Slinn must have said he was no danger to the public and that he wasn't going to run away. He can go home, but there'll be conditions like he probably has to check in at the local polis every day." He took a long slurp of lager. "But it might be that he's told them Stiff confessed because he was a nutter rather than 'cos he really killed Skilling, and they can't bear to just drop the charges." Craig smiled. "DCI Blackie will be going mental."

A waiter put a plate of onion bhajis in front of Craig and some poppadums for Flint. Between mouthfuls, Flint said, "What did you mean about the reporter helping us?"

Craig spoke quietly, although the hubbub in the curry house was building and it was unlikely he could be overheard. Flint had to lean across the table to hear about Craig's suspensions and how meeting Jordan in Bertie's bar had led to his return to work.

"It meant I had to come to this shitehole of a place, but it was better than not being in the police."

"You seem to have made a good few pals, though."

"Aye, it's getting better. When we were driving down into Aberdeen the other day it felt quite good to be coming back."

"I'm not surprised. You had a night with Mo to look forward to. She's braw."

They ate on, and soon their curries and rice appeared.

"I don't know how you can eat that," said Flint as Craig wolfed into his Madras. "I've never got past mild curries."

"You should try Vindaloo, that'll really nip yer arse the next day."

They ate on in silence apart from ordering more lager. When their plates were scraped clean of the last rice grains Flint belched and leant forward again.

"If Professor Slinn is killing off his list of targets one by one, why didn't he make sure Stiff stayed locked up? I mean, having someone else blamed for it means no one is going to catch him. Now he's let him out."

"God knows," said Craig. "Maybe there's some good in him even if he is a serial killer."

"Probably thinks he'll never be caught. Like he's sort of invincible." Flint's mind had flipped back to the Limb Collector. Until he and Craig had confronted him at the top of The Mount, he had thought no one could touch him. Typical psychopathic behaviour, Dr Sutton had said. And if he and Craig were correct about Slinn, this psychopath was a psychiatrist himself.

"How come you're not seeing Mo tonight?" They were climbing the stairs to the flat and Flint was lagging behind, despite Craig being the one with the broken leg.

"She's out with some work pals. Asked me if I wanted to come but I could tell she didn't want me to." Craig turned to throw a sardonic grin at Flint, who was just reaching the top landing. "'A lovely girly night', she said. I can pass on that. I'm going to see her tomorrow afternoon."

As Craig opened the flat door Flint caught up.

"I'm knackered after that. It's amazing how a big meal makes you tired. It's only the back of nine o'clock, and I could sleep."

They slumped in front of the telly, each with a can of McEwans Lager.

"There's bugger all on until Sportscene starts," said Flint. He reached for the *Evening Express* and looked up at Craig after a moment.

"Bit of a coincidence, that journalist you mentioned reporting on Skilling and you've met him before," he said. "And you say you haven't told Davy or anyone you know him?"

"Yeah. I've only told one sergeant."

"You said you didn't want anyone to know in case they thought you'd leaked stuff to the papers. But if you go to ask the guy for help won't all that come out? About you knowing him, and your suspensions."

"Journalists never reveal their sources." Craig pictured the smug P&J editor and his 'journalist's integrity' speech.

"It's a bit of a risk, though, if you still want to keep it quiet," said Flint.

"Aye, I suppose. But it's worth it, for Stiff's sake." Craig let out a long belch.

"That's what I'm needing to do," said Flint, his hand on his belly, "I feel like I'm going to burst."

Flint went back to reading the *Express* article. After a few minutes he looked up at Craig. "It doesn't say much here about Soutar. You saw him at the Police Station, right? What did you think of him?"

Craig put his can down on the floor beside him.

"It was actually at his home. Miltonfold, Bucksburn. I felt a bit sorry for him. The first thing I thought was he was too wee. There's no way he could have overpowered the man Skilling." Craig's head was shaking as he spoke. "And he was an obvious nutter, in and out of the loony bin and all sorts of stuff in his medical notes about dreams, and him wanting to cut men's cocks off. Mental stuff." Craig turned to Flint, rolling his eyes. "I'm not even supposed to speak about any of this. But you know it already." He got up. "I'm going for a slash before the football starts."

Chapter 38

Sunday 9th May

Flint lay in the sleeping bag, wondering what time it was. He'd forgotten to wind his watch and it had stopped at ten past one. The green curtains didn't meet, and a shaft of sunlight streaming in told him it was morning. A steady flow of traffic was passing below.

His mood was lower than it had been for weeks, and he felt like he had been awake all night. For the first time in months, he'd had some of the disordered dreams about his past. Not the bad one. At least that had stopped. As usual, the details were just out of reach. It was a familiar feeling of frustration. His mind meandered, scenes from his childhood melting into memories of his tumultuous time at university.

When he'd resorted to hypnotherapy it helped his phobias and cured his fear of heights. A side effect, though, was discovering the meaning of disturbing dreams. Shocking truths from the past about himself and his family emerged, things he had buried away under his phobias. Confronting them unmasked the Limb Collector, but also led to his cruel father's death.

Then the new dream had started. The bad one that told him he had killed his father. And made Isla break up with him.

Trying to distract himself, he picked up the *Express* again.

###

"Tell me what you can remember about Stiff's dreams," said Flint.

Craig had just come out of his bedroom, trouserless and his blue leg cast highlighting the whiteness of his legs. "My ankle's itchy as hell. What did you say?"

"Stiff. Ian Soutar. You said something about him having nightmares he couldn't remember. Isn't that what the psychiatrist said?"

"She wanted to have him hypnotised. Something about buried trauma in his past. That's what I was going to ask you about when I came to visit you in Auchmoor. But you told me to bugger off."

Flint said nothing and looked out of the window. Then without looking back at Craig, he said, "Remember I told you and Jack about my own 'buried trauma'? And it was only hypnotherapy that unburied it. Explained my mental dreams." He turned back to Craig, whose brow was furrowed.

"Erm — are you still having trouble?"

"No. Well, some I suppose. But d'you think Slinn actually hypnotised Soutar when he saw him?" Flint paused and turned a questioning look towards Craig. "I keep meaning to ask. What's this 'Stiff' thing about, anyway? Why does Soutar get called Stiff?"

"Dunno. Seems to like it. When me and DS Ovenstone went to visit him, his mother called him Ian but he asked us to call him Stiff."

"Anyway, I've been wondering if Professor Slinn hypnotised Stiff and discovered something. Something to explain why he's obsessed with cutting off men's tackle."

"We couldn't find that out without getting into the medical report he sent to the Fiscal." Craig looked hard at Flint. "I'm not trying anything, if that's what you're thinking."

Chapter 39

In the early afternoon, Craig set off to meet Mo. He had changed into his clean tracksuit bottoms, and said proudly he was going to walk all the way to Rosemount.

Davy was out on shift, and Flint sat in the empty flat until he thought Craig would be far enough away, then reached for his jacket. As he pulled the door shut, he realised he didn't have a key, and tried the handle in case the snib was off. It wasn't, and he was locked out now. He shrugged and then started down the stairs two at a time.

Ten minutes later he was on Rosemount Viaduct. He turned round as he climbed the steps to the Central Library, and looked out across the busy Union Terrace junction. To the left, and behind the imposing bronze figure of William Wallace with his outstretched hand and sword, were the Union Terrace Gardens. Flint smiled briefly at the memory of his Glaswegian student friend Nudge climbing to hang a Celtic scarf over Wallace's arm, before being chased. To escape angry Dons fans, he had jumped over a wall into what he had thought were bushes, only to fall fifteen feet through trees. Flint and his pals had known the spot as Nudge's Leap ever since.

The library doors were closed. He had forgotten it was Sunday, and he wouldn't be able to look at the electoral roll. He considered giving up, but remembered a phone box in Glasgow, four years ago when he'd been hunting for the man he'd thought was his mother's lover. He crossed the road and strode along Union Terrace. At the junction with Union Street there were two red phone boxes, and one of them had a directory.

###

Even though most of the shops were shut, the No. 17 bus was slow as it went along George Street. When it passed The

Rubber Shop, Flint recalled visits there with Isla, smiling to himself. The first time they had gone in was not long after they had met and both were new to the city. Intrigued by the name, Flint had pulled her away from the packed window display of dolls, trikes and model cars and in over the tiled threshold. He could still remember the mixed smells — leather and the damp Saturday doormat — and the shrieks of children being pulled away from the china displays as they rushed to make their lists for Santa. Flint had bought new studs for his football boots.

Not far along, the bus stopped outside Arnotts, a posh department store. He remembered lingering in its doorway before dawn one Sunday morning, waiting for Isla's train. She'd set off back from Edinburgh as soon as he'd called her. He'd spent the day before being interviewed by police, after he'd found his flatmate's body.

Flint spent more of the journey reminiscing. He made plans to visit Isla again, then dismissed the idea. When he'd spied her in Jamaica Street, she'd been on the way out, dressed up. She must be seeing someone else.

He was drawn back to the present by a woman across the aisle shouting at her two moaning children. "Shut it! We're goin' tae Bucksburn tae see yer grannie like every Sunday. Stop yer girnin', will ye."

The bus was already on Auchmill Road, and Bucksburn wasn't much further on. Flint still didn't know what to say when he got there and began to regret setting out to find Stiff. He knew he couldn't ask Craig to take any more risks with his career, but thought if he could meet Stiff he might learn more. He wanted to know why Professor Slinn had intervened to have Stiff released from jail.

"Excuse me, are you going to Bucksburn?" Flint knew that was where the tired-looking mother was headed, but didn't want her to think he had been listening.

"Aye, son, this is oor stop." She pressed a bell and started to gather her kids and their toys.

"Can you tell me where to get off for Miltonfold?"

"Aye, son, get aff here. It's just up past the polis station."

Flint felt conspicuous as he walked past Bucksburn Police Station, and tucked the piece of paper he'd torn from the phone directory into his pocket. Towards the end of a curving row of squat blocks, he found a building with the sign 'Miltonfold 58-66', separated from the main road by a strip of grass. It needed mowing, he noted.

On the first-floor landing, he took a deep breath before tapping on the door of number 64. Shouts and applause from inside became muted and he could tell a TV game show was being turned down. The smell of smoke intensified when the door opened.

"Err, Mrs Thomasina Soutar? I'm one of Professor Slinn's students. I'm doing research and—"

"You found him? You here about Ian?" The woman opened the door a little more and leaned out to look behind Flint. "Far is he?" She started coughing.

Flint's nerve held, and when she paused to take another drag he went on.

"I wondered if I could come in Mrs Soutar and ask a bit about Mr Soutar, Ian I mean—"

"Call me Ina, loon. A'bdy else does. C'mon in, d'ye ken far he is?"

Ian and Ina, thought Flint. No wonder he calls himself something else. Guessing Stiff wasn't at home and that his mother didn't know where he was, he followed her in. Before he could think of a question to ask, Ina Soutar said, "Big Jock was here a couple of hours ago. Said Ian didna turn up this mornin'. For his bail, y'ken?"

Flint's face must have told her he was confused.

"Ian's got tae check in at the polis station every day, and he didna go the day. He'll be the death o' me, that loon, I can tell ye. It wis better when he wis in the jail, at least I kent far he wis. He wis bad last night. Kept goin' on about havin' to speak to yer boss, this Dr Slinn. Said he's got magic powers. Ah tell ye, he needs his injection again."

"Big Jock? Erm — is that the policeman?"

"Aye, the sergeant, Jock Tawse. He's a good one. He kens Ian, sort of looks out for him, y'ken."

As he processed what Mrs Soutar had said, Flint's scalp prickled with a new growing fear.

"Is Sergeant Tawse out looking for Ian?"

"No, he said he'll give him until tonight before he reports him for nae checkin' in. He's good that way. Anyway, we ken far he'll be. He'll have gone on the bus to that bloody golf course again."

Flint took ten pence from his pocket and held it out. "Mrs Soutar, do you have a telephone I could use?"

Conscious of Ina Soutar hovering behind him in the narrow hall of 64 Miltonfold, Flint stared at a framed poster of Elvis Presley, inches from his face. The phone kept ringing in his ear and cigarette smoke drifted around him. He was about to hang up and accept that Craig wasn't back from Mo's yet when he heard the receiver being lifted.

"Hello. Craig?" he said, leaning even closer to the picture and turning away from Ina Soutar.

"Nah, he's nae in. Fa's iss?"

"It's Flint, Davy. Listen, quick, I need to speak to Craig."

"I've nae idea far he is, min. Fit's so urgent? I was just haein' a crap."

Flint turned back towards Ina. "Mrs Soutar, I'm afraid I have to speak to Professor Slinn's secretary and it has to be confidential. It's important medical details I need to discuss. Would you mind leaving me alone for a moment?"

"Aye, son, but dinna be ower long wi' the phone." She squeezed herself past him and into her living room. The TV went back on.

"Listen, Davy, remember the man Soutar? Stiff? The one out on bail?"

"Aye, why you whisperin', min? I can hardly hear—"

"Davy, listen. He's missing, and I think he might be dead soon if we don't find him."

"What? I've just come off shift and I never heard anything."

"No, the police don't know."

Flint could feel his pulse rate increasing and the grimy receiver was getting damp with his sweat. An idea occurred.

"Davy, could you take Craig's car and come and get me? It's important. I think I know where Stiff is."

Flint heard a sigh. "Aw fuck. I should report you both. Aye, I'll come. Far are ye?"

Chapter 40

Having excused himself from Mrs Soutar, Flint walked towards the Four Mile Inn. Davy had said he would prefer to meet him there instead of near the police station. Davy had guessed that what Flint wanted to do might not be approved of by Grampian Police. Flint had got Davy involved, another policeman, and was worried about what Craig would say.

His heart sank when the Escort drew up. Craig was in the passenger seat. Instead of berating him, though, Craig wound down the window, saying, "Davy came to Mo's and said you were up to something. Get in."

When Flint was in the back seat, Craig stretched round to him. "You think Stiff's in some kind of danger?"

Flint threw a quick look towards Davy and back to Craig, his eyebrows raised. Craig took the signal. "I think Davy knows enough already. We can tell him more later. Unless he takes us straight to Queen Street."

Davy kept looking ahead but Flint could see his resigned smile. "You buggers have got me in this deep, I might as well go down with you."

"You told Davy you think someone's going to kill Stiff?" Craig was still twisted in his seat.

"Something like that."

"Me too. I've been thinking the same. It explains why Slinn got him out of jail. He couldn't kill him in Craiginches, so he got him out."

Davy spoke again. "Hang on a minute. Are you saying this Professor mannie is going to kill the loon? Why would he do that, it disna make sense."

Now the look of resignation was on Craig's face. They were going to have to tell Davy.

"We think Slinn is a serial killer."

"I worked that much out from what you two have been goin' on about. I'm nae that stupid, even if you think I am," he said, glancing at Craig. "But surely if the Prof is the killer it's better for him if Soutar goes down for it? It's hard enough to understand why he arranged the bail, and I canna see why he'd want to kill him."

"I'm going to tell you," said Craig. He closed the car window, although there was no one passing in the pub car park. "I've been reading a psychology book I found in Mo's flat. Her flatmate's still at Uni. Anyway, there's a chapter on psychopaths. They think they're untouchable, the book says. Like no one else matters but them, and they are smarter than everyone else. You said the same last night, Flint. I was thinking about it today, and read the chapter again while Mo was away getting her hair cut by a neighbour."

"Get to the point. Do you mean Stiff's not a psycho but his shrink is? Or what?" Davy said, "And why are we in Bucksburn?"

Craig shifted in his seat and looked back and forth between his two friends.

"I think Slinn is playing games, like he's taking the piss out of everyone. He's going to kill Stiff. I don't know how, but I think he's just going to prove to himself he can do it and no one will catch him. The book says when they get caught it's because they think they can take risks."

"I still don't get it," said Davy. "If he's just helped him out of jail, why is he going to kill him?"

"When they get a taste of it, killing's like a drug to them, and they need more and more."

"This is mental." Davy looked at Flint. "Don't tell me you agree with this crap?"

Flint thought for a moment before speaking. He looked at Craig. "I think Stiff might die if we don't do something," he said, watching Craig nod in agreement, "but I don't think Slinn will be anywhere near when he does."

Craig now sat back with a surprised, questioning face.

Flint went on. "Think about it. Slinn is a psychiatrist, but he's also into hypnotherapy. Stiff told his mum that Slinn's got 'magic powers'."

"For fuck's sake, min. This is—"

"Go on," said Craig, shooshing Davy with a waved hand.

"I think Stiff's going to kill himself. Do Slinn's work for him. Then Slinn will come out and say he'd got it wrong about Stiff, and that he must have killed Ivan Skilling after all, and then the guilt made him top himself."

"Aw, for fuck's sake. I'm telling you, it's you two that's needin' a shrink. Yer each as bad as the other."

"Just drive, Davy," said Craig. "You think you know where Stiff is, Flint, right?"

"Some golf course he always goes to, his mother said."

"Girdle Ness. And that's where they found Skilling's body."

Still wary of being spotted by Sgt. Tawse, Davy detoured through Bankhead to avoid passing the police station. The Sunday traffic was light, and as they made their way across town Craig and Flint outlined to Davy what they knew about Slinn.

"You mean you broke into his desk and found a list of names? And that made you decide this Professor Slinn was killing them one by one?"

Flint said, "Yes, but there's more to it. All three of the murders we know about were done exactly the same way, head injury and their genitals cut off, and at least two of them had daughters who were patients of Slinn."

"That disnae mean he killed them."

Craig backed Flint up. "But he's definitely connected to all three of them, and as far as we know he's the only one who is."

"The quines could have done it. The daughters."

"But not all in the same way, and in different areas. Being Slinn's patients is the only thing that connects the girls," said Flint. "It's got to be Slinn. Otherwise, why does he keep that list?"

"Ach, dinna get me any more involved. I'm just the driver, right?" said Davy, shaking his head.

All three said no more until they crossed the River Dee.

"Turn left here, Davy," said Craig, "I know where they found the body."

Davy drove along Greyhope Road. To their left was the entrance to Aberdeen harbour, with Fittie and the city beyond. A red and white ship, smaller than a ferry but bigger than a fishing boat, was powering its way out into the North Sea, hardly moved by the swell. Flint watched it as they wound their way along the narrow road that hugged the coastline. Beyond the ship, he could count four helicopters going to and from Dyce Airport. Like the oil supply vessel in front of him, he knew the Chinooks and Sikorskys served dozens of drilling and exploration rigs dotted between Scotland and Norway.

As the car drew along below the Torry Battery, Craig said, "Not far from here, on the right." A flat area opened up in front of them as they rounded a bend. Above and beyond it a red flag protruded from a turfed crest. Nearer, at the foot of the slope, a streamer of blue and white crime scene tape was flapping from an old, angled fence post. Flint's eyes were drawn beyond its ragged end as if it were showing him where to look. Long grass was blowing in the wind, rippling like the waves on the sea. As it wafted to and fro, a dark shape flashed in and out of view. Davy stopped the car.

"Is that what I think it is?"

"It's a body," said Craig. "He's topped himself already." He was pushing the car door open. "Flint, help me out, quick!"

Chapter 41

Flint took Craig's arm and helped him out of the car, looking over his shoulder at the figure lying motionless at the edge of the car park.

When he thought about it later, he realised that while he had gone numb, Craig and Davy had put their police training to use as if without thinking.

Davy had restarted the engine almost as soon as it had gone quiet. "There'll be a phone in one of those cottages back near Torry. I'll go and get help," he said.

"I don't have my fucking stick. Flint go on, I'll catch up." Craig's commanding tone compelled him to run forward towards the body. He approached the supine figure with his throat clamped shut and his breath held. Two yards away he stopped, and shouted behind him.

"Davy, wait!"

Davy had just reversed the car to turn it and was revving the engine, about to pull forward.

When Craig caught up with Flint, he turned round, calling out, "Aye, Davy, stop. It's OK, he looks fine."

Flint saw Davy shaking his head in confusion. He turned back to look at the little boy on the ground. Craig was kneeling down awkwardly, one ankle held at a rigid right angle by the blue cast.

"Hello, Ian. Remember me? It's PC Masson. Are you OK?"

"You came tae ma hoose. I telt ye then, call me Stiff."

Flint realised the child's body he thought they had found was a man who had just spent months in jail. Ian Soutar's face was pale and made to look even smaller by his mop of black hair. Flint stood back, aware that he must be towering over

Stiff and likely to scare him, but Stiff wore a serene smile as he looked at both of them in turn.

"Is he OK? He's nae deid?" said Davy, gasping as he approached. "Christ. Ma heart's in ma mooth."

With both hands, Craig motioned Davy and Flint to stay back, nodding reassurance.

"He's OK. Aren't you, Stiff," he said as he turned back to face him. "What are you doing lying, there, though?"

"I come here all the time. Or I used tae, afore I was — ye ken — in there." He waved an arm in the direction of Torry, where the prison was.

"How long have you been lying here?"

"Since this mornin'. I got the number 12 bus like usual. First one on a Sunday's a bittie later."

"Did you forget you were meant to check in at the police station? With Sgt. Tawse."

"Aye, but Big Jock'll ken far I am."

"You have to keep to the rules, Stiff, or you'll get sent back into Craiginches."

"Doctor Slinn can keep me oot. He's magic. He can dae onythin'."

Craig looked at Flint who stood nearby. Davy had gone back to the car and was pulling his jacket on. Behind the car he could see the outline of the city, now grey against the sky. The breeze had dropped, and out to sea a bank of fog had appeared. The haar was coming in.

"It's getting cold, Stiff. Are you not freezing lying there?" Stiff was wearing just a lightweight, navy shell suit.

Stiff had a satisfied smile and said, "Naw, I'm just fine." He turned to look at Craig. "Dr Slinn made me all warm inside. Still am, ever since he did his trance thing on me."

Craig looked at Flint again who caught his eye and moved a pace closer.

"Did Professor Slinn hypnotise you, Stiff?" Craig asked.

"Aye, that's it. Hypnostise. Like the mannie on the stage." He was still smiling, his eyes wide.

"A man on stage?" Craig had a look of confusion when he glanced towards Flint again.

"Ah canna mind he's name, I wisna allowed tae go tae see him, when he wis on at the big stage in the toon. But ah seen him on the telly one time."

Flint spoke. "The Great Romano?" Flint had a flashback to his first date with Isla at the Music Hall, when he'd finally learned his flatmate Miles's name. It had been Miles who'd sparked Flint's interest in hypnotherapy.

"Aye, min, that's it. I mind noo. A loon in Kingseat used tae rave aboot it."

"And 'Kingseat' is the hospital you were in, right?" Flint had moved in to crouch beside Stiff.

"Aye. Fa are you, onywye? You polis in aw?"

"Erm, no, I'm a friend of PC Masson's. My name's Flint."

Davy came back from the car and whispered to Craig, who stood up. Flint thought he heard Craig saying, "No, Davy," as they moved a few yards away. He couldn't hear more, but thought they were arguing.

"Fa's 'at?" Stiff looked alarmed.

"That's Davy," said Flint, "he's another policeman."

"Fit wye are they nae in their uniforms?" Stiff looked at Craig and Davy while they continued to whisper. "They talkin' aboot me? I dinna like them." He started to sit up from where he'd been lying since they found him.

"No, they're fine. They're, erm, working undercover. Like detectives. They're looking after you."

"Are they goin' tae get me the jail again?" Stiff drew his knees up and curled his arms around them, balling himself like a hedgehog.

"No, really, Stiff, we want to help you." He took a chance, and went on, "Like Professor Slinn. What was it like when he hypnotised you?"

Stiff's head came up and his small, dark eyes fixed on Flint. "The trance thing?"

"Yes, how did he do that? What was it like?" Flint glanced back at Craig and Davy whose whispered exchange was still animated.

"He sent the screw out, telt him tae leave us alane, like. Then he sat real close and said stuff. Made me feel right fine, like I was all wrapped up and comfy."

"Is that what you meant when you said he made you feel warm inside?"

He could see Stiff relaxing, his limbs loosening and his face softening.

"Aye. I can feel it now."

"I can do that, Stiff. I can hypnotise you."

"Really? Dae it the noo." A child-like, pleading face looked up at Flint, who was out of his depth and wishing Craig and Davy would decide what to do.

As they walked away, leaving Flint crouching over Stiff, Craig caught hold of his friend's sleeve.

"No, Davy."

"Dinna try and stop me," hissed Davy, still pulling away.

"Listen Davy, you can't call Blackie, he'll wonder how you knew where to find him. You know more about Soutar's case than you should."

"I wish you'd never got me involved."

"I wish I *wasn't* involved, but we know Slinn's a serial killer and no one else does."

"Then we go to Queen Street and tell them everything."

Craig put his hands on Davy's elbows. "They'd lock *us* up, Davy, not Slinn."

Davy said nothing, shook himself free of Craig's grasp and stared out to sea.

"You know they would, Davy. We've got to get more on Slinn, and before he kills his next victim. At least we've got to Stiff before anything happened to him."

Davy turned back. "You really think Slinn's killing all these men? And getting away with it?"

"He's got to be. Remember the list of the victims Flint found. He's scoring them off one by one."

Davy's shoulders slumped. "I don't like it. What do we do?"

"We need to let Sgt. Tawse know Stiff's OK. Tawse knows him and has probably guessed he came here. That's why he gave him some leeway, but he'll only give him so long."

"We need to let his mother know as well."

Stiff smiled up at Craig when he walked back and sat down on the grass beside him.

"This mannie's going to do the hypnostisms on me. What's that blue thing on your leg?"

Flint saw puzzlement and surprise on Craig's face before he turned back to Stiff, saying, "Erm — I broke my leg — it's a new sort of plaster cast."

"Magic. A loon at school broke his arm and he hit me with his big white stookie. I got a black eye and my mither said I'd been fightin'."

"Stiff was telling me about Professor Slinn hypnotising him in the prison," said Flint, "and I said I knew a bit about hypnotherapy and how to help people."

"That would be good, but we've got to get you back home, Stiff. Davy — that's PC Jepson — he's just gone to speak to Sgt. Tawse and let him know you're ok. Then we'll get you back to your mum."

"But I don't want to go home. I want him to trance me." Stiff pointed at Flint.

"I can't hypnotise you here," said Flint. He was already regretting offering to hypnotise Stiff. It was dangerous to hypnotise anyone with a psychotic illness. Slinn could get away with it, being a specialist in psychiatry and hypnosis.

"Get Dr Slinn to do it again. He'll do it. He said he's going to see me again and do it more."

Flint said, "Really? When's he going to see you again, Stiff?"

"I dinna ken. Get him to do it now."

"Let's just get you back home, Stiff, get you warmed up and your mum will give you something to eat."

"I've told you, I'm all warm already."

"I don't want you to get in trouble," said Craig. He looked at Flint, raised his eyebrows and added, "Or me."

Chapter 42

Davy pulled the door of the phone box on Victoria Road and scanned the list of local numbers on the back wall. Someone had scrawled the word 'FERGIE!' on it in red felt pen, but he could see enough to tell that under 'P' there was only the number for Queen Street. He reached for the directory and found the number for the Bucksburn station.

"Hello, it's PC Jepson here, can I speak to Sergeant Tawse?" he asked when a deep voice answered.

"He's off duty, constable. This is Sgt. Rettie. What is it?"

Off guard, Davy pictured Michael Rettie with his crew cut, and remembered his bad breath. They'd spent several weeks paired together shortly after Davy finished his probation, and it was typical of Rettie not to acknowledge him by name.

"It's about Ian Soutar, I—"

"He's turned up, has he? Little bastard, wasting our time. Ought to be back in Kingseat. Is that where he is? Have they picked him up again? I knew it. Best place for him."

"Erm — can you leave a note for Sgt. Tawse? When he's on shift tomorrow—"

"Jock won't be here tomorrow, constable, he's on annual leave for two weeks, lucky bastard. Leave it with me, I'll pass it on that Soutar's back in the nuthouse. Save us all a lot of time."

Rettie ended the call and Davy stood looking at the receiver in his hand wondering what had just happened. He hadn't needed to tell Sgt Tawse his prepared lies about having found Soutar when he was playing golf. Davy didn't play golf.

###

Craig and Flint persuaded Stiff to come down to the car park on Greyhope Road to wait for Davy to come back. When he arrived, Davy climbed out of the car and explained what had happened when he called Bucksburn.

"That Rettie's an obnoxious prick," said Craig, who had come across the sergeant before. "And Mrs Soutar wasn't in? Christ, what do we do now?" He looked out into the fog over the sea.

"My ma goes tae her bingo on Sundays," said Stiff, yawning.

"We'll need to run him back home later," said Davy.

"Can we get in the car? I'm freezing." Flint pulled the back door open and climbed into the Escort.

Craig and Davy remained standing, with Stiff between them.

"Fuck, this is mad. The police think he's back in Kingseat — except for us," Craig said, rolling his eyes, "and we've got him here. What do we do?"

"Take him back to the flat? We can wait there and run him tae his mither later." Davy waved a thumb towards Flint. "And he's right, it's bloody cauld."

None of them spoke as they drove back to Esslemont Avenue. Stiff fell asleep, slumped in against Flint. Minutes after they had shaken him awake and climbed to the second floor, he was snoring on Craig's bed.

"For a wee man he maks a hell of a racket," said Davy.

"What time d'you think his mother'll be back home?" Flint asked.

"Dunno. Ma grannie does the bingo and she's usually a couple of hours," said Davy.

"Right, as soon as I've had this coffee I'm going out for suppers. There's a chippie in Rose Street. What are you wanting?"

"Red puddin' supper. I'm stervin'," said Davy.

"Smoked sausage again, Craig?"

Craig looked deep in thought, and Flint chose for him. Twenty minutes later he returned with three suppers and a stain on his jacket. "Bloody fat leaked through the paper," he said as he set them down on the coffee table.

Flint and Davy tore into their suppers, but Craig put his down after a few chips.

"This is a nightmare. We can't take him home."

"Why not? We just wait 'til his mither's back." Davy had red sauce on his cheek.

"The police think he's in Kingseat, and they won't expect him to report in every day for his bail. What if they see him going about? Or if someone mentions him? Bucksburn's a small place."

Davy chuckled, shaking his head. "Christ, that bastard Rettie'll say I lied about Stiff bein' in Kingseat. Fuck, what a mess, eh? And I'm in it up tae ma neck."

Flint stopped eating. "But Stiff's mother's going to wonder where he is."

"We'll need to tell *her* he's in Kingseat," said Craig, staring at the darkening window.

"This is getting mental," said Davy. "What the fuck are we going to do?"

Flint stood up and took a folded piece of paper out of his pocket, walking towards the hall. "Just got a quick phone call to make."

When he came back in five minutes later, he said, "Sorted."

Davy had finished his supper and Craig was picking at his. They both looked up with quizzical faces.

"I just tried phoning Mrs Soutar. She's back." Flint was holding the page he had torn from the telephone directory a few hours earlier.

They waited for him to say more, Craig looking concerned.

"When I spoke to her before, I told her I worked for Professor Slinn. I said when I found Stiff I was worried about his mental state and asked Slinn to get him taken back into the hospital. She was delighted. 'Better for my nerves,' she said."

"Fuckin' hell." Davy was laughing.

Craig looked even more worried. "We'll have to keep him here."

"It's alright, Craig. I've got an idea."

Craig looked at the floor and muttered, "Oh fuck."

Craig said Flint's plan would never work, but couldn't suggest anything better. With no choice but to keep Stiff in the flat, he left to spend the night with Mo, saying he wouldn't be back until afternoon because Mo was off work. The next day was a local holiday.

Chapter 43

Monday 10th May

Davy and Flint took turns to check on Stiff until he finally woke up mid-morning. Davy was on his days off between shift changes, and went out to buy a paper.

When Stiff had finished beans on toast, Flint asked him, "Why do they call you Stiff?"

"The big boys at school called me it."

"Why'd they call you that?"

"Ah dinna ken. It made them laugh, so I laughed an' aw." Flint thought he looked even smaller, and even more like a child. His voice sounded higher. "And they didna batter me so much, so I liked it." His face brightened and he went on, "Are you gonna hypnostise me now?"

"I don't think I'm clever enough, Stiff. It's not right, when someone's ill like you."

"Ah'm nae ill. As long as they keep giving me the stuff."

"Stuff?" Oh shit, thought Flint. None of them had thought about Stiff's medication. "Are you on tablets every day, Stiff?"

"Naw, nae noo. Used tae be. Then they got me injections." He put his hand up to his opposite shoulder and made a stabbing motion. "A big jab."

"Every day?"

"Naw, just every twa weeks. I got ane afore I came oot o' Craiginches, and I've just tae go down the doctors in Gilbert Road for the next ane. My ma's got the appointment sorted." He looked up at Flint, pleading. "Can ye no dae the trance thing on me? Go on."

"What if we could get Professor Slinn to come here and see you?"

"Aye! Magic. When? Today?"

Flint heard the flat door closing and Davy came in.

"Craig still not back?"

"No, no sign of him yet. I thought that might be him when I heard the door."

"He'd better bloody come soon," said Davy. "He's got to be here if this is going to work."

Flint looked at his watch. It was nearly half past four and Slinn's lecture started at six.

###

He knew it was a gamble, and Craig and Davy had taken a lot of persuading.

The idea was far-fetched, to say the least. But he had managed something similar at Liff, and with Patricia Gaska. Why couldn't he put on his act again?

But it had been one thing when he had misled hospital secretaries and taken advantage of one of Slinn's poor patients. It was going much further to imagine that he might be able to persuade Professor Dante Slinn, a distinguished psychiatrist and clinical psychologist, to interrupt his busy schedule to come to the Esslemont Avenue flat.

As he drove towards the university in Old Aberdeen, Flint reminded himself that the biggest risk he was taking was driving Craig's car with only a provisional licence. Making a fool of himself in front of a lot of students and academics was nothing. Craig and Davy were gambling with their careers to show that Slinn was a serial killer and Stiff was innocent. As Davy had said, they were in it up to their necks. Flint owed it to them — and Stiff — to get this right.

His plan was to hint that Stiff had remembered something more about the murder of Ivan Skilling, but was only willing to reveal details to Professor Slinn. It might be enough to entice Slinn to the flat if he thought he could manipulate Stiff even more, and cover his tracks. And demonstrate to himself once again how invincible he was.

Flint rehearsed his approach to Slinn as he walked from the car to the auditorium. He'd been in the enormous psychology lecture theatre before when he was a student, having sneaked in to listen to a second-year students' introduction to hypnotherapy. He smiled as he remembered thinking that by that time he'd known more about the subject than the young, spotty lecturer.

Shaking himself back to the task in hand, Flint made his way to the front row. He looked over his shoulder at the steep tiers of seats that reached up far behind him. The hall was only about one-third filled, but there must have been about a hundred people, of all ages. The lecture was open to the public. As well as the obvious students who lounged over seats in casual clothes, there were several pairs and threes of smartly-dressed older people.

A man in a gown Flint vaguely recognised as a university grandee walked onto the stage with a sheet of paper, and paused to read it to himself. He was about to look up at the hushing audience when Professor Slinn strode across the stage, seizing the crowd's attention. From the head and shoulders picture on the flyer, Flint had expected Slinn to be a slight, bookish intellectual. His athletic build was a surprise. Standing at the lectern in his tan leather sports jacket, with his collar-length dark hair and neat moustache he looked like Burt Reynolds. Flint had a fleeting memory of his boyish jealousy when he'd discovered Reynolds was Isla's secret heart-throb. Two middle-aged women along the row made appreciative noises.

"Good evening, ladies and gentlemen, I am Professor Dante Slinn of the Department of Clinical Psychiatry at the University of Dundee," Slinn said. He had introduced himself, Flint thought, instead of letting the meeting chairman do it. A porter in a grey overall brought a chair into the shadow of the lectern, ushering the discomposed man to sit down with his notes.

Smooth, thought Flint. He doesn't want anyone stealing his limelight.

Slinn's lecture fascinated Flint. He had no notes to read from or slides to show, and the Professor's easy manner and charisma kept his audience rapt. Flint thought the whole performance was like a gripping one-man play. He had to remind himself why he was there.

He took his chance when Slinn asked the audience if anyone had experienced hypnotic regression.

"Fascinating. Fascinating," said Slinn, when Flint had outlined in a few sentences how his repressed memories had been brought to light under hypnosis.

Slinn waved expansively around the auditorium. "Listening to this young man's first-hand account of his experiences, so honestly set out for us in such an erudite way, is a privilege we should all thank him for." He clapped his hands and the audience joined in. Flint was blushing when Slinn went on.

"May I ask you who your therapist was?"

"Erm — I didn't have one."

"You have misunderstood. I meant who hypnotised you and regressed you?" Slinn looked expectant.

"I didn't have one. I couldn't afford it." There was a ripple of laughter and some knowing nods. "I taught myself."

Flint saw Slinn's thick, brown eyebrows rise in surprise, and for the first time, he looked lost for words. After a pause, he said, "Really?" He glanced at Flint before turning his attention back to his audience, recovering as if nothing had happened and continuing to enthral his fans.

As the lecture drew to a natural close, with all Slinn's threads and theories tied together and the audience's questions answered, Flint's discomfort grew. He now had to approach Slinn and entice him, or scare him, into coming to Esslemont Avenue.

Everything now depended on Slinn's arrogance, his need to take chances. Agreeing to come and speak to Stiff would mean he could flaunt his brilliance under the noses of the police and Procurator Fiscal.

Once he was in 20 Esslemont Avenue, Craig and Davy would confront Slinn with the information they had about the list from his desk drawer, details that linked him to three identical murders. The two cops were going to bet everything they had. If their misdemeanours and accessing confidential papers brought a serial killer to justice, there might be a chance of saving their careers.

The more Flint went over the plan the more ridiculous it became. His oxters* began to sweat in the air-conditioned theatre. As the audience's extended round of applause died down Flint started to move towards the end of the row. He had to get out. He would admit to Craig and Davy he had over-reached himself, and they'd need to think of something else.

The stern chairman rose to approach the lectern, presumably to give thanks to the illustrious professor. Flint thought that was his chance to escape, but Slinn intercepted the man, shook his hand briefly as he stood nonplussed once more, and carried on past him looking straight at Flint.

"I must thank you for your contribution to my talk. Most interesting. I'd love to hear more. You really taught yourself?"

The lecture theatre was emptying and Flint struggled to hear Slinn's soft-spoken words over the chattering and shuffling of feet. The magnetic charisma of his stage presence was gone, but his tilted head and expectant eyes still demanded Flint's attention and response.

"Yes. Well, a friend showed me the basics and I read a bit about it. I think I was quite good at it."

I can't help myself, thought Flint. He's amazing.

"And I think you mentioned you uncovered some trauma from your past?"

"Yes. 'I'd seen my mother with ...'" What am I doing? he thought. Slinn's focus was irresistible and Flint found himself continuing, "When I went further in — you know — regressed myself, I began to make connections."

"Go on." Slinn had sat down at the end of the row and Flint couldn't have left if he had wanted to.

"Yes, I began to link things I had seen in my dreams with things that had really happened." He was back in his student residence room in Hillhead, inducing his trance by picturing scenes from his childhood. If he had continued, he knew he would soon be seeing a severed hand wearing a gold ring. He managed to wrench his eyes from Slinn's.

"Can I ask you for help with something, Professor Slinn?"

"Of course. I'm in no hurry. Would you like me to regress you? I have a private patient to see tomorrow afternoon but I am free in the morning. There would be no charge, of course, as you are a fellow practitioner."

Flint was taken aback, and flattered.

"Erm — no. Well, I hadn't thought of that." The opportunity to banish the dreams about his father's death was tempting. Isla had been driven to break up with him by what his dreams had been doing to them. "But it was someone else I was going to ask you about. Ian Soutar. I think you know him."

Slinn stiffened in obvious surprise. Flint wondered if, somehow, he had got the plan back on track.

"No, I can't discuss a patient. Confidentiality precludes…"

Flint was going to fall at the first hurdle.

Slinn sat back, his brow furrowing before his face relaxed into a wry smile. "But then, of course, my involvement with Mr Soutar has been reported widely in the press, so it is hardly a complete secret, is it?"

Flint couldn't tell where this was going. He could think of nothing to say, but Slinn went on.

"What exactly did you want? Help with something, I think you said? Have you been hypnotising Soutar?" Slinn was sitting forward again, waiting for Flint to go on.

"Erm — no. But — I think Stiff's bizarre ideas about having killed Ivan Skilling are something to do with buried past trauma." Relieved, Flint took a deep breath. He knew he'd rushed out his prepared lines, but he hadn't stumbled over them.

The professor looked around the lecture theatre. Only the porter remained, working his way along each row of seats as he cleared up. "No one will overhear us anyway, and we are, after all, two clinicians discussing a case," he said, tapping the side of his nose and winking. Flint felt himself drawn in by the professor's confident, conspiratorial manner.

Slinn continued. "Mr Soutar - or 'Stiff' as he prefers, is a fascinating case. There is something very deep in there. It is to do with his name, I am sure. The reason he calls himself Stiff. I mentioned it when he was deep in trance, in the jail cell, and he became very obviously agitated the longer I persisted. I had to bring him up from his trance and use positive suggestions. Warm and comfortable, the usual kind of thing. Prison was not the ideal setting for a session, but I gleaned enough to know the lad is most definitely not a murderer."

Slinn had intertwined his fingers and was rolling his thumbs as he spoke.

"I'm very much looking forward to working more with Stiff. Muriel Trickett had asked me to assess him professionally and my next session with him is being arranged by my secretary. It's frustrating there will be some delay." He sat back, looking Flint in the eye. "Are you involved in his care?"

"No, he's — a friend of mine. I know his mum. He's staying with me at the moment."

"Really? Really? Tell me how you think I can help. I would relish the opportunity. He is a fascinating subject. As I said, I am free tomorrow morning if we could arrange something."

Flint didn't need to scare Professor Slinn with the unlikely story about Stiff naming the killer. He volunteered to come to the Esslemont Avenue flat.

(Some notes on Doric Scots are included in a Glossary at the end of Flowers for the Slaughterman)

Chapter 44

The only sound was a reggae beat from downstairs. He could feel it in his soles as he entered the flat.

"Craig? Davy?" he called out as he opened the living room door. They were standing by the window, and both turned to look at him when he entered. Davy was in his uniform and Craig was turning his warrant card over and over in his hand.

"Is he coming in his own car?" said Craig, looking back down at the street.

"No. Not tonight."

"Fuck! Why not?" said Craig. He limped over and sat on the couch, looking up at Flint.

"He'll be here tomorrow morning. 11 o'clock. He wants to help Stiff. I didn't have to—"

"What? I don't get it," said Davy, "He just agreed to come?"

Flint sat down and outlined what had happened after the lecture.

"He volunteered. He seems to think I'm quite an expert. Called me a 'fellow practitioner'."

Davy had stayed standing near the window and now came to sit, putting his police cap on the table. Its distinctive checkerboard 'Sillitoe tartan' band clashed with the polka-dot design on the Formica. They had tidied the flat while he'd been at the lecture.

"What did you think of him?" Davy said.

"I dunno really. He was—"

The door opened and Stiff stood looking around the room. "Is he here? Is he going to trance me?" He looked at Davy. "Are you going to work now?"

"Professor Slinn's not coming tonight, Stiff. He's going to be here tomorrow morning." Flint stood up. "I'm starving. Is there food?"

Tuesday 11th May

Flint heard a church bell chiming the half hour and wondered what time it was. It was still dark. He could hear Davy snoring in one bedroom and Stiff duetting with him from the other.

A few hours earlier, Craig had left to go to Mo's. "Last night of freedom," he'd said, with a roll of his eyes. They knew they were going to be in trouble, even if things worked out the way they hoped. When Flint had spoken of his idea about going to Slinn's lecture, Craig had wanted to confront Slinn there to get it over with, but Davy had refused. Doing it in public, wearing his uniform, was one unofficial step too far.

Now the agreed strategy was for the two cops to surprise Slinn, interrupt while he was seeing Stiff and catch him off guard. Confront him with the list, and intimidate him into letting something slip that only the killer could know. Having met Slinn, experienced his supreme composure and confidence, Flint now thought this was likely to fail. He was beginning to doubt the idea that Slinn intended to kill Stiff at their next appointment. Slinn was too earnest and genuine. Christ, maybe I'm under his spell now, he thought, before quickly trying to dismiss the thought. Anyway, he concluded, we're all up to our necks in it now. Can't back out now.

Soon fed up with the TV, Stiff had gone back to the bedroom with a pile of old magazines Craig had said he could take clippings from. Flint had then sat with Davy discussing the evidence against Slinn.

"We should have waited until we could get the list," Davy said.

"There wasn't time. Stiff could have been dead by then. We had to do something. Getting Slinn to incriminate himself is our only hope." Flint didn't find his own words convincing, and Davy showed he was of the same mind.

"This is mental," he muttered, harumphing to his room.

Flint tried to settle himself on the couch to sleep. The circumstances linking Slinn to the deaths were convincing, but something else wasn't right. Again, Flint thought the smooth professor just didn't seem like a ruthless killer. It was hard to accept that he could have selected men who had abused their daughters, then castrated them before smashing their heads.

Now, at half-past whatever, Flint lay wrestling with the fact that he had found himself liking Slinn. The way the psychiatrist had commanded the audience in the vast lecture theatre was impressive, but within seconds he had transformed himself. When he sat beside Flint, he was no longer a six-foot-three Burt Reynolds and instead seemed to match Flint's size. Slinn was an actor, a magician, and he had taken Flint into his confidence by engaging him with sincere, if misplaced, flattery. They had discussed Stiff like 'two clinicians discussing a case'.

When the church bell struck three times Flint was still wide awake. Out of his depth, he knew that in a few hours, he had to continue with his charade even if he was having doubts.

###

"Is this him?" asked Craig.

Flint checked his watch. Exactly 11 o'clock. He moved closer to the window to look down on Esslemont Avenue, and Davy edged in beside him.

"Christ, min, the loon's got an Alfa Spyder."

The three of them watched Professor Dante Slinn climb out of his flame-red convertible holding a briefcase. After taking a black holdall from the boot, he stood in his glossy leather jacket and looked along the main doors for number twenty. He glided across the road like a skater, disappearing out of view at the foot of the tenement.

"Smooth-looking fucker, right enough," Davy continued.

"OK. This is it," said Craig, stepping from one foot to the other by the door to the hall. "Flint, you greet him, and go in with him and Stiff—"

"I know. I know, Craig, we've been over and over this. I'll do it exactly like you said." *I don't think Slinn's a killer, though.*

"This is going to be brilliant." Davy was grinning and holding up his handcuffs.

"Put them away!" Craig was looking again at the notes he'd made on a scrap of paper.

Flint stood behind the door, holding on to the wall with one hand. Footsteps on the stairs seemed to echo as they got louder, and it felt like hours as he waited for the doorbell to sound. Don't faint. Don't faint.

He jumped when there were three loud knocks on the door. The metal door handle lever was cold as his fingers closed around it. As he pulled that door inward the door to Craig's bedroom flew open. Stiff skipped out into the hallway just behind Flint.

"Ah canna wait. Is the mannie here? The doctor. Ah canna wait!" He was dancing like a kiddie on Christmas Eve.

This wasn't supposed to happen.

"Oh, hello again, Mr Soutar. Remember me?" Slinn was smiling, looking at Stiff and then turning towards Flint, who could make no sound. "I see our patient is keen to proceed, Mr Flint. Perhaps I'd better get straight to it. Where shall we —"

"In here. In here, Professor Doctor, in here." Stiff was pulling the psychiatrist's sleeve.

"You can call me Dan, Stiff." Slinn handed Flint his briefcase, smiling and saying, "I'll see you in an hour or so." He closed the door in Flint's face.

When Flint went back into the living room Davy and Craig were both sitting on the couch with their heads in their hands. They'd guessed what had happened.

"It's not my fault," said Flint. "Stiff was supposed to fucking wait in the room. Fuck!"

Craig waved his hands and hissed. "Sshh. Keep your voice down. Slinn's not supposed to know we're here." Two closed doors separated them from Slinn and Stiff who were on the other side of the hallway. Craig's room faced the rear.

"What do we do now?" Davy whispered.

"Slinn said he'd be about an hour. Wait half an hour then you two barge in?" Flint shrugged. "Nothing's changed except I'm not in there to witness what he says to Stiff."

"Don't s'pose there's much else we can do. Fuck, this is a nightmare." Craig put his head back in his hands.

"I'm needing the toilet," said Davy.

"You'll just need to hold on to your pish, said Craig, looking up now and shaking his head.

"It's not a pish I'm needin'."

The three of them sat in silence, listening to muffled voices from within the bedroom. Davy took his tunic off and rolled up his white sleeves. Flint kept looking at his watch. After twenty-five minutes Craig and Davy were whispering to each other when there was a sudden shout and loud thud from across the hall.

"What was that?" said Craig, standing up. Silence resumed, and Craig was lowering himself to sit back down when they heard a shriek, footsteps and the sound of shattering glass.

Davy was first to reach Craig's bedroom door. "It won't open."

"Shove harder," said Craig, and they both pushed.

A weight seemed to be against the door. The two of them could only force it open a couple of inches and Davy said, "Fuckin' hell, get this door open quick!"

Flint joined in, and they open the door far enough to allow Davy to squeeze in before it whumped back shut. Flint heard him grunting with effort, and retching.

"Fuckin' hell! Craig, get an ambulance!"

Flint watched Craig reach for the phone, his mind numbed. When he shook himself, Davy had somehow managed to move the obstruction. Flint was able to open the door wide. As he entered, he was reminded briefly of opening Miles's door in Hillhead, when he'd found his flatmate's room festooned in red crepe paper, and his body in the wardrobe. This time there were no maggots, no rotting smell, and the red decor was blood.

Davy looked up at him with his eyes and mouth wide open. He was kneeling beside a body, red spatters over his white shirt. A large pair of scissors was embedded in Dante Slinn's neck, blood pulsing feebly from around the blade. The same blood had been spraying the room seconds earlier, draining Professor Slinn of his life. Dark eyes looked up at Flint, becoming glazed as Slinn's gaping mouth tried to speak its last words.

"The window," said Davy, as he pulled the scissors away and pressed on Slinn's neck.

Flint hadn't yet noticed that there was no sign of Stiff in the bedroom. His feet squelched in Slinn's blood. A Hitachi portable cassette player was lying on a chair, its reels turning, and on the bed were dozens of bloodied magazine clippings.

The forceful pumping of Slinn's heart had sprayed the whole length of the room. A tapering arc, crimson on magnolia, decorated the far wall. It was interrupted by the gaping, jagged maw of the shattered window. Dreading what more he might see Flint inched forward, stretching between glass shards that were like shark's teeth, to lean into the cold fresh air.

Two floors below, on the corrugated roof of an outhouse, lay the body of Ian Soutar, his legs bent at impossible angles. The last things Flint heard before he vomited and passed out were the screams of a woman from a downstairs window, and sirens.

Chapter 45

DCI Stuart Blackie stared across the table at Craig.

"We've listened to the tape. We know what happened in there, but what in hell was going on in that flat? Why was Professor Slinn there? And Soutar, for fuck's sake!"

Craig had been taken from the cell in Queen Street after sitting for more than three hours wondering what had happened to Stiff and whether he was still alive. It had taken less than five minutes for an ambulance and a police car to arrive simultaneously outside 20 Esslemont Avenue, but to Craig it felt like hours. While Davy had continued to apply pressure to Slinn's neck, Craig had tried to perform the chest compressions he'd been taught at Tulliallan. Every time he squeezed where he thought Slinn's heart must be, bubbles of foaming blood frothed in and out of the dead man's mouth. Craig didn't need to be a doctor to know Slinn's life had ended.

"Is Soutar still alive?" Craig looked Blackie in the eye for the first time since he'd been escorted into the drab room. He was more used to escorting others in.

Blackie stared at Craig, before saying, "Little bastard was lucky. Apparently, he'll live."

"Thank fuck. Sorry, sir, I mean—"

"Mind you, he'll do time for two murders now. Might have been better for him if he *had* died." Blackie was smirking as he continued, "And it serves the posh professor right for getting him out of Craiginches, stupid bastard. It was obvious Soutar killed Ivan Skilling, even if the shrink thought he could get him off for being a nutter."

Craig was certain his police career was finally over this time. He had no idea what Davy or Flint had said in their statements, or even if they had been questioned yet. He had intended to say as little as possible until he had been allowed to speak to a Police Federation representative or a solicitor. Now, though, he was sickened by Blackie's smug disrespect for Ian Soutar and his dismissal of the possibility he might have charged the wrong person for Skilling's murder. He could hold back no longer.

"Soutar may have killed Professor Slinn, sir, but he didn't kill Skilling. There's been a serial killer at work, and it wasn't Ian Soutar. You got it wrong, sir."

Blackie was quiet for a moment before scowling at Craig. "A *serial killer*, for fuck's sake. Jesus wept, don't tell me you're as mad as that nutcase Flint?"

There was a knock on the door before Craig could think of how to reply. A uniformed constable poked his head into the interview room.

"Sir, Detective Superintendent Morrice would like to speak to you."

"Don't go anywhere." Blackie jabbed a thick finger at Craig before leaving him in the secure room. Craig stared at the closed door and heard the lock turn. *Don't go anywhere.*

He knew now that Flint had already given a statement. He, too, had told Blackie that a serial killer was at work, and it wasn't Stiff. While he waited for the interview to resume, Craig decided he was going to disclose to Blackie every detail he could remember about the linked murders. He was resigned to his own fate, but owed it to Davy to make it clear that the tragedy in the flat had been down to himself and Flint. He would try to persuade the top brass that Davy had played little part in their unofficial police work. That way his friend and colleague might escape with a short suspension.

He rehearsed how to explain why they suspected a serial killer was at work.

By chance, he'd read on his chip wrapper about an unsolved crime very similar to Ivan Skilling's murder. When he read in Stiff's file about his fantasies of mutilating men's genitals, he had contacted Flint to ask if hypnosis might explain why the dreams made Stiff confess to a crime he was physically incapable of committing. But that was as much as he could tell Blackie; he couldn't admit that Jack had used the PNC to find other killings identical to that of Skilling.

A short burst of loud voices in the corridor outside made Craig lose his thread. For a few minutes, his thoughts jumped back and forth as he tried to put a coherent statement together before Blackie returned.

Something was bugging him. Something Blackie had said.

We've listened to the tape.

What tape? What did he mean?

The brown door swung open and DS Ovenstone walked in. Confusion at seeing Murray Ovenstone was mixed with relief that Blackie wasn't back yet. Murray raised his eyebrows and shook his head as he walked the two paces to the table to sit down. With a wry smile, he looked across at Craig for a few seconds before he spoke.

"What the hell have you been doing, Craig?"

Craig felt his mouth drying. It would be easier coming clean to Murray than to Blackie, but it came to the same thing. He still had to tell his prepared story. His right hand gripped the leg of the table. Someone had stuck a knob of hard chewing gum on it.

"Stiff — I mean Soutar, sir — he's innocent. I know he is, and the real killer—"

"I know he is, Craig. We know what DCI Blackie did."

"What he did?" Craig sat back from the table, his head spinning. What did Murray mean? Do they think Blackie is a killer?

After a pause, Murray Ovenstone went on. "I shared your doubts about Soutar, Craig, and we weren't the only ones. Blackie was so hell-bent on charging Soutar that he ignored the obvious. And worse than that, he altered evidence."

For a moment, Craig forgot his own predicament. *Blackie altered evidence?*

Murray Ovenstone leaned forward, and Craig felt himself do likewise. In quiet tones, the DS went on.

"In his report to the Super, Blackie left out the fact that the bus driver had seen Soutar getting on the first No 12 bus at about 7 am and that the newsagent had seen him return to Bucksburn a couple of hours later."

Craig was trying to understand what this meant.

"The body was discovered at 8.15 am by the first of the morning's golfers."

"So?" He couldn't see how this helped Stiff.

"Blackie stated the time of death was consistent with Soutar's presence at the locus, but the pathologist's report wasn't produced until after Soutar had been charged. The fiscal was never given Dr McHardy's report, even when it was available."

"But Detective Superintendent Morrice must have seen it?"

"No. It was only when Chic Morrice bumped into Bill McHardy and joked about how long it was taking to get his report that we knew he'd already sent it. We found it in Blackie's desk."

"Fuck! — erm, sorry, sir."

Murray laughed. "And guess what? The pathologist said an accurate time was impossible to give, but that Skilling had been dead for at least six hours when he was found."

They both sat back. Craig was thinking about all the time Stiff had been in Craiginches when he should have been being helped. And it was all down to Blackie.

"But surely, sir, that would have come out in court, wouldn't it?"

"Aye, Craig, if the Fiscal didn't notice it before that and drop the case. Blackie was stupid. Arrogant prick!"

"What'll happen to DCI Blackie, sir?"

"Off the case. We've been building a case against him — Chic Morrice took me in to help him. But with the Federation to deal with and the Fiscal's dithering it was taking forever. Now this has happened things started moving. Blackie's been suspended."

The thought of suspension brought Craig's mind back to his own situation, and his spirit slumped. Murray seemed to sense what he was thinking.

"You'll be suspended as well, Craig, but not for long." He smiled kindly. "We know you were trying to prove Soutar's innocence, and once we've taken a full statement about how you persuaded poor Professor Slinn to back you up it'll all be OK."

Craig couldn't find words. Was now the time to expose Slinn as a serial killer? Before he could think further, Murray went on.

"Thank God you hadn't discovered another serial killer this time, eh?" he said, laughing. "Once in your lifetime is enough."

Craig decided to leave it at that. Flint and Davy were bound to have disclosed Slinn's crimes, but for now, he would keep quiet.

"DCI Blackie mentioned a tape, sir. Can I ask you what tape?"

"Professor Slinn taped his meeting with Soutar. Taped his own death. I've listened to it all, and that was another thing that helped catch Blackie out. On the tape, Soutar described finding Skilling's body. When he was in this trance thing, I mean. He didn't say anything about killing him. Said the body was just lying there, next to the car. And he said the sun was up. It was daylight. He couldn't have done it."

"I knew he couldn't have overpowered Skilling," said Craig.

Craig could see from Murray's face that he was quite disturbed by what he'd heard on the tape. "Then he went mental and killed the professor. The prof kept asking him about his name. Stiff, I mean. Soutar's voice became louder, and when Slinn kept asking him he went into a rage. You can hear Professor Slinn gasp, just before some shuffling and then a thud." Murray was reporting what he had listened to as if he was describing it live. "Then footsteps before the window smashes." He cleared his throat. "It's obvious what happened in there. Bloody awful. He must have flown across the room at the prof." Craig could remember the thud just before the glass shattered. Then they found Slinn's body slumped against the door.

They were both quiet for a moment.

"Can I go, sir?"

Murray shook himself as if he was returning to the present. "Yes. As I said, you'll likely get some sort of suspension, but for now, you can go. Not to your flat, though. It's a crime scene."

Chapter 46

Flint had started his interview with a disordered ramble about hypnosis, repressed dreams, and genital mutilation. DCI Blackie had sat shaking his head, silent apart from impatient humphing and sighs, before standing up and heading for the door. As his chair clattered to the floor, he'd said, "Ah canna listen tae this shite. I'm going to speak to fucking Masson," before walking out. The embarrassed-looking young detective who had been seated next to Blackie said, "DCI Blackie will be back to continue the interview soon. I'm going to get us cups of coffee. I'll be back in a couple of minutes to carry on." He had then also left, locking the door behind him.

Flint then sat waiting in the bleak room. There was a smell of cigarettes. He had heard a church clock chime two o'clock shortly after Blackie left. When it had marked two more quarter hours, still no one had restarted his interview. He spent the time worrying. What had they been thinking? Professor Slinn was dead, and so was Stiff as far as he knew. The police were bound to think they had killed Slinn.

Davy had been in police uniform, and the first police to arrive thought he had got there before them somehow. The little flat had soon been congested with paramedics and more police, and when they worked out that Craig, Davy and Flint had been present when Slinn died the three of them were handcuffed and huckled down to a police van. There had been a crowd of schoolkids gawping through the railings of the Grammar School opposite, and Flint had briefly been transported to the last time he'd been handcuffed, four years before when he'd been taken to Cupar police station. Craig had been there that time, too. He looked at the marks where the heavy cuffs had hurt his wrists, and wished Isla was there to comfort him again.

It was all his fault. He had been the one who had linked the killings to Slinn, when he'd played the big man and breezed into Slinn's workplace and sneaked a look in his desk. Now Craig would be in awful trouble again, and Davy as well. And it was all his fucking fault. If he could say as little as possible about their involvement, he might limit the damage.

The lock on the interview room door made a tinny sound, at odds with the heavy clanging he was used to from watching Z-Cars and Softly Softly. The door opened, and instead of DCI Blackie a woman in a dark blue skirt and grey blouse entered. She looked at him for a second, then clip-clopped the short distance over the lino and sat at the table opposite him. A uniformed policeman followed her in and stood against the door.

The woman sat silently, looking at Flint who felt a tremble in his back muscles and a moistness on his palms. Then she smiled.

"Mr Gordon Flint?"

"Yes." His voice echoed in his ears.

"I am Detective Inspector Sangster, Grampian Police. I've been asked to take over. What were you doing in number 20 Esslemont Avenue, top floor left, today?" DI Sangster spoke precisely, but softly.

"Erm — I've been staying there." She remained silent, an eyebrow raised inviting him to continue. "I was visiting Craig."

"PC Craig Masson?"

"Yes."

"Who else was there this morning?"

"Davy."

"Do you mean PC David Jepson?" Flint realised he hadn't heard Davy's surname until then. His mind flashed images at him of Davy's big, gurning face and his long ears, followed by his petite, beautiful sister. Her full name must be Mo Jepson.

"Erm — yes, I think so."

"Who else? There were two others I think?" Both eyebrows were up now, and her lips were pursed. She didn't look threatening, and Flint's thoughts flowed out of his mouth as if a dam had broken.

"I'm sorry it was my fault I thought Slinn I mean Professor Slinn could help Stiff if he could hypnotise him and find out why he had those dreams and why he — why he — why he said he killed that man on the golf course I don't think he did and neither does Craig and—"

"Stiff?"

"I mean Ian Soutar, he's called Stiff, and it's something to do with—"

"Slow down. You're giving me a headache." DI Sangster's stare dried Flint's flow of words. Tears gathered and his head slumped forward, sobs escaping.

"Sorry. I'm sorry." His cheeks were wet when he lifted his head to look at the detective.

"It's a tragedy. A man is dead. But we know from the tape what happened in that room."

The Hitachi tape recorder. Flint now remembered seeing it lying on the chair in Craig's room. Slinn must have been taping the consultation.

DI Sangster continued. "From what we understand, Professor Slinn came to that flat of his own accord, and he knew Soutar was there, right?"

"Yes."

"When the three of you have been interviewed, you'll be allowed to leave. For now. We'll want more from you. You are in trouble, Mr Flint."

###

Craig walked downstairs in Queen Street heading for the exit, unsure what to do next or where to go. DS Ovenstone had told him not to go back to Esslemont Avenue. Davy was using the phone behind the front desk, and Big Kenny nodded recognition at Craig, indicating to his right. Looking that way, Craig saw Flint sitting at the end of a row of chairs against the wall.

"You been interviewed?" he asked, sitting down beside Flint.

"Aye." Flint nodded.

Craig suspected Flint had been crying. There was a grubby line from his eye to his cheekbone which stopped where he must have wiped most of it away, and a faint stain on the right sleeve of his army surplus jacket.

"What do we do now?" said Craig, shrugging. "They told me not to go back to the flat."

"You could go to Mo's," Flint said, looking at Craig.

"Rigman have sent her away on a course all week. New software."

"What's software?"

Craig rolled his eyes, and before he could answer Davy approached. He still had blood on his white shirt.

"It's alright, boys, we'll go back to my place. Big Kenny let me phone."

"Your parents' place?"

"Aye. C'mon, let's get out of here." Davy stood up and moved towards the big glass doors.

Chapter 47

"That was great, Mrs Jepson," said Craig, scraping the last of his gravy from the edge of his plate.

"Want some more, son?" Marie Jepson pointed to the pot on the stove, "There's plenty."

"No, thanks. Two plates were enough. You're a great cook."

"Too right," added Flint, "I've not tasted lamb like that since I left home."

Davy grinned and said, "I've had that every Tuesday night for years unless I was on shift, an' there's aye plenty left for seconds."

"Aye, yer Dad's appetite's no as good as it was, but I still make the same amount as I did when a'body was still at hame."

A short time later, Davy, Craig and Flint were alone in the living room of the three-bedroomed flat Davy had grown up in. Marie and Davy's dad Walter had gone out with the dog. The nine o'clock news was on the TV, and the three had barely spoken since their dinner.

Craig stood up and switched the TV off. Sitting back down and laying his cast on a footstool, he said, "What the hell are we going to do?"

They hadn't mentioned Slinn, Stiff or their afternoon in custody since they'd arrived at Davy's family home in Hilton Terrace. Now, all three sighed in unison, Davy muttering, "Fuck knows," and Flint shaking his head.

"What do we do about Slinn?" Craig said. "I can't believe he's got off with it."

"Got off with it? The mannie's deid! He's hardly got off with it."

"Aye, but, you know what I mean."

Flint spoke up with a question he had been desperate to ask. "Did you two tell the cops about Slinn? I didn't."

"Me neither," said Davy, and they both looked at Craig. Flint thought Craig looked uncertain, or guilty. They both waited for him to speak.

"Not exactly."

"What d'you mean, 'not exactly'?" said Davy. "For Fuck's sake, min. I just telt them aboot tryin' to help Stiff. I wisna goin' tae say onythin' aboot serial killers."

"Me too," said Flint. "I didn't want to get you two into any trouble, for — you know — doing unofficial stuff." Davy was nodding, and they were both still looking at Craig.

"I didn't say it was Slinn. But I said something to Blackie before he was called away. I think I said we knew there was a serial killer." They both kept staring, silently. "Blackie was being a real prick. Gloating about Stiff, that sort of stuff. I was just about to tell him how wrong he'd got it all when he was called away."

Davy stood up and walked to the window. Without turning to face the other two he said, "They still think Stiff killed Skilling, and now he's killed Slinn as well. They'll lock him up forever."

"No, they don't," said Craig. He explained to Davy and Flint what Murray Ovenstone had told him about Blackie altering evidence, and that it was clear to the police now that Stiff was innocent."

"Fuxake," said Flint. "You hear about dishonest police but I thought they were just made up for TV."

"Blackie! The stupid bastard." said Davy.

"We all know Stiff killed Slinn, but at least they know now that he didn't kill Skilling," said Craig. "It still means they don't know Slinn's a serial killer, though."

"Was a serial killer, you mean," said Flint.

Davy came and sat down, and they were quiet for a few minutes.

"You know what it means?" asked Craig. They both looked at him, his fists clenched. "It means we know there was a serial killer at work, but the police don't. Because the bloody PNC doesn't get used properly. He got away with it. Slinn could have been stopped. Just like four years ago. Nothing's got any better."

Flint's mind returned to The Mount, Cupar and Auchmoor.

"Davy, can I use your parent's phone for a minute? I've got twenty pence."

"Aye, help yersel. No need tae pay. It's cheap rate now anyway."

Flint had begun to think about what to do next. Though they had failed to bring Slinn to justice, the killings would stop and there was nothing to keep him in Aberdeen now. He wondered if there had been any mail for him. He still hadn't remembered to call home since he'd walked out of his job at Hamlyn's and gone to Dundee. It was only a week ago, but he knew he should have let his mother know where he was.

"Hello, Mum."

"Gordon! Where have you been?"

"Sorry, Mum, I got distracted. I've been helping Craig with something."

"Craig? PC Masson? You're in Dundee again?"

"Well, I was. I'm in Aberdeen now."

"Aberdeen? Are you seeing Isla?"

Flint swallowed. "Erm, no, mum. Listen, has there been any post for me?"

"Only a letter from the Job Centre. Nothing from Isla. When are you coming home?"

"I can't really talk too long, mum, I'm using Davy's mum's phone."

"Davy?" He heard the 'hmph' noise she always made when she was becoming angry. "Gordon, at least tell me where you are staying!"

Flint had to ask Davy for the address.

Press and Journal

Wednesday 12th May 1982

SOUTAR KILLS AGAIN
Prof Murdered in Aberdeen Flat
Killer seriously ill in hospital
2 Cops were witnesses

Exclusive report by Tom Jordan,
Senior Crime Reporter

Tragedy struck at a city centre flat yesterday morning when a respected Psychiatrist was slain by a man he had just had released from prison.

Professor Danté Slinn of Liff Hospital, Dundee, (*pictured*) was visiting an Esslemont Avenue flat to try to help Ian Soutar, 22, who was charged last year with the gruesome murder of Ivan Skilling. The mutilated body of Mr Skilling, from Newmachar, was found near the Torry Battery last September.

Police sources have indicated that they believe Professor Slinn was giving Soutar therapy. Last week the specialist intervened to have Soutar released on bail. *But yesterday the crazed beast went wild and killed his saviour.*

Soutar is understood to have jumped from a second floor window attempting to escape. He has been detained in hospital.

In a bizarre twist, sources report that Soutar was being housed in the flat by two Grampian Police officers. PC D Jepson and PC C Masson befriended Soutar when he was freed from prison, only last week. Also present was Mr Gordon Flint, 24. It is not known why the officers were present. The P&J understands they were off duty.

Four years ago, PC Masson was involved in the unmasking of the serial killer known as the Limb Collector.

(*continued on Page 2*)

Chapter 48

Wednesday 12th May

Tom Jordan decided he deserved a second pint. He might even have a pie. He didn't usually eat after his breakfast until evening came, but today he was congratulating himself for having dominated the front page again. He put his copy of the P&J down on the bar, making sure the headline and byline were visible to anyone nearby, then signalled to the barman.

Things are going well. I'm getting good at this. The stories just keep coming. I can't help it if I'm lucky.

While he watched the Guinness being poured, a large man walked past and took a seat at the end of the Prince of Wales bar. Jordan's nose wrinkled at a curious chemical smell.

"Hiya, George," the barman said, before putting Jordan's pint down. "There you are, a Guinness." He stood waiting for the money.

"And, my good fellow, there *you* are. Keep the change."

Taking Jordan's pound note, the barman beamed, and said, "Thanks min! You celebratin'?"

Jordan indicated the newspaper and said, "Only that." While the man scanned the front page Jordan took a mouthful of his pint and wiped the foam from his upper lip.

"Jeez. I never saw the paper the day. A man killed in Esslemont Avenue. How come you're so pleased? It sounds hellish."

Jordan pointed to his name under the headline. "I wrote it."

The barman's eyebrows rose and he looked back at the paper. After reading the introduction again he turned the page. Jordan smiled to see him searching for the rest of the piece.

"Christ, min. I can hardly read it, all that gory stuff aboot blood."

Jordan laughed. "I grew up hearing things like that. My father was a surgeon."

"The police gave you a statement, I guess?" the barman said when he looked up.

"No. Well, not exactly." Jordan was halfway through his pint already. "I know a few people. Come to think about it, I know quite a bit about the murders."

"Murders? You mean there's more than just the mannie Skilling?"

"Erm — it doesn't matter." Jordan put down his unfinished drink and reached for his jacket.

Flint, Davy and Craig spent Wednesday morning watching TV. Mr and Mrs Jepson were both out at work, and Mac the collie dog was sleeping in the corner, one eye open.

Towards lunchtime, Flint asked if he could go for a shower. Davy went to buy a paper, and when Craig saw the front page, he threw the P&J on the coffee table, knocking a mug over. Mac gave a cursory bark.

"Hey! Watch it, Craigie. My ma's carpet." Davy mopped up the spill.

"Sorry. It's just that bloody Tom Jordan. Naming us in the paper. Bastard."

Davy picked up the P&J. "And where did he get that from? 'sources', it says. He doesn't say anything about an official statement."

"But he gives our bloody names," said Craig. Then he mumbled, "They'll just blame me again, I suppose."

Davy looked at him, head tilted and eyebrows down.

Craig glanced at the paper's headline, then looked at Davy, who was chewing on a buttery. After a pause, he said, "Did you know about the leak? A while back, all the details about Skilling?"

After swallowing some cold coffee, Davy said, "Aye, but I never heard if anyone got caught for it."

Craig shook his head. "As long as you don't think it was me. Blackie suspected me but DS Ovenstone put them right on that."

"Aye, he's awright, Ovenstone, eh?"

"Aye. He was good to me when I first arrived here. He even knows about my previous suspension."

Craig watched Davy stand up and go for a fresh cup of coffee. He liked him more and more as time went on.

When Davy returned with the mugs, he said, "Flint telt me it was that Limb Collector case that you got suspended for."

Craig felt sick. "He told you? How much?" Have you told anyone?" If he ever did get back to work, he would never be trusted if his links to Jordan were common knowledge.

"It's nane o' ma business."

Craig breathed out slowly. He owed it to Davy to tell him more. And it would be good to confide in him.

"I might as well tell you," he said, "As long as you don't tell Barry."

"Cummings? Ach, I learned at primary school never tell that loon onythin' ye want kept quiet."

Craig smiled.

"How much d'you know about The Limb Collector?"

"Just what Flint telt me. I'd heard of him afore, like. One of his victims was a lassie fae Fraserburgh, I think?"

"Yeah, that's him. Well, listen to this…"

###

"Christ, min! I'm nae surprised ye got suspended," Davy said when Craig had summarised his troubles after The Mount, and later for using the PNC again in Haddington. "But the bastards suspended you a second time cos they didna want tae be shown up aboot the PNC?" He sat back, shaking his grinning head.

Craig smiled himself, reaching for his cooling coffee.

"And when you met him in a pub, this reporter mannie, Jordan, he wrote about your suspension in the paper and got you your job back? That's amazin'."

"Yeah, and you can see why I was worried when I was sent to interview him after the leak. It was bad enough when I heard he'd come to Aberdeen."

"Ha ha! Maybe he's followed ye here, min. Wants ye to leak him anither big story." Craig couldn't help smiling at Davy's kind, teasing face. He shook his head, trying to think of a smart response to Davy's joke, but Davy continued.

"Or maybe he's repaying ye the favour? He's daein' the killings for ye so ye can catch anither serial killer!"

"Oh, for fuck's sake, Davy." It was all he could think of.

Flint came into the living room. "Brilliant shower. Electric. I had to fiddle with it to get the heat right but it was great. Has everyone got them in Aberdeen?"

"Nah, it's a new thing. My da heard it's cheaper than putting the immerser on. 6p a shower. He never shuts up aboot it."

"When will we get back into the flat? I've had the same Y-Fronts on for four days now. I've got another pair in my bag. I meant to change them yesterday."

"Dirty bastard," said Davy, laughing.

"And I don't fancy another night on that floor," added Flint, looking at Craig who had bagged Mo's bed.

Mac stood up, alert. He barked a second later when the doorbell chimed. Davy went to answer it, muttering, "Fuckin' Moonies, never awa' fi' the place. You'd think they'd get the message, the brainwashed basta—"

As the door closed behind him Craig and Flint were laughing.

A moment later the door opened and Davy's head poked in. "Flint, there's a braw-looking lassie asking for ye. Quine says her name's Isla."

Chapter 49

Flint looked out of the flat window. A red taxi was drawing away. He could feel Craig watching him.

"Go on. Don't leave her standing there."

"I — don't know if I..." It was all he could think of to say, but his feet were already taking him to the door. When he reached the hallway Davy was returning.

"I didna let her in. Gave you time tae escape oot the back," he whispered, winking.

When Flint pulled the front door open, Isla was silhouetted by sunlight, her dark chocolate hair shining. Her face was in shadow, but her expression didn't matter. She was the most beautiful sight he had ever seen. His chest filled with joy and he couldn't speak.

"Thank God you're alright," she said, stepping forward and embracing him. Flint felt his body slacken as he exhaled, his arms moving themselves around her shoulders and pulling her tight against him. He felt her hair brushing his cheek and leant down to bathe in its aroma.

Isla had tears when she let him go and stood back. "What's going on? Why didn't you come to see me? That flat? I saw the paper. I didn't know..."

Their tears mixed when they held each other again.

"How did you know where I was?" he said. She had tucked her head under his chin, where it belonged.

"I phoned your mum. I got a taxi. I didn't bring enough money to get back. Oh, Flint."

"It's OK. It's OK."

It was OK. It was the most OK Flint had felt in months. OK doesn't come anywhere near it, he thought, as he gripped her again.

When Flint opened his eyes a boy of about ten was walking past, wearing a grass-stained red tracksuit and smoking. He stared at them before stopping and asking, "You goin' tae shag her?" He ran off laughing.

"We'd better go in," said Flint, taking Isla's hand.

As they walked along the hall Flint heard shuffling in the living room. Davy and Craig had been listening behind the door. When he opened it, Craig was in a different seat and Davy was standing by the window holding the folded P&J upside down.

Davy excused himself not long after he'd been introduced to Isla. Craig shook hands with her and sat back down, and Flint thought he looked as uncomfortable as he was himself. Craig knew why they had split up and about Flint's feelings for Isla. The three of them were silent for a moment before Isla picked up the newspaper.

"That poor Professor. And that awful madman! I can't believe it."

Flint saw Craig open his mouth to speak, and said quickly, "Yes, it was hellish. I can't believe it myself." With his eyes, he motioned Craig to say nothing.

It was all too weird, the three of them together for the first time since four years before when they'd teamed up to unmask a different serial killer. And now there was another one they couldn't tell Isla about. Flint was elated that she'd been concerned for him and had hugged him. If it meant there was even a slim chance of reconciling, he wasn't going to spoil it.

The break-up with Isla had resulted from his night terrors. If Flint explained to her that Stiff's nightmares had made him believe he had mutilated and murdered Ivan Skilling, Isla was bound to think he was still obsessed with dreams and hypnosis.

He would definitely drive her away if he mentioned another serial killer.

"I'd better get ready to face the music," said Craig, standing up and heading to the door.

"Oh, what happened to your leg?" said Isla.

Craig looked down at his blue cast. "Car accident," he said, "I can't wait to get this bloody thing off."

After he'd left, Isla looked at Flint and said, "What did he mean, 'face the music'?"

Flint looked at the floor. "He's in a bit of trouble at work. Davy is, too." He knew she was waiting for him to say more, and said, "What did you tell my mum when you called her?"

"I didn't tell her your name was in the paper, if that's what you mean. Look, what the hell is going on, Flint?"

He sighed, looked up, and said, "It would take a while to explain it." She came across the room and sat beside him on the couch. He wanted to take her hand.

"I've got all afternoon," she said.

Davy came in wearing his uniform. "No tie," he said, pointing at his neck. "They took it for blood grouping. You two want a lift somewhere?"

"No, thanks, I'm going to walk Isla home." Flint glanced towards Isla as he spoke, and saw her smile in agreement.

"Ach, well, just put the snib on when you leave. Me an' Craigie-boy are away tae get sacked."

How can he be so relaxed about it all? thought Flint. As if Davy had read his mind he went on, "I never really wanted tae be a polis forever, onywye. A change'll dae me good." He turned and called out into the hall, "C'mon, Craig, let's go."

Flint watched the red Escort pull away from outside the flat. Craig looked small in the passenger seat of his own car, his shoulders slumped and head bowed. He'd borrowed a white shirt from Davy and one of Mr Jepson's ties, but with his cast he still had to wear the tracksuit bottoms.

Isla walked across the slabbed parking area towards the pavement as Flint pulled the door closed. As he followed her, he felt like he was being watched. He turned to see a frowning face looking down from a window of the flat upstairs. Mr and Mrs Jepson's neighbours would all have read the P&J.

He hurried to catch Isla and they walked down the sloping street. Neither of them spoke until they had gone a few hundred yards.

"I'm pretty sure if we turn right and then left we'll be somewhere near the top of St Machar Road. Then along towards Kittybrewster."

Isla looked at him briefly and said, "Or we could take a walk through Old Aberdeen."

That was a detour, and Flint hoped it was a sign she was happy to spend a bit more time with him.

The traffic was heavy and they didn't try to speak much until they were past the Zoology building. Nearing the Central Refectory, Isla laughed and said, "D'you remember that disco in the Ref when you and Nudge nicked the pint glasses?"

"Aye, and Nudge dropped one out of his jacket pocket just as we were passing the porter. That was a great night."

She was still laughing. "I thought we'd get banned from the Ref."

It was a story they'd told each other before and Flint began to relax. He felt even better when, a few moments later, she asked, "Have you got any money on you?"

"Only a few quid, I think," he said, feeling in his back pocket for his wallet. "Why?"

"The Machar's just round the corner," she said, with a cheeky, beautiful smile he hadn't seen for too long.

They found seats in the bar, and the smells and sounds took Flint back to their student days and happiest times. They chatted and laughed as they reminisced, and Flint wanted to hold her hand and kiss her. When he came back from the bar with their second drinks, Isla said, "Are you going to tell me why you were in that flat?"

He looked at the table. A sliver of foam trickled slowly down the outside of his glass and soaked into the beer mat.

"We were trying to help Stiff — that's Ian Soutar, the one who jumped out of the window."

"Help him how?" Isla's brow furrowed. "He's a murderer."

"Well, he is now, I suppose, but we were trying to prove he didn't kill the man Skilling."

Her quizzical expression intensified.

"Craig's pretty sure he confessed because he dreamt he did it."

"Dreams?" She frowned.

Flint went on quickly, watching Isla's face as he outlined Stiff's history. He knew he had to go on, but his leg was shaking when he told her that something dark in Stiff's past had sparked his obsession with male genitalia and made him confuse his dreams with reality. Isla listened, only interrupting for clarification when he had gone too fast. From her nodding and the raising of her eyebrows, he could tell she was focused. Flint felt himself relax a little.

"And you got that poor professor to come to the flat to hypnotise him?"

"Yes. And he agreed that Stiff was innocent."

"But now he's dead. How awful. The poor man."

Flint couldn't bring himself to tell Isla that Slinn was a serial killer.

It was after five o'clock when they left the Machar. As they walked down High Street towards King's College, three pints made Flint confident enough to risk taking Isla's hand. She let him, and squeezed his. She had a new ring on her middle finger, but otherwise, their hands fitted together as they always had. He couldn't have been happier.

"Flint. There's something I've got to tell you."

Dread poured into him, filling him from his toes with cold numbness. Something I've got to tell you. I know what it is. Oh God, I know what it is. I know what she's going to say. There's someone else.

"About someone else."

He dropped her hand, but somehow his legs kept walking.

"Oh, Flint, I'm sorry. I have to tell you. There was someone else. Look at me, Flint."

Was?

He couldn't speak, but they both stopped and turned to face each other. A man on a bicycle whizzed by, his wheels drumming on the cobbles. He must have a sore arse, Flint thought, before the reality of what he was about to hear returned.

"I went out with a guy a few times, and we — you know — a couple of times. Oh, I don't know why I had to tell you. I'm sorry, Flint, I'm sorry, I had to tell you. You hate me now."

Words still wouldn't form. Was?

"It's over, though, I promise. I finished with him last Thursday." She reached for his hand. "Say something."

"Last Thursday?" It was the night he'd seen her leaving the flat in her new jacket.

"Yes. I went to meet him and told him I didn't want to see him again."

They walked on in silence. When they reached Mounthooly Flint asked, "Why did you finish with him? Was he bad to you?"

"No, nothing like that." She stopped and gripped his upper arms, shaking his shoulders. "It was you I wanted. You. No one else."

A car whizzed past on the roundabout, wind catching her hair. Flint pulled her away from the edge of the pavement.

"I'm better now. Really. And I'm hardly drinking."

"I wouldn't care. I just want you back. I've missed you so much. When I hadn't seen you for so long, I thought I never would. The girls at work told me to move on. That's why I didn't write. I wanted to. Please don't hate me." She was sobbing into his neck.

"I'll never hate you." He held her tight, also weeping. A woman in white boots walked past and tutted. Flint laughed at her through his tears. "Miserable old git." The woman hurried on.

Chapter 50

Craig was exhausted by the time he'd walked from Queen Street back to Esslemont Avenue. When he'd left the flat the day before, handcuffs meant he couldn't have picked up his stick if he'd remembered to. It would have helped on the long walk up Union St.

He was also dejected. Suspended for the third time. At least Davy had escaped with a disciplinary warning. Ruining his own career was bad enough. It was Davy's first offence, he told himself, and not because he was Aberdonian.

When he entered the flat there was a strange smell. A bit like over-ripe apples, he thought, but also a distinct smell of sawdust. He'd smelt old blood before and didn't like to think of what the inside of his bedroom was like. The door had police tape over it, and for good measure, a joiner had sawn two lengths of timber and nailed them to the door frame. He guessed the window would also have been boarded up.

He spent the evening trying to concentrate on the TV and going back and forth to the bread bin. By nine-thirty he was in Flint's sleeping bag on the couch, going over and over what he knew about Slinn's crimes. He hadn't been able to tell any of it to Detective Superintendent Morrice and Murray Ovenstone. He had played down Davy's part, and not mentioned Jack or the PNC at all. His suspension this time was for "inappropriate contact with a suspect". They had accepted the truth that Flint had invited Slinn to visit Stiff to try to help him.

As far as Grampian Police were concerned, Professor Slinn had been wrong to call for Stiff to be released on bail when he was. The case against Blackie was moving forward, and Stiff's innocence would soon be disclosed. Without saying so explicitly, Detective Superintendent Morrice had made it clear he thought the interfering specialist had got what he deserved.

The late Professor Slinn would be lauded as a misguided genius devoted to helping others. Craig knew Slinn was a vicious serial killer.

Chapter 51

Thursday 13th May

When Flint woke in the bed he hadn't lain in for seven months it felt like he'd never been away. The clock radio, a present from his mum when they had moved into the flat, clicked as it flipped to 6.09.

Isla's head was against his chest, and he smiled at the serene look on her sleeping face he knew so well. Her hair tickled under his chin and when he tried to move Isla stirred, opened her eyes and smiled back at him, pulling him closer to her.

"It's been too long," she mumbled, kissing him and running her hands through his hair. "I missed your freckles."

He moved against her and he saw her pupils dilate, one hand stroking down his body to reach for him.

Half an hour later, they rolled apart and lay on their backs.

"Is there any food?" Flint asked.

She laughed. "You're always hungry. But I'm pretty starving, too. I was going to go to Safeway yesterday but then I read the paper. I haven't eaten since."

Flint made toasted cheese for them both. Tomato sauce for him and brown sauce for her. When he'd finished it, he put the plate down on the floor beside him and started to speak. Isla interrupted him.

"I'll let you off with just a warning, but it's the last time." She handed him her plate and indicated the kitchenette with her smiling eyes. When he returned from the sink he sat down beside her and tried again. All the while he was eating, he'd been trying to gather the courage to tell her, and to decide how to say it. He owed it to her.

"While I was at home I — well, there was someone else." He'd not meant to use the same word she had. Someone else. It sounded so meaningful.

She said nothing and stared at her hands.

"It didn't mean anything."

After a few interminable seconds, Isla turned towards him. He couldn't read her face, and the feeling of dread, of having blown it all again, began to recollect.

"Is it over?"

"It was over the next morning."

Her dark eyebrows descended, her head tilting.

"A one-night stand?"

"Yes, I suppose so." Oh God, why did I tell her?

"And you haven't heard from her since?" Her olive green eyes were moist. She was silent for a moment, before looking directly at him. "What's her name?"

"I don't know."

Confusion clouded her face, until her eyebrows rose and the corners of her mouth twitched up. "You don't remember?"

"Not a thing."

Isla laughed, and he exhaled the breath he hadn't noticed he was holding before laughing with her.

"Where did you meet her?"

"I've no idea. It might have been at the Royal Hotel disco."

In between bouts of giggling, she teased him for more details. He told her about finding the girl in the bed, and that she had gone when he'd next woken. He didn't say it was his mother's bed he was in, or his brief suspicions of who the body beside him might have been, but when he spoke about Craig arriving he let slip about the knickers against the skirting board.

"I'm going to ask Craig for more details. He's a policeman, he's bound to have made notes," she said with a wicked, lovely grin he couldn't resist. He grabbed her and she let him, both of them tickling and sniggering.

MY BEST YET

Number seven!
I'm too good at this.
Four more since I hit the target.
And this one's the first after...
Since there's been no one to *save* me! Ha ha.
I had to hurry up after he was gone.
Doing them from memory now.
The next one's the last.
I posted him another letter this morning.
His appointment.
It'll be hard to beat this one, though.
Look how neat he is down there.
And his cheeks all puffed out and round.
Like a hamster.
Like a cover star.
Shame he won't look so good on the front page.

Chapter 52

A phone was ringing. As he surfaced from sleep Craig returned from his childhood home in Dalkeith to the Esslemont Avenue flat. He tried to put in order the pieces of reality as they came back to him in random order: he had a broken leg; he was in Aberdeen; he had been suspended again. Fuck.

The phone stopped ringing, and he heard a deep voice from the hall. "Aye, I'll just get him."

Davy. He hadn't heard Davy come in after his shift last night. Lucky bastard, straight back to work. He peered at his watch. Twenty-past seven.

The big face and the ears appeared round the living room door, "It's for you-hoo, Craigie-boy. C'mon, min, the man's in a call-box." Davy's face disappeared, and Craig heard, "Hang on, pal, the lazy bugger's just comin'."

Craig's cast got stuck in the sleeping bag as he tried to struggle out of it. He was cursing when he passed Davy in the narrow hallway.

"Who the hell's phoning at this time of day?"

"Ah didna ask, min."

"Hello?" said Craig, taking the receiver. "Who's this?"

"Craig, it's Jack. Listen."

Flint drifted awake. There was music in the background. The time on the radio alarm clock read 8.15. They must have drifted off again. Isla rolled over and silenced it.

"Damn. I left it on again." She rolled back and closed her eyes, pulling the duvet around her.

He knew her morning routine by heart: by half-past eight she would have showered, dressed and put on make-up. After a cup of tea, she would leave at 8.40 to walk to the town centre. She had got the first job she'd applied for after graduating, he remembered, with an American-owned recruitment company establishing a base in Aberdeen. After she'd gone, he would quickly dress in time for the van to pick him up outside. At least being the gaffer of a Parks Department team had had some perks.

He stretched his arm out and stroked her shoulder. "Hey, don't go back to sleep. You'll be late for work."

"Mmmm — I'm on holiday all week. It's Thursday already and I still haven't remembered to switch the alarm off."

"You don't have to go?" He pulled her towards him and she resisted, weakly.

"Sleep a bit longer," she said.

Flint kissed her neck. Her hair fell over his eyes and blocked all light, its scent heavenly.

"Mmmm..." she murmured, turning to him.

Loud, urgent rapping on the flat door made them both jump.

"Who's that?"

"I don't know. No one ever comes. This time of the morning?" Isla pulled her dressing gown around her and headed out towards the flat door. There was more frantic banging.

"Hello? Who's there," she called out.

"Is that you, Isla?" A man's voice.

Flint jumped out of bed, hackles up and worried. The boyfriend?

Isla had her eye to the peephole.

"Who is it?" Flint shouted, holding the door before she could open it.

"I can't see," she said, taking the chain off.

"That you, Flint? It's me. Craig."

"Craig? What the...?"

Isla pulled the door open and Flint ran back to find his Y-Fronts. When he returned, Isla was filling the kettle and Craig was standing, dripping on the living room floor. Flint now noticed heavy rain streaming down the kitchenette window.

"What—?"

"Jack phoned me. I came to find you. Drove myself." Craig was breathless. "Couldn't get parked, had to walk in the rain." He pointed at his cast. "I can drive, though." He looked excited.

"But what the fuck are you doing here? How did you know where..."

"I'd been here when I tried to visit you last year. But you'd moved out." Craig glanced over towards Isla who was facing the window. He turned back with a questioning expression. Flint had no idea what was going on and shrugged.

Craig lowered his voice and looked Flint in the eye. "There's been another one."

"What?" Flint was shaking his head.

"You're a bit early, Craig, but sit down anyway," said Isla, reaching for mugs and tea bags.

"What are you talking about?" said Flint.

"It wasn't Slinn."

"The Professor? That poor man. What about him? What are you talking about, Craig?" said Isla, her eyebrows coming together.

Flint was beginning to suspect what Craig was going to tell him. His mind was racing. Not Slinn?

"Jack phoned me. Another man has been killed, in Dundee. Exactly the same."

Flint said nothing. Isla stopped, a mug in each hand and her mouth open.

"Exactly the same," Craig repeated. "Head smashed, balls in his mouth. Lying at the side of his own car. Exactly the same. And after Slinn was dead."

Flint saw disgust on Isla's face. Putting the teas down she faced Flint and said, "I want to know what's going on. What have you been doing?" She looked almost fierce. Flint's eyes met Craig's, and Craig shook his head.

"Tell me what's going on!" In the glare of her fixed expression, Flint's shoulders slumped.

"There's a serial killer," he said.

"Oh, God." Isla turned back to the sink, holding on to its edge. Flint knew she would be recalling the events leading up to The Mount. He looked at Craig, who shrugged.

Flint was desperate to know more about the latest murder, but it was obvious from Isla's reaction that he couldn't ask until they'd explained some of what had gone on before.

"Ivan Skilling, the man Stiff confessed about, he wasn't the only one. There were two more before him. Same bizarre injuries. It has to be the same killer."

"Oh, God, it's all happening again." She was still looking into the sink, shaking her head. He touched her arm.

"Come on, Isla, sit down," Flint said, looking at Craig, "We'll tell you it all."

When Isla turned round there was a look on her face he thought was a mix of anger, fear and resignation.

"At least put your bloody clothes on," she said.

Over the next half an hour, between them Flint and Craig told Isla everything they had discovered. At first, she was incredulous, frowning and sitting back on the couch, making brief objections to what she was hearing. Flint knew her interest was growing, her questions focusing.

"But why couldn't this Stiff Soutar man have done them all? I mean, I know you said he's too small, but there might be a way he could have done it."

"He was in hospital when one of the killings took place."

"And we know from the time of death that when Stiff found Skilling he'd already been dead for six hours," Craig added. Flint raised his eyebrows at this, and Craig went on, "Aye, DI Ovenstone told me that."

Isla sat back, looking puzzled but interested. "But why did you think Professor Slinn had done it? Or done them, I mean."

Flint smiled. "You still think he's just too good-looking, like Burt Reynolds," he said.

The P&J had printed the publicity photo from Slinn's lecture flyer, and Isla had already remarked on the resemblance. Imagine if she'd seen him on stage at the lecture, Flint had thought.

"Remember we said about the list? Flint found it in Slinn's office."

"Oh, yeah. Names being scored off. Same names as the dead men," Isla said, talking to herself. "But it can't have been him — now that there's been another one."

Jack's call to Craig was to tell him Tayside were investigating the murder of a man in a park in Dundee. Jack wasn't on the case, but he had seen the early reports. The injuries were the same, and it was another middle-aged man who lived alone. Jack wanted to know what else Craig might have discovered. Then he planned to use the PNC, officially this time, to 'uncover' the three previous linked murders.

"Is it the same Jack from before, Craig?" asked Isla. Jack had accessed the PNC to help them track down the Limb Collector.

"Yes, that's him. At least he'll be able to demonstrate what the PNC can do. Maybe they'll take notice this time." Craig put his head in his hands. "And I've been suspended again, fuck it!" He looked round at Isla. "Sorry, it's just…"

Isla handed Flint her mug and pointed to the kitchenette. "What are you going to do?"

"Nothing," said Craig. "I came round here thinking there's been another murder and that we should keep trying to work things out. But having spoken about it all I realise there's nothing more to do. Tayside will use the PNC and make the links, and they'll find the serial killer." He looked out of the window.

When Flint turned round from the sink, he could see Craig's eyes were moistening.

"Think of it this way, Craig. At least Stiff will be off the hook. That's what you wanted. Even before we knew there were other killings."

Craig stood up. "Yeah. For that one at least. He killed Slinn, remember." He looked towards Isla. "Sorry I disturbed you both. I'll get back to the flat."

Flint had finished washing the mugs. "D'you want me to drive you?"

"Yeah, you probably should. My cast got stuck between the clutch and the throttle and I nearly ran into the back of a bus."

Flint looked at Isla now. "D'you mind if I go back to the flat for a while? I could do with picking up a change of clothes."

"You're not joking. Your Y-fronts! Eeugh."

"You come as well, Isla, if you want," said Craig.

Chapter 53

"Is that where...?" Isla pointed at the boarded and taped door.

"Yes. Come along to the living room," said Craig, walking straight past. Flint was behind and noticed Craig turned his face away when he passed his bedroom, saying, "I'm just going to put the kettle on."

Isla sat on the couch. "Quite a nice flat, for blokes," she said, looking round the room.

Flint had come in, and said, "You should have seen it when I first came. A real tip. Didn't take me long to tidy it up."

Isla looked askance, rolling her eyes.

"He's joking, Isla," Craig called over his shoulder.

"That's obvious. Unless he's had a personality change."

"Shit! The immerser's been left on. Two whole days."

"Good, that means I can go straight in the bath," said Flint.

"Thank God," said Isla, smiling.

While Flint was in the bathroom, Craig went out for milk and bread. Isla looked around the room then stood for a few minutes looking down on the traffic toing and froing. A bell rang and she saw streams of uniformed schoolkids passing between classes at the Grammar School opposite. She found herself wondering if she and Flint would one day be able to move to a bigger flat like this.

Within less than 24 hours, she realised, she had reunited with Flint and plunged straight into another bizarre situation. She, Flint and Craig knew about an active serial killer. Until now, the police knew nothing of it, but at least they would soon. This time, she and Flint weren't going to be involved.

Turning away from the window, her eye was caught by a glint of sunlight reflecting from something on the floor next to the couch. Bending over, she was able to see it was the brass lock of an attaché case. It looked identical to the one her father had cherished. Presented to him by a rich aunt on the day he graduated in accountancy, it was a constant in Isla's childhood.

Now looking at the briefcase in front of her, she imagined the feel of its fine leather, cracked and old though it clearly was. Each brass hasp would open with a satisfying click at the touch of its own brass button. She smiled, recalling the effort it was for her little girl thumbs to press those buttons, and her delight at the achievement. She knew from toddlerhood the importance of not lifting the case's lid open. Whatever was inside it was Very Important, and Secret.

Unable to resist, Isla reached for the padded handle on the briefcase. She remembered being barely able to lift her father's, but this one was lighter. Aged or not, they both retained their stylish luxury.

She placed the case on the coffee table, mesmerised by the aroma and compelled to run her finger over the embossed Dunhill logo on the bottom right hand corner of the lid. Lost in nostalgia, she clicked each of the locks. They both opened with the lightest touch. Overcoming the urge to look inside, she swung the hasps back into place, surprised when they didn't click as they closed. She lifted the case to replace it between the couch and the wall next to the window.

When the lid swung open and a flurry of papers scattered out onto the dusty carpet between the couch and the table, Isla's mouth dried and a bubble of panic swelled in her chest. After a quick look towards the door, she crouched down and started to gather together the contents. It was awkward in the narrow space, and some of the papers had slid under the couch. She was half lying down, stretching to reach them, when Craig's voice said, "Lost something?"

Isla pulled herself up quickly, closed the case, pressing hard until she heard the locks click, and slid it back into its space. Turning, she stuttered, "Sorry, erm, I dropped your briefcase, it wasn't shut—"

"Briefcase?" Craig was smiling and shaking his head. "You mean Flint's grip?"

Isla could see Flint's holdall was on the other side of the room. She was confused for a moment.

"No, the briefcase." She pointed down beside her. "I'm sorry, it can't have been closed properly."

Craig put the milk, rolls and bacon he'd bought on the worktop by the sink and came across to look. He pulled the case out, looking at it suspiciously, as Isla went back to retrieving the rest of its contents.

"Bloody hell," said Craig.

"What's going on?" Flint was standing in the doorway, a towel round his waist.

Craig held out the attaché case. Barely readable, Isla could now make out 'D.S.' in cracked gold leaf.

"Slinn's," said Craig.

Flint now remembered Professor Slinn handing him his briefcase when Stiff interrupted them at the flat door.

"I just put it down there and forgot about it," he said as he sat down. "He handed it to me before he went in with Stiff." The attaché case was now sitting on the coffee table, closed and with all its contents back inside. The tan leather was the same shade as Slinn's jacket. Isla was staring at the case, redness fading from her cheeks.

"We should take it to the Police," she said.

"Fucking Blackie!" Craig raised his hands. "Some fucking search they did, eh? Fucking incompetent bastard."

"What fell out of it?" asked Flint.

Isla looked uncertain. "Erm — a couple of photos of him, and some notes and things. Oh, and a newspaper cutting." She turned to Craig, who was now staring angrily at the case.

"You think you'd better hand it in?" she asked.

Craig sighed. "I'm in enough trouble I don't deserve. They'll just fucking accuse me of hiding it."

Flint was surprised by the intensity of Craig's fury. "We can't just keep it, though. Can we?" he said.

Craig reached out, grasping the handle and pulling the case towards him. "Whatever we do, I'm having a look at what's in it."

He clicked the two latches, inverted the case and tipped its contents onto the coffee table. They all sat looking at the jumble of papers. First to reach for something was Craig, who took the corner of a photograph and pulled it out. Standing on pebbles at the edge of a loch, Slinn had his arm around an auburn-haired woman who exuded glamour, even in sweatshirt and jeans. They both looked straight at the lens with film star smiles, Slinn looking equally beautiful in denims and suede boots.

"Wow. What a couple." Isla took the picture and turned it over. On the back, neat handwriting read '*Mr and Mrs on honeymoon, 1973*'. Isla had a tear in her eye. The poor man was married. His poor wife.

"She died. I remember Granville told me," Flint said.

"Oh, no. How could a man like that be a killer?"

Flint had been sifting through the pile on the table and was reading a newspaper clipping.

"What's that, Flint?"

"A report on a killing. One we hadn't heard about, but it's the same."

"What's the name?" said Craig, pulling another photo from the pile.

"Cornelius Thake. Found lying outside his own car, in a lay-by near Connel. Same injuries. I—" Flint sat back, clenched his fists and looked upwards with a satisfied grin. "Thake! That's it. The name I couldn't remember. From the short list. Now I see it in writing it's…"

Isla and Craig smiled with him, grimly.

"We were right about that list," said Isla.

"Looks like it," said Craig. "Can I see?"

He reached out and took the *Daily Record* clipping from Flint. "'the mutilated remains of Cornelius Thake, 61, were found on Sunday morning'," he read out. "Killed on the Saturday night, it says."

Craig put his finger to the tiny caption under a photo of a steel bridge spanning a wide expanse of fast-flowing water. "'Connel Bridge, Oban, Argyll.'" he read. "That'll have been Strathclyde case, then."

"I've been to Connel." said Isla. "We stopped in a lay-by to eat our sandwiches and I saw a heron fishing. And there was a smell of seaweed. I was twelve the next day."

Craig continued as if Isla wasn't there, his finger now at the top of the news page. "Monday 18th September 1978." Laying the cutting down on the table, he said, "Christ, that's four years ago."

"Look at this." Flint was holding another sheet of paper from the pile.

"What is it?" Isla sat forward.

"A list. 'Survivors of Childhood Trauma'. There's dozens of girls' names, addresses, and dates of birth."

"That's awful. You shouldn't be looking at that, Flint." She was frowning, motioning to him to put the list back in the briefcase.

"But it's got the surnames of the dead men on it. Skilling, Gaska, Narloch." He looked again. "And Thake."

"Let me see." Craig's words sounded strangled and he cleared his throat. He took the list and scanned it. "Is this the same list you found in Slinn's desk?"

Flint saw Isla's mouth fall open in disbelief. "You went through his desk?" He looked at her, nodding as he answered Craig's question.

"No. I told you. It was shorter, and just three columns, erm — surname, date of birth and a number."

Craig ran his index finger down the page, turning it over to continue. "You said there was about half a page of names? There's a lot more here."

"Aye, it was a much shorter list. Probably about ten. Maybe less."

"So, there's two lists, a long one and a short one. And the dead men's names are on both," Craig murmured.

"Are you thinking what I'm thinking, Craig?" said Flint. Craig frowned, but said nothing. "I mean, why was Slinn carrying about that news report on Thake? He's got to be the killer, but he's dead, and there's been another one, so he can't be. Can he?"

Craig looked at the window, mumbling, "Something like that."

No one spoke for a moment, until Flint said, "Oh fuck, what the fuck's going on?" reaching for the long list. Eyebrows down, he examined it slowly, his finger tapping on each line. "For one of these it only gives the initials 'R.F.'," he said. "And an asterisk. Why's that one different? Oh, hang on, there's another asterisk, down here — 'see private staff file'."

Isla sat forward. "Was the new one on the shorter list," she said.

"New one?"

"The one in Dundee, the man Jack told you about."

"I dunno. I don't think he told me the name. Why?" Craig said.

"Keep up! It's you two that have been working on this." They both turned to Isla. Flint saw the same excited look she wore when she was beating him at Scrabble. "Because if it's only the names on the shorter list that are getting murdered it means someone has selected some for a shortlist. A kill list."

Flint nodded. "And still working through it," he said, looking at Isla.

"And it's in Slinn's desk," she said. "It's got to be him — but it's not…"

"We need to see that shortlist again," said Craig.

"It'll still be in Slinn's desk at Liff Hospital." Flint was looking at Craig and Isla in turn. The three of them were a team again.

"We need to go back to Dundee." Craig was gathering up Slinn's papers. Isla looked at him, her head to one side, eyebrows down.

"Now?" she said. "It'd take hours to get to Dundee. And we can't just go to the hospital. Anyway, by the time we got there the office might be shut. We'd just have to drive back to Aberdeen." She was looking back and forth between Craig and Flint. Flint was watching Craig, who was smiling, holding the briefcase.

"Okay then, we can stay at Jack's. Flint can do his medical student impersonation again at Liff tomorrow. But let's get going."

"Make sure that case is shut properly," said Isla. "And can we at least stop at my flat to pick up some clothes?"

Chapter 54

Driving south out of Aberdeen was always slow, and that Thursday afternoon was no exception. It was over an hour by the time they were passing Brechin, where they came on yet another length of major roadworks.

As Flint pulled up in the slow queue, Isla said from the back seat, "I'm still amazed that you can drive, Flint."

"I like it. We should get a car."

"You need to get a better job first. I can't afford a car."

Flint looked across at Craig. He had fallen asleep with his head resting on the seat belt.

In a low voice, Flint said, "I haven't told anyone — well, except my mum who made me do it — I've applied for teacher training."

Isla reached forward and squeezed his arm. "That's brill! Oh, Flint, that's fantastic. Why didn't you tell me?"

Craig stirred. "What? Sorry, must have fallen asleep. Tell you what?" He was rubbing his eyes.

"It doesn't matter." Flint glanced back between the seats and told her with his eyes not to say more. He knew she would be wondering why it was a secret, but he couldn't bear to tell her the course was in Dundee. They'd only just got back together and he was going to mess it up.

Their progress was faster when they had passed the roadworks, but it was after four o'clock before they entered Dundee, and the traffic became thick and slow again. Isla had been right; it would have been pointless trying to go to Liff that day.

"I didn't realise Dundee was so big," said Isla. "Are you sure Jack won't mind us arriving out of the blue?"

"No, he'll be fine. His flatmate's away."

Flint found a parking space opposite Jack's flat. As he got out, a net curtain moved and the old woman who'd looked after Craig's crutches waved.

"I've got competition," said Isla, laughing. She handed Slinn's attaché case to Flint and slung the rope of her duffel bag over her shoulder.

When Jack answered the door, he raised his eyebrows in surprise. "Jeez, I didn't expect to be seeing you. You didn't say when we spoke this morning."

He waved them in, and soon the four of them were seated in the living room.

Jack shook hands with Isla. "We've never met, but I remember your name. Craig told me everything about that Sunday."

"Ah, yes. The Mount. Don't remind me," she replied.

None of them spoke for a moment. In the car, they'd decided to tell Jack as little about their plans as they could. He seemed to have other ideas.

"Are you going to tell me what you're up to? I know it has to be about the serial killer, but what do you think you've got that Tayside CID haven't worked out?"

They told Jack about the two lists, and Flint's impersonation of a medical student the previous week.

"And if we can get another look at the shorter list, the *kill list*," Flint said, looking at Isla, "we might be able to get to the men on it before the killer does."

"You think this list means the killer's going to go for more?" Jack's eyebrows were raised.

Craig spoke. "He's ticking them off one by one, Jack, and you know serial killers can't stop. Even Tulliallan basic training taught us that."

"And you say this shortlist was in Professor Slinn's desk?"

"Yes. And Flint's going to Liff tomorrow to try to get it."

"It won't be there." Jack was shaking his head.

"I know which drawer it's in," said Flint.

"That's just it. When Slinn was murdered, Grampian asked for his work files. They wanted all correspondence with the shrinks in Aberdeen. About Soutar."

"So, where is it?" said Craig, shaking his head. "Don't tell me it was all sent back to Aberdeen."

"Everything in his office. There were three boxes, Grampian sent a van for them yesterday."

"Fuck," said Flint, punching the couch.

"I'm going down to the corner shop," Jack said. "Anyone want me to pick anything up?"

"If they've got tomato sauce crisps I'll take a couple of packs," said Flint.

When Jack had left, Craig said, "We're back to square one."

Isla reached for the briefcase. "We might be able to do something. I hate the thought that we know someone's being lined up to be killed, and that we could maybe stop it."

She was spreading the contents of Slinn's case on the tartan carpet. Flint and Craig looked at each other, shrugging.

"Did you say Jack's got notes about the killings?" asked Isla.

Craig said, "Aye, but he'd get hellish trouble if Tayside found out he'd used the PNC before he had permission. We can't use it. We know what's in it, anyway."

"He might have added something about the new one, though," said Flint. "I'll just get the pages, leave the folder."

The front door handle turned before Flint reached Jack's bedroom door. Jack went straight to the kitchen with two bags of shopping. Flint joined Isla and Craig to gather around the pile of papers on the floor.

Craig started notes on what they knew about the killings.

1. 16th Sep 1978 Cornelius Thake, 61, Connell (Strathclyde Police)
2. July 1980 Harkan Gaska, 49, Stirling (Central Scotland Police)
3. 31st Jan 1981 Alex Narloch, 58, Tentsmuir (Fife Police)
4. 30th Sep 1981 Ivan Skilling, 53, Newmachar (Grampian Police)
5. May 1982 Name Unknown (ask Jack) Dundee (Tayside Police)

They didn't realise Jack was back in the living room until he put two bags of crisps down on the table. "What are you up to?"

"Erm — " Flint looked up. Isla was engrossed in one of the newspaper cuttings, and Craig appeared to be staring into space, deep in thought. "Erm — gathering as much as we know about the victims. What was the Dundee man called?"

"Robert Currid."

"Thanks." Flint added it to Craig's list. "What else can you tell us? How old was he?"

Jack walked to the end of the couch and reached down. "There you are, last night's paper has it all." He handed Flint a copy of the *Evening Telegraph* and walked towards his bedroom. "I'll get my notes."

Robert Currid's body had been discovered by a gardener working in Camperdown Park. The body was lying outside the driver's side of a car. He was 53, the paper said, and lived alone.

Craig woke from whatever reverie he'd been in when Jack brought his notes. "What were his exact injuries?"

"The station was buzzing with it yesterday," said Jack, "I haven't seen a PM report, but the uniforms first on the scene said he looked like he was sleeping. A single mark on his head, probably a hammer, I heard. But wait 'til you hear this."

Jack had an audience of three.

"He was naked from the waist down. The PC who found him said they didn't realise he was injured apart from the head wound, but they heard the Police Surgeon saying he'd never seen anything like it."

"Go on," said Craig.

"His balls were in his mouth, like your Aberdeen man, but his lips had been carefully stitched together. His ball sack was repaired, too. A real neat stitching job, the doctor said."

"Eeuch!" said Isla.

"Fuxake," said Flint. "They didn't say that in the *Telegraph*." He was eating his crisps.

Jack looked pleased with himself.

"My head's nipping with all this," said Craig. "I don't really want to read any more tonight." He was staring at the papers on the table, biting his thumbnail.

"We could go for a pint?" Jack looked hopeful. "I haven't been out for weeks."

They didn't spend long in the Polepark Bar. Jack was on an early shift the next day, and keen to get back after two pints. When he had gone to bed, Craig soon followed suit and went to the other bedroom.

Flint and Isla made up a bed of sorts using the cushions from the couch and two armchairs. Jack had brought three blankets from his room. After they made love quietly, Flint soon went to sleep. He woke in the early hours to find Isla sitting up, reading by the glow of a streetlight outside the uncurtained window.

"What are you doing?" he mumbled.

"I couldn't sleep," she whispered. He reached up to stroke her bare shoulder, but she didn't turn away from the notepad she was writing on. "I've been looking the notes we made. I've drawn up this table. Dates, injuries and as many details as I can find in the news cuttings. I think there's a pattern. Or at least a sort of progression."

Flint sighed and pushed himself up to sit. "I don't know how you can see what you're doing."

"Your eyes adjust to it after a while, but now you're awake I'll put the big light on." She stood up and he had to shield his eyes when she clicked the switch. She was wearing only her knickers.

"Oh, come back here," he said, reaching his arms out.

She smiled but said, "Maybe later. Look at this." She pulled a T-shirt on.

"You're a cruel woman, doing that to me," he said, shuffling over to see what she had written.

"Look, the first one, Thake, was butchered. Read that." Isla pointed to the *Daily Record* article from Slinn's briefcase. She had drawn a line round one paragraph. Flint read, 'the victim's genitalia had been removed. A Police witness told me he saw multiple slashes on the lower torso and that he'd never seen so much blood.'

"Sounds hellish. But I don't see—"

"Compare that to what we know about Currid. Neatly sewn up and hardly any blood. His bits carefully hidden in his mouth."

Flint waited for her to continue.

"I found this in Jack's notes." She was still whispering. "Details of the injuries."

Flint hadn't looked again at Jack's notes, having assumed he was already familiar with them. She handed him the page. He read the familiar words.

'Alex Narloch, widower, from Cupar, Fife. 58. Body found beside car. Head mashed with a rock.

Now, though, Flint could see Jack had added more details. In the same black ink he had written, '*(from PNC): Penis missing. Testicles in trouser pocket!*'

Flint sat back and exhaled, trying to put all this into a pattern. Isla helped him.

"The killer is perfecting his technique. The first one is rough. 'Crude' the paper says. The last one was put back together with 'a real neat stitching job'. And Narloch is somewhere in between."

"It's pretty convincing. But what does it tell us?"

"I don't know, but any links we can find can only help."

Flint smiled at her. "Come back to bed."

To his surprise and disappointment, Isla was asleep within moments of lying back down. It was his turn to writhe around on the lumpy cushions.

Friday 14th May 1982

Flint heard Jack creeping around between the bathroom and his bedroom at just after half past six. It was a relief to have an excuse to get up. He'd kept trying to read Slinn's papers and Jack's notes, but his eyes hadn't adjusted in the way Isla said they would, and the cloudy dawn had barely thrown more light than the street lamps.

"Morning, Jack," he said from the hallway. The bathroom door was open and Jack was cleaning his teeth with one hand, buttoning his tunic with the other.

"Hi, Flint. Still hoping to catch the killer before we do?" He flashed a frothy white smile.

"Just frustrated we can't get hold of that list from Slinn's drawer. I've got no idea why he had it. He's obviously not the killer — seeing as he's dead now. But it might have helped us warn whoever's next."

"It'll all come out soon enough. At least now three forces are working together. I want to make sure it's Tayside that catches the bastard." He pointed at papers Flint had in his hand. "Then you can stop poring over those."

Flint hadn't even realised he'd taken the newspaper clippings with him when he came out of the bedroom. He held them under the hallway lightbulb. "At least I can read them properly now. Wait a minute — these two pieces are by the same reporter." Jack came to look over his shoulder.

"'Tom Jordan'," said Flint. "His name's at the top of the *Daily Record* report about the 1978 killing. Y'know, Thake. And look, the same bloke wrote the one about Robert Currid in the Dundee Telegraph one."

"It's the *Evening Telegraph*," said Jack. "Hang on a minute." He ran back into his bedroom.

Flint sat on the bath edge, going through the articles again. *Have I heard that name before somewhere? 'Tom Jordan'...*

Jack appeared. "I've really got to rush, but have a look through these. I'm pretty sure I remember that name from *The Courier*. I think the same guy might have written about Narloch's killing at Tentsmuir. Pretty weird if he has." He thrust a pile of clippings towards Flint. "Got to go."

Flint was already searching for the *Courier* article.

Chapter 55

Flint barged into the medical student's room waving the *Courier* cutting, telling Craig about the journalist's connection to the deaths of Cornelius Thake, Alex Narloch and most recently Robert Currid.

Craig was awake, sitting on the edge of the bed. "Fuck," he said, looking down and sighing.

"But, don't you see? He could be the—"

"And Ivan Skilling," said Craig, looking up now, with a grim face.

Craig's reaction took an edge off Flint's excitement, but he went on. "So that's four. All by the same man, this—"

"Tom Jordan."

Flint paused. "The same reporter who helped you get your job back." He was nodding as he spoke, realisation dawning.

That's where I knew the name from. The sorry tale Craig had told him in the curry house. Craig being suspected of leaking to the P&J.

"It was bound to come out," said Craig, lying back on the bed.

By ten to eight they'd talked of nothing else. Flint was stretched out on the floor beside the bed.

"It doesn't have to mean Jordan's the killer," said Craig. He was facing the ceiling and Flint couldn't see his expression. "I agree it's pretty suspicious that he was first to report on them," Craig went on, "but it could be a coincidence. Or he's just quick off the mark. A good reporter, I mean."

"But first to know about *four* of the murders — *at least* four," said Flint, "he's got to be connected somehow."

"Who has?"

Flint twisted round and looked at the door. Isla was standing wrapped in a blanket. "I heard you talking and wondered what was going on," she said, yawning.

"Let's get up and go through it all," said Craig.

While Isla got dressed, Flint made coffee and toast. Craig knocked on the living room door before joining them. When he came in, he looked at Flint. "I sometimes forget you ever wear trousers."

"I've got a T-shirt on," Flint shrugged as he brought the toast to the table. The look on Isla's face made him reach for his jeans.

Craig laid the three news clippings side by side, with a gap between Narloch and Currid. "Remember Jordan also wrote the Skilling article."

Isla put her toast down. "Jordan? Sorry, who's he?" When Flint had explained, she said. "If this Tom Jordan isn't the killer, he's *got* to be connected somehow."

"Erm — wait a minute. What if..?" Craig put his cup down. He was looking straight at Flint but his eyes appeared to be focused on the wall behind.

"What?"

Craig's gaze made Flint look away. Isla's toast was halfway to her mouth.

When Craig spoke, he was biting his lip, his eyebrows low. "Jordan might not be the killer," he muttered.

"I can't hear you, Craig," said Isla.

Craig exhaled. "Jordan — he might not be *the* killer."

"So?" said Flint. "We know he *might* not be the killer, but we also know it might *be* him." He was looking at Isla who appeared rapt, but was chewing slowly.

"What if Jordan's the killer's accomplice? They could be working together."

"Aw, come on!" said Flint. "That's taking it too far—"

"Flint, quiet a minute. Go on, Craig."

Craig looked at Isla, then at Flint. "It might explain how the killings are continuing."

"I don't follow, Craig," Isla said.

"If Slinn and Jordan were in it together, that means Jordan could be continuing now that Slinn's dead."

They went on discussing the idea. Craig had to explain to Isla about his previous contact with Jordan, and the journalist's part in bringing Craig's suspension to an end. "I wasn't sacked. That time, at least," he added, groaning.

"If they are — were working together, it might also be why Slinn had the Thake article in his briefcase," said Flint.

Isla changed the subject. "Craig? Is it alright if I go and have a bath?"

"It's not my flat, but I don't see why not."

"I'm still starving," said Flint. "We should have brought the rest of that bacon with us." Craig gave him a pound.

When he came back from the shop, and while they waited for Isla, the conversation reverted to Slinn and Jordan.

"Let's say they were working together," said Flint, "I mean, I'm not sure I believe it, but let's say they were. It doesn't help us. Or the police. Someone's still got to catch him out. Get to the next victim, I mean, before he does."

"Aye. If only we could have got to that bloody list before it was sent to Aberdeen. I bet Grampian haven't even looked at Slinn's files. All they're interested in is making sure they nail Stiff for Slinn's murder. Like it doesn't matter that he didn't kill Skilling." Craig turned his hands up and rolled his eyes. "Fucking saving face! That's all they're doing. What a fucking mess."

Flint exhaled through pursed lips. "Yep. The list's the link. Jordan's connected somehow, but we canny fuckin' do anything."

"We might as well just head back to Aberdeen," said Craig.

Isla came in, dressed but with a green towel round her head. Where her wet hair showed, it looked black instead of brown. "I've been thinking. There's something different about one of the murders."

Neither of them answered. Craig sat looking out of the window and Flint got up to pour Isla tea and check the bacon in the grill.

"We need to face it, Isla, there's nothing we can do," Craig said.

Flint was back with her tea. "What was different?"

"All of them had head injuries, right?"

"So?" Craig shrugged.

"Four of them were done with a hammer, but one of them had his head mashed with a rock. What was different about that one? Why didn't he use the hammer?"

Flint was nodding. "Which one was it again?"

"The one in the woods near a beach. Narloch, I think," said Isla. The news clippings were still where Craig had arranged them, and Flint picked up the folded broadsheet *Courier* page.

"'The victim's head was smashed to a pulp, a Police source told me'," he read, unfolding the page to see more.

"It doesn't make sense, right enough," said Craig, "but I don't see how it helps."

Isla was drying her hair with the towel, and now sat down at the table. "But if Slinn — whoever — was perfecting his technique, getting better at his murders, neater and tidier, I mean, why would he go from using a hammer to mashing the next one's head with a dirty great rock? And then back to the hammer."

Craig was reading more of Jordan's *Courier* report. "Listen to this," he said. "'When I visited the scene, I was struck by the beauty of the idyllic spot the killer had chosen. Amid majestic pines, sandstone rocks mark out the parking area where Mr Narloch's mutilated remains were discovered. Those rocks are now forever stained by his blood.'"

"It's like Jordan's writing a novel," said Isla.

"He's been to the crime scene," Flint said, sitting forward. "If Jordan—"

"You mean Jordan did the Tentsmuir one? Isla said, shaking her head. "But Slinn was still alive."

Flint shrugged. "It might explain the difference." He reached for *The Courier* and read Jordan's words for himself. "Is the bastard bragging about it?"

Isla said, "But I don't get *why* Jordan would be involved. And anyway, there's nothing to say there's any connection between him and Slinn."

"Erm — maybe there is," said Craig. He was holding the flyer advertising Slinn's lecture, reading the flip side. "I didn't notice there was anything on the back. There's a load of quotes from other professors and folk, saying how smart Slinn is."

"What of it? He was trying to get more private patients," said Flint.

"Aye, but listen to this one: 'I interviewed Dr Slinn in his office near Dundee, and he told me in layman's terms about his fascinating work with survivors of abuse.'"

"So? Someone gave him an endorsement." Isla shrugged.

"The quote is from 'Tom Jordan, Investigative Journalist'." Craig looked up, wide-eyed and mouth open.

347

"So they *do* know each other." Isla reached for the flyer. "Or did, I suppose."

Flint felt a rush of excitement. "Jordan's written about the killings, and been to Slinn's office. And to Tentsmuir!"

Craig sat back from the table. "God! That's it. It's been bugging the life out of me." They both looked at him.

"What?"

"I couldn't remember what it was. I knew we saw something else weird at Tentsmuir. I've remembered now." He looked relieved, and they both waited for him to go on. "That bouquet on the tree. Sorry, probably nothing."

Flint explained to Isla about their trip to Tentsmuir two weeks before, and the thistles tied with baler twine.

"This Tentsmuir, is it far from here?"

"Not far. It was one of my driving lessons. Over the Tay Bri—"

"Let's go today. We might get some ideas." She was on her feet.

"But why?" Flint shrugged again.

"I've just got a feeling about it," said Isla.

Chapter 56

Of the three of them, Craig was the least enthusiastic. As his car proceeded down the winding road through the trees he said, "I still think this is a waste of time. I don't want to spend long here."

"Are you scared, Craig?" Flint was laughing. He was just happy to be driving again, pleased that he was managing better than last time.

"It is a bit creepy," Isla said. "Especially knowing…"

As the track approached the clearing near the beach and the trees thinned, Isla leaned forward from the back seat.

"But this is beautiful. Look at that beach." The sky had cleared, and sunshine lit the white sand, the sea beyond it navy blue below a pale sky. Flint stopped the car at the edge of the parking area. There were a handful of other vehicles, and an elderly couple were trying to coax their spaniel into a Vauxhall.

"It's hard to believe something so awful happened here," said Isla, opening the door.

"I'm just going to stay in the car," said Craig. He looked at his watch. "It's nearly one o'clock. Don't be long. We still need to drive back to Aberdeen and I want to see Mo tonight."

Flint and Isla strolled across the clearing and as they neared the beach she took his hand.

"It's lovely here, but I don't like it," she said.

"That doesn't make sense."

She pulled his hand. "Let's not stay long."

Flint had hoped to have a walk to the water's edge. The tide was receding, the sky reflected in the flat, wet sand.

"What's the hurry? Just a wee walk?"

She pulled him round. "No, let's go."

Heading back in the direction of the car Flint said, "What's the matter?"

"I don't know. I just feel…" She picked up the pace.

"I know that man was killed here, but it was over a year ago."

"It's not just that," Isla said. "It was me that wanted to come here. It seemed important. But now I'm here, I don't like it."

Flint shrugged and walked along with her. They were halfway back to the car when she stopped and turned to him. She lowered her voice. "There's something else about this place. I can feel it. Don't tell Craig, he'll think I'm mad. But this place is important."

Flint looked at her. His face didn't know which expression to display.

"And it's not just because Mr Narloch died here. I think whoever killed him has been here again."

"Like Jordan? He wrote about being here in the paper."

"Maybe. But it's something more than that. I can feel it."

Flint said nothing but squeezed her hand. He was glad when they resumed walking.

Craig had wound down the car window. As they approached, he pointed to the edge of the clearing. "Look."

They both turned towards the trees.

"Fuck!" Flint said. He let go of Isla's hand and walked a few paces to his right. On the tree where he and Craig had seen the bouquet of thistles hung a bunch of purple tulips, suspended upside down by the same blue, nylon baler twine. The dry thistles were scattered amongst pine needles below.

"D'you think it's like a 'calling card'? Don't serial killers do that?" Isla asked when they were passing through Tayport.

"But why return and update it? Why would he do that?" Craig had regained some of his enthusiasm. "It means Jordan's been back here. How old d'you think the flowers were?"

"No more than a day or so. The petals were still quite firm."

"Jordan was back here. Yesterday."

None of them spoke again until they were on the Tay Bridge.

"How old were the thistles?" Isla asked.

"They were last year's. They had the remains of old flowers on them. They flower late summer, and because they are moderately well lignified they last a long time when cut, although they obviously lose their colour quite soon. That's why the remnants would have survived as recognisable, even after the winter."

Flint saw Craig looking askance from the passenger seat.

"I just meant roughly, Mr Botany Man," said Isla, laughing. Flint felt his face heating.

"I suppose I meant they were probably hung there late last summer."

"Narloch died the previous January. And Jordan was back at Tentsmuir last summer. Why?" Craig turned round to face Isla.

"I don't know. I'm just sure there's something important about that place."

"Something's making Jordan keep going there," said Flint.

Craig turned back, sighing. "It's still all a waste of our time. We can't do anything. We don't know who's next for the knife."

Chapter 57

It was nearly two-thirty before Flint pulled up outside Jack's flat. The door was unlocked and Craig called out, "That you home, Jack?"

Jack came out of the living room.

"Where have you been? I've been waiting to give you your present." He wore a sly grin, and nodded towards the living room.

"What?" said Craig, nervously opening the door. Jack was known for his practical jokes.

"On the table."

It was a sheet of paper.

"Christ! How did you get this? Flint, Isla, look."

Jack smiled as he spoke. "When Flint showed me the links to Tom Jordan I couldn't stop thinking about it."

Flint and Isla had joined Craig at the table.

"Is that the list from Professor Slinn's desk?" Isla looked at Flint, who was already sitting at the table running his finger down the names.

"It fucking is, yes. Brilliant!"

Craig persisted. "But how did you get it, Jack?"

"I was alone in the office for a while. I phoned Grampian. Said I was working on the Currid case and that my bosses were looking into a possible connection to Slinn."

Craig was shaking his head. "But—"

"It's OK. I got a civilian clerk who was really helpful. I think she liked me. I asked her if there was anything in Slinn's files from Liff that listed his patients."

"Fucking hell, Jack," Craig said, sitting back.

"She said there were a few. She looked through them all for Currid's name. She knew that was the Dundee case. She faxed me the two lists she found. One was the same long list you've already got, although this version had dates of appointments handwritten down the side. I shredded it so no-one would find it. I guessed it was this short list you were looking for." Jack looked pleased with himself.

"Currid's on it," said Flint. "And Skilling, Narloch, Thake."

"Gaska?" asked Craig. He was still staring at Jack.

"Aye. They're all here," said Flint. "And some I don't recognise."

Jack left the flat soon after to play football. "I don't want to know any more," he'd said. But before he closed the door he called over his shoulder, "Just go and catch the bastard."

The three of them now sat round the little table with both lists side by side, and Slinn's briefcase open on the floor.

"Is that definitely the list you saw?" asked Craig.

"Aye. I told you there were more scored off." He was running his finger down the list. "There's a Fenton, and a Beveridge."

Craig was counting on his fingers. "Six dead. Bloody hell."

"Seven."

Flint and Craig now both looked at Isla. She went on, "You forgot Currid. He's there, but he's not scored out." She pulled the longer list they'd found in Slinn's case closer to her and pointed. "Look. Currid's on both, that's why the clerk gave two lists to Jack." She concentrated on the long list, moving her finger slowly down the names, before turning over to continue. Flint was distracted for a moment by her green eyes.

"We need to focus on the short list," said Craig. The ones who've not been — erm — scored out."

"Hang on, Alex Narloch's not on the long list," said Isla. All the others are."

"He's on the short list, though, the *kill list*. And scored out," said Flint.

"There's something different about Narloch. I know it."

"Woman's intuition?" Flint grinned.

"Don't take the piss, Flint, I told you, that Tentsmuir place —"

"Can we just stick to this, for fuck's sake?" Craig slapped the short list down, covering the other.

When Flint had glanced at the list in Slinn's desk drawer in Liff Hospital, the names Skilling, Narloch and Gaska had jumped out at him, the rest a blur. Now, focused on it, he could see there was a total of eight names.

"We can cross off Robert Currid," he said, looking across the table at Isla and Craig.

"Only one alive," murmured Isla.

"Jordan will be going for this bloke now," said Craig, "James McWatt. We've got to find him."

All three were silent until Flint exhaled and let his head drop forward. "Could be anywhere in Scotland. We've no chance."

"We can't give up," said Isla.

"I'm going to make a call," said Craig, and went out into the hallway.

"We've got no chance. He could be anywhere."

"Stop saying that, Flint." Isla drew the two lists toward her, muttering, "Let me look at these again." Flint watched her, one finger on the long list and the other pointing to one of the dead men's names. The tip of her tongue was protruding between her pursed lips, the way it sometimes did when she was deep in thought.

"The dates of birth on the kill list are different. The men's." She reached for the *Daily Record* page from the briefcase. "Yup. Cornelius Thake, 61." She was talking to herself now. "He died in 1978, aged 61. Born in..." She looked at the list again. "Yes! Born 8th March 1917."

She sat back, a satisfied grin lighting her face.

"Well done. But I don't see how it helps."

"No, but it shows we can find out more from these lists. Don't give up."

Flint sat forward. "Oh God."

"What?"

"It's obvious. Why didn't I realise? The connection's Fife. Slinn worked in Fife. Stratheden Hospital, Dr Sutton said. That's where he started his clinic. All the abuse victims came from Fife."

"But their fathers have moved all over," said Isla. "Mr Skilling was in Aberdeen, Gaska was Stirling. One of them was near Oban, for God's sake."

"Fife's got to be the most likely, though. That's where we should start. At least there's a chance we might get to the mannie McWatt before Jordan."

Isla looked uncertain, but reached for the *Record* article again. "I suppose it does say here 'Thake, who lives in Oban, was known to have moved to the west from Leven, Fife, some years ago. He lived alone.'"

"Fife it is, then?"

"Fife it is." Isla shrugged.

Flint grinned, winking. "We make a good team. The woman does the donkey work and the man does the brainwork, eh?"

She punched his arm, and he giggled, grabbing her.

"Fife it is," Craig said as he came back in. Flint and Isla stopped mid-embrace, looking at him with questioning expressions. "I've just phoned the P&J. Tom Jordan is in Fife. Working on a big story, they said."

They both gawped at Craig, who was grinning. "I told them who I am. PC Masson. Said I was following up on something and needed to speak to Jordan."

"He's in Fife?" Flint looked at Craig, then Isla.

Craig sat down at the table. "He's going for Mr McWatt."

"McWatt could live somewhere else, though," Isla said.

"It's possible, yeah, but everything points to Fife. Anyway, we might not have time to look wider," said Flint.

"We might be too late already," Craig said, reaching for the list, "but even if we are, we need to find Jordan. And McWatt's the only target still alive."

"Is there a phone book in the flat?" Isla had stood up and was looking out into the hall. "There's not one by the phone."

"I've seen one somewhere," said Craig. "I think it was when I was rummaging about in Jack's room. Why?"

"We could look up all the McWatts."

Craig found the tattered phone book holding up a leg of Jack's bed. He brought it through to the living room shaking his head. "Shite. It's just the Dundee one. There'll only be a few Fife numbers in it."

"I'm going to make a quick phone call," said Flint. "Anyone got a pen?"

His call was answered after two rings. "Auchmoor 2764."

"Hello, Mum. It's Flint."

"Gordon? Where are you? Are you alright?"

Eleanor Flint's questions kept coming, and Flint knew he just had to let her finish.

"Sadie said she'd seen your name in the *Press and Journal*. What has been going on? I've been frantic, Gordon."

"Erm, sorry, Mum. It's a long story." As he said it, he heard his words echoing on the phone line. *It's a long story.* Before she asked to hear it, he rushed on. "Mum, can you look something up in the phone book for me?"

After several more 'What are you up to?'s and 'What's going on?'s, he heard and pictured Eleanor reaching to take the phone book from its shelf under the telephone table in the hallway. Between her mutterings he heard the pages turning. "McPake". A few pages forward. "McWilliam." A page turning back. "Ah, McWatt. Ooh, there's a lot." Flint was shifting his weight back and forth between his feet, and gripping the receiver tight.

"Look for J. McWatt, Mum. Or James."

"You still haven't told me what this is all about. Is he a friend of — ah — here we are."

Flint dropped to the floor under the wall phone and held his pen ready. "Can you read me out the address and phone number, Mum?"

"There are three. Well, one James and two Js. Which one?"

"All of them. Please." Flint's jaw was beginning to cramp. He tried to unclench his teeth.

"Gordon, don't be so impatient."

"Who's going to phone them?" asked Craig.

"I'll do it." Isla took the scrap of paper Flint had written the details on. "Which one first?"

"Try the James. The Auchtermuchty one."

Craig and Flint gathered round Isla at the wall phone.

"Hello?" A woman's voice. There were noisy children in the background. "Be quiet! I'm on the phone."

"Erm, hello, is James McWatt there, please?" Isla glanced at Flint and Craig. Flint thought there was a slight tremor in her voice.

"Hang on, he's in the garden fixing the pram. JAMES!" Isla shrank back from the phone. The voice went on. "He'll be in just the now. It's mental here, sorry, we've just had another baby and the other two are driving me — Tommy! Get down off there."

"Sorry to have bothered you, I think I've got the wrong number," said Isla, her finger ready to dial the next number.

"Hello. Who's there?" A refined, female voice.

"Hello, I wonder if I can speak to J. McWatt, please?"

"I am she. Miss Jemima McWatt. Now, who is this and what do you want? Are you selling something?"

"I'm sorry. Wrong number."

Isla was giggling when she ended the call, quickly dialling the third number.

Long, nervous minutes later, she shrugged, lowering the receiver. "It's no use. There's no one there."

They sat at the table, silent until Flint took the list. "It can only be this one." He scored off Jemima and young James from Auchtermuchty.

"What do we do?" said Isla.

"We go to his door. It's all we can do," said Craig.

"What if he's not there?" said Flint.

"What if he *is* there? What do we say?" Isla was frowning, shaking her head.

"We ask him if he has a daughter," said Craig, "and take it from there. We've got to do something if he really is Jordan's next victim."

Chapter 58

The rush hour traffic meant it was after five o'clock before they were even on the Tay Bridge. As Flint pulled off the roundabout at the entry point to Fife and started up the dual carriageway, Isla spoke.

"What if it's not him? There might be other James McWatts who're not on the phone."

"Or ex-directory," said Flint.

"Listen," said Craig. "We've got to do something. We only know of three J McWatts, and one of them's too young and the other's called fucking Jemima."

Flint laughed, but soon they were quiet again.

As they neared Dairsie, Isla asked, "Will we have to drive past The Mount?"

"It's hard not to see it from anywhere round Cupar, but we won't be near it." Flint glanced at Isla in the back seat.

"Eyes on the road. My car, remember."

"I don't want to think about it," said Isla.

"Like old times, though, eh? The three of us chasing around Fife," Flint said. "Depending on which way we go I could let you have another look at Cupar Police Station if you like?" He laughed.

"Don't remind me," said Isla.

"It's OK. There's another way."

"What time is it," Isla asked. "My watch has stopped."

"Twenty-to-six."

Cupar was busy with traffic, and Flint turned left off Bonnygate.

"Where are you going?" asked Craig. "I thought we had to go past Cupar?"

"Quicker this way."

"You wouldn't think so," said Craig. Just after the turn off they had to sit and wait for a reversing Danskins Transport lorry to manoeuvre its way into a yard.

A few minutes later, though, Flint turned into a narrow road between tall hedges. "Drum Road," he said.

"This is it? There's nothing here." Craig said.

"Cupar Muir's just at the bottom of the brae. Just a few farm cottages and a couple of workshops," said Flint, heading down the sloping road.

"There must have been a quarry somewhere," said Craig.

"It's so dark," said Isla. "It's not even six." Heavy-looking, black clouds were gathering.

No. 1 Quarry Cottages was at the foot of the slope. Two low-set houses adjoining each other were the first dwellings they came to. As they approached, ahead of them a dark green Austin 1100 pulled out of a narrow driveway beside No. 2 and drove away. Flint noticed its exhaust was hanging off.

They parked in a farm gateway past the cottages. Craig turned round to look back at James McWatt's house.

"Well. Now we're here we'd better get it over with," he said opening the car door. His cast caught on the sill and he nearly fell. "Fuck!"

"I'll go, Craig," said Flint, climbing out.

"I'm not going to have to run anywhere," said Craig. "Fucking leg."

"Stay with the car, Craig," said Isla, also getting out. Flint stared at her in surprise, and she went on, "I'm not letting you go on your own."

They walked thirty yards or so back along to the cottages. A wooden gate hung between overgrown privet hedges. As Flint swung it open he thought it might fall apart. Green-painted woodwork around the sash windows was flaking and cracked, the door the same.

"God, imagine living here," whispered Isla.

Flint knocked and they stood back from the step. A wind was getting up, ivy around the door rustling.

"Come on. Answer the door, Mr McWatt. I think it's going to rain." Flint realised he was opening and closing his hands. He knocked again, louder this time. There were no lights on and the only sound was the Crossroads theme tune from an open window next door.

"He's not in." Isla turned to go.

"I suppose we can wait in the car and try again later," Flint said, following her down the weedy, crazy-paving path.

"Are you looking for Jimmy?"

Flint jumped. He hadn't realised how tense he was.

"Hello. Jimmy's not in."

When he turned round, a short woman with white hair and a cigarette was on the doorstep of the adjoining house. It had fresher paintwork but the number 2 above the door hung upside down on one screw.

"Oh, hello, yes. Sorry." Flint was turning away again when the voice went on.

The woman had stepped onto a path worn into the turf between the front doors.

"You just missed him. He's gone to meet his daughter." She took the cigarette out of her mouth. "He got another letter from her yesterday. He's excited, hasnae seen her for years." She paused, and looked down at her hands. "He's not a bad man really."

"Oh, right, thanks."

"Who are you?" She was looking at Isla, who was at the gate. "Are you his daughter? Didn't he find you?" She started coughing.

"No. No. Sorry. I think we got the wrong house. Sorry."

Flint put his hands up in apology as he backed away. Isla was beckoning him through the gate. She had a folded piece of paper in her hand.

###

Rain hammering on the car roof made it hard to hear. In the seconds it had taken to walk and run back to the car, the sky had darkened further, huge raindrops dotting the dry road.

"You found it where?" Craig said, his eyes on the letter in his lap.

"It was under the bushes by the gate. He must have dropped it. I picked it up while the woman next door was talking to Flint."

"She said he was excited," said Flint.

"Thank God we found it before the rain started. Let me read it again." Isla reached through between the front seats. "'I'm ready to meet you, Dad', she says. Then 'Friday evening at Scotstarvit. Park by the main road, facing Craigrothie where I'll see you. I'll come after work. Wait if I'm late'."

"At least if he's gone out to meet her, Jordan won't get to him if he's not at home," Flint said.

"Jordan — or Slinn *and* Jordan — don't kill them at home. They kill them in their cars," Craig said.

"I think we've got something wrong here," said Isla. "I mean, I don't know why Jordan would get involved. If somehow he knew Slinn was working through a list of abuse victims to kill their fathers, he'd report it, not keep it going. It's too far-fetched."

"I know, but he's connected to Slinn, and he's been to at least one of the murder sites," said Flint.

"There's something not right," said Isla. "Tell me again how you know Jordan, Craig."

Craig explained briefly about meeting Tom Jordan in the pub in Edinburgh and telling him about the Limb Collector. "He did a big article on the cases and how the police hadn't linked them."

She said, "Maybe he got a taste for it, and hooked up with Slinn so he could get the scoops on Slinn's murders."

Flint was rolling his eyes and shaking his head.

Isla shrugged back at him. "There's got to be something we can do," she said.

Craig was still holding the letter. "If you were writing to your estranged father you hadn't seen for years," he said, looking at Isla, "it would be very personal, right?"

"I suppose so, but I—"

"Would you type it?"

"No, of course not. But — oh, I see what you mean." She looked at the letter on Craig's lap. "But how does—?"

"Skilling's letter — the one from his daughter — was typed as well. I saw it in the file. I thought it was a bit odd. And I think it was on the same sort of paper as this. Same size and colour, anyway."

"Let me see again," said Flint, taking the letter. "It's signed. 'Sarah'. That's handwritten."

"Signatures are easy to copy," said Craig. "And Jack's notes about Harkan Gaska said something about a letter."

"Maybe Jordan has been writing to the fathers. Then luring them to meet him?" said Craig.

"Or Slinn. Or both of them," Flint said.

"Oh, for God's sake," Isla hissed, "we're going round in circles. We're all taking turns at being the one with doubts." She grabbed the letter from Flint, who wound down the window.

"The car's steaming up. At least the rain's gone off."

"Where's Scotstarvit?" Isla asked.

"No idea," said Craig.

"It's got to be Scotstarvit Tower. It's near Craigrothie," said Flint. "I used to go there on cycle runs."

"We can't go there. The man's meeting his daughter." Craig looked at Flint, and then round at Isla. "Can we?"

"You just said Jordan was luring the men, pretending to be the daughter," said Isla.

Flint started the car.

Chapter 59

Turning a hairpin bend after climbing a long hill, Flint said, "When you're cycling up the Sandy Brae you know when you reach this bit you're nearly at the top. The tower's just along there to the right."

"I can't believe you cycled up here," said Craig.

"You're a soft city boy," Flint laughed.

It was nearly ten minutes after they left Cupar Muir, and Isla had been quiet. "This Scotstarvit Tower, it's not going to be like The Mount?" she asked.

"Nah. There's a wee parking bit by the main road. I bet that's where they're meeting."

Flint slowed the car as it entered a shady stretch between tall beech trees and stone walls. On the right, the wall curved inwards, forming a semicircle broken by the entrance to a track. There was space for three or four cars to park, but only one sat on gravel under the dripping tree canopy. It was the green Austin they'd seen leaving Quarry Cottages.

"You can't park beside him," said Craig.

After turning the car in a farm entrance, Flint drove back past the Austin. They parked outside a field gate, on the hairpin bend they'd rounded minutes before.

"What do we do?" asked Craig.

"There was only one person in the car. Jordan hasn't got to him yet," said Isla. "But we can't just sit here."

Inside, Flint was churning. It wasn't like The Mount. That time he'd been knocked unconscious and kidnapped by a crazed killer. This time things were calmer. He had a choice.

Isla seemed to read his mind. "Shouldn't we just go and get the Police?"

Her words seemed to affect him like a shot of adrenaline. In milliseconds, his mind flashed images: severed testicles; the kill list; Slinn's pumping blood; Stiff's broken body; DCI Blackie shouting at him; a purple tulip bouquet. The mental slide show ended with the exhaust hanging off James McWatt's car as he waited for a daughter who wouldn't arrive.

Flint looked at Craig, then turned round to Isla. "No time," he said, opening the car door. "You stay here. Craig'n'me'll go and have a look. He's the cop, and he'll manage to limp along."

"We can get a bit closer," Flint whispered.

Keeping low, they had scrambled along the edge of a field, brushing against dripping potato plants and long grass.

"Bloody mud!"

"Ssh."

Now in shade of the trees, Flint crept on his hunkers towards the car park wall, stopping when he thought he was opposite McWatt's car.

"What are we going to be able to do from here?" murmured Craig, catching up.

"When Jordan arrives, we wait until he approaches the car then jump over and tackle him. Got your police badge?"

Craig patted his pocket. "Yes, but I don't see me jumping a wall." His cast was caked in claggy, clay mud.

###

Isla sat in the car, staring after Flint and Craig. They'd moved out of view and she thought they must be near the car park by now. Her left leg was shaking, and she held it with both hands trying to calm herself.

"I can't stay here," she said out loud, opening the car and hurrying up the slope towards the main road.

"What does Jordan drive?" Flint whispered, sneaking a look over the wall.

"No idea."

"A yellow car's coming. Pulling into the car park." Flint lowered himself. Through gaps between the stones topping the wall, he could see the back of the green Austin. He heard the other car on the gravel, slowing to a stop, its engine still running.

"I can't see if it's him," he whispered. He edged his head up an inch.

"Fuck!" he hissed, ducking down.

"Did he see you?" Craig asked with his eyes.

"It's a fucking woman," whispered Flint. "Just sitting there. She'll scare Jordan off."

"Maybe it *is* his daughter."

They heard music, a radio jingle. Seconds later it quietened when a car door clunked shut.

"She's getting out." Flint turned to Craig shrugging, his eyebrows tilted. "What…?" he mouthed. Turning back, between the gaps he could see a slight figure in black walking towards the Austin. A young woman, with blonde, almost white hair, and a leather bag in her left hand. The daughter?

Isla walked along the road looking for the Scotstarvit Tower signpost. She'd seen it earlier, on the right. The first sign she came to pointed left. 'Hill of Tarvit', and underneath, 'Marie Curie Home'. She hadn't noticed it from the car, but a few paces on the Scotstarvit sign came into view. The sound of a car engine behind her made her dodge between the wall and a gorse bush. A yellow car passed, before pulling off to the right where Isla knew James McWatt's car was. She quickened her pace.

Time seemed to slow. Flint watched the blonde woman walk in between the car and the wall, just a few feet away from him. She reached into the bag, taking something in her right hand. The bag dropped to the ground beside the car. She tapped on the car window, and the driver flinched. Turning towards her, he smiled, wound down the window and pointed to a large pink hearing aid behind his right ear. McWatt hadn't heard the woman approach. His smile changed to a look of confusion. Then horror. He drew back from the window he was still winding down.

The woman lifted a gun, pointing it straight towards McWatt's head. She extended her elbow to reach inside the car. Point blank.

Flint's legs propelled him over the wall. His voice screaming, "NO!"

Isla peeked past the corner of the wall where it curved in to enclose the parking area. A yellow Mini Clubman sat behind McWatt's car. A dark figure was leaning towards the Austin's front window.

Flint's head and torso shot up above the wall. She saw him scream out before the sound reached her. He dived over, disappearing between the cars and the wall. As Isla ran forward, she saw Craig clamber awkwardly over the wall, falling flat just as a blonde head rose between the cars. Ducking behind the Mini, Isla peered through the car's windows. A slight, black-clad girl was scurrying towards her, holding a gun. As if in slow motion, Craig scrabbled up to a crouch, lunging forward as the girl passed him. She body swerved his attempt to rugby tackle her.

Beyond, motionless on the gravel beside the green car, Isla could now see Flint. Prone, his legs were at odd angles, his head to one side. There was a red stain on his temple.

Isla screamed. The girl reached the yellow car, pulling the door open. The radio was playing, engine running. Desperate to stop Flint's killer, Isla darted forward, grabbing the passenger door of the mini as it started to move off. Still screaming she threw herself into the moving car. The woman swung a black handgun up to meet Isla's forehead, and fired.

As the mini drove away with gravel spraying from its front wheels, Craig pushed himself up to stand. Turning, he saw Flint on the ground. Above him in the Austin, James McWatt was slumped, his hands holding his chest, face contorted and lips blue. There was vomit on his chin and shoulder.

Craig crouched down, shaking Flint.

"Flint! Flint!" There was a bloody mark on his head, a triangular, oozing graze.

Flint's eyes opened, glazed and rolling. He moaned, raising a hand to his temple. "What happened?" His body jerked alive and he tried to sit up.

"She's gone," Craig said. "Who the hell was she?"

Flint pushed himself up against the Austin, still rubbing his head. "Dunno." He frowned at Craig, craned to try and see McWatt, then looked back at Craig. "But I think I might have seen her before."

"Where?"

Flint shook his head, moved it back and forward a little, and peered. "I can see you now. Fuck, what happened?"

"She hit you on the hea—"

"She had a gun!" Flint jumped up. "She had a gun!"

Craig grabbed Flint by the shoulders. "Flint, she took Isla."

"What? From the car? What?" He was looking back across the field to where Craig's car was.

"No, Flint, Isla came here. She tried to stop the woman. Flint, I think Isla was shot."

Flint shook Craig away and ran towards the road, in the direction of Craig's car. A van passed as he emerged from the car park, swerving, horn blaring.

"Fuck off!" he shouted after it, still running.

Craig looked at McWatt, who was now sitting back, holding the steering wheel and breathing heavily. Turning, Craig hobbled along behind Flint, mud falling off his cast.

"Flint. Don't go without me."

Chapter 60

Adrenaline did its work again, clearing Flint's head. He had to get to Isla, and he had an idea.

Craig was just arriving at the junction with the main road as Flint drove up to it.

"Are you OK to drive, Flint?"

"Get in. I need your help. Get in!"

They set off down the long slope towards Cupar, Flint leaning forward over the steering wheel.

"She's got a fucking gun. It must've been the gun she hit me with. She fucking shot Isla? I'll fucking kill her!" He was spitting the words.

"Slow down a bit, Flint, you'll kill us."

He sped up.

"What the hell, Flint? Where are we going?"

"I know who she is," he said, throwing the car round a bend. "We've got to find out where she's gone with Isla."

"Who is she?"

"Slinn's secretary. I saw her at Liff. It's definitely her. She's the link to Slinn. And all the men."

"But how's Jordan involved?"

"Fuck knows. Who cares?" They'd stopped at a junction. Flint hammered the steering wheel, shouting, "Get a fucking move on!" at an approaching Kirkcaldy-bound bus. "Aw, fuck it," he said, screeching out across the main road in front of the oncoming bus, before accelerating towards the centre of Cupar.

A few seconds later he stopped the car outside a little shop opposite a Y-junction. Craig saw a sign for Ceres and a stream of traffic splitting either side of a small off-white cottage on the corner.

"Phone box," Flint said. "Change?" A red telephone box stood outside the shop.

Craig handed over a pile of coins from his pocket. "But we don't need money for 999 calls," said Craig, surprising himself at how quickly he was able to exit the car.

"It's Jack I want to call," said Flint.

Craig reached the heavy door of the call-box before Flint, and insisted on calling an ambulance for James McWatt. As soon as he put the receiver down Flint pulled him out of the box and said, "Jack's number."

Craig reeled off the number from memory. Flint dialled, pounding his fist against the directory board on the wall in front of him.

"Jack?" he shouted, ramming in two 10p coins to stop the pips. "Jack!" He punched the air and mouthed 'he's in!' to Craig who was standing holding the door. "Jack write this down. It's important."

Flint read out the number of the call box first, and then told Jack to ring Liff Hospital and get the name and address of Professor Slinn's secretary.

"They'll never give that out," said Jack.

"Just fucking get it. Quick. We're waiting here for you to call back. Do it!" He slammed the receiver down.

While they waited, Craig had to show his warrant card to a red-faced man who wanted to make a call.

"You're not a polis. Look at you!" red face said.

Flint opened the callbox door to say, "Just fuck off!"

The phone rang.

"Jack, tell me now," Flint said after one ring.

"I had to tell the evening receptionist I was investigating the death of Professor Slinn and needed some inform——"

"Shut up, Jack. The name and address."

Minutes later Flint had turned the car and they headed west out of Cupar.

"Where are we going?" asked Craig.

Flint's mind was racing. *Roza Fraser!* In Liff Hospital, he'd heard her say, 'I'm Rosa. I used to work for both of them.'

"She told me her name when I met her in Slinn's office," he said, more to himself than in answer to Craig's question. "Lives in Pitlessie."

"But we don't know that's where she's gone," Craig was holding on to the car seat as Flint accelerated.

"You got a better idea?" said Flint.

"But she could be anywhere."

"You got a better idea?"

Chapter 61

Every part of her hurt, but her head was worst. She had the impression she was sitting, but she might have been upside down for all she knew. She drifted into unconsciousness again.

The next thing Isla became aware of was a voice. Not talking to her, and only one voice, but a continuous flow of words. Someone talking to themself? Herself? It became clearer as she was able to concentrate on it.

"Who?...it should be done...where did they?...over the wall?...who?...what am I going to..?"

When she remembered she had eyes, Isla forced them open. That tiny movement brought pain rushing to the front of her head. Before she snapped them shut, she saw a shadow to her left. Small. Pacing.

Then nothingness again.

The next time she roused there was silence. She had an itch she had to get to, but didn't know where it was. It strengthened to become a searing, caustic irritation. Her arms. She had to scratch them.

I can't move my arms.

Her fingers gripped something smooth, hard. Wood?

Awareness seeped in, diluting her pain. A beating started in her chest.

Where am I?

Opening her eyes was not so bad next time. The pacing shadow had gone. Dim light came from her right, through cracks in a shuttered window.

Fraying twine bound her wrists to the wooden arms of a chair, the cause of the itch still demanding to be scratched. And her bottom was sore, like it was grazed. An absurd laugh rose in her, a strangled hiccough escaping into her gagged mouth.

A voice behind her.

"You're awake?"

Isla moaned into fabric. Footsteps. Hands at her neck, scruffling. The gag falling away and her own coughing. And coughing, and slumping.

"Who are you?" The voice was closer, to her left. Then, "Who? Why were you there?" Isla felt hot breath, and inhaled perfume.

As her eyes adjusted to the dimness, a little figure took form, gliding over to a huge armchair. A woman, definitely, but slight. Her hair grabbed attention. A frizz of blonde — no, white — curls, surrounding a small, pale face with black doll's eyes. Isla had seen her somewhere before.

"Where did you..? Who are you..?" the woman asked, fidgeting with her hands.

She's nervous, thought Isla. Poor thing.

Poor thing? She tied me up. Where am I?

"Why did you get in my car?" The voice sounded tinny, speech pressured. "I had to deal with you somehow. I had to drag you out. Had to make sure nosey neighbour Mike didn't see me."

She dragged me. My sore backside.

Fraser continued. "You jumped into my car. But I was leaving." She paused. "And was someone hiding behind the wall?"

A yellow car. A mini. The memories flooded back. The wall. The girl in black. That's where I saw her. The gun coming towards her face. *Flint! Oh God!*

"Who are you? Let me go!" Isla made her voice work but she wasn't sure if it made sound. Her head reeled, her wrists fighting against the bindings. She screamed, and the woman rose from the chair.

"Shut up!" Small hands took the nylon scarf from Isla's lap, retying it. "My bitch mother's. No help from her." Isla wailed. The woman was whispering as she pulled the gag even tighter. "Ssshh. There's a car outside."

"You know where it is?"

"I know Burnside. Malt Place must branch off it. That's how the address reads," said Flint.

Flint slowed as they approached Pitlessie, turning right opposite the maltings with its three paGoda roof peaks.

"Burnside's just up here," he said. After passing low stone cottages on the left and flat fields to the east, Flint turned slowly into an unmade side road. Malt Place. Beyond two houses, the yellow mini was parked outside a squat, sandstone dwelling with shuttered windows. Flint drew in behind the mini, outside a derelict workshop, its peeling plank door askew. He stopped the engine, and above recent rain dripping from gutters, heard a muffled wail.

"Did you hear that?" Flint threw the car door open.

Isla watched the girl-woman standing in front of her. Wringing her hands, she was trembling, looking from side to side as if seeking escape. Her captor's fear seemed to overflow into Isla. She couldn't breathe, but her chest was inflating. I'm going to wet myself.

Loud rapping on the door. Shouting. "Isla! Isla!"

Flint!

She exhaled at last, another strangled moan escaping through the choking gag.

More bangs on the door.

"This is the Police. Roza Fraser! Unlock this door!"

Footsteps and shouting. Banging, crashing, louder. The shutters splitting. More light. Glass breaking.

"Isla!"

Flint's body crashed through the window and landed on the floor.

Isla watched as he got up onto his knees, his desperate eyes fixed on hers.

Roza Fraser strode towards Flint, held the gun to his head, and fired. Flint slumped to the side, his body jerking weakly for only a moment before he became deathly still.

Chapter 62

Craig's foot caught on the splintered shutters as he pushed himself through the smashed window. He fell onto the floor, his warrant card held outstretched. "Police," he said, scrambling up to stand.

Isla was tied to a chair. The blonde girl, Roza Fraser he now knew, stood behind Isla. Her delicate right hand pressed the gun to Isla's head, while the left held the point of a carving knife to her neck.

To Craig's left, Flint lay flat out, head to one side and eyes open, his mouth frothy. Craig started to walk towards Flint, bending down.

"Leave him. He'll be OK soon." The girl had a sing-song voice, and Craig felt compelled to stand back.

"You shot him," he said.

Isla was moaning through the gag, tears streaming down her face. The gun was still pressed to her temple, and Fraser was now pointing the blade at Craig.

"How d'you think I got those men to lie still while I cut them? I wanted them alive. To suffer."

Craig's confusion must have shown. Fraser went on, "You still haven't worked it out, have you?"

Isla struggled against her bindings. Fraser looked down at her, gesturing towards Flint with the knife point. "I guess that's your boyfriend?" There was a sneer in the tinny voice. "He'll live. It's only a stun gun."

Isla's eyes didn't leave Flint, who wasn't moving.

Craig said, "You admit killing those men? All of them?" He edged half a pace towards Isla and Fraser.

"Stay where you are!" Fraser swung the blade back to Isla's neck.

"OK. OK." Craig put his hands up, and Fraser lowered the knife, until a tense, furious, frightened look took over her face. Looking quickly side to side, waving the knife again, she jabbered. "How did you know? Be quiet. I need to work out... I haven't finished... you lot interfering... my plans... bastard McWatt..."

She paused, then grinned, but with dead eyes. "I can't kill all of *you* as well? Can I?" Craig could see her thinking, biting her lip. *She's totally insane. This could go either way.*

Flint moaned. In the corner of his eye Craig could see he still wasn't moving. He kept his focus on Fraser. If he could help her work out what to do it might buy them some time. She doesn't want to kill us, he told himself.

"You worked for Professor, Slinn?"

"Yes, the great man." Her face changed again, sardonic now.

"You didn't like him?"

"Oh, I liked him. He was gorgeous, obviously, and great to me, but..."

"But?" This was good. She was engaging in a dialogue with him. Craig's only training in negotiation was the brief notes they'd been given at Tulliallan.

"He only did half the job. I know he couldn't do more, but someone had to finish it for us." Fraser was looking at Craig, but talking to herself. "We were still left with the cause."

"We?"

She looked at Craig now as if he was stupid.

"Us. The victims. Slinn thought he'd cured us, '*helped us accept, adjust*'," she sneered. "But the cause was never addressed. The bastards who raped us were still alive."

"I'm sorry if you were abused," said Craig.

"Sorry? Sorry!" She laughed.

Craig shrugged.

Her anger was back. "If I was abused? If! The one who raped me every time he could was the real target. The one I had to get."

Her father, Craig thought.

A shaft of sunlight slanted through the window like a spotlight on Roza Fraser. Craig hoped she would keep talking. He wondered if she might be relieved to be sharing her awful secrets.

"Go on." Her penetrating gaze now fixed on Craig and it was an effort for him to maintain eye contact.

"I dreamed of doing it for years. The best way. The most pain. His death had to be perfect."

From his left, a scraping noise and low groaning told Craig Flint was coming to. Fraser appeared not to care, and carried on with the story she seemed compelled to tell. Craig was happy to let her.

"I used his toy." She let out a short laugh, waving the stun gun. "I had to overpower him somehow. He *had* to be alive." Fraser took a step to her left, looking at Isla as if she needed to know her audience.

Isla coughed.

"Roza, do you think you could take the gag off?" Craig asked. "Isla won't make a sound." Isla was nodding.

Still with the gun to Isla's head, Fraser leaned away to lay the knife down on a sideboard. With her free hand she removed the paisley scarf, holding it up for a second and shaking her head. "My mother's. She left him. Left me with him. She knew what he was doing." The scarf fell to the floor.

"Thank you," Isla croaked.

Craig glanced at Flint who had pushed himself up onto his elbows, his head lolling. With Isla tied up and Flint probably still unaware of where he was, only Craig could do anything, unless he gave Flint time to recover. He tried another tentative step towards Fraser.

"Stay where you are," Fraser snapped, reaching for the knife and prodding Isla's temple with the stun gun.

"Sorry. Just shifting my weight. Legs stiff." He was babbling, his hands raised in submission.

"You have a broken leg?" Fraser nodded towards his cast.

"Erm — yes, car crash." said Craig. This is bizarre, he thought. I don't know how much longer I can keep her talking. "You were telling me about your father. How you, erm…"

She returned readily to her subject.

"I had to get it right. I had to know it would work." Her gaze was fixed on Craig again. "If I was going to get practice, I thought it had better be on someone who deserved it." She chuckled. "But thanks to the great professor, I was in the right place. Slinn even suggested I apply for the job, when he thought he'd *fixed* me."

'R.F. (see private Staff File)', thought Craig. The penny had dropped. Roza Fraser was on Slinn's clinic list, her details obscured to maintain confidentiality.

The stun gun was inches from Isla's head, the knife pointing at Craig.

"I had dozens of girls to choose from. I read the Prof's letters as I typed them. It wasn't difficult to find some of the abusers. Fathers, stepfathers, uncles."

She turned to look at Isla, flicking the knife point towards Flint. "You can never trust them, remember that."

Isla nodded, and flitted her eyes towards Craig.

Isla's helping me with this, Craig thought.

"Which one was your father?" he asked. "We didn't know about a Fraser."

"Aleksy Narloch. Everyone's favourite Polish fighter, welcomed here after the war. Or welcomed a bit. The only job he was allowed to apply for was in the slaughterhouse." She spat on her own floor. "Too good for him."

Alex Narloch! Tentsmuir. Slaughterhouse. The stun gun. 'His toy'. Craig could see his realisation mirrored on Isla's face as more pieces fitted into the jigsaw.

"I dropped the surname as soon as I got away. Fraser's my middle name. My bitch mother's name. Her family couldn't stand her marrying a Pole."

Isla cleared her throat. "Can I ask something?"

Fraser nodded.

Isla's voice was croaky. "If Mr Narloch was the most important victim, why did you — erm — do him with a rock instead of a hammer? And why did you go on killing more?"

Fraser laughed. "Ah, yes. The rock. That was funny, looking back on it. I was so organised! I'd practised on two others by then, knew I could stun them to get them out of the car."

She was shaking her head, eyebrows raised, but her eyes remained focused on Craig. She flexed her knife arm with an ironic grin, and Craig noticed for the first time that Fraser's slight frame was muscular. "I had worked hard on getting strong enough, but it was the adrenaline! You wouldn't believe it. I could have dragged two of them out!" Fraser now flashed a smug smile, nodding slightly. "And I was even getting better at the surgery bit."

Flint moaned again. Fraser glanced at him, tensing. Craig thought she looked like she had lost her thread. We might be able to distract her, he thought.

"The rock?" he said.

Fraser nodded, then rolled her eyes. "Oh, yes, sorry. When it came to the one that mattered, the one it was all about, I was so excited when I got him to turn up that I dropped the flaming hammer! I couldn't find it. Nearly broke my back lifting that flaming rock!"

She laughed again. When she continued, the corners of her mouth were raised, talking as much to herself as her audience. "Mind you, it was satisfying. Really mashing his head in, I mean. The others I only wanted to disguise the stun mark." Fraser looked at Craig now. "To put your lot off. Didn't want you clever detectives looking for people with stun guns, did I?" She cackled, then with a vicious look into the distance, said, "I used his special Polish vodka to clean their skin."

There was a short silence, and Craig caught Isla's eye.

"Did you go back to Tentsmuir?" It was Flint's voice. He'd managed to sit up.

"I told you he'd be OK," Fraser said. Looking at Isla and waving the stun gun. "This is just meant to be used on rabbits or chickens."

Fraser turned to Flint, looking over Isla's head to answer his question. He was to be included in her audience now, Craig thought. "I went back a few times. I had to go and find the hammer. I couldn't believe the police didn't find it in the '*fingertip search*'." Another laugh.

Craig's mind flashed back to Slinn's attaché case, missed in another search.

"I knew they wouldn't find his — thing." Fraser's voice was rising. "The thing he put inside me, made me suck. Evil bastard!" She exhaled through gritted teeth, then smiled, continuing more calmly. "*That* went into the woods for the foxes or crows." She had a wistful look on her pretty, pale face. "I tucked his balls in his trouser pocket. I couldn't resist leaving a tribute to my father. I did something better with the ones after that."

"And when you went back to look for the hammer you left another tribute?" Craig said.

She nodded, her eyes glazing.

She's miles away, thought Craig. Should I go for her now? Isla was looking up at the glinting steel blade, still inches from her neck.

"That was when you left the thistles," Craig said.

"No, daffodils. It was in the spring. I put the thistles up after I did Skilling."

"And tulips for Currid," Flint said.

"Well done! You are back with us, right enough." Flint was now on his knees, and Fraser put the knife against Isla's neck. "But if you move again, she gets it. Stay still and listen."

She's enjoying holding court, thought Craig. But how is this going to end?

"It became a sort of tradition. After I did each one, I went back to Tentsmuir and left a bouquet. But you lot have sort of spoiled it now. McWatt was going to be the last. No reason, he was just the last one that answered one of my letters."

She typed the letters, Craig thought. Kept writing to them. Lured them, as Isla had said. We thought it was Jordan.

Roza Fraser was still in full flow. "And the pathetic bastards fell for my letters. I kept writing until I'd convinced them they were forgiven. Some even smiled at me, even though I can't have looked anything like their precious daughters. Except my own perfect Polish daddy."

She cackled, the knife wavering in her hand. Then silence. She looked around the room, hooded eyes focusing on each of them, flitting from Craig to Flint to Isla, and on round again. "You spoiled it all," she hissed, spitting.

She's getting angry again. Panicked. Keep her talking, keep her talking.

"Why was the list in Professor Slinn's drawer," Craig asked.

The sly smile returned, eyebrows raised. "You knew it was there? Ha! That worked then. I kept it in his precious, neat desk. Tucked away under other files, but easy to find." Now Fraser had a sardonic look, "not that *he* would ever see it. Never used his desk. Keeps everything in his pretty, brilliant head. Or kept, haha."

Craig waited for her to go on.

"But if anyone caught on, worked out the link was Slinn's clinic, I mean, they would think it was him." She was talking to herself, rambling.

"Sometimes, I thought someone was already on to me. That reporter didn't know what he was doing, but he was fishing around…"

Craig glanced at Flint and then Isla. Their faces said they had both picked up the reference to Jordan, who had been to Slinn's office.

"…and when I found one of Jordan's articles in the Prof's briefcase I got a bit worried for a minute." She chuckled, and then hesitated, looking directly at Flint, pointing the knife. "*You!* You were at Liff. I just realised it was you. Were you there because…?" The laughing started again.

She really is mad, thought Craig.

"And then some nutcase in Aberdeen killed the great professor. It was all getting very strange," she said, shaking her head.

Craig had no idea what to do, but thought he should say something. "And they took away your list."

"Hmph. I didn't really need it. I keep them in *my* pretty little head." With an irritated look, she jabbed towards Craig with the knife. "I've already *told* you, the list was only there to implicate Slinn." The sly grin returned slowly. "I liked ticking them off, mind you. One by one." More cackling.

"When they came for it, I even worried a bit. But the stupid police just packed it all up, smiled and said, 'Sorry, Miss.' Probably haven't even looked through it all."

Craig thought she might be right, but was a little hurt by the jibe.

Fraser was miles away again, reminiscing. "There was only McWatt left. I hadn't even got round to scoring Currid off yet. But I'd been busy. Even though he was dead, it was me that had to type and send all the Prof's clinic letters, put all his notes in order. Wonder who I'll be working for next?"

She's fucking insane. She thinks this is all just going to go away, thought Craig, though he was lost for what to do or say.

"Why did you go on killing after you'd murdered your father," Isla asked.

Fraser exhaled, looking at each of them in turn.

"It was just that by the time I got my father done I realised how easy it was. Apart from forgetting the hammer." She laughed again. "But I was good at it. After Harry Gaska parked the wrong way round, I even learned to make sure they parked driver's side away from the road." Isla lowered her eyebrows in confusion, and Fraser must have noticed. "Keep up," she said, rolling her eyes. "After I had him on the ground I had to drag him round to the other side of the car. I managed, but I had to get my breath back before I got on with the cutting."

Craig realised Gaska was the only body found on the passenger side. *Park by the main road, facing Craigrothie,* the letter to McWatt had read. He had to admire Fraser's attention to detail.

She went on. "I suppose I thought the other girls on the list I'd drawn up deserved what I had. Revenge. 'Justice?' The stupid *closure* they go on about." She turned to Isla. "But women have got to look after each other, right?"

"You're mad," Isla said.

"Haha! I don't think Professor Slinn would agree with you. Mad or bad? Schizophrenic or psychopathic? I think he'd say I was a sociopath. Nurture, not nature. That's the way he spoke." She paused, then waved the stun gun and knife, sniggering like a child, "I suppose I'm not quite right, though, getting a taste for this sort of thing."

"Are you OK, Roza? Your window's smashed?"

The voice came from outside, and all four in the room turned to look towards the broken shutters.

"There's a man here looking for you," the voice went on, closer now.

"It's fine. Stay away, Mike, you'll cut yourself. I'll come to the do—"

The 'nosey neighbour', thought Craig.

It was all over in seconds. Craig took his chance. He dived across the space between him and the distracted Fraser, head-butting her in the stomach. As they crashed to the floor, he was vaguely aware of the stun gun clattering on the floorboards and Flint pulling Isla and the chair away. Craig pinned down Roza Fraser, who didn't struggle. Flint grabbed the knife and started to cut the baler twine around Isla's wrists and ankles.

"Call the police," Craig shouted towards the window.

"What's going on?" The voice of Mike the neighbour.

Then another voice. One Craig recognised.

"Stand back. Let me have a look." A head poked in through the window. "Oh Christ!" Get the police! Someone's been kidnapped."

Chapter 63

After Roza Fraser was arrested, Flint, Isla, Craig and Tom Jordan were kept apart until they had been interviewed. They were transported to Cupar police station in separate cars.

Fife CID initially doubted Fraser's willing confession, but decided to believe her bizarre story when it was backed up by four witnesses whose accounts matched down to the fine details. She was then detained, waiting to be charged.

As they finished their statements, one by one they were released but told inquiries would continue until facts were verified. When Flint was shown into a waiting room, Isla was already there. They held each other tight.

Flint was first to speak. "Thank God you're OK. I thought you were dead."

"I thought you were." She began crying. "That gun..."

"I know. A stun gun for rabbits. Even when I was beginning to hear and think, I couldn't move."

"I know, but you could feel pain. My God, think what those men must have gone through. Even if they deserved—"

Craig Masson walked in. "Bloody hell! Tom Jordan, eh?" He looked around him, shaking his head and exhaling. "Jeez, it's the same room they put us in after The Mount."

They all sat down. Flint and Isla both spoke, Flint saying, "I couldn't believe it was him—", at the same time as Isla's "When you said that's who it was, Craig, I—"

Craig was smiling and shaking his head. "Me neither, I thought at first he was coming to help Fraser, that the three of them were in it together, but when he dived through the window, helped me hold Fraser down, not that she was resisting, but Jordan helped me, tied her hands with the nylon rope—

Craig's rapid, animated account was interrupted, allowing him to draw breath when the door opened and Tom Jordan was shown in. He had a fresh bandage on his upper arm.

They all bombarded him with questions.

"Let me speak," Jordan said, his hands up to ask for silence. "I've got just as many questions for you. When I saw a girl tied to a chair, I thought it must be Roza Fraser, but the hair was different. Then I recognised you, PC Masson. Nothing made sense, but I could see we needed the police." He pointed to the bandage. "Did this getting through the broken window."

"Why were you there, though? How did you know Roza Fraser was the killer?" asked Craig.

"I didn't. It never occurred to me for a minute."

"We thought *you* were——"

"Go on, Mr Jordan" said Isla.

"Tom's fine," said Jordan, looking at each of them in turn with a half smile. "I was coming to see if she'd let me interview her, given her connection to Slinn."

"So even though he was dead, you thought Slinn had something to do with it? Because all the victims had daughters who were his patients?" asked Flint.

"Did they?" Tom's head tilted to the side, then his brow furrowed and he began nodding. "That explains the Fife and Dundee connection."

The others waited for him to go on.

"I'd reported on Thake's murder, and Narloch. I knew the injuries were very similar. Then when Ivan Skilling was done the same way I knew there had to be a serial killer. A little digging told me the victims had all lived in Fife."

Flint and Craig looked at each other. While he and Craig had been probing for links between the cases, Jordan had been doing the same in his own parallel investigation.

Craig cleared his throat, and said, "Why had you been to Slinn's office?"

"God, that was years ago. Before I met you for the first time, Craig. I was working for the *Record* at the time, and doing a piece about child abuse. Someone had recommended Slinn as an expert. It must have been not long after the Thake murder."

"But what *was* it that made you suspect Slinn?" Flint asked.

"Just a kind of hunch. I had given Slinn my Thake piece as an example of my recent writing, and remembered how he'd reacted. It was like he knew something. We were in his office and suddenly there was a kind of, erm, atmosphere." He shrugged. "It was weird. But now you tell me he was treating the daughters, that probably explains his discomfort. Patient confidentiality."

Flint thought Jordan seemed to be putting things together for himself as he spoke.

"Was Roza Fraser in the room?" asked Isla. "She had a weird air about her,".

"Maybe, I can't remember." Tom smiled. "Aye. Anyway, I'd connected Slinn to the murders. When he was killed I thought the murders would stop—"

"So did we," said Flint.

"And when the Dundee murder happened, we thought you had done it," said Craig.

"Aye, carrying on Slinn's work," continued Flint, "or you and Slinn had been working together all along." He was shaking his head.

Tom's mouth was gaping in disbelief. "Bloody, hell. What made you think that?"

"I'm sorry, Tom," said Isla, "But we wondered why you were always the first reporter on the scene."

"And you were quoted on his lecture leaflet, saying what a great man he was," said Craig.

"He took that from a draft of the child abuse article I wrote in '78. He didn't even ask me. It was never printed, mind you, the editor didn't think it was steamy enough." He rolled his eyes. "The great *Daily Record.*"

"Slinn had your Thake article in his attaché case."

"Did he? Why would he have that with him?"

"Maybe he suspected you were the serial killer," said Flint, laughing.

"Don't joke," said Tom, exhaling. "Christ, he might have."

"There's got to be some reason he had it in his case." Craig was shrugging, shaking his head. "He's bound to have seen the Skilling report you wrote."

"We'll never know. But really, Tom, how come you were able to report on all of them?" said Isla. "First to get the story."

"A bit of luck, and contacts. I was sent to cover the Thake one for the *Record*. By the time Aleksy Narloch's body was found I had moved to *The Courier*, and the editor thought I should do it. It was a friend at *The Courier* who called me in Aberdeen to tip me off about Currid. He owed me."

Craig asked, "Who leaked information to you? About the Skilling murder."

"Oh, poor old DC Cummings. PC Cummings I should say, now he's back in uniform. I tried to contact him the other day but they told me he's been transferred out to Inverurie."

Craig couldn't help smiling to himself. Barry Cummings wasn't that bad, but he must've been unable to keep his mouth shut and been found out.

They were all quiet for a moment.

"We've all been chasing the wrong people," said Isla.

"Fuck, we were lucky," said Flint. "We were waiting for you to come and get McWatt," he said, looking at Tom, "but then Roza Fraser turned up."

"Tell me how that all happened," said Tom.

Flint, Isla and Craig explained their afternoon and how they had ended up at Scotstarvit watching James McWatt's car.

"Bloody hell," said Tom.

"What'll happen to Fraser now?" Isla asked. "She did it all because she'd been abused."

"All that stuff she went on about, 'mad or bad', and 'sociopath' and the rest, maybe that'll make them lenient," Flint said.

"She's still evil." said Craig. "Killed six times. She'll be locked up somewhere for a long time, that's for certain. Like Stiff."

"It's two o'clock in the morning," said Isla. "I want to go home."

"We can't go back to Aberdeen tonight."

A uniformed constable Flint realised he knew from school in Auchmoor was told to drive the four of them back to Pitlessie to collect the cars. Flint sat in the front of the Transit van and chatted awkwardly with the PC, whose first name he couldn't remember. As they turned onto the bumpy surface of Malt Place, he could see another cop leaning against the wall of Roza Fraser's home, presumably guarding the premises and the cars. He shook himself awake as the van approached.

Tom Jordan drove Craig back to Jack's flat, and Flint and Isla took Craig's car to Auchmoor. "One more time driving without a proper licence, Flint. The *last* time, OK?" said Craig before they parted.

"I'll have to drive it back to Dundee for you tomorrow." Flint shrugged.

Craig rolled his eyes as he wound up the window of Tom's car.

On the way to Auchmoor, Isla said, "Won't your mum mind us turning up in the middle of the night?"

"She'll cope with it. She'll be glad to hear we're together again."

EPILOGUE

Three Months Later

"I can't thank you enough, Mr Flint," said Dr Muriel Trickett, putting her coffee cup down and reaching for another buttered roll. "Ian's talking about it freely now. We'd never have got through to him without your help. Are you sure you wouldn't consider training? You'd be a credit to us."

In June, an envelope had arrived for Flint. He was at home in Auchmoor, drawing dole while he waited to start his Teacher Training course. In between his fortnightly giros he would hitch-hike to spend time with Isla. The typed address and the Aberdeen postmark had made him think it was from his former employer. Instead, he'd found a letter from Dr Trickett, asking him to telephone her about one of her patients. Flint remembered Craig mentioning Dr Trickett's report, and though she hadn't named Ian Soutar, he knew it could only be him.

When Flint called, Dr Trickett asked him — implored him — to come to Kingseat to assist with Soutar's care. As soon as his leg injuries had been attended to, Stiff had been transferred to the secure unit at Kingseat, under Dr Trickett's care. He had been withdrawn, almost mute. When he did make eye contact and speak it was to ask for 'the trance thing'.

Several attempts at hypnosis had been made by local psychologists, but Stiff had refused to cooperate, repeatedly asking for 'Dr Slinn's friend'. From police and press reports about the events at 20 Esslemont Avenue, Dr Trickett had worked out he meant Flint.

"It's very unconventional," she'd said, "but if I can't help him out of his current state I fear he will remain in institutional care for the rest of his life."

Flint had reluctantly agreed to travel to Kingseat. Expenses were paid and he was offered a room in the Nurses' Home, but he'd chosen to stay at Jamaica Street with Isla. He saw Stiff daily at first, always with two male nurses standing guard. From the outset, it was clear that Stiff was going to respond. He'd smiled at Flint, saying "Make me warm inside, mannie."

Flint made it up as he went along. His nightly reading was his old copy of Hartland, the textbook he'd first been lent years ago when he started experimenting with self-hypnosis.

What worked for Stiff was always what he built on at the next session. At about their tenth meeting, Stiff let him ask about his nickname. His closed eyelids had twitched and his limbs had stiffened, but after several more gentle relaxation and deepening exercises he was regressed enough to answer Flint's questions.

'Physio', was the first clue he'd given when asked how he'd gained his nickname. Flint had been given access to Soutar's medical records, under Dr Trickett's supervision, and discovered Stiff's childhood diagnosis of juvenile rheumatoid arthritis. Eleven years old, he'd been hospitalised and missed the start of secondary school. When he did attend Bankhead Academy, he had required daily physiotherapy sessions.

Flint focused the hypnotherapy on Stiff's daily stretching exercises, delivered in the school medical room by a man Stiff called 'The Hornet'. On one occasion, Stiff now revealed, a boy called Peter had been waiting outside for the school nurse to bandage his knee, and overheard The Hornet working with Stiff.

Deep in trance, Stiff quoted the physio, "Oh, you are a big, stiff boy today. Let me give you a nice rub. That's nice isn't it? Let me rub that stiffness until we make it go away for you." The physio session ended as usual, but when Stiff returned to class there was giggling and pointing. Over the next days he had been relentlessly hounded by gangs of little boys chanting 'Soutar got a stiffy', and 'Hornet wanked him o-off, Hornet wanked him o-off!'

Stiff's arthritis worsened and he was off school for weeks. School refusal and truanting then meant he was held back when he did return. The teasing died down, though, as the bullies moved on to someone else and as Ian Soutar grew used to his nickname. Flint remembered what Stiff had told him in Esslemont Avenue back in May. *And they didna batter me so much, so I liked it.*

But Stiff's dreams, which under hypnosis Flint was able to tease out in detail, became vivid. Disturbing enough for him to be scared to sleep. Dreams and reality became hard for him to distinguish, to the point where he firmly believed he had carried out ritual genital mutilations. Flint had discussed with Dr Trickett the idea that in Stiff's mind, it might be like revenge.

Now it was August, and Flint was meeting with Dr Trickett. "You really should consider formal training, Mr Flint. It's thanks to you that Ian is now discussing his dreams with me. My formulation is that he repressed the experience of his humiliation so deeply that he had no conscious memory of it. He didn't even associate his nickname, Stiff, with the event.

"His subconscious, however, has been tormented ever since," Trickett continued. "He developed an intense revulsion focused on his own genitalia, and in fact all male genitalia, which his childhood mind blamed for his humiliation. Whether he did or did not have an erection in the presence of the physiotherapist is irrelevant, in my opinion, but I consider it unlikely. His dreams — fantasies if you like — developed into a kind of horror film that played nightly, in which he took his revenge by butchering men."

She paused, tapping her pen on the desk. "I may be putting two and two together, and my job is not to do the work of the police, but I suspect he heard or read about the unfortunate Mr Skilling, seeing similarities to his dreams. He believed he had inflicted Skilling's fatal injuries himself."

Flint had come to enjoy Dr Trickett's precise, expansive explanations. He didn't understand all of the psychiatric terms she used but his reading of Hartland helped.

Muriel Trickett sat back, smiling warmly at Flint. "Ian is so much better," she said "he is on no medication. We are anticipating his return home soon."

She lowered her head, looking at Flint over her glasses. "Now that you have exposed the cause of Ian's mental problems, I can send my further reports. He is fit for court, and of course will be convicted. I will strongly recommend lifelong forensic psychiatry review, and no custodial sentence."

"Dr Trickett, can I ask something?"

"Of course."

"Why do you think Stiff — I mean Soutar — killed Professor Slinn? I don't think he'd ever been violent before, had he?"

He watched Dr Trickett's lips purse, her brow furrowing while she appeared to weigh up whether to speak.

"Between you and me only, having listened repeatedly to the tape of their interaction, I think Dante pushed Soutar too hard. When he found Soutar's trigger — the interaction with the physiotherapist which led to his being bullied — Dante honed in on it, made Soutar re-live it. I know Dante was a proponent of what psychologists call "Flooding Technique", the rapid and intensive exposure to triggers of distress. It's used in an attempt to desensitise the patient."

Flint remembered reading about "flooding" when he had been searching for solutions to his own problems.

Muriel Trickett continued. "It can be very effective, or so enthusiasts of the method believe, but I know it has to be done in controlled, safe circumstances. On his first meeting with Soutar, and in an unconventional setting, Dante went too far and much too quickly. He was — and I don't like to speak ill of a colleague, especially a deceased colleague, but it has to be said — Dante was a fool. Too cocksure."

She took a handkerchief from her blouse sleeve and dabbed her eyes. Flint looked at the floor.

"Your own approach was much more measured, Mr Flint. And successful."

Flint felt his face heat up.

"I mean it, Mr Flint. You would make — you already are — a wonderful therapist. You are more than capable of qualifying as a clinical psychologist if you were to undertake the training."

"Thank you, but I am all set for my teaching course in September."

There was a knock on Dr Trickett's office door, and a nurse poked her head in.

"That's Mr Flint's taxi here, Dr Trickett."

"Thank you, Rebecca."

As Flint was slipping on his jacket, Muriel Trickett said, "May I ask you something now, Mr Flint?"

"Erm — yes?"

"I saw in the news reports that two policemen were present when Dante Slinn died."

"Yes."

"What happened to them? I mean, were they in big trouble? I know you were trying to help Ian Soutar."

"Davy, that's PC Jepson, was given a warning. PC Masson was off work with a broken leg. They suspended him but he's pretty sure he'll be allowed back to work. He's nearly finished all his physio."

"Good, I am glad. And what are your plans before you start your course?"

Flint held up both hands with his fingers crossed, smiling. "I'm going to keep trying to persuade my girlfriend to move to Dundee with me. I'm pretty confident she's going to say yes."

THE END

Glossary

A note on Doric Scots

Doric is an ancient dialect still spoken widely in the North East of Scotland. It can be hard to follow at times, and there are hundreds of unique words and local derivations.

Some basics:

The sound **'wh'**, as in who, is usually substituted with **'f'**. (Although some might say the substitution went the other way.)

The sound **'th'**, however, is commonly dropped altogether.

Who? — *fa?* *(Fa's 'at?* = Who's that?)
What? — *fit?* *(Fit's 'at?* = What's that?)
When? — *far?*
Why? — *fit-wye?*

However, **'f'** is also sometimes used for **'h'**.

Think *foo?* for 'how?' *(Foo's 'at?* = How's that?)
and 'f' can replace 'fr' *(fae* = from.)

loon means 'young male person.'

quine means 'young female person.'

ootsider means 'outsider' (Alternative: *fae ootbye* = 'from elsewhere.'

feel means 'daft' or 'crazy'

A common greeting is *foo's yer doos?* meaning 'How are you?' or 'How are you doing?' But, *doos* is a Scots word for pigeon, so *foo's yer doos?* literally means 'How are your pigeons?' A common answer to *foo's yer doos* is 'aye peckin'. (meaning 'still pecking' or in other words 'doing OK, thank you.')

It took me years to adjust to Doric, as an *'ootsider'*, but it is a beautiful and historic dialect that is far from dying out. It's not, I understand, such a heinous crime to use it in schools. I hope that continues.

A good reference tool is: *doricphrases.com*

Notes:

Though not only in Doric speaking areas, "messages" is commonly used in Scotland to mean shopping. "My ma sent me doon the road to get the messages."

Likewise, in Scotland and some parts of North England, the word "oxters" is used for armpits.

About the Author

Nick Edmunds enjoyed decades as a doctor in Scotland. He now lives in Stirling with his wife and spaniel.

His other published work includes:

- **MILES AWAY — Memories Can Kill** (Book 1 in the Flint&Masson Series)
- **RAGGED ISLAND**
- **Short Stories**

Read more at *njedmunds.com*

Reviews and any feedback are always welcome

Acknowledgements

Before, during, and after I wrote Flowers for the Slaughterman I had help, advice and encouragement from more people than I can reliably remember. I have listed many below, and apologise to anyone I may have omitted.

John Harkin advised me on 'polis' matters, correcting many of my misconceptions.

Niall Farquharson, a former flatmate of mine in 20 Esslemont Avenue many years ago, gave his permission to use the address as an important location. The story is set in 1981/82, at which time the flat was owned by Niall or his family.

Phil (Kaf) Leckie gave me the benefit of his knowledge of the pubs in Haddington.

Stephen Rule told me about pubs in Dundee.

(If you are seeing a pattern here, I didn't need to ask anyone about pubs in Aberdeen.)

Once again, **Sandy Paterson** told me which end of a gun was which.

Rachel Edmunds (**@r.eds.art**) provided the background image for the cover of Flowers for the Slaughterman, another example of her endless artistic talents. Painted in acrylic, it shows the iconic granite tenements of Wallfield Place in Aberdeen, near a key location in the story, Esslemont Avenue.

All of following people read, commented on, and suggested improvements to my writing:

Sue Leckie, (there are two references that only Sue, Kaf and Helen might spot) **Laura Edmunds, John Bell, Marlene Pitcher, Sue Partridge, John Petrie, Jenny Richards, Sonny Kohet, Robin Tones, Bron Hogan, Bridget Scrannage, Ellie Ness, Isabel Flynn, Joe Durham, Philip Highway, Donna Best, Stephen Granville, Sue Boddy, Sarah Smith.**

And of course my wife **Helen.**

Nick Edmunds, September 2025

SouthToll
2025

Printed in Dunstable, United Kingdom